THE FINISHING TOUCHES

HESTER BROWNE

ISIS
LARGE PRINT
Oxford

First published in Great Britain 2010
by
Hodder
An imprint of Hodder & Stoughton

Published in Large Print 2011 by ISIS Publishing Ltd.,
7 Centremead, Osney Mead, Oxford OX2 0ES
by arrangement with
Hodder & Stoughton
An Hachette UK Company

British Library Cataloguing in Publication Data
Browne, Hester.
The finishing touches.
1. Single women - - Fiction.
2. Etiquette for women - - Fiction.
3. Chick lit.
4. Large type books.
I. Title
823.9'2–dc22

ISBN 978–0–7531–8898–9 (hb)
ISBN 978–0–7531–8899–6 (pb)

Printed and bound in Great Britain by
T. J. International Ltd., Padstow, Cornwall

For Maggie, with love and thanks

Hester Browne's polite thank you notes

These thank yous are heartfelt, even if they're not delivered on correspondence cards attached to bunches of violets, as per Tallimore Academy instructions. I'm v. grateful to Sara Kinsella and Isobel Akenhead, who edit with such humour and encouragement, and, as always, to the incomparable Lizzy Kremer, the best agent anyone could wish for.

Also, thanks to Mrs X, the beautifully-finished lady whose anonymity I will protect, but whose naughty recollections over a long lunch at le Gavroche were better than anything I could invent. The day I can host a party as well as her will be the day I hang up my ice tongs in triumph. (Note to self: buy ice tongs.)

Prologue

21 July 1981
Mayfair, W1

Deep in the discerning matronly bosom of Mayfair, Full Moon Street hid the last remaining secret of London society. Between buzzy, chaotic Soho on one side and the discreet gentlemen's clubs of St James on the other, Full Moon Street's elegant Georgian townhouses rose behind curled iron railings, while, high above the pavement, pigeons perched on tight-packed rows of red chimneypots. Four storeys below, at Number 34, was the only surviving finishing school in London.

The Tallimore Academy for Young Ladies had occupied the same double-fronted townhouse since 1880. It had once been *the* place for England's oldest families to send their daughters for a year of pre-marriage-market polishing — Tallimore girls had a reputation for never letting a conversation die over dinner, no matter how curmudgeonly or drunken the guests, and maintaining a cheerful attitude and ramrod deportment well into old age.

Now, one hundred years later, enrolment was well down from the Academy's post-war heyday, but a steady trickle of jolly blond girls still tottered in for the year's course in minding one's house, family and manners. Lately, the trickle had become a stream, thanks to Lady Diana Spencer, the most famously finished girl in England, and the Tallimore Academy was enjoying something of a mini-revival.

Although the boarding girls didn't stumble down for their full English breakfast till eight, every morning at twenty to seven, Kathleen Connor, the cook, opened the front door to collect the milk. This morning — 21 July 1981 — was no different, except Kathleen discovered, to her annoyance, that the milkman had ignored her note requesting orange juice, and left a box of Cooper's fine cut marmalade instead.

"Fine cut? I'll give him fine cut," she grumbled to no one in particular, and started to scoop up the milk-bottles, stuffing them in the ample crook of her arm, when a distinct cough from the box almost made her drop the lot.

Kathleen stared into the marmalade box, uncharacteristically lost for words. One of her most secret, heartfelt prayers seemed to have been answered, in the oddest fashion.

She looked up and down the street, in search of the box's owner, but the pavement was deserted, the only sound a distant rattle of traffic already crawling down Piccadilly.

Meanwhile, the box coughed again. Kathleen could restrain herself no longer.

"Jesus, Mary, Joseph and all the saints!" she breathed, crossing herself as she bent to pick it up.

* * *

Upstairs, in the morning room, Lady Frances Tallimore was tapping her red lips with a silver fountain pen.

How best to comfort a girl suffering an unfortunate eyebrow wax? So far, all she'd come up with was a photograph of Marlene Dietrich and a vague memory that a drop of castor oil speeded up regrowth. Or was that eyelashes? Frances made a note to check with Nancy, the Academy's matron. Nancy knew all sorts of useful little nuggets, most involving malt vinegar.

The finishing school had been in her husband Pelham's family for generations — ironic, really, since Pelham himself had the social ease of a penguin who'd stumbled into the lion enclosure, much like every other Englishman she knew. Frances wasn't the principal — that was Miss Vanderbilt, who had been correcting the girls' tea drinking technique since before colour television — but Frances had wanted to be involved from the start. She was eager to pass on some of the mysteries of modern life that her own finishing school had failed to explain, like how to extricate yourself from a blind date. Or make an instant supper from five eggs and a kipper.

Though Frances always said that she pitched in for the sake of the family business, she loved her mornings at the Academy, particularly the giggling atmosphere that fifteen or so teenage girls carried round like their clouds of perfume. The Tallimores had one child — a son, Hector — and Frances would have dearly loved a daughter, but to her great sorrow, the Hon. Hector was her lot. She was pragmatic, though, and Frances' silver lining now was to be a sort of wise aunt who could offer some proper advice to the rich but neglected teenagers who were sent to Full Moon Street for finishing off. Some of them, she thought sadly, were barely started.

There was a knock on the door, and Kathleen appeared, as she always did at nine o'clock. Frances noted that she wasn't bearing the usual tray of morning coffee, but was clutching a box of marmalade.

Behind her, bobbing up and down nervously, was Nancy. From the anxious way she kept glancing into the box, Frances assumed, with a sinking heart, that either Harrods' delivery system had broken down badly, or else one of the girls had let her cat have kittens again.

Kathleen seemed flustered, chewing her lip and flushing pink to the roots of her jet-black hair. "Sorry to interrupt, but I think you ought to see this, Lady Frances. I found it on the doorstep."

Kathleen placed the box on her desk and Frances found herself looking into the round, blue eyes of the most beautiful baby she had ever seen. She knew at once she was a little girl, just a few days old: the pink mouth curled up at the edges and her eyes were thickly fringed with pale golden lashes. Before Frances knew what she was doing, she had lifted the baby out of the box, and was cradling the warm weight in her arms, marvelling at the peach-down softness of her pearly skin.

The baby didn't make a sound, but gazed up with serious eyes, the colour of navy blue school shirts. Frances' own eyes brimmed with tears, and her heart flooded with a fierce, protective yearning. The baby was dressed in a clean cotton romper suit and wrapped in a pashmina, with her fragile fingers opening and closing like sea anemones. Her feet were, Frances was relieved to see, covered with pink cashmere socks, and from her heavy contentedness, she'd obviously just been fed.

"Hello," she murmured, stroking the porcelain cheek with the back of her finger, taking care not to graze her with her diamond rings. "Where's your mummy, darling?"

Frances cupped a tiny foot in her hand and squeezed, transfixed, as the baby sent invisible tentacles of love into her heart, wrapping round so tightly she could hardly breathe.

"We've called the police!" wailed Nancy. She flapped across the room, and hovered over the box like a mother hen in support tights. "But it's dreadful! Poor wee mite! Just that blanket, in this weather, with those filthy pigeons everywhere! I don't know what sort of irresponsible —"

"It's good cashmere, that scarf. And there was a note," said Kathleen, more matter-of-fact. "Whoever left her isn't coming back, if you ask me."

But Frances was only half listening. The scarf had fallen back to reveal a fine covering of red-gold hair curling around the baby's delicate ears, and by then she was absolutely lost. This tiny vulnerable scrap needed her, and she wasn't going to let her down! Not like whoever had left her there, helpless and alone on the doorstep of a strange house.

Kathleen was speaking again. ". . . tried to find Lord Tallimore, but the man at his club says he's not there. I gave a message to telephone at his earliest opportunity."

Nancy stepped forward to take the baby from her arms, but Frances turned slightly, unwilling to break the spell. "Pelham's busy this morning," she said.

Kathleen and Nancy exchanged a look. Frances knew they knew exactly where Pelham was: trying to find Hector. They'd been part of her family for too long not to read between the lines. When it came to Hector the lines were drawn pretty far apart, just to fit everything in.

Even Frances had to admit that Hector was getting to be the sort of junior cad she warned the girls to avoid at all costs. Handsome, charming, utterly irresponsible and not to be trusted in moonlit gardens. It didn't help that some of her charges already had wild crushes on Hector and his circle of young earls and millionaires' sons who fell in and out of the gossip columns and rehab clinics as often as they were in and out of the casinos and cocktail bars of Mayfair. They were getting to be quite notorious, and it gave Frances insomnia. It *wasn't* how he'd been brought up. It *wasn't* what she wanted for him. And yet she still hoped he'd grow out of it.

Or find a girl who'd make him grow out of it.

"I'm expecting Lord Tallimore back this afternoon, with Hector," she added, more confidently than she felt. Hector had had been AWOL for a week now, and so had his two best friends, Rory and Simon. Last time Hector had gone missing, Pelham had had to spring him from a police cell in Venice. The *Daily Mail* was delighted to print that the Hon. Hector Tallimore had been arrested in full dinner dress, complete with a tutu.

"What will Lord Tallimore say?" wailed Nancy. "What will it look like, abandoned babies on the step! They'll think it's one of the —"

"Nonsense," said Frances, briskly. "The poor soul who left this baby knew this was a place where young women are well looked after, and she was quite right. Nancy, we're going to need some supplies, so perhaps you'd be so good as to pop to Harrods for the necessaries? Did you say there was a note, Kathleen?"

Kathleen fished a folded piece of writing paper out of her apron pocket and handed it over.

"Well, the mother had a fountain pen at least," Frances observed. "*Please look after my baby. I want her to grow up to be a proper lady. Thank you,*" she read. "Polite and to the point."

"The bee, Kathleen," whispered Nancy, urgently. "Show her the bee!"

"It was fastened on this." Kathleen produced a kilt pin from her apron. "I took it off for her own safety."

"Poor wee mite could have had her eye out!" exclaimed Nancy, then clamped her mouth shut under Kathleen's glare.

Frances frowned as she examined it. It was a common-or-garden kilt pin, and attached to it was a gold charm, in the shape of a diamond-studded bee. An expensive one, definitely.

"No name?" she said, turning the paper over. "That's very odd. You'd think a mother would want her little girl to have a name, at least." She looked down at the baby, who was making the occasional mewing noise. "We can't have an angel like you without a name, now can we?" she said, softly, tracing the faint golden eyebrows with her fingertip. "What will we call you?"

The smell of lavender, bleach, and shortbread was getting stronger. Frances looked up at the two middle-aged spinsters, hovering closer as they'd hovered for most of her life, and she could tell that they were yearning to cuddle the baby too.

They were the two kindest women Frances knew. Between us, she thought wryly, the poor desperate mother couldn't have picked three women keener to love an unwanted baby.

"What do you think?" she asked. "Something royal? After Lady Diana, maybe? With the Royal Wedding in the morning, after all!"

"No. Elizabeth," said Kathleen at once. "After our own dear queen."

"I don't know if she's quite an Elizabeth," mused Frances, unable to tear her eyes away from the baby's face for more than a moment. "She's too pretty for such a long name. She's . . ."

Not Lizzy, or Bessie. Or Beth.

"Betsy?" suggested Nancy.

"Betsy," Frances repeated, in a whisper. "Yes, I think she is. Bee for Betsy."

The baby blinked her navy blue eyes, and for a fleeting moment, Frances thought she opened her mouth into a smile. Frances didn't know who'd brought Betsy to the Tallimore Academy, but she made a silent promise that from now on, even if someone came to take her away, it would be her home.

CHAPTER ONE

The only truly waterproof mascara is an eyelash tint.

"If you want a sneaky cry at weddings and funerals, dye your lashes." That was probably one of the best tips Franny gave me, out of the thousands she passed on over twenty-seven years.

Other pieces of useful advice included, "sun screen now saves face lifts later" and "never trust a man with a ready-made bow tie".

I stared blankly out of the window at the red London bus idling next to our taxi. For once, I didn't mind the clogged-up traffic on the Brompton Road, because it gave me time to pull myself together between leaving the church and arriving at the memorial tea, where I'd have to hear how elegant and inspiring my mother was, all over again, this time while juggling canapés and a wine glass.

Tears prickled treacherously along my lashes. They weren't the same miserable tears I'd cried six months ago, when Franny's headaches turned out to be a tumour, but they were sad ones, because now it was real: I'd never feel her elegant, comforting presence behind me at memorials again. Franny always knew what to say, the kind word to murmur at the right time. She handled awkwardness gracefully.

I blinked hard, knowing that at least I wouldn't be given away by telltale panda eyes. I hadn't had time to buy a new outfit for the memorial service, but I had made time for a lash tint. I could almost see Franny's familiar smile that twisted up one corner of her mouth. I knew she'd know. It was one of her lifelong quests: the unsmearable mascara that would let you cry at Red Arrows flypasts without anyone knowing.

That thought *really* set the tears off. Oh, *nuts*.

A hand clamped on my knee and shook it. "Betsy? Betsy, will you pack in that stiff-upper-lip bollocks? It's *us*! If you can't let your nose run with your best friend, when can you?"

I turned my face back into the cab, swallowing my tears. "I'm fine! Honestly!"

"No, you're not. You've been wobbling your lip for the last five minutes." Liv's words were brisk but her voice was gentle and concerned. "You're *meant* to cry at these things. The whole *point* of memorial services is to let everyone have a good howl. It's good for the soul. Then the women can repair each other's make-up as an ice breaker after, and get on with the hilarious memories. I'm sure you told me that."

Liv was balanced on the taxi jump seat opposite me, her long legs arranged like Bambi's, and a mixture of concern and proudly smudged mascara all over her beautiful face. Apart from the lack of a lash tint, Franny would thoroughly have approved of Liv's outfit. The dress code had been "celebratory" and Liv was wearing a sunshine yellow miniskirt and a selection of perfectly chosen accessories, including gloves and a gold sequinned beret on her straight blond hair, as her tribute to Franny's devotion to the Tallimore Academy finishing school and its "Hats for All Seasons" lesson.

It made my simple blue coat and shift dress look rather sober in the grudging January light, but I'd barely had time to think about what to throw on before the taxi came for me that morning. I didn't have Liv's panache for accessorizing, *or* her wardrobe.

There was a discreet cough from my left, but I didn't turn my head, because that would mean looking at Jamie, and I wasn't sure whether that was a good idea. I hadn't known Jamie was coming along today. If I *had* known, I might have distracted myself with hours of worrying about what to wear. And done something about my puffy eyes, at least. I angled my head so he couldn't see my dark circles.

"What my darling sister means is that after everything that was said about Lady Frances, you'd need a heart of pure concrete not to be weeping like a burst drain," said Jamie. "Even I cried when you read out that letter she sent you at school, about making friends with bullies by complimenting them on their shoes. And you know what a heartless bastard I am."

Liv wiped under her eyes with a finger, and smeared her mascara. "It was such a lovely service," she sniffed. "It was like Franny was *there*. Those lilies she loved, and that Bach solo and everyone in beautiful little hats with veils . . ."

“Here,” I said, reaching into my bag, glad of the distraction. “Have a handkerchief.”

“But what about you?”

“I’ve got two.” I waved mine, a big white gent’s hanky. “Always carry two: one for you and one for a friend.” I managed a watery smile. “A top tip from the Academy.”

“Franny told you such useful things.” Liv’s face disappeared into the hanky. “I wish I’d grown up in a finishing school.”

“So do I,” said Jamie.

“Shut up, Jamie,” said Liv, blowing her nose with a trumpeting sound. “No one in their right mind would let you into a finishing school. It’d be like letting a fox loose in a hen house.”

“A fox?” I could tell by his voice that he was joggling his eyebrows. “Why, thanks!”

I risked a sideways glance. I hadn’t really expected Jamie to come to the memorial service — in fact I’d thought he was in New York, working — but he’d arrived with Liv, looking devastating as usual in a dark suit, his blond hair cut slightly shorter than I remembered but still falling into his eyes. When he brushed it away from his handsome face with a tanned hand, my stomach still flipped over, memorial service or not.

It was a habit, I told myself. My stomach had flipped over at the sight of Jamie O’Hare’s floppy hair since I was fourteen years old; if only he was as easy to knock on the head as nail biting.

"I meant I wished *you'd* grown up in a finishing school, you plum," said Jamie. "It'd have done you good to have learned some manners. And how to arrange flowers and . . ." He turned to me and gave me such a charming smile that I forgot to look away and disguise my puffy face. "What exactly did they learn at the Academy? I'm afraid my knowledge of finishing schools is limited to, um . . ."

"Dodgy DVDs and his own private fantasy world," Liv finished. "You *knocker*."

"They learned how to dine with royalty, and talk to anyone, and arrange flowers," I said, promptly. The Academy and its fairytale lessons had been such a big part of my childhood, it merged in places with storybooks. "They used to rehearse proposals, too, accepting and declining without hurting anyone's feelings, that sort of thing. What to wear to the opera and to Ascot."

"How to be a princess, basically," sighed Liv.

"Sort of," I agreed. "I think there was some useful stuff too. Franny was quite keen for the girls to have things to talk about, in between the proposals and flowers. The girls were there to be finished, you know. Polished up."

"Turned into the perfect wives?" asked Jamie, with a leading wink.

"Nnngh," I agreed, as my brain registered that his knee was almost touching mine and conveniently went blank.

It said something about my distracted state of mind that I hadn't already mumbled something moronic to

Jamie. Whenever I saw him normally I acted as if I was suffering from an incapacitating hangover; Liv, who had no idea how I felt, always mistook it for supreme indifference, something she felt Jamie didn't get enough of in the general scheme of things.

Now, for instance, my face was grinning, but my brain was pretty much white noise.

"And it's still going now?" he went on, gamely making conversation to haul us through this sticky moment. I admired people who could do that, but then Jamie had to be sociable professionally. "What sort of finishing do the girls get these days? Do they still do curtseys?"

Guilt at my long absence jerked me into focus. "I haven't been back in years . . ." I began.

"Before you ask," Liv interrupted, leaning over to rap his knee with her clutch bag, "they *don't* learn how to mix cocktails while waxing their own bikini lines, so if you're coming along to the reception to check them out, you're going to be disappointed. We all know what *your* ideal woman is. And you won't find her type here."

I glanced between Liv and Jamie as the penny dropped. I'd wondered why he'd been at the service — though it was lovely of him to pay his respects to a woman he'd rarely met, Jamie was very busy. He and his friend, Howard, owned a company that arranged parties for the sort of clients who were mad enough to demand special cocktails to be served at their Shih Tzu's third birthday party — and rich enough to pay for them. But when Liv put it like that . . . He wanted to see inside the Academy for potential conquests and/or posh waitresses. My heart deflated a little.

"That is not what *my* ideal woman . . . oh, forget it, Liv," said Jamie, seeing my crestfallen face. "I came because I know how much Franny meant to Betsy, and I happened to be in London this week. I'm glad I did." He turned to me, and said, with the grave charm that kept a stream of Olympic skiers and party girls swooning in glossy heaps all over London's hottest nightclubs, "She was obviously a real lady of the old school, and if it's any consolation, I think she passed on a great deal of that to you."

I blushed, and Liv coughed, hard, to disguise a snort.

The trouble with Jamie's famed charm was that it was hard to take him very seriously off duty. Besides, it wasn't true. Franny had done her best to pass on a lifetime of hints and tips, but I just didn't have her natural grace. That wasn't something any finishing school could teach; it was something you were born with.

The traffic began to move again and I grabbed the chance to stare out of the window so he couldn't see my expression. We were moving up Knightsbridge now, getting nearer Mayfair and the tall townhouses near the Academy, and my heart began to thump in anticipation of the moment when I'd have to get out of the car and not have Jamie's leg pressing against mine.

I mean, face the other guests at the reception.

"He's right, for once, Betsy," said Liv. "You *are* like her."

"That's really sweet of you to say," I squirmed. "But Franny was gracious and chic and had fabulous parties and knew everyone. I never know what to say and I'm still doing my holiday job after five years, even though I'm a university graduate." I sighed, not wanting to go down that particular route. "She just knew how to make people feel better about themselves. That's proper manners."

"But you're . . ." Liv began.

"I'm *not*," I said flatly. "I wish I was."

"She didn't manage to teach you how to accept a compliment," said Jamie. He nudged me, until I turned back and had to look at him. His greyish eyes twinkled with a sad sort of friendliness, and I wished he'd been paying me the compliment under happier circumstances. I managed a small, non-stupid smile, then readdressed my attention to the traffic lights on Piccadilly, so he couldn't see the gormlessness that broke through.

"Anyway!" said Liv, slapping her tiny, tanned knees. "We've done the sad part, let's concentrate on remembering the good bits! Let's talk about the way Nancy and Kathleen used to throw duchess parties for you when you were little and Franny would lend you her tiara and fur coat!"

"Really?" Jamie cocked an eyebrow and something melted inside me. "Any chance of doing that . . . Oh, excuse me." He reached inside his suit pocket and took out both his phones, then answered one. "It's work. Hello, Jamie O'Hare speaking. Lily! Hello! Yes, the ice sculptor should be with you any minute; the question is, are you ready for him?"

Liv rolled her eyes at me. “When you turn your social life into your job, I suppose the fun never stops. Or the work never starts, whatever.”

I rolled my eyes back. We’d turned down Full Moon Street now, and were only moments away from the reception.

“Are you OK?” she mouthed, all concern, and I nodded bravely.

“Let’s stop here,” I said. “I’d like to walk.”

Jamie leaned forward to talk to the driver, phone still clamped to his ear. I could hear the distant honking of Chelsea panic. “Can you drop these two lovely ladies here, please, then take me back to Cadogan Gardens, mate? Cheers.” He sat back. “Sorry, I can’t stay for the bunfight, I’ve got a hostess in distress with an engagement party at seven. Themed round *Dirty Dancing*. You don’t want to know what I’ve had to arrange.”

“You came to the most important part,” I said. “Thanks.”

Jamie smiled and rubbed my upper arm. “My pleasure.”

Liv was busy getting out and paying the driver, and for a second or two, my eyes locked with Jamie’s as his hand rested on my coat sleeve, and I thought he might say something else. Or the conversation fairy might help me out with a witty comment. But the silence stretched, and then Liv’s hand grabbed mine and we were walking down Full Moon Street, towards the Academy.

* * *

Although I'd often been back to the mews cottage where my adoptive grandmothers, Kathleen and Nancy still lived, I hadn't set foot inside the Tallimore Academy itself since I was twelve years old — for various reasons. Their cottage was warm and cosy, full of cakes and impenetrable nannyisms about "not being at home to Miss Rude", whereas the big house was much more imposing altogether. An old chill of anticipation fluttered in my stomach when I spotted the familiar brass plaque next to the red door.

I'd felt the same flutter as a little girl, walking down the street after my afternoon turn around Green Park with Nancy. There was always something intriguing to spot in the upper windows of the Academy, some romantic lesson in the mysterious grown-up world awaiting the shrieking Sloane girls I saw streaming in every morning, with their padded jackets and long hair.

In winter, the four-storey facade was like a living advent calendar with a different scene behind each lighted square: blond girls waltzing together in the old ballroom where moulded plaster vines were picked out in gold above glittering crystal chandeliers, and on the floor beneath them, the Social Dining class, struggling with a plateful of oysters and seven different glasses.

On *very* hot summer days, the sash windows at the front were opened, and Nancy and I would catch the sounds of a piano being hammered and enthusiastic singing as we walked down the street. Not that we ever went in through the red door; we took a side alley two houses down that ran into the mews behind the street, and from there let ourselves into Kathleen's kitchen, where table manners were more rigidly enforced than they were in the class. Both Kathleen and Nancy were well into their sixties when I arrived, and were fond of the "elbows off, napkins on, plenty of prunes and early nights" approach to child-rearing.

Now I thought about it, I'd had a very *Bridehead Revisited* sort of childhood, though it had seemed perfectly normal at the time . . .

I was jolted out of this daydream by Liv nudging me.

"I said, did it take you long to get everything arranged, Betsy?" she asked, in a tone that suggested I'd probably done everything in an hour. I had a reputation for organising which, to be honest, wasn't one hundred per cent deserved.

I shook my head. "I didn't do very much, really. I did offer, but it's been so busy in the shop, and Lord T insisted that he'd manage it all himself. In fact, he specifically told me not to take time off work and come down." I paused, wondering now if I'd done the right thing. "I thought it was best to let him, you know, keep busy."

Keeping busy was my personal therapy when things were bad. Right now, my flat and the shop were absolutely gleaming, with every account filed and shelf spotless. A couple of days after Franny's funeral I'd even arrived early and polished the windows, to the amazement of the assistants. I'd used vinegar and newspaper. That was one of Nancy's Good Housekeeping tips, not Franny's.

"Probably for the best," Liv agreed. "I suppose there'd be people at the Academy to help? The headmistress?"

"Mm," I said, distracted by the middle-aged ladies with "good legs" already heading towards Number 34 like honey-blond bees: obviously old Tallimores from their confident sashay in high heels.

"And there's always Kathleen and Nancy," she went on. "I can't imagine they'd stand by and let him undercater a party. You know what Kathleen's like," Liv went into a terrible impression of Kathleen's Lancashire solidness, with her hands on her non-existent hips, "If a party's worth having, it's worth having wi' lots of sandwiches. A cake shared is a pleasure halved. Better to feed the birds after, than starve the guests before."

Kathleen and Nancy communicated entirely in pithy sayings, most of which I now suspected them of making up to suit the occasion.

"At least there'll be plenty to eat," I said. "That's one thing you can be sure of. That and the three hundred thank-you notes Lord T will get in exactly twenty-four hours' time."

We were nearly outside the house, and as we approached, our pace slowed as we tried to pretend we weren't looking at the famous Doorstep of the Abandoned Child.

Over the years, Franny, Nancy and Kathleen had told the story about the Cooper's marmalade box left on the Academy's front step so many times that it was sometimes hard to remember it was actually me inside it. Obviously, I had no memory of it myself, and what I'd *really* wanted to hear wasn't what had happened, but how excited and delighted they were to find me there, and how Franny had sent to Harrods for nappies.

I'd told the tale quite often myself at school, admittedly with a few elaborations involving cloaked figures and tearstains on the blanket, and there were times when I'd even made myself cry with second-hand pathos, along with everyone around me. But as I got older, and started thinking more deeply about *why* my mother might have left me, and where she might be now, I wasn't sure it was healthy to feel so detached. The simple truth was that I wanted to feel something — but there was nothing there, except the little bee pendant that I wore every day around my neck on a gold chain Franny had given me.

I tried to feel a flicker of something now, seeing the front doorstep where the box had been wedged against the bootscraper, but all I could see was tatty ivy clinging to a frontage that needed a lick of paint.

"Head up, shoulders back, chest out," said Liv, as she rapped the lion's-head door knocker. "Just remember the happy times, OK?"

It wasn't quite so straightforward as that though, I thought. Much as I loved Franny and the graceful, white-shouldered vision of high-society elegance she represented, there were other memories attached to the Academy for me. Painful ones that I thought I'd put to one side, but which were now rising up inside my chest like acid reflux.

The red front door was opening. The nostalgic smell of polish and high ceilings and fresh flowers rushed out to meet me, making my head spin with recognition.

"Betsy?" Liv's voice sounded far away. "Are you all right?"

I took a half-step back away from the black-and-white tiles of the entrance hall, but then I saw a familiar face and my manners took over. Without thinking, I stood up straighter, pulled my shoulders back and put on my best smile.

Lord Pelham Tallimore, my adopted father and the official host, stood at the door, his wiry frame thinner than normal in his dark Savile Row suit. He'd put a crimson silk hankie in the top pocket, in a melancholy attempt to comply with the cheerful dress code, but his face was grey and tight with strain beneath his white hair.

I wished I could hug him, but the only time Lord T voluntarily submitted to having anyone put their arms round him in public was when his tailor took his chest measurement. His expression, though, softened when he saw me, and I smiled, hoping he'd read the hug in my eyes.

"Betsy," he said, reaching out for my hands, "and Olivia, how lovely. Come in."

There's an irony, I thought, as he kissed my cheek and welcomed me inside. Me, being welcomed into the Tallimore Academy by the very man who'd decided, nearly a decade ago, against his own wife's wishes, that it wasn't appropriate for me to attend.

CHAPTER TWO

A good handshake should be firm but not tight, with three shakes up and down, hinging at the elbow, and plenty of eye contact.

The day I found out that I wasn't allowed to join the Academy girls in their napkin-folding, prince-meeting etiquette classes was the day my life stopped being like something from one of Nancy's well-thumbed Georgette Heyer novels, and turned into something more approaching real life.

Actually, I'm being melodramatic. I was eighteen. Real life had definitely cut in — I'd already failed two driving tests and had my ears pierced. What I mean, I suppose, is that, for the first time, I was forced to consider the possibility that I might not be the abandoned baby of a wronged actress/brokenhearted heiress/tubercular ballerina. I might not be special at all.

Up till then, I'd enjoyed the luxury of a mysterious past that made first the Academy girls, and then my own school-friends go gratifyingly misty-eyed, but with the comforting safety net of Franny, Nancy and

Kathleen's absolute devotion. Franny treated me exactly as if I were her own little girl, and, to be honest, I felt as if I was. It's hard to miss your "real" mother when you don't even know what colour her eyes are, and Franny couldn't have loved me more than she did. Lord T and I weren't what you'd call close, but he sorted me out with a dog and made sure my pocket money was up-to-date.

I went to a smart primary behind Buckingham Palace until I was eleven, and then Franny sent me to her old boarding school in Yorkshire. I met Liv on our first night, tearfully scoffing a Pot Noodle and chicken nuggets because "it reminded her of home". Liv's dad, Ken, was an Irish property wideboy who'd made a pile from correctly guessing which areas of London would go from scummy to trendy in the time it took him to install Ikea kitchens and new loos, and her mum, Rina, was a retired fashion model who'd been the "legs" of various famous stockings. Liv and I were both outsiders, among the 24-carat posh girls: Lanky Liv had a half-Irish, half-London accent that didn't fit in with everyone else's drawly yahs; I had carroty hair and dressed just like you'd expect someone who'd grown up in a finishing school would: pearls, kitten heels, Laura Ashley floral skirts. We clicked at once.

I tried hard at school, knowing how expensive the fees were, and I was popular enough, given that my best subject was Maths, which I loved because everything added up, there was always a right answer and no room for mystery whatsoever. But as my final year approached, and we started to talk about jobs and university, something strange happened. I started thinking about my mother, and the Academy and that sad hope she'd written on the note: *I want her to grow up to be a proper lady*. I hadn't really followed what was happening at the Academy since I'd been away, and from what I remembered, I wasn't sure if I needed to learn half the stuff on offer, unless International Economists also had to lay the dinner table before hosting summits. But it seemed like the only way I'd ever connect to my shadowy birth mother, even if she never knew I'd been, as well as pleasing Franny, who ran it, so I decided it'd be as good a gap year as any.

It didn't work out like that.

At the end of the summer, Franny and Lord T took me out for lunch at the Savoy Grill to celebrate my A-level grades, and after some discussion about what kind of dog would result if Lord T bred his Great Dane with their neighbour's evil little Border Terrier (a Great Derrière, we decided), the conversation turned to my "future plans". The atmosphere up till then had been quite merry, and I was sure that Franny was hinting that I should get myself a cashmere twinset in readiness for some tea strainer and placecard action.

I beamed at her over the cheese platter, and said, "Liv reckons we should drive across America and make a road movie, but she's failed her test again, so that's not on. I thought I might have my gap year in London and learn some manners?"

Franny smiled sadly and pulled her triple string of pearls tight, and I knew something was wrong.

I followed her gaze to Lord T, who was gouging awkwardly at the Stilton in a fashion that wouldn't have passed muster in the Academy's Social Dining class.

"Finishing school's wasted on a girl like you," he mumbled, flushing and spraying a tenner's worth of crumbs over the tablecloth. "Get yourself a degree, something useful . . . How about Durham? Know some people there . . . My old college, jolly good Maths faculty . . ."

I felt as if I'd just swallowed a wasp. *A girl like me*? What sort of girl was that?

Even though I had every intention of going to uni, thank you very much, I was stunned. I tried to tell myself that it was a compliment, that he was proud of my academic achievements, but I couldn't get round the fact that he clearly thought there was no point wasting time or money trying to turn me into something I wasn't.

I'd never felt more *adopted* in my whole life. I wanted to slide under the table with humiliation.

Franny leapt in at once. "Pelham, it's up to *Betsy* where she studies!" She glanced at me and her eyes were full of something I hadn't seen before: frustration. "How about LSE, darling, nearer home? With your grades, they'll be *begging* you to apply!"

But she didn't try to talk him round and something inside me curled up into a tight ball.

Well, I thought, grimly, if he wants me to go away, I'll *go* away.

That afternoon I applied to St Andrews — the furthest British university I could find — and moved up to Scotland where I turned my back on everything the Academy stood for. Manners, etiquette, twinsets, behaving like Audrey Hepburn — it hurt even to think about it. Much to Liv's horror, I gave all my kitten heels to Oxfam, and bought cargo pants, and vowed I'd never, *ever* write a stupid bloody placecard.

It broke my heart that I hadn't been able to be what my mother wanted, but if she'd known what the entry requirements were, maybe she should have thought about putting a pedigree in the Cooper's marmalade box with me, not a plea for help and a necklace.

I got over it, of course. Franny refused to acknowledge my hurt silence and sent me Fortnum & Mason hampers and funny letters full of advice and gossip and passed on worried queries about whether I was eating enough (from Kathleen) and wearing thermals (from Nancy). In the end, as I told Liv, I was *glad* I hadn't wasted precious time on curtseying: I learned more useful things in one Freshers' Week than I would have done in a year of napkin-folding. I left with a first-class degree and ten different hangover cures, and started my life over again in Edinburgh, where no one would have believed the "left in a box at a finishing school" story even if I'd told them. Which I didn't.

I *thought* I didn't care about the Academy any more. And yet, standing there on the doorstep, a grown woman with a proper job and her own flat, I felt a weird sense that there was something waiting for me behind the door that I didn't even know about yet. Like one of those spooky "and this is how your life *could* have gone" films.

"Come in, Betsy," said Lord T and I realised I was hovering, blocking his polite attempts to shake Liv's hand. "And thank you for coming, Olivia."

"Oh, my pleasure," said Liv and I could see Lord T melt under her most concerned smile. Liv had that effect on people, even men who usually talked to women as if they were dangerous.

I took a deep breath and stepped over the threshold, looking round at the reception unfolding beneath the old crystal chandeliers. Between the swooping staircase on one side and the table of wineglasses and teacups on the other, the hall was packed with women, all somewhere between the ages of thirty and seventy, although you couldn't pin an exact age on a single one of them. They were stylishly dressed in flattering pastel shades, engaged in animated conversation, and most were wearing nude shoes to elongate their legs.

Lord T stuck by my side, seeming a bit lost amidst the female hordes. "What on earth are they laughing about?" he asked, more bemused than upset. "Half of them were in floods half an hour ago. I'm down to my last handkerchief and I brought *four*."

"Drinks!" said Liv, stealing my own "get out of jail free" conversation card. "That's what we need! I'll go and get some tea!"

Before I could reply, two sisters beetled up and accosted us with outstretched hands to shake. Tallimore girls were not backwards at coming forwards in a cocktail party situation.

"Betsy! It's Marcia Holderstone!" said one of them. "You won't remember me but I used to plait your hair, do you remember, in Personal Grooming! You must have been about six! How lovely to see you again!"

I found myself smiling as my hand was grasped and shaken warmly. There was something effortless about confidence like that. I really envied it. Franny taught me all the tricks about walking through a party, head high, pretending you knew everyone, but women like Marcia really did know everyone; she'd probably been networking since she was knee-high to a Shetland pony.

"Oh, we had such a wonderful year here, didn't we, Kate?" Marcia turned to her sister, and then suddenly turned serious and sympathetic as her funeral manners kicked in. "We're so sorry for your loss, Lord Tallimore. And you, Betsy. Lady Frances was *marvellous*. I still think of her every time I pack my suitcase. Shoes at the bottom, clean knicks in the . . ."

"I don't think Lord Tallimore needs to know the details," said Kate, quickly.

I glanced at his frozen expression. In Lord T's circles, the women were trained for social occasions and the men drank port and communicated about death and childbirth via grunts. It must be torture, I thought, hearing how everyone adored his wife and not having the faintest idea what to say.

"That's the secret of a well-packed case, isn't it!" I interjected, in a voice that sounded a bit higher than my normal one. "No one sees the details!"

"Absolutely! Oh, it's such a thrill to be back!" Marcia's eyes darted around. "Can we see the old ballroom, do you think?" she asked, already gazing up the curving staircase to the teaching rooms on the first floor. "Do you remember, Kate, learning the fashion catwalk?"

"Ah no!" Lord Tallimore sprang to life with a sudden cough. "No, I rather think Miss Thorne has decided to keep the reception to one room . . . health and safety, you see . . ."

"Oh! Of course, yes." Marcia recovered but looked disappointed. "What a shame." She shook his hand again. "Mustn't monopolise you, I'm sure everyone wants to share their condolences."

I spotted the hovering line of women waiting to have similar conversations, all primed with kind comments. Funerals, broken engagements, hairs in soup: Tallimore girls were well briefed on every awkward situation up to and including alien abduction. No cringe-making silences with unintroduced Martian warlords for *them*. I touched Lord T's arm as Marcia and Kate swayed towards the buffet and the next commiseree approached. "Would you like a moment on your own? I know it's a strain thinking of new things to say every time. If you want to slip out to the library, I can bring some tea . . ."

"No, duty first." Lord T grimaced as if he were about to be shot at dawn, then dropped his voice. "Maybe in quarter of an hour? If you see me trapped in a corner? Frances used to wait for me to put my spectacles on, then she'd shimmer over and save me. Subtle, you know." He looked forlorn, and I suddenly saw what a team they'd been for forty-odd years.

"OK," I whispered back, and he squared his shoulders and went back to his task.

I was gasping for a cup of tea, though, and my eyes darted greedily around the hall as I headed for the table. I kept seeing things I'd forgotten about: the moody painting of the first Lady Tallimore draped on a chaise longue (her magnificent Georgian bosom painted over by a disapproving Victorian ancestor), the china bowls of potpourri on dark oak sidetables, the framed photographs of each year's intake adorning the deep red walls. All just as I remembered.

Liv was deep in conversation with a flamboyant-looking granny, so I picked up a cup and drifted over to the wall of photographs, which began with pre-war smiles and neat ankles and ended around 1995, in a cloud of Ellnett hairspray. Automatically, I looked for the 1981 photograph, "my" year — a dozen or so girls arranged around the rose garden seats, all looking up from under their floppy Duran Duran fringes with bashful expressions and pearlised pink lipstick.

I wondered what they all looked like now — how many of them were here? And whether they would remember me, and my arrival on the steps. Whether, in fact, they knew who might have put me there?

Ever since Franny's funeral, I'd been having the same nagging thought: who knew where my birth mother was now? Over the years, I'd daydreamed various dramatic meetings with my biological parents but I'd never thought seriously about actually tracing them. As far as I was concerned, Franny was my "real" mother, and though she'd never made a secret of my mysterious beginnings, her eyes filled with unbearable sadness whenever I asked about it, so I rarely did. But now Franny wasn't here to be hurt, I'd started to wonder if it mightn't be the time to start investigating. The only trouble was, I thought, staring at the Class of '81, I had nothing to go on but a note, and a necklace. But if anyone was going to know something, surely it would be here?

I peered closer at the frilly collars and blue eyeliner. Maybe even in this very photograph . . .

"Oh my God! Didn't we all look *awful*! Look at me in that ludicrous ruffly shirt. I look like someone's just assaulted me with aerosol cream."

I jumped as a woman in a Pucci print dress loomed up behind me. She'd taken the "cheerful" dress code to heart, and added turquoise shoes and perched a jaunty feather fascinator in her black geometric bob in case her swirly dress wasn't quite cheerful enough. She was carrying it off, though. Her eyes twinkled naughtily, as if she knew me, but I wasn't sure whether we knew each other well enough for me to agree with her about her hideous blouse, or not.

"Oh, um, I think ruffles are coming back in," I hazarded.

"Only if you're a female impersonator, darling." She waved her hands in the air, nearly spilling her wine. "But you're *far* too young to know how embarrassing these clothes are! If you're who I think you are, you popped up about three days after that photograph was taken! While we were all queueing down the Mall to get a peek at Charles and Diana, the real excitement was unfolding on our doorstep! Quite literally! It's Betsy, isn't it? The Tallimore baby?"

I felt my cheeks go hot under her frank gaze. Seriously posh people could be incredibly direct, even with intensive finishing, it would seem. "Um, yes. I'm very sorry, but I don't remember . . ."

"Well, how *would* you, darling? You were teeny enough to stash in an evening bag last time I saw you." Her eyes creased up as she smiled. "I'm Nell, Nell Howard. Or Eleanor, as I was here. Are you still Betsy Tallimore, or have you racked up some double-barrels yet?"

"No," I said, "I'm still Betsy Tallimore."

"Ah, not a *true* Tallimore girl until you've bagged a few spouses," she said, with a sardonic flick of her black brows. "Miss Thorne must have had shares in The Great Trading Company wedding list, the way she banged on about the importance of getting ourselves shacked up. Well, hello, Betsy."

I juggled my teacup and biscuit while she expertly juggled her wineglass and sideplate, and we shook hands.

"So, do tell," she went on, chattily, "did you ever track down your real ma and pa? Oh, sorry! Personal questions!" She slapped her own wrist and looked slightly, but not very, remorseful. "I'm not the most tactful conversationalist — used to get some dirty looks from Miss Vanderbilt. But if you don't ask, and all that . . ."

"No, I never tried," I admitted. "I was very happy. The Tallimores were all the family I needed, and Nancy and Kathleen looked after me . . ."

"Oh, I can imagine those two! Mother hens! But you never even looked?" Nell squinted at me as if I was standing in front of a bright light. She had the squinty tanned face of the habitual ski/sun/sand Sloane, who'd happily take a few wrinkles in the name of snow, wine and shrieks of hysterical laughter.

I shook my head. "I think it would have hurt too many feelings."

That wasn't the whole truth: I had to admit to a fair bit of suspicion about my father's identity, at least, though I'd never have said.

Everything pointed to feckless Hector, Franny's runaway black sheep son, with the aristocratic good looks, and the debt management problem. Why else would the Tallimores have taken me in and looked after me like their own if they weren't secretly sure that he'd had a hand — at the very least — in my arrival? From what I'd managed to glean from Kathleen, he was irresponsible enough, had access to a veritable sweet shop of impressionable girls, and he'd skipped off to Argentina years ago, which in Nancy's book(s) was standard Guilty Rake Behaviour. If there were any photos of Hector twiddling a moustache while posing next to a sportscar, the evidence would be complete.

Sadly for my detective ambitions, there were no photos of Hector, because Franny had hidden them all, apart from the one by her bed — which, to my mind, explained why she doted on me the way she did. I was the last link with him. Nancy had looked after Hector as a baby and missed him too, so I couldn't ask, but a couple of times, I managed to enter into a dark hinting exchange with Kathleen. She insisted she didn't know my father's identity, but that she could "feel it in her water that whoever it was, wasn't a million miles away from here. If you know what I mean."

Nell didn't need to know the complicated emotional reasoning behind all this though.

"Besides," I said, as lightly as I could, "I didn't mind not knowing. It meant I had nothing to live up to, or down to. I was just me!"

She tipped her head on one side and her feather fascinator bounced. "Fair enough."

"I did wonder whether it might be . . ." I hesitated, surprised at myself. "Whether my mother might have been at the Academy? Someone who knew what time Kathleen collected the milk in the morning? Did anyone else wonder that?"

"God, yes!" Nell nodded. "Quite possible. Bit of an scandaloso year, that — tons of really gorgeous girls who ended up as models, three-second roles in a Bond film, Flake adverts, that sort of thing. And of course they went round town with the Kensington Hunt. Gosh." She fanned herself with an enthusiastic hand. "They were even more divine than the girls, to tell the truth. We'd be in some tedious dress-making lesson, and the horns would honk outside, and there they'd be — Rory, Simon, Hector . . . All floppy-haired and *disgraceful*, but so much fun. Everyone would squeal. Apart from Miss Vanderbilt, obviously. But even she went a bit pink around the gills, old Vanders."

"The Kensington Hunt?" I repeated. "I didn't know there were foxes round here."

Nell fixed me with a look. "Did Lady Frances keep you in a bunker all your life, darling? They were terribly notorious in their day, always hot on the trail of *girls*. Foxy girls, I suppose. Hence the nickname. They used to hang out at the Admiral Cod, mostly, but any party would do. Hilarious up to a point, but they always went a bit too far — not much common sense. Hector Tallimore was the worst of the lot, which would explain why Lady Frances never mentioned it. He actually had a horn he'd blow if . . ." She looked more curiously at me. "Now, did *he* ever turn up? The bold Hector?"

I shook my head. Nell had an outrageously forthright manner, but I was too curious to be offended. I just wanted her to keep on talking. It was like a gossip sugar rush. "He's still in Argentina, as far as I know. Didn't even come back for the funeral." I bit my lip. "It was very sudden, though — a brain tumour. By the time . . ." I gulped. Even I had missed the very end.

"I heard." Nell sighed. "He always was utterly unworthy of his mother, darling. Anyway, moving on . . ."

"So, you think my mother was one of these girls?" I asked, pointing at the photograph, my pulse hammering with the thrill of asking proper questions at last. "One of your friends?"

Nell barked with laughter. "*My* year? I don't think so! Look at us!" She gestured at the photograph with her glass. The wine sloshed. "Bunch of heifers! The only film *we'd* end up in would be *Alien*! No, they were a year older. We all got mixed up, you know — some people did one term, some did three or four."

But I was already searching for the 1980 photograph. "1979 . . . 1982 . . ." I turned to Nell. "It's not here."

"Isn't it?" Her cat's eyes widened and she put a finger on her chin. "Ooh! The plot thickens. I must say, they weren't the most popular year. Not with the staff, anyway." She winked.

"Elizabeth! And Eleanor Howard! What a nice surprise!"

I whisked round to find Miss Thorne, the new headmistress, right behind us.

No, not new headmistress, I corrected myself. She'd been running the place for four years, since Miss Vanderbilt retired. The trouble was, it was very hard to think of the Tallimore Academy without thinking first of Franny, then of Miss Vanderbilt. I imagined Miss Thorne was probably more aware of that than most.

Nell discreetly tipped back the remains of her wine then looked in surprise at her glass. "Goodness! I've run dry! Miss Thorne, can I get you a cup of tea? You must be parched. Betsy? No? Excuse me for a moment, won't you?"

And she slid off into the throng, leaving me with Miss Thorne, who I could tell was marking my outfit out of ten. I didn't care: my brain was still whirling with drunken hi-jinks and cads in dinner jackets, and the possibility that I might have Bond girl blood running through my veins. Was that better or worse than impoverished ballerina? It certainly felt more real, all of a sudden.

I concentrated on standing up straight and saying the right thing to Miss Thorne. She had been the Nice Cop to the redoubtable Miss Vanderbilt's Really Rather Disappointed Cop and although Miss Thorne was generally much freer with her compliments, they tended to be the sort of compliments that exploded on closer examination. She also had favourites, of which I knew I wasn't one, not being tiny or fabulously wealthy or related to a polo player (as far as anyone knew).

"Elizabeth! You read very nicely, dear," she said, offering a small soft hand and I managed a nod. "Don't take this the wrong way, but I must say, I wouldn't have recognised you! So chic!"

Miss Thorne stood back so she could get a proper professional view of me. I was at least five inches taller than her, despite her stout heels.

"Thank you," I said, pleased despite the obvious way she was marking out of ten. I tried hard to be chic. After my angry university grunge phase, which only made me look like a lumberjack Ronald McDonald, I'd settled back into a sort of Jackie O middle ground of simple neutral separates — which had the added advantage of not costing much and being easy to match first thing in the morning — and minimal make-up, just crimson lips and mascara, which I normally ended up doing on the bus. Just enough to make me look coloured-in.

"But where's all that adorable curly hair?" Miss Thorne went on, taking in my blue shift and gold flats. "What was it the girls used to call you?" She affected not to remember but I knew she knew. "The film, you know, with the ghastly dog and the dancing . . ."

"Annie," I said, reluctantly.

"Yes! Little orphan Annie! How funny."

The warmth drained out of my smile, though I didn't let it drop. It wasn't a nickname I liked for a number of reasons, but I could hardly pretend I didn't remember. It was largely because of that nickname that I'd spent two arm-wrecking months teaching myself to blow-dry my coppery frizz into submission. I could do a salon-perfect finish in under fifteen minutes now, and my hairdryer doubled as a crème brûlée torch.

Miss Thorne either didn't see my awkwardness or chose to gloss over it. "So what are you up to now?" she went on. "Is there a lucky chap? Or are you still working?"

"I'm focusing on my career at the moment," I smiled, so my voice would sound cheerful, though I didn't feel it. "It keeps me very busy." There was no way I was going to tell Miss Thorne that not only was I conducting a one-woman survey into the very good reasons why the remaining single men of Edinburgh *were* still single, I was also using my famous Maths degree to work out sale discounts on diamante sandals.

She carried on staring at me, which was the socially acceptable way of saying "and?" My mouth started moving on its own under the force of her gaze. "I work in brand positioning and market analysis," I stammered, crossing my fingers and thinking of the January sales plan I'd just drawn up for Fiona, the somewhat highly-strung owner of the shoe shop where I work. I did sometimes wonder if Fiona had won The Glass Slipper in a raffle, rather than made a conscious business plan.

Miss Thorne's bright eyes glittered and she tilted her head to one side, watching my face. "How *marvellous*! Who are you working with? Is it one of those big companies I might have seen on the news?"

"I don't think so . . ." I flushed even more. That's the worst thing about having skin the colour of milk: no fake tan, no sunbathing and absolutely no blushing. "It's a shoestring operation."

I was saved from having to think up further shoe-related semi-fibs by a slender forty-something woman in a pink boucle suit, who sailed up behind us and touched Miss Thorne on the arm. "Miss Thorne? Julia Palmer? From the Somerset Palmers? So sorry to hear about . . ."

"Piggy *Palmer*!" cried Miss Thorne, turning away from me as if I'd never been there. "Look at *you*, my dear!"

Piggy — who must have been piggy a *very* long time ago from the state of her toned calves — flinched, then gamely reengaged her warm smile.

I took the opportunity to slide away, scanning the room for any sign of Nell Howard, but she'd vanished into the sea of silk dresses and Chanel jackets. My brain was buzzing with questions I desperately wanted to ask her: it might just be old gossip to Nell, but to me, it was the first direct connection to the flesh and blood woman who'd dumped me here.

Had there been one red-headed girl she might remember?

And exactly what sort of things went on with these reckless rich boys?

Did Hector Tallimore have a particular girlfriend?

Did she recognise my little bee necklace, the one I was wearing right now, and never took off?

I nudged my way into the throng, conscious that my stomach was making most inelegant noises. I hadn't had anything to eat since lunch the previous day, which was highly irregular, since Getting A Good Breakfast was something Kathleen had drilled into me from an early age. "The bigger the day, the bigger the breakfast," she'd insist, shovelling three different types of egg on to my plate. I'd skipped breakfast with her this morning for that very reason — I was far too tense to eat, much less deal with roaring indigestion.

Now, though, I was starting to feel decidedly peckish, and I headed towards the sandwiches. If I knew Franny, I thought, she'd have left specific instructions about the catering: no crusts, plenty of tiny cakes and cloth napkins all round.

The post-memorial spread was laid on a long table beneath the first Lady Tallimore's lascivious oil portrait, and I began helping myself to the cucumber sandwiches and scones. I was disappointed to see that the plates were already looking rather picked through, with telltale spaces between the parsley sprigs. Out of habit, born from Kathleen's catering tips, I shuffled the remaining egg and cress sarnies together, so they'd look nicer, when suddenly the silver sandwich platter slid backwards out of my reach and I heard an audible tut.

I looked up in surprise. A dark-haired man in a black suit and tie that, going by the clashing colours, seemed to be from a very, very minor public school, was standing behind the table, holding the other end of the platter.

"Two," he said, nodding at my plate. "Two sandwiches per person. And one scone half. Jam or cream?"

"*Excuse* me?" I said, in surprise.

"Two sandwiches," he repeated. "You've got two there."

I didn't recognise him. Apart from Lord Tallimore, he was the only man in the sea of oestrogen and cashmere, which would have explained the nervous air on its own, but his brown eyes were darting back and forth, as if something was just about to go wrong, but he didn't know where.

"Are the sandwiches *rationed?*" I said in a joking tone and tugged my end of the platter, which — I couldn't believe it! — he refused to let go of. I tugged again, more meaningfully. "What if I don't like egg and cress?"

"There are enough sandwiches to go round," he said, "as long as people aren't greedy. This is meant to be a quick buffet, not afternoon tea at the Ritz."

I put my hand to my mouth in shock, and he took advantage of my confusion to seize control of the platter. Triumphantly, he pushed his wire-rimmed glasses up his long nose with one finger. I made a determined grab for another sandwich, but he was too quick and moved the platter just as a woman approached from my right; he made it look as if he wasn't actually snatching the platter away from me, but offering it to her.

"How *rude!*" I gasped.

She looked at me before accepting the two (curling) egg and cress quarters and moving off, hurriedly, casting glances over her shoulder as she went.

Did I imagine that? I wondered, bewildered. Did I really just fight over the sandwiches with a *caterer*?

"Have you had a cup of tea?" he asked, politely.

"One — so far." I glared at him. "Is that also limited?"

"No, there's plenty of tea," he said, then paused. "If you could just stick to one glass of wine, though. And keep your glass to save on washing up, if you don't mind."

What sort of firm *was* this? I put my plate down and sized him up. He seemed quite posh, but then most caterers I'd met in my attempts to cater launches for Fiona were posh bankers' wives doing it for a hobby — maybe this was his post-Crunch career. It would explain the obsession with sandwich equity.

"I don't know what Miss Thorne's instructions were about catering," I began in a friendly voice, "but I'm sure she wouldn't want Lady Frances to be remembered as the woman who made her guests share one scone between two at her memorial tea . . ."

I felt a tray in the small of my back.

"Ooops, sorry!" said a loud London accent. "Mark, I've run out. I kept moving fast, like you said, but the big one in the hat like a satellite dish took all the salmon ones, said she had a dairy allergy, so what could I do? I tried to move on, but she got her mate to block me while she cleaned out the scones. This lot are like piranhas, I'm telling you. So much for posh women's eating disorders!"

I turned round. A short girl with a pixie crop stood about ten centimetres away from me with another platter, containing only crumbs and parsley. "Are you after more grub?" she enquired, with a disarming beam. "Only we've run out of bread and there's no petty cash. Did the whole thing for sixty quid, mind. But sshh!" She held a finger up to her lips. "No one will notice if we just keep moving the plates round!"

"Sixty quid?" I repeated. "That's all they paid you to cater the whole tea?"

The man looked horrified, then furious. "For God's sake, Paulette. Is there any point telling you to keep things like that to yourself?"

I was rummaging in my bag for my purse. I couldn't stand it any longer. If Kathleen heard any paid catering professionals carrying on like this she'd explode right out of her corselette, memorial or no memorial, and that would spoil everything. "Here . . ." I handed over the forty pounds I'd earmarked for dinner with Liv that evening. "There's a Tesco Metro round the corner — get the fanciest, smallest cakes they have, and some wine, and run back here as soon as you can."

"There's really no need for guests to pay for food," the man — Mark? — began, but I stopped him.

"I'm not a guest, I'm Lady Tallimore's *daughter*. I don't want anyone being told they can't have a third sandwich. It's not the sort of hostess she was."

As I said it, the pair of them exchanged horrified glances, and Paulette slapped her head with her palm.

Mark closed his eyes, squeezed his nose, then opened them again. He looked as if he'd hoped the room would have vanished in between.

"I'll go, shall I?" asked Paulette.

"Yes," I said at the same time as he did, and she grabbed my money and scuttled off.

"I can explain . . ." he began, but I shook my head. It wasn't my job to start yelling at the caterers but honestly — sixty pounds? What sort of budget was that? And what sort of caterers did you get for sixty quid anyway?

"Please don't," I said, feeling desperately sorry for Lord T. I *knew* I should have come down earlier and done more. "Just make sure the sandwiches are circulating before the wine runs out. No crusts, filling up to the edge, please. And if you could refresh the tea, that would be great."

I turned to go but he coughed, embarrassed.

"I don't suppose . . ." he began, then gestured at the plates. "You could give me a hand?"

"What?" Now I'd heard everything. "Are sandwiches not lesson one at Catering College?"

I think he tried a smile, but it came out more like a grimace. "Probably. Only I'm not a caterer, I'm the bursar. And my lovely assistant there is no waitress, as you can tell. Paulette's the headmistress's PA." He ran a despairing hand through his thick brown hair. "Before you ask, yes, her telephone manner is just as discreet as her waitressing. She's more of a before than after, when it comes to the Academy's professional services."

"Oh," I said, surprised, and a bit embarrassed at the way I'd glared at him before. Now I looked at him properly, I realised he was younger than I'd thought, around my age, with nice brown eyes and the sort of honest, outdoorsy face you tend to see on porridge boxes. A bit rugged, and slightly cross, but honest. "Lord Tallimore didn't get this properly catered?"

"There was some confusion, because Miss Thorne wanted to hire some old girl who plays at . . . who has a catering firm, but it *seems* there was a communication breakdown." Mr Bursar-Caterer was clearly trying not to be rude from the way his thick eyebrows kept leaping up and down behind his glasses, but he obviously hadn't had a Tallimore training in keeping his face straight while manipulating the truth into politer shapes. "I found out this morning that nothing had been done, so I stepped in, rather than add to Lord Tallimore's worries on a day like this. There was only me and Paulette and we didn't have long, while everyone was at the service . . ."

"Hence the rationing," I said. I was touched at his concern, and felt bad. "I see now. Sorry."

"Well, I prefer to call it portion control." He pushed the glasses back up his nose and gazed at the massed guests. His bewilderment reminded me of Lord T. "For a bunch of women who aren't meant to eat, they've gone through this in no time. I thought we'd done *more* than enough."

"Always make half as much again. First rule of throwing a party. Do they still teach the Party Planning course?" I asked, half-joking. "Calculations for sandwiches per head, according to time of year, mean age of guests, whether people would abandon crab paste sarnies after one bite, et cetera. Proper mathematical equations and everything."

"Maths? Surely not," he said drily. "That sounds almost useful."

I couldn't really disagree — even aged seven I'd thought it was blindingly obvious to count your guests before "instructing your cook" — but at the same time, something in his tone meant I couldn't stop myself leaping to the Academy's defence.

"Well, it *would* have been useful today, wouldn't it? I'm sure Miss Thorne would have told you, if you'd asked," I retorted.

Even as I spoke, his gaze was following a guest towards the drinks table, and when she picked up two glasses, he took an involuntary step forward.

"Whoa, there!" I grabbed his arm to stop him interrogating her about her actual thirst requirements. "She might be taking one for a friend. Or she might be trying to escape from a party bore, and is pulling the, 'I'm just on my way to give this to someone' trick. I learned that here." I paused and let go of his suit sleeve. "And that *is* actually quite useful."

He turned back to me, and the stern expression had softened into something nearing amusement, but not quite.

"You're funny," he said.

"We've missed out proper introductions," I said by way of distraction, seeing a gaggle of guests head towards the wine. "Let's do it now, before it gets embarrassing. I'm Betsy." I extended a hand to shake, and added, encouraged by his cautious smile, "I'm sorry I didn't recognise you. I haven't been back here for a while. The last bursar I remember used to wear terrible check sports jackets and called every woman under fifty Popsy. Colonel Montgomery? Did you meet him?"

"In passing." His expression stiffened. "My father."

"Oh." I wilted. And I'd been doing so well. "Sorry."

"Don't be. My mother's not keen on sports jackets either. I'm Mark, Mark Montgomery, obviously," he said, and as he shot out his hand, I saw silver cufflinks and a crisp white cuff. "I'm a bit more enlightened, I like to think. I'm not a big believer in this sort of place, to be perfectly honest with you, but I have a good deal of time for Lord Tallimore. I drop in once a month, keep the books ticking over."

Mark Montgomery scored highly on the handshake test, having both a firm grip and warm but dry hands.

I fell back on busy-ness to cover my embarrassment, and focused on the depleted sandwiches. "Good, well, now we've got that sorted out, shall we do something about the food situation?" I said, wishing I didn't sound like such a bossyboots, but not being able to help myself. "I know where I can find some bread before — was it Paulette? — comes back. My godmothers live in the mews cottage; they've got the sort of pantry that could survive a nuclear winter." I looked up at him, hopefully. "I'm sure you're much more expert with a bread knife than you're letting on. If that doesn't sound wrong?"

Mark had relaxed enough to manage a smile at that, but he still looked uptight around the forehead. He had one of those faces that always looked a bit cheesed off, I decided. Either that, or he was allergic to expensive ladies' perfume.

"Wouldn't it make more sense for me to stay here and supervise the distribution of what's left? It needs a firm hand."

I bit my tongue. That was exactly what I didn't want, Mark Montgomery adding a tasteful "Red Cross food aid" theme to Franny's memorial tea. Besides, the sooner this was done, the sooner I could get out there and find Nell Howard again and see what else she could tell me.

"Well, a helper makes half a job?" Mark opened his mouth to argue, so I quickly tried a different tack. "Or you could stay here and circulate with the sandwiches? And make conversation with the old girls?"

I'd hit a nerve. He blinked rapidly, revealing surprisingly long lashes behind his bookish specs, and generally looked as if I'd just suggested he cover himself in mustard and thrown himself to the lions.

"Egg and cress or cheese?" he asked, and handed me the empty platter.

I found Kathleen and Nancy in a corner surrounded by adoring old girls, all of whom were insisting they didn't look a day older than sixty, which they didn't, despite being well into their eighties.

The pair of them had taken the reverse approach to ageing; instead of desperately clinging to thirty-two while the tides of time swept them into their forties, they'd plumped for looking fifty-three from the age of thirty, and had stuck there. In Kathleen's case, regular applications of Nice and Easy kept her hair a startling jet black, and regular partaking of brown ale and Lancashire hotpot kept her skin unlined, whereas Nancy's bird-like nerves maintained her miniature pepper-grinder frame. They looked the same to me now as they had done throughout my childhood, and in turn, they liked to think I was still twelve.

"Betsy! There you are! What have you done to your hair?" said Kathleen, right on cue when I approached. "Where are those pretty curls? Have you been ironing your hair again?"

Kathleen thought I was making hair straighteners up. She couldn't believe anyone could be so stupid.

"Where've you been?" demanded Nancy, reaching up to smack a kiss on to my cheek. "You read so beautifully. Everyone said you were the best. We were proud as punch, weren't we, Kathleen?"

"We were." Kathleen nodded. "And Frances would have been very proud of you. I said to Fenella Rickett, as was, our little Betsy's running her own management company up in Edinburgh, all on her . . ."

"Um, listen, can I ask you two for some help?" I interrupted hurriedly. I didn't want to get into the whole "management company" misunderstanding just yet. "They've run out of sandwiches."

"I knew it!" said Kathleen triumphantly. "I said Geraldine Thorne wouldn't order enough. Right, then — we'd better crack on, hadn't we?"

She was more than happy to rush me into her walk-in larder of delights, as an excuse to interrogate me about my eating habits, and in fifteen minutes, Mark Montgomery and I were marching up the garden path with enough sandwiches to choke an elephant, just in time to meet Paulette returning with twelve boxes of after-dinner mints.

"On sale," she said, pouring my change into the pocket on my dress. "Better value than cupcakes, I reckoned. And no need to ration them out!"

"Oh, well, on that basis, why didn't you just get cornflakes . . ." Mark began, but I leaped in. There was no point having a row now.

"What an unusual idea!" I said, quickly. "Take them round with coffee, Paulette, and make sure everyone gets *as many as they want*. Ah, now here's a man who needs some refreshment!" I said, seeing Lord T back away with some difficulty from a little knot of guests. They were all patting him, like a sick dog. "Sandwich?"

"Oh, marvellous!" he said gratefully. "Sandwiches, yes."

Lord T looked as if he'd just spent seven hours trapped in a lift with the entire Women's Institute of Great Britain. His hair was ruffled and he was definitely wearing his spectacles. In fact, I'd never seen such an emphatically worn pair of specs.

"No crusts," he said, rather wistfully. "And cucumber, too. Frances' favourite." He looked over at me and Mark and managed a weak smile. "Jolly good show, cucumber. Can't beat it. Enough to go round, I hope?"

"Everything's under control, food-wise," said Mark. "So long as people don't . . ."

I kicked him, discreetly.

"We're fine," he finished.

"Splendid," said Lord T, with visible relief. "Good. "Betsy, could I have a quiet word?" he said. "In the library?" I wondered if he realised he had pearly pink lipstick on his cheek. Two different shades.

"Of course," I said, handing my teetering platter to Mark who promptly swept it out of the way of some poor guest's optimistic reach.

I let Lord T usher me down the corridor to the quiet rooms at the back of the house, and tried not to look too obviously at the walls for the missing year's photograph.

In his youth, Pelham Tallimore had been a Home Counties version of Roger Moore: piercing blue eyes and a dark quiff, but with tweed jackets not safari suits. Like Franny, he had the sort of aristocratic good looks that age turns into silvery foxiness and throughout our adolescence, Liv claimed she had a real older man crush on his "brooding silences" and impeccable manners.

I'd always thought of Lord T as handsome, but today, I noted sadly, he looked handsome *for his age*. There were bags under his eyes, and shadows where I'd never seen them before. Still, his shoes shone like a Steinway piano. That was something.

He waved me into the library, then leaned on the door for a split second, his shoulders dropping with sheer relief to be away from the noisy chatter of the hall.

"Think today went off well?" he asked, with a touching nervousness.

"I do," I said. "Franny would have been so thrilled at the turn out."

"Excellent, excellent." He stepped nearer the empty fireplace and fidgeted awkwardly with the back of a leather armchair. "I appreciate the help, you know. It's good of you, when you're so busy. How *are* things at the moment? Expect you have a New Year rush as all the Christmas bodge-ups come to light and you have to charge in and sort them out! Eh?"

Now it was my turn to start fidgeting with a chair.

Despite my fertile imagination, I was a terrible liar. Terrible in that I really wasn't very good at it, having been assured from an early age by Nancy that magpies pecked out fibbing tongues. Had I been even a mediocre liar, when it came to covering up my stuck-in-a-rut shop job, I'd have made up a glamorous career that I actually understood, instead of letting Franny — and hence Lord T and Kathleen and Nancy — create their own impression that I was a hotshot management consultant.

The only silver lining was that they had slightly less idea of what management consulting involved than I did.

I wasn't a management consultant. I managed the same shoe shop in which I'd done my holiday work as a student. Admittedly it was a very smart shoe shop, but somehow, after five years, I was still there. The misunderstanding had come about because, in my *very* selected highlights of what I'd been up to, I'd told Franny about Fiona's hopeless filing system and how I'd halved her tax bill, and set up a loyalty card scheme. Maybe I overstated it a bit, because somehow Franny got it into her head that I'd stormed in with my calculator blazing, as a professional troubleshooter, not a helpful assistant manager. She'd been so proud of me that I'd never had the heart to point out I was window-dressing driving shoes, not overhauling multinationals.

The painful thing was, Franny's misapprehension wasn't so far off what I actually wanted to do. My ambition was to have a business of my own, something that was all mine — what, though, I wasn't quite sure. I'd really enjoyed sprucing up Fiona's accounts as well as her stockroom, but how can you set yourself up as a business spring cleaner when you haven't any actual experience? Liv said I should just make up some references and go for it, but, as I say, lying convincingly wasn't my strong suit.

Lord T was looking at me, waiting for me to say something thrusting and professional about "my workload". I swallowed. Now probably wasn't the best time to clear up the confusion. "I'm dealing with some very well-heeled clients," I managed.

"Good, good," he said again, distractedly, and rubbed his hands together. "Good."

"Should we sit down?" I suggested. It was my top tactic in the shop. Once you had someone sitting down,

I told the salesgirls, they relaxed and felt more inclined to try things on. And buy things.

Lord T's face brightened and he sank into one of the leather armchairs. I sat on the edge of the one opposite, knees and ankles somehow clamping neatly together in a proper manner, and we faced each other across the empty marble fireplace.

He took a deep breath. "There's something I'd like to talk to you about. As . . . family."

My heart bumped, and I wondered, with a tingle, if he was about to tell me Something Significant. Maybe this was going to be the moment he admitted Hector was my father. Or tell me that my mother had been in touch, seeing Franny's obituary in the paper. Maybe there had been something in Franny's will: "six months from my death . . ." or something. It was coming up to that now. From the tooth-pulling expression on Lord T's face, it had to be something emotional.

"Really?" I said, trying to keep calm. "Go on."

Lord T smoothed his silvery hair back with his left hand. "It's about the Academy."

"What? I mean, oh." My heart stopped bumping and plunged with disappointment. "What about the Academy?"

"I need a favour, Betsy," he said, fixing me with an honest look. "I don't mind telling you that I sat down last night and thought to myself, what would Frances do? And I knew she'd ask you."

My defences had risen at the sheer nerve of being asked to do a favour for the snotty "not for a girl like you" establishment, but then I thought of Franny, needing me, and I heard my voice say, "Of course I'll help."

The expression of unashamed relief on Lord T's face, though, made me wonder if I should have waited to hear the favour first.

"So long as I can," I added, meaningfully. "I mean, I'm not exactly an expert on finishing schools, am I?"

Lord T wasn't tuned in to conversational subtleties like irony. "Which is precisely why I'm asking you," he went on. "I'd very much appreciate it if you could take a look around. I think the Academy needs . . . what's the right way to put this? A spring clean, if you like."

"You want me to *clean* it?" I blurted out, in horror.

Lord Tallimore's smile evaporated. "*Clean* it? Good Lord, no! Whatever gave you that idea? No, it's . . . I need your *professional expertise*, Betsy. I need some good honest business advice. Miss Thorne's been doing her best, I know, but if we don't get some more girls for next term, then . . ."

He raised his hands, then dropped them on his knees with an empty slap. "Place is falling down round our ears — that's why we can't let the guests upstairs, you see. Buckets in the ballroom." He managed a wintry smile. "Roof's been leaking so badly even the mice have water wings."

"Oh!" I was taken aback by how upset I felt, not just for Franny, but for the big house itself. How humiliating to go from glamorous society beehive to a creaky old wreck. Buckets in the ballroom! Franny would be mortified. The ghosts of Lady Tallimores past would be clutching their pearls in shame.

Lord T sighed and I could feel sadness thicken the air between us. "Between you and me, Betsy, there's not much time left. What the Academy needs is something new, some . . . *oomph*. I'd get one of those fancy consultancy firms in, but I can't bear the thought of some smart-arse Soho johnny in German spectacles running round the place, totting up the assets." He rubbed his nose. "No offence!"

"God, no," I said, then remembered he was talking about me. Would it make him better to know he was getting a pretend consultant, for free? I thought not.

"I know Frances would trust you," he said, solemnly, "not just to get the figures adding up again, but to set the Academy on the right lines. So we can carry on into the twenty-first century with something she'd be proud of. Otherwise . . ." His voice trailed away.

I started to nod, in a wise, management consultant fashion, but then a cold chill settled on me, as the enormity of what he was asking sank in. The Academy was in real trouble, serious trouble, and I had even less idea of what to do to help than they did! Lord T needed proper advice. Not me pretending.

I tried to backtrack as calmly as I could, given the way my insides were now twisting with guilt. Nancy was right: little liars *did* start big fires.

"I'm honoured that you think I could help, but I'm not a teacher," I stammered. "I don't know where I'd start."

Lord T waved a dismissive hand. "Miss Thorne can take care of any teaching. Frances wasn't a teacher — she just had her good ideas of what young girls should be told, what they needed to know to set them up in life."

"I know," I agreed, thinking of the things she taught me, the trade secrets of womanhood that were so much more useful than marriage proposal lessons. Prompt thank yous written on funny postcards; Vaseline on the inner heels of stiff new shoes; apples as emergency breath fresheners. Little touches that had got me jobs and good friends. Far more important than giving someone the wrong fork.

I had to give it a try, I told myself, for Franny. Maybe there was *something* I could do. It was just a shop, after all — one selling manners. A real consultant would probably just shut it down straight away.

And, I thought, with an illicit twinge, I might find out a few more things about the 1980 girls and their outrageous boyfriends. Not that I would mention that to Lord T. Not yet, anyway.

"What would you want me to do?" I said, trying to remember what the people on *The Apprentice* said before they were set ludicrous tasks they didn't know how to deal with. "I mean, it's not a normal, er, productivity assessment."

Lord T seemed impressed, but then I didn't think he watched much television. "Well, no. I suppose you'd need to see some lessons, talk to the staff and the current students . . ." His face brightened. "I'd leave it up to your professional experience, Betsy."

"Oh, good," I said, faintly. "Fair enough."

"It's always been a peculiar business for a chap to be involved in," he went on, more cheerily, "but it's been in the family since the year dot, and I don't want to be the one in charge when the ship goes down. Frances poured her heart and soul into — well, I don't need to tell you how she felt about this place, now, do I?"

He managed a wistful smile, and I suddenly saw that it wasn't just the Academy he'd be losing if it closed, but the happy days of his marriage: the sparkling cocktail parties they'd thrown here for London friends, the graduations and presentations, the balmy summer evenings in the garden. The days *I'd* spent with Franny, playing in the roses. She'd spent hours and hours here, guiding and advising and roaring with infectious laughter, the one unladylike thing about her. Franny *was* the Academy.

"After all she did for me? Of course I'll do what I can — for her. And for you," I said impulsively, and leaned forward to grab his hand. It felt thin but strong and his signet ring dug into my palm.

Lord T's eyes met mine, and I was surprised, as I always was, at how bright blue they were in his baggy face. They were still young, even if the rest of him, through stress and grief, looked a hundred.

"Thank you," he said, simply. "I'd be very grateful for whatever you can do."

We held the moment for as long as his Englishness could stand it — about five seconds — then he coughed and said, "So, when could you start? Do you have clients to postpone?"

I thought quickly. I had quite a lot of holiday stored up, and I was off so rarely that Fiona could hardly protest if I pleaded for some compassionate leave.

"What if I come back at the beginning of next week?" It was the third week in January, and The Glass Slipper's sale was drawing to a close. I couldn't leave her in the middle of the second markdowns. That's when prices were almost reasonable, and the shoving got serious.

"Marvellous," he said again. "Of course, you must invoice us — wouldn't expect you to do it for nothing!"

I started to protest, then remembered that actually, the council tax was due, along with my post-Christmas credit card bills. Franny had left me enough money in her will to pay off the mortgage on my minuscule flat, but my budget still required skilful juggling each month. And doing it for nothing would *totally* give away the fact that I wasn't a self-employed professional.

"Whatever you like," I said. "But I can't make any promises."

Lord T gave me a sad smile. "So long as you do your best, Betsy, that's all we can ask."

That's what Franny would have said, I thought. It made me try harder than any threat or bribe, and had done since I was about four.

CHAPTER THREE

Never economise on sushi, sunglasses, or legal advice.

In my absence, the crowds around the refreshment table had swelled considerably, and Liv had joined Kathleen and Nancy at their gossip station by the tea urn. They were hanging on her every word and Nancy was sewing a button back on Liv's gorgeous, probably vintage Dior, jacket.

"And then I said, Finn, please stop sending the flowers, I've got no more vases! So — this is so ridiculous — he sent me a tree. A tree. What am I meant to do with a tree? Then I realised it had this necklace on it . . ."

I'd heard this story earlier in the week, but with much juicier details: it was the tale of Liv's most recent boyfriend Finn, the last solvent banker in Europe, whom she'd met on the Eurostar when her suitcase got stuck in the overhead compartment, and he'd gallantly unjammed it. One short channel hop later, he was filling her sitting room with orchids for five days straight until she'd agreed to have dinner with him — in Rome. Seriously, I had no idea how she did it.

"Heavens above, Liv!" Nancy bit off the thread and sighed with delight. She had a terrible weakness for historical romances. My tuck box at school was filled with Kathleen's cakes and Nancy's tear-stained novelettas. "You are *just* like a Regency heroine!"

"But without the corsets," said Kathleen pointedly. "You should be wearing a vest under that, Olivia. You'll catch your death."

Kathleen and Nancy hung on every breathless word of Liv's action-packed love-life: she lived the kind of bodice-ripping existence that Nancy literally couldn't hear enough about, and which, if I wasn't witness to, I'd suspect her of making up. She'd been engaged five times, for a start. Liv looked cool but was surprisingly old-fashioned underneath, and she found it easy enough to say no to everything except a proposal, to which she felt obliged, out of politeness, to say yes. It helped that she also attracted the kind of men who could lay their hands on Cartier solitaires at short notice.

My love-life, in comparison, was more like a series of short stories. Funny stories, with some unexpected twists, but so far, lacking in happy ever afters. Liv (or rather, Liv's advice books) said I didn't invite romance into my world, which was sort of true; I loved the *idea* of men dropping at my feet, like they did for her, but when it actually happened to me, I panicked. Something froze inside me. I didn't know much about my mother, but I got the feeling that I'd probably inherited a weakness for unsuitable charmers, along with whatever philanderer genes runaway Hector had donated. I wanted to fall in love, more than anything, but I was terrified of it turning into the sort of love that ended up with babies abandoned on doorsteps.

Not that it stopped me trying. Over the last few years, I'd had several short, uncomfortable flings and a couple of long, reassuring but actually quite dull relationships, and, of course, a long-standing crush on the most unsuitable man of all: Jamie. And that only confirmed my worst suspicions about myself.

"Betsy!" Nancy spotted me and waved. "Have you heard about Liv's new chap?"

"There's a ring," said Kathleen, meaningfully.

Liv looked shifty and tucked a long strand of blond hair behind one ear. "I accepted it as a *friendship* ring. I told him I'm having a break from serious relationships right now."

"Weren't you engaged to that *last* fellow?" asked Kathleen. "That chap with the fancy car that blew up?"

"It didn't blow up, I just didn't . . ." Liv's hair fell over her face. "I didn't put the right petrol in it. Or I forgot to, or something. Anyway, no, that's off."

"But you kept the ring?" Nancy enquired anxiously. "Or was it his grandmother's again?"

"Or his current wife's?" I couldn't help it. I'd had to disentangle her from the would-be bigamist myself, and it hadn't been pretty, pretending to be your best friend's psychiatric nurse.

"Er, let's not talk about me," said Liv. "What we really want to know is what happened in the library? Let's go back to Kathleen's and you can give us the goss."

"I should really say my thank yous to Miss Thorne . . ." I said, looking round for the principal, or any of the teachers, but they were nowhere in sight. Someone had cleared the room with top-drawer hostess efficiency. I couldn't even see Mark Montgomery, let alone Nell Howard and her Pucci print dress.

I felt suddenly bereft, as if I'd come very close to learning something important, but now it was slipping away from me and I had no idea how to get it back.

"Come on, we're dying to know," Liv added, tugging my arm. "You were in there ages. Was there a will, with conditions? Have you been set tasks before you can claim your massive inheritance?"

"And what sort of tasks do you think Franny would have had in mind?" I enquired. "Running an etiquette assault course around Knightsbridge? Arranging the top table seating at a fourth marriage?"

"Catering a reception using only one white loaf and a jar of peanut butter?" Liv pulled a face. "Can you have a word with those caterers, by the way? I went to get some food for Kathleen and Nancy and that grumpy bloke acted like I'd just tried to shoplift the silver. I only took two sandwiches!"

"You were lucky you got two," I said. "He's got a measuring jug for the wine. Seriously. I found it next to the tea urn."

"Hello, Mark," said Kathleen, gazing very obviously over my left shoulder.

I spun round, embarrassed. Mark Montgomery was standing there with four ten-pound notes in his hand.

"Here," he said, "from petty cash. Forty quid."

I thought of what Lord T had told me about the echoing Academy coffers and blushed. I wondered if by "petty cash" he meant his own wallet. "No, honestly, it's fine . . ."

"Please, take it," said Mark, thrusting it at me. "I've just been trying to get it through to Miss *Thorne* that balancing the books does not mean walking round the ballroom with Chambers *bloody* English *bloody* dictionary on your head. Paulette got a receipt."

I wondered what had happened to make Mark so cross. Any traces of good humour that had emerged over the sandwich-making had now vanished and now even his garish tie seemed to be quivering with barely suppressed irritation. He looked less like a wholesome Scots Oats advert and more like he was about to take my head off with a caber. Whatever conversation he'd just had with Miss Thorne had made his mouth go very thin, but not, I noted, in an entirely unattractive way.

"OK," I said, slowly, and pocketed the notes.

"You're not going to count them?" Mark glowered at me, and I realised that some of his irritation seemed to be directed at me. I took an involuntary step back, nearly knocking over a flower arrangement. "I wouldn't want you to find any problems in the *audit*," he said, and nodded politely to Kathleen and Nancy before turning on his heel and marching off.

"Ooh," said Liv. "You don't normally see flouncing like that in a suit. No wonder he's got vents in his jacket — plenty of room for the stick up his —"

"Liv!" said Kathleen. "Manners!"

"Sorry," she said, looking about as far from sorry as it was possible to be.

"You can tell *you're* not a Tallimore lady," said Kathleen. I tried not to catch Liv's eye. Or Nancy's.

Liv and I went back to Kathleen and Nancy's for a cup of tea, which, as usual, wasn't so much a cup of tea as a selection of food that would have fed all the memorial guests, plus a passing orchestra, accompanied by a light grilling about whether I was "regular".

Every time I tried to quiz them on the state of the Academy, though, they became very evasive and dragged the conversation back to how much I was eating, whether I'd met a nice young man, whether any of Liv's nice young men would do for me, and so on. It was very frustrating and I didn't really understand it; they'd both been retired for nearly twenty years, and although Nancy was generous to the point of lunacy when it came to giving the benefit of the doubt, Kathleen usually had no trouble speaking her mind.

"I'm just glad poor Frances retired when she did," was all Kathleen would be drawn to say, and then, promising I'd be back soon, Liv and I had to leave while we still had room left for supper.

I didn't see enough of Liv, being up in Edinburgh, so staying with her in Clapham was a treat; even without the enormous Chinese banquet she insisted on ordering for us from one of the four takeways she had on speed dial. Liv was as generous as someone with her allowance could afford to be: since Rina and Ken's divorce, Ken had devoted much of his considerable energy to making sure his princess wanted for nothing. Consequently, Liv had more spending money than Paris Hilton, mostly in used notes held together with an elastic band.

"I should warn you, the place is a bit of a mess," she said, as we approached her house, down one of the pretty terraced streets near the Common.

"A mess? Don't be ridiculous," I scoffed, already mentally sinking into one of her deep cream sofas. "You've got the only flatmate in London who's in some kind of competition with the cleaner."

"What, Erin? No! Didn't I tell you? Erin's not here any more. She got a promotion — some law firm in Chicago headhunted her." Liv made the sort of bunny ears with her fingers that Erin liked to make, usually when referring to their "housekeeping rota" or "shared cleaning responsibilities". Only Erin's fingers managed to be sarcastic. "Packed up her cross-cut shredder and moved out about three weeks ago." She fumbled in her bag for her keys, looked cross, pulled out a fancy gold lipstick, looked pleased, then cross again, then dumped the bag on the step while she scrabbled inside it with both hands.

"You never said! Did she give you notice?"

"Well, I reckoned you had more important things to be worrying about than my flatmate leaving. Bloody hell! Where do keys go?"

"You know you should clip your keys to the inner pocket zip," I pointed out. "Then no one can steal them and you always know where to look."

"Yeah, yeah, send it to *Take a Break*," said Liv, still searching. "Aha!" She waved the bunch at me. They were on the huge diamond-ring keyring I'd given her, on the basis that her magpie eye would be drawn automatically to a giant solitaire. "And," she added, letting us in, "can you believe this for timing? Erin bailed on me the same week *Joan* handed her notice in too. Retired!"

"Joan *retired*? How are you managing?" I said, now genuinely concerned. Erin's mania for bills and rotas had just about contained Liv's domestic oblivion, but saintly Joan was the only thing standing between full-on chemical warfare breaking out in the fridge. She'd cleaned for the O'Hare family for years, and was the sort of Heritage Cleaning Lady even Kathleen would approve of.

"I'm not managing," said Liv. "I never thought she'd retire. She said she wanted to go on Hoovering someone's stair runner to the end. Die on the job, mop in hand."

"Although there was always the risk that you might finish her off with your mess," I added, following her into the kitchen.

A faint whiff of unemptied bin cut through the scent of the white lilies on the counter. It was a gorgeous kitchen, all reclaimed retro units and granite work surfaces, with a bold, square window looking out on to a tiny patch of garden, stacked with tumbling pots. Ken's crack squad of Polish builders had knocked it off in a fortnight between conversion jobs and had transformed the grubby back room into the kind of space you could do fashion shoots in. Just as well, since now Erin had gone, there'd be no cooking going on.

"Well . . . she was eighty, you know? Fair dos. And then Dad's gone to Spain . . ." Liv went on, opening and shutting drawers in search of a corkscrew.

This really was getting surreal now. "*Ken? Spain?*" With his freckly skin and innate suspicion of foreign water? I balanced myself against the huge reclaimed table, and kicked off my shoes. "I thought he hated abroad."

"Yeah," said Liv. "I thought that too. But you know what he's like . . . Maybe he's some villas going cheap. Oh, sorry, the oven's not working," she added, seeing me putting plates in to warm up before the takeaway arrived.

I turned it on at the wall switch, where Erin had probably turned it off for safety reasons. "When's he back?"

Liv stared at the oven as if I'd performed some magic trick on it, then shrugged and opened the wine. "Dunno. He just said, 'Off to the sun for a few weeks, princess', then handed me the usual roll of fifties." She did an eerily accurate Ken O'Hare wideboy wink, then smiled, untroubled. "Told me not to get into any trouble, or get engaged to anyone he didn't know. Tsk! As if!"

I frowned, my imagination already running amok. Ken usually left his princess with very detailed instructions about his whereabouts, in case she needed Emergency Dad Assistance. "But I thought he'd just been away for Christmas? Did he leave a number?"

"He's got his mobile! Honestly, Betsy, you're such a drama queen. You should know us better by now. 'Don' arks', that's the O'Hare family motto."

I opened my mouth to suggest that, this once, maybe she *should* ask what on earth Ken was up to, then closed it again. Apart from the stream of suitors and the handbag collection, that was the main difference between me and Liv. I was constantly wondering whether I was doing the right thing or imagining what could go wrong next, whereas Liv never did. She had simple faith in things sorting themselves out, or at least, someone leaping in to sort them for her.

Then again, if I had men falling over themselves sending me trees with necklaces on, I probably wouldn't waste time worrying about stuff either.

Liv saw my brow furrow, and she did what she always did when she saw me worrying — she rolled her huge eyes goofily, and changed the subject. It made her look like a duck, albeit one with killer cheekbones. "God, what am I like? I should know how to turn the oven on, shouldn't I!" she said. "Do you have any idea where Erin left the manuals for the kitchen stuff?"

"You don't need manuals, Liv," I said. "There are pictures, on the appliances."

She giggled, as if I were joking, and poured us both a big glass of Chablis. "Is that something they teach at that Academy then? Ovens and whatnot?" She pushed the glass over to me. "Maybe I should go there for a bit. Get myself some stir-fry skills now Erin's packed up her wok and left me to the mercy of Takeaway Alley. Will you let me in, now you're in charge?"

"It's canapés, mostly," I said, trying to remember what exactly they *had* taught in the cookery classes. I'd learned my proper cooking from Kathleen downstairs. It involved a lot of potatoes and had been my saviour during many a budget-strapped week at uni. "They learned meringue swans and hard-boiled eggs in aspic . . . Nothing you'd really want to *eat*. I mean, I don't know what they do now." I took a sip of wine. "Besides, I'm not going to be in *charge*. I'm just going to . . . look round. And . . . advise."

"You'll have to be a bit more executive than that," Liv retorted. "Didn't you tell Kathleen and Nancy you were going in there to hit them with your magic consultancy stick?"

"Well . . . yes." I cringed and took another, bigger, sip of wine. "Don't remind me."

"Look, you could just tell them the truth," said Liv, gently. "Come on, Betsy, it's nothing to be ashamed of. You don't even lie on your car insurance — this must be killing you!"

"No!" I said at once, spluttering wine everywhere. "No, I can't tell them. It's gone on too long. I mean, it's bad enough that Franny died thinking I was some hotshot business guru instead of a shop assistant . . ."

"Now that's just stupid!" Liv pointed her finger at me. "You're not just a shop assistant, you're the manager! And you know what Franny was like about shoes; she'd have *loved* what you've done with that shop. I never knew a woman with better shoes than Franny. Didn't she always say that the right heels were the first step in the best outfits?"

My mouth twisted into a sad smile. "Yes. And that you could tell a lady from the state of her heels. And that good shoes turned high street into Bond Street."

Liv made an "awww" face and swung her long legs up on to the table. "Do you think she guessed? Do you think she used to go on about shoes to make you feel better about The Glass Slipper?"

"No." I shook my head. "She said all that because she believed that trainers were the devil's own footwear. She left me custody of all her Ferragamos in her will, and told me to find a women's charity where they'd be appreciated." I sighed. "Poor Franny. I hope she had no idea how bad things were at the Academy after she left."

"But you can *fix* that!" Liv's eyes were full of the sort of puppyish trust and enthusiasm that made law partners run to Tiffany's with their cheque books flapping in the breeze. "You can make it up to her by doing the job *she thought* you were doing, on the Academy! Go in there, and . . . I don't know . . . make them tackle their filing, like you did with Fiona and her accounts."

"Oh, Liv, that was different! It's a tiny shop, not a finishing school . . ." I started, but Liv wasn't having any of it.

"They obviously don't have a clue, so what difference does it make if you don't either?" Liv tried to look motivational. "You don't know what you can do till you try — that's what you're always telling me."

Well, actually, that was what Kathleen was always telling *me*.

"And . . ." Liv rapped the table with her finger, then pointed at me to indicate that she'd had an idea. "You know you're always going on about how you can't start your own consultancy when you've got no experience? Well, look — you've done Fiona's boutique, and if you do this too, you've got references, right? I bet Dad'll let you overhaul his office if you want, and there's three! There's your business plan! This time next year, you could actually be doing the job everyone reckons you are, and you'll never have to come clean!" She paused. "It's a fairly elaborate way of getting out of telling a lie, I'll give you that, but you're such a rubbish liar, anyway . . ."

A slow excitement began to burn in my stomach. It was so ridiculous, it was almost reasonable.

Liv saw she had me on the ropes and went in for the killer blow. "I mean, have you applied for any proper jobs recently?"

I squirmed. Every couple of months, I told myself it was about time I kicked my life into gear, and had a furious week where I applied for "proper jobs" — accountancy, legal retraining, even the tax office. But when I actually had the biro in hand and the application form in front of me, I froze. I'd spent my whole life spinning wild possibilities about who I might be, and now it came down to boxes. It felt so final. Was I letting down some ballerina blood inside me? Was I *really* an actuary at heart?

"But I can't decide what I want to do," I whined, then reminded myself that Liv was hardly one to talk about career drift. Neither of us had exactly set the world on fire so far, although in Liv's case, Ken's regular bundles of fifties kept her pretty toasty. "Have you?"

"No," said Liv, with absolute serenity. "I'm happy with my two days behind the bar at Igor's. It gives me time to pursue my dreams of becoming a top photographer. Or possibly a poet slash muse."

"As well as time to be Eurostarred to Paris at the drop of a hat," I pointed out.

"That too." She shook her long fringe out of her angelic face. "We're not talking about me though. This is one of those chances of a lifetime! I mean, I think Lord T's got a bloody nerve asking you to go back there when he wouldn't let you in to begin with, but if the place is going down the toilet, what harm can it do for you to go and look round?"

I pulled the horrified Cat's-bum face Miss Thorne would have made at the merest mention of the T-word. "It's going down the *lavatory*, Olivia. Not the *toilet*."

"Whatever. Oh, come on! You keep telling me you don't want to be handing pop socks to women with bunions this time next year — isn't this a great chance to get out of that?"

The doorbell rang before I could answer, and Liv swung her legs off the table. "Think about it while I get the takeaway," she said, lifting a finger in my direction.

I reached into my bag for my purse. "Liv, here's my half, at least . . ." I started, but she waved my money away.

"My treat," she said.

Liv padded down the hall and I heard the door open, and the sound of distant flirting as I pulled open drawers in search of forks and spoons. I wasn't really listening, though — I was quailing at the prospect of marching back into the Academy in under a week's time and telling Miss Thorne where she was going wrong.

In the drama of Nell Howard's revelations, and the weird half-dream of seeing inside my childhood memories, and the glow of helping out the Tallimores, I'd sort of forgotten I'd be expected to *do* something. More to the point, I'd have to deliver the bad news myself — once I'd worked out what it was. I mean, how was I meant to know why they weren't making any money? I didn't even know what the Academy did these days. I'd never seen a brochure.

And it didn't look as though Mark "Butter the bottom bit of the sandwich only" Montgomery was going to be much help, if he thought it was all a useless waste of time.

I chewed my lip. But would I ever get another chance to ask questions?

The front door banged and Liv reappeared with three bursting bags of Chinese food.

"You know what? I think I've over-ordered again," she said, dumping them on the counter. "I never know how much rice is enough . . ."

My silence must have unnerved her because she stopped unpacking the cartons and looked me in the eye with a remorseful expression. Liv had a very open, honest face. She didn't get it from Ken.

"Was I out of order just then?" she said. "Sorry. It was really insensitive, to go on at you about work and stuff, when you're only just back from the memorial. I just thought . . . well, isn't it what Franny would want? You saving their bacon by being practical and smart, not toffee-nosed and dumb? She thought you were brilliant like that."

"I know," I said. "But that doesn't actually make me feel better? It just makes me wish I'd told her the truth before . . . Before she . . ."

Liv grabbed my hand as my eyes filled, and I went on, quickly. "There is another reason why I said I'd go back to the Academy. But it's completely secret, and you can't let on to a soul. Not even Nancy or Kathleen. I might . . ." My stomach felt quite fluttery, saying it out loud. "I might have found someone who knows who my mother might have been. Be."

There were a lot of mights in that sentence.

"Oh my God!" Liv covered her mouth. Above it, her eyes were perfectly round. "No! You're going to look for your mother, finally!"

"Well, maybe. It's just a rumour." I told her what Nell Howard had said about the 1980 glamour girls and their out-of-control Hooray boyfriends. "I didn't get a chance to ask her any more. She'd left. But I can get her address from the office, I bet. If I go back . . ."

"I always *knew* you were seriously posh underneath!" breathed Liv. "Abandoned by a cad in a Miami Vice jacket! Or a top hat and tails! That is like a romance novel! Nancy's going to be *thrilled*!"

"Yeah, well, don't get carried away — it doesn't sound like any of the girls were exactly Mother Superior material," I said, turning my attention back to the rice, making neat portions to calm myself down again. "And don't tell *anyone* just yet. I'm not sure . . . how Nancy and Kathleen would feel about me looking. I don't want them thinking I'm going to trace my parents and abandon them. Neither of them have families, you know, apart from me."

"As if! Oh, you *definitely* have to go back now," said Liv. "What?" she added, seeing my expression. "I need to know how it ends."

"This isn't a detective novel," I said faintly. "It's not going to be Lord Farquhar in the billiard room with a candlestick and Miss Scarlett. This is my *life*."

"I know. I've been there for the last fifteen years, watching you pretend you're not really interested. It's been the longest trailer in existence." Liv pointed a chopstick at me. "I will do everything I can to help you. Even if it means going undercover at this."

I looked at her over the crowded table. She flicked her perfectly arched model eyebrows up and down until I had to laugh.

"In that case, you can start by not pointing your chopsticks," I said, helping myself to sweet and sour pork balls. "It's the height of rudeness."

CHAPTER FOUR

If you're wearing very high heels, fishnets are easier to walk in than sheer stockings, because they slip less inside the shoe. They're also surprisingly flattering . . .

As soon as I got back to Edinburgh, I bit the bullet and asked Fiona for ten days' leave.

Fiona was about as calm as a shop owner in the end throes of January sales could be, which is to say she couldn't speak for five minutes and when she did, it was in tiny squeaks, punctuated by wild gestures towards the till. However, when I explained what I was going back to do — save a finishing school from ruin, using only my Maths degree and my glass-polishing tips — she gave me a look that clearly said, "You're checking into rehab, aren't you?" I didn't need to add anything else, and she even pressed a pair of black patent court shoes into my hand, "for luck".

I spent the rest of the week looking up what I could find about modern finishing schools on the Internet. There wasn't very much. That didn't surprise me, because for one thing, who on earth needed to be taught the Secret Language of Fans any more, and for another, surely the whole point of social coaching was to give the impression that you'd *always* been so poised and elegant, not that you'd bought your manners? Besides, Miss Thorne didn't seem to be the type to embrace the technological age. No one needed to email a bishop.

Turning myself into a credible troubleshooter was another matter. The night before I flew down to London, I watched every episode of *The Apprentice* and *Dragons' Den* that I could find on YouTube. Then I hauled every navy item of clothing out of my wardrobe, and practised scraping my curls into a sort of bun until I looked almost severe. I packed some Georgette Heyer romances to read on the plane to get me in the mood for finishing school, and some Post-its that I'd borrowed from the shop stationery drawer for efficient note-making.

And I packed another notebook, a smaller one that I could sneak into my bag for taking covert notes. On the first page, I'd written: *Nell Howard's phone number*? Google had let me down, for once. I'd have to be much more Nancy Drew, starting in the Academy's files.

At half past nine the following Monday morning, after catching the first Edinburgh — Heathrow flight, I stepped bleary-eyed out of Green Park underground station and on to Piccadilly, with its bright sales signs and coffee shops glinting in the winter sunshine.

As I passed a café full of suits queuing for their morning espresso, I checked myself out in the glass: I was wearing a fitted wool suit I'd bought from Hobbs in one of my "proper job" application phases, with my best crisp white shirt and Fiona's sympathy shoes. Over my arm, as the key "finishing touch", was my big leather handbag. It was a properly expensive bag, a Christmas present to myself, and it was pillar-box red. Franny said that red was a neutral when it came to bags and shoes. Personally I liked the way it was a flash of scarlet woman-ness you could hide under the table if necessary.

I turned down Full Moon Street, where the shadows cast everything into black and white, and while I was still admiring the sun streaming through the iron railings, I came face-to-face with the lion's-head knocker on the door of number 34 and suddenly my confidence deserted me.

I hadn't actually rehearsed what I was going to say. For some stupid romantic reason, I'd imagined the right words would just pop into my head, and now all I could hear in my head was the Britney Spears track that had been blaring out of the coffee shop on the corner.

Just get on with it, I told myself sternly and rapped the brass ring hard against the door, before I could think twice. Then I stepped back, and took a deep breath as I distracted myself with details.

The Academy hadn't got any cleaner since the previous week. The murky windows were positively spooky, and next to the discreet smartness of the townhouses on either side, the house had the look of a mad old aunt with wild ivy hair and slept-in make-up flaking off the windows.

The door was yanked open and I took a step back.

"Sorry, sorry, sorry, I'm just about to move it!" It was Paulette, the girl with the pixie crop from the reception, the one who'd let the cat out of the bag about the budget. Her mouth was smiling, but her sharp black eyes darted back and forth as if she half expected someone else to leap out from behind me.

I held out my hand, and tried to say hello, but she was talking and casting worried glances up the street at the same time, while blocking me from entering the house. "I know you've spoken to Anna about it before, but I don't think they have parking restrictions where she lives in Moscow."

"I'm not here about any parking," I said. "I'm here to speak to . . ."

Paulette looked confused, then looked aghast. "You're not a bailiff, are you?"

Bailiff? How bad had things got here?

"No, I have an appointment with Miss Thorne," I said, extending my hand again. "She's expecting me." I paused, in case she didn't recognise me. My hair was tied back so hard I'd given myself a facelift. "We met briefly at the memorial service here, last week, but I don't think we were properly introduced. Is it Paulette? I'm Betsy Tallimore."

Paulette clapped both hands to the side of her face, dragging her chipmunk cheeks down in horror. "Oh my

God! You're the orphan who the Tallimores took in off the steps! The ginger love child!"

"Well, yes," I said, because none of that was technically untrue.

"And now you're some kind of consultant busybody type who's come here to kick everyone's arse! Like on television!"

"Who told you that? I mean, no, it's really not . . ." I tried again. "I'm just here to have a look around and a chat with Miss Thorne. Can I come in, please?"

As I stepped inside, I tried not to let the shock of familiarity undo the cool, collected image I was working hard to present. It still felt strange, being in the Academy again as an adult, and my first emotions were a mix of nostalgia and fresh curiosity. Without the crush of ladies reminiscing about the good old days, the empty hall seemed much more "Monday morning" — echoing and somewhat chilly.

I noticed Paulette was wearing two jumpers, and very thick tights beneath her tweed skirt, as well as her regulation single string of pearls. She didn't give the impression that either the pearls or the tweed skirt were the sort of thing she'd normally wear.

"Would you like a cup of . . . No, hang on, I should let Miss Thorne know you're . . ." Her forehead creased. "She's not at her best first thing, I'd leave it half an hour if I were you, give her time to digest her croissant. Coffee?"

"Yes, I'd love a cup," I said, smiling as reassuringly as I could. "Why don't you let Miss Thorne know I'm here and I'll wait in the reception room?"

And have a snoop about, I added to myself.

"Good idea," Paulette agreed and, without realising, she let me direct her through the hall towards the headmistress's office, a large room towards the back of the house.

As we clicked our way across the black and white tiles, my eyes flitted from portrait to portrait, sweeping around for clues as to why the Academy was in such dire straits. The pedestal plant holders still trailed ivy down the magnificent staircase, but I spotted cobwebs veiling the higher chandeliers. Next to the old grandfather clock, there was a museum-piece vacuum cleaner with a fraying power cord, and a suspiciously waxy arrangement of out-of-season roses dumped in a large urn.

I pretended to inspect the oil painting of the first Lady Tallimore, but really so I could take a deeper breath. The Academy smelled almost as I remembered, but not quite. Something was slightly off.

I closed my eyes, and rolled the different components around my nose like a wine taster. Beeswax wood polish. Old books. Several toxically clashing perfumes — Chanel No. 5, always a favourite, a new one that smelled like loo cleaner, some vanilla body oil. There was always one girl with a vanilla smell. But that potpourri — it wasn't right. When Franny had been in charge the entrance hall had smelled of garden flowers: roses, peonies, sweet peas. This smelled stale and slightly . . . pine fresh.

I spotted a telltale air freshener half-hidden behind the urn of roses on the sideboard. They were *fake*. And not even good-quality fakes! And the air freshener wasn't even hidden!

Paulette had stopped a few feet away from the office door, and dropped her voice conspiratorially.

"Now, just so you know, Miss Thorne's got a dental appointment this afternoon, so she might be in one of her moods. Abscesses, you know. From all the mints, I reckon. It's like an *addiction*."

"Paulette," I said, dropping my voice too. "Don't take this the wrong way, but does Miss Thorne know you're telling me about her abscesses? She always used to tell the students that the best secretaries have secrets in them — does she still say that?"

"What? No. Are you sure you're not an inspector?" Paulette gazed up at me like a puppy who's done something unpleasant in a shoe you've just put on. "I didn't mean to apply for the secretary's job," she confessed in a rush. "I thought this was a hotel. No one even checked my references! Nuts. I shouldn't have said that either, should I?"

I shook my head quickly. "Don't worry, it's fine."

But she hadn't finished. "Please don't tell her what I said about the traffic wardens, I'm not meant to be covering up for Anastasia, but she's had them round here twice this month, and she won't listen to me when I tell her she needs to sort it out, and her dad's quite big in the Russian mafia. She says."

"I won't," I promised. Oh my God, I thought, my voice spiralling into a squawk in my head, what's going *on* here?

I reminded myself that at least it would make a good story to tell Liv. In the meantime, I had to start small, just like I did with the Saturday girls at The Glass Slipper.

"Now. Can I give you my coat? Great! Do you have any wooden hangers?" I guided Paulette gently to the cloakroom. "They're much better for the shape than metal ones . . . No? OK, don't worry about it now, I'll find you some later. Now, if you could tell Miss Thorne? Give us both time to check our lipstick . . ."

Paulette flashed me a quick, grateful smile, which made her seem about twelve, and rushed off.

While she was busy in the headmistress's office, I did the old Tallimore BLT check (Buttons, fastened; Lipstick, fresh; Teeth, clean), then pulled myself up to full height, filled my lungs, and tried to breathe out slowly. Miss Thorne had known me since I was little — what on earth did I have to get het up about? Besides, I now knew she had abscesses and a mint imperial addiction.

And then Paulette was back, looking flushed.

"I'll get the coffee," she said, ushering me through, and I knocked on the white door.

After a count of four, a voice trilled "Enter!" from within, and I opened the door and walked in.

I didn't have a strong memory of the headmistress's office, since it had always been Miss Vanderbilt's domain, and I'd never had cause — good or bad — to be summoned to it.

It had once been a drawing room, and was painted in Wedgwood blue, with one wall taken up by a full-length bookshelf and another by a pair of French windows that led into the enclosed garden where students were supposed to cultivate herbs and definitely *not* sunbathe.

Dominating the far end of the room was a massive antique desk, behind which Miss Thorne was just visible in her sugar-pink cashmere ensemble. Her white hair was set like swirls of whipped cream around her doll-like face, beneath which a triple string of pearls balanced on a shelf-like bust. There was no computer in sight, only a silver desk set, three Art Deco Rolodexes, and a Limoges bowl full of mint imperials.

Miss Thorne looked up as I stepped into the room, and her expression of welcome had just the right mixture of pleasure and surprise. She didn't rise as I approached the desk, my hand at the ready for shaking, but instead added a flourishing signature to some document and pressed an old-fashioned blotter over it.

I felt as if I'd wandered uninvited into a state opening of Parliament. Immediately, I felt too tall, too clumsy, and wearing all the wrong clothes. The thick pile carpet was almost impossible to walk on in my new slippy-soled high heels and I was terrified I'd slip and go tumbling over her desk.

"Elizabeth!" she said. "Do have a seat! You've caught me finishing some letters — would you excuse me a moment?"

"Of course," I said, retracting my hand self-consciously and taking a seat in the spindly chair opposite. My accent had shifted a few postcodes nearer to Buckingham Palace. "Am I early?"

"Ohh, no, no. Well. Maybe by just a moment or two."

I am *not*, I thought. I knew I was dead on time, because I always was. Punctuality, as I'd had drilled into my infant brain, was the politeness of princes.

Miss Thorne certainly wasn't as friendly as she had been at Franny's memorial tea. But maybe she was dealing with some of the nightmare bills Lord T had hinted at. Even Fiona forgot to call everyone "darling" at VAT time.

While she carried on scribbling, I smoothed down my skirt, put my bag down by my side, and scanned the room discreetly for any photos of a 1980-ish vintage. Miss Thorne's office was full of silver-framed portraits of old girls, on the walls and propped up on the bookshelves. "Dear Miss Vanderbilt, with much love, Ninks Harrington (nee Featherstonehaugh!!!!) xxx" read the nearest, scrawled in a round hand over a photo of a jolly brunette posing with her feet splayed in the deportment class's classic photograph position (standing). She was proudly holding a baby, who already looked like a weeny merchant banker, in front of a Range Rover parked outside a large house, with two black Labradors at her feet.

Mid-eighties, judging from the peplum and shoulderpads. Too late.

I kept looking, trying not to make my tilted head seem too obvious: squeezing all your worldly goods into one photo seemed to be a theme: ballgowns, tiaras, yachts and, in one case, a helicopter featured, as did teeth, well-trowelled makeup and a faraway expression, as if the real photographer was standing somewhere to the left of the one taking the picture. I was surprised to see one graduation photograph positioned almost out of sight, and then realised it was my own.

"So sorry! Now! How lovely to see you again so soon, Elizabeth," said Miss Thorne, a benevolent smile lighting up her soft cheeks as she clicked her fountain pen shut.

"Thank you," I said. "It's so nice to be back and see so much just as I remember it."

"Although you were never actually a pupil here, were you? Strictly speaking."

I was somewhat caught off balance by that. "Well, no," I admitted. "Not strictly speaking. But, you know, I spent so much of my childhood around the teachers and girls here that . . ."

"Yes." Miss Thorne's smile became more rigid. "You always were sitting in the classes, weren't you? And running up and down the corridors."

Was she being friendly? I wondered, or was that *rude*? But Miss Thorne wasn't finished.

"And playing in the beauty studio. And getting in and out of our practice car as if you were at a premiere."

I could feel my face getting pink, and reminded myself that the girls had *loved* having me around, and the teachers never complained. I counted to five in my head, and tried to give her the benefit of the doubt, as Nancy would. But Miss Thorne carried on smiling in that strange indulgent way, as if she was determined to put me in my place, right from the moment I sat down.

What on earth had Lord Tallimore told her about my visit to put her back up so much? I wondered. Had he embroidered my already over-embroidered credentials? What was I doing now, working for the Bank of England?

All I could do was be polite, I reminded myself. Put a good thick coat of manners over everything.

"Well, it was quite a few years ago now!" I said. "We've all changed since then, haven't we?"

"Dear me, yes," nodded Miss Thorne, but in a way that made me wonder if she was actually answering a different question.

I unclipped my handbag and removed my leather-bound notebook and pen, ready to take notes. It gave me a moment to get a grip.

Think consultant. Think professional.

All I could think of was *The Apprentice*, but that would have to do, for the time being.

"I'm sure Lord Tallimore's discussed why I'm here," I said. "He tells me that the Academy is going through something of a tricky patch? He asked me to come in and see what I can do to help. Fresh eyes, new . . ." I scrabbled around for some suitable jargon. "Initiatives."

"And is that your field these days?" asked Miss Thorne.

"Yes," I said. "I specialise in . . . creative re-positioning."

That was true. Literally, in the case of Fiona's stock. I was in charge of all the window displays, thanks to my skill at both arranging shoes to their best advantage, and getting a really good shine on the glass.

"Do you indeed?" Miss Thorne looked unconvinced.

"Yes," I said. "I help businesses showcase their star products to their best advantage by spotlighting key strengths and discounting outdated stock. I mean, outdated ideas. Window-dressing! Which isn't," I added, with a flash of inspiration, "unlike what the Academy does for its students."

"Well, I don't claim to understand the cut and thrust of corporate life, but that sounds very . . . challenging." Miss Thorne's pursed lips curved, but she didn't seem very amused. "*Entre nous*, dear, I think Lord Tallimore is over-reacting a teeny bit. We're just going through one of our sporadic intake dips — I've seen it before! Often happens when the foreign money markets wobble, but there's nothing to worry about. Good manners will never go out of fashion now, will they, Elizabeth?"

I wished she wouldn't call me Elizabeth. It made me feel there was someone else in the room. "Do call me Betsy, Miss Thorne," I said, with a smile. "Everyone does."

"Do they?" she mused. "I suppose those olde-worlde names are coming back into fashion. Lily, Daisy, Ruby . . . We used to call them parlourmaid names!" She paused just long enough for me to wonder if I was supposed to take offence at that or not, then, just as I decided I could hardly take it any other way, she added, "Very fashionable now, of course!"

"Do you think I could have a guided tour?" I asked, trying to focus on the task in hand. "To refresh my memory, you know, before we talk about what the Academy does these days?"

Miss Thorne looked as if I'd just asked to see her bank statements. "Is that necessary? Surely I can tell you everything you need to know?"

She increased the wattage of her smile but as she did, something inside me stiffened. I'd come to nose around those classrooms, and nose around I would.

"I'm sure you can, but Lord Tallimore asked me for my professional opinion about the whole business, and I'd love to see what the Academy is offering in the twenty-first century." I checked my watch. "Isn't it about time for the first lesson?"

"Oh, but my dear, we shouldn't interrupt them! I'll have Paulette bring us some coffee and biscuits, and we can have a nice catch-up." Miss Thorne's beady eyes took on a steely glimmer of resistance beneath her pastel eyeshadow and her little hand gripped her Mont Blanc pen. "We're not quite the same proposition as a baked *bean* factory, or whatever concerns you're used to . . . inspecting."

It suddenly dawned on me that maybe my impression was *too* convincing. Maybe she thought my next move would be to impound the petty cash box. Did she have a minor petty cash/mint imperial scam going on? That would explain the defensiveness.

I tried a different tack: shameless flattery, the secret skeleton key of conversation. According to Franny, "absolutely everyone" opened up with a little sweet talk.

"Oh, gosh, no! Of *course* it's not the same thing!" I raised my hands in apparent horror. "I'm not here to criticise, Miss Thorne, I'm here to see if I can *help*. I'm sure no one knows more about the Academy than you do, after all your years here . . ."

Miss Thorne's pink lips pressed together and I could tell her brain was whizzing round faster than she could spin her Rolodex of florists and emergency viscounts.

"How long have you been teaching now?" I enquired.

"Twenty-nine years," she said, and her cashmere bosom puffed out as if inflated by an invisible pump. "I was terribly young, of course, when I arrived . . ."

And the rest, I thought. If she was under sixty-five, I was the editor of *Evening Gloves & Opera Glass Collector*.

"I'd love to see some of the teaching rooms." I went on, persuasively. "I don't want to keep you from your schedule but it would be *lovely* to see the ballroom again."

That was true. I really did want to see it again. Not to mention the photographs on the wall outside it.

"Where you danced with, now who was it with . . ." I played my trump card, as she pretended to blush. "With the Prince of Wales, was it? Wow."

"Yes, but it was a private ball and I really don't like to talk about that, as you know, Elizabeth. But, very well," she sighed, and pushed back her chair to rise, revealing two large booster cushions. "We can make a very quick visit, but I have a great deal to do . . ."

As she swept past me, Miss Thorne's smile remained impeccable, but I didn't miss the metallic note in her voice or the way she locked her desk drawer before we left the room.

Either way, we were finally heading upstairs, into the heart of my childhood memories and the cauldron of possible gossip about my past.

CHAPTER FIVE

Only take one canapé at a time and avoid anything that requires biting in two. Caviar is a good cocktail party choice, as the oil soaks up the alcohol as you go.

My pulse galloped as we made our way up the staircase to the classrooms. Everywhere I looked were things I'd totally forgotten about until that moment. There was the creepy Georgian portrait of the Tallimore twins and their three gormless pugs, whose boggly eyes followed you up the stairs. I had to stop myself touching the heavy red velvet curtains on the long window looking on to Full Moon Street; the polished oak banisters still made part of me long to run up all four flights of stairs and slide all the way down the centre of the house.

I didn't, though, obviously. I was too busy keeping up with Miss Thorne, who moved very quickly for a woman with legs like a pair of skittles, while looking out for clues and noting, with despair, how the house seemed more run down the higher we climbed.

I'd been brought up downstairs to "see jobs that need doing" and there were jobs *everywhere*. Moth-eaten patches on the curtains and dead flies inside the windows. The picture glass needed polishing, and the woodwork needed a lick of fresh paint. I was disappointed. It felt like the house had let itself go.

As we approached the first classroom, I heard a familiar voice. Posh Scottish — Morningside Edinburgh — like most of Fiona's customers.

"Can one of you tell me how we might eat asparagus?" the voice enquired, with a touch of weariness. "Yes, Divinity, this *is* asparagus."

Ooh, Table Etiquette, I thought.

"Miss McGregor is taking the first class this morning," Miss Thorne said, seeing my face light up. "I'm sure she won't mind if we pop our heads round, but we don't want to disturb the girls, now, do we?"

"Of course we don't," I said, still listening to see if anyone knew what to do with asparagus.

Inside, there was a faint sound of reply, and Miss McGregor's voice snapped, "Whatever asparagus may or may not do to a lady's digestive system does not affect the tool with which she eats it, Clementine!"

Miss Thorne coughed, then rapped on the door, and pushed it open.

The main classroom had once been a breath-taking reception room, with full-length windows stretching from red-carpeted floor to moulded ceiling, offering a view of Green Park, if you craned your neck sideways. School legend had it that this was where proposals were expected to take place: the last official proposal of any note made at the Academy was by Hereward, Earl Newent, in 1969, to Lady Penelope Hinton-Scott. Even when I was there, it was spoken of in the same hushed tones reserved for the last woman hanged in Great Britain.

Now, however, the Lady Hamilton Room was thoroughly stripped of any residual romance, and instead held four grey desks. The windows were dressed in mould-green velvet curtains held back with elderly gold tiebacks. Three majestic crystal chandeliers were still in place, missing a few dusty drops here and there, and the swirling burgundy wallpaper was punctuated with framed oils of Tallimore Ladies of the Past. In the centre of the room, rather incongruously, was a dining table, set with white napkins and candelabra, and at it sat four teenage girls, two with their elbows on the table, one with a spear of asparagus on a fork, and one texting on her mobile.

By the way the heads swivelled towards the door as we entered, I didn't think the girls had been particularly gripped by the lesson, although just seeing the silver dishes on the table made me feel excited. I loved Table Etiquette as a little girl. Oysters, lobsters, asparagus, prawns, caviar were brought up from Kathleen's kitchen to be scoffed elegantly — most of the Academy's courses were covered in a term, but Table Etiquette seemed to require a lot of repeated practice.

But they can't really still be teaching *Table Etiquette*, I thought. Does anyone still *care*?

Maybe it had been updated, I reasoned. Modern food was quite complicated too, what with sushi and pasta and canapés . . .

Miss McGregor, undisputed heavyweight champion of fish knives, was standing at the front with a pointer and a clipboard, squeezing her eyes tightly shut as if in silent prayer. She was rangy and sleek but with a "racehorse-gone-to-pasture" slope to her bony shoulders. As Miss Thorne stepped in, her head bounced up, letting a few more grey flyaways loose from her bun.

"Now, please don't mind us, ladies," cooed Miss Thorne, ensuring that everyone noticed her. "We just want to pop our heads around . . ."

But Miss McGregor's face had gone from "weary horse" to "horse seeing feedbucket" in an instant. "Betsy!" she cried, dropping her pointer, and holding out her arms to me in welcome. "How lovely to see you!"

"Hello, Miss McGregor," I said, feeling about ten again.

She swept across the room with the grace of a lifetime's deportment lessons and gripped my hands. "Look at you! So grown up!"

I felt a smile spread across my face. "You haven't changed a bit," I said.

I wasn't sweet talking this time: Miss McGregor was absolutely no different from the last time I'd seen her — her salt-and-pepper hair pulled back into a cottage loaf and her red tartan maxi-kilt and half-moon glasses on a long gold chain were no different. Obviously all that flower arranging fluid was acting as a preservative.

"Girls," she said, turning to address the class, "this is Betsy, one of my very favourite and best pupils."

Miss Thorne murmured, "Not strictly speaking an old pupil . . ." but Miss McGregor pretended not to hear her, and instead gestured towards the dining table.

"Now, Betsy, I'm sure you can tell us: asparagus, finger or fork?"

"Fingers," I said, at once. "Fork if it's an accompaniment, but if it's a starter and the hostess uses her fingers, go ahead and pick it up. *Debrett's* says yes to fingers, so long as you've got something to wipe them on."

"Very good. Banana?"

The tallest and most beautiful of the four girls, a long, languid honey-blonde whose hair — someone's hair, anyway — tumbled expensively down her back, answered, without taking her eyes off her phone. "You use the special fruit knives and forks provided. You peel, then cut into slices and eat with the fork."

"Like, not being funny," said a girl with jet-black hair and more eyeliner than even Amy Winehouse would consider appropriate for daytime. She pointed at her own temple with a long blue nail, like someone on daytime TV. "But if I went to someone's house for *dinner*, and they gave me a *banana*, I'd be like, what is this? Is this a *joke* or what?"

The other two — a diminutive blonde in a fur gilet and a doll-like girl with gorgeous coffee-coloured skin — made noises of agreement, and Miss Thorne's lips tightened with displeasure.

"Right?" The blue talon was pointed towards me. "You'd be like, I got tarted up to empty your *fruit bowl?*"

I nodded, conscious of Miss Thorne's furious expression burning over my shoulder towards the girl. "It is a bit out of date," I said, diplomatically. "I think if you're out for dinner, and someone's giving you a banana for pudding, you have to assume there'd been some disaster with the *real* pudding, in which case I don't think your hostess would care how you ate it, so long as you looked like you were enjoying it. That's the good manners, not the fruit knife."

The blonde in the gilet slid her almond eyes sideways with a sly nod towards the girl who'd answered first. "Venetia," she said in a heavy Russian accent, "I bet you could look like you were enjoying a banana."

Venetia snapped her attention away from her phone and delivered the sort of venomous stare that could melt plastic. It didn't fit very well with her otherwise demure appearance. "Meaning?"

Eyeliner girl took up the innocent expression. "Meaning, you're good at peeling things . . . off?"

Venetia pushed back a thick hank of hair from her face. "Don't bother trying to be funny, Clammy. Save it for your wardrobe."

"*Clemmy*," snapped eyeliner girl.

"What did I say?" Venetia looked confused. "Oh, did I say Clammy again? So sorry. Slip of the tongue."

"Another of your specialities!" sniped the Russian, triumphantly. "You are quite the expert today!"

Miss McGregor clapped her hands together sharply. "Anastasia! Venetia! That's enough!"

"*Not* the sort of repartee I expect from Tallimore ladies," added Miss Thorne, pursing up her face and folding her arms as if her control pants were pinching. She rather spoiled the effect by glancing at me to check my reaction, and to wind her up, I opened my notebook and jotted down some scribbles.

In actual fact, I was noting the girls and their names and any other details I remembered, like Anastasia's parking fines and Paulette's wide-eyed terror of her.

The black girl, who seemed vaguely familiar from somewhere, turned her head madly between her classmates, so her ringlet extensions tangled in her long earrings.

"What is it now, Divinity?" said Miss Thorne.

"Someone tell me what I should write down, OK?" she pleaded. "Banana knives or what?"

"Stick to grapes, you're safer," I said. "Pull off a clump, not single ones, and don't spit the pips."

"Moving on," said Miss McGregor. "Oysters?"

"Oh my God!" Divinity almost leaped out of her seat with delight. "I know this. Oysters — you should say, no, right! Because he's trying to get you into bed! It's a sign, isn't it? Like car keys!"

"Divinity!" Even Miss McGregor looked embarrassed. "That *isn't* what I was asking."

"It's true," Divinity nodded. "Didn't that happen to you, Venetia? When you went out with that film producer? The one with the hairpiece? He ordered oysters for your starter, and then you found a room key underneath your serviette?"

"Napkin!" snapped Miss Thorne, then added almost as an afterthought, "And I'm sure that's not the case."

"I don't want to talk about it." Venetia played idly with some speckled quails' eggs on the plate in front of her, then without looking up, breathed, "Berkeley Hotel. Chelsea suite."

"Wow!" Divinity looked at the other two to check their reaction. She seemed impressed, even though they weren't. "You've been propositioned in all the best hotels, Venetia."

"Well, all you have to do is swallow a couple of oysters and you could be admiring the en suite with her," said Clemmy. "Have you still got his number, Venetia? Can we Facebook him?"

"That doesn't happen *every* time you order oysters," I pointed out hastily, seeing Divinity scribbling notes. "Especially if you get a dodgy one. That can end a date pretty quickly, believe me."

"And how do you know if you've got a dodgy one?" Clemmy had stopped baiting Venetia, and was peering under the silver dome that presumably contained the oysters they'd be practising on. "How can you tell when they all smell like . . ."

"You vvvomit," said Anastasia, slapping her hands together and beetling her dark eyebrows. "All over the eediot who brought you to a restaurant that didn't check their supplier. It happened to me once. Only once."

She sounded so terrifying that we all flinched; at which point she giggled uproariously, then resumed her fierce expression. "We laughed eventually. And then my father had the place closed down."

"Your father works in environmental health?" I asked, rather hopefully.

"No," said Miss McGregor, before she could reply. "Anastasia's father is . . . in oil, I think."

"Officially, yes," said Anastasia, with a charming smile.

"Now then, girls: where would you find your bread roll in a formal place setting?"

I knew the answer but didn't say anything as the four girls searched under glasses and plates, still arguing about whether oysters made you horny or pukey, and if pukey, whether that was necessarily the end of the date anyway.

Miss McGregor turned to me and raised one of her eyebrows in silent query.

"In the napkin?" I murmured. Sad, I know, but I couldn't stop myself.

"Oh, very good, Elizabeth," said Miss Thorne, rather snippily, I thought. "You should be taking the class."

The weird thing was, I couldn't remember actually learning where the bread roll hid — it had all been a fascinating game to my little eyes, with rules that seemed to come from *Alice in Wonderland*. Where to seat barons and colonels, the family of different sized crystal glasses, fairy-sized spoons for salt, and napkins with bread rolls hidden in them; everything polished downstairs with boring bicarb and toothbrushes until the light bounced off the glass and silver and it turned into Cinderella's fairytale table.

I mean, it was completely irrelevant now, when your biggest eating concerns were how many canapés was greedy or what that sushi actually *was*, but so romantic and magical . . .

Miss Thorne broke through my thoughts with a pronounced sniff. "So, have you seen enough, Elizabeth? As you can see, we stick to the traditional feminine accomplishments. It's what we're famous for, after all. I don't think you really need to . . ."

"Are you a new teacher?" Divinity demanded. She sounded rather dubious, as if she wasn't sure what I could be teaching them. "Or a new pupil?"

"No," I started, "I'm . . ."

Miss Thorne interrupted me, but put her hand on my arm so I'd know she wasn't being rude out of choice. "Elizabeth is here to assess us, on behalf of Lord Tallimore," she said. "She's a professional consultant — whatever that means! So best behaviour, everyone." She paused. "Clementine, please don't take that as a challenge."

The girls were really staring at me now. Venetia was giving my outfit a sorrowful onceover; Divinity was smiling so hard I could see the white gum in her back teeth; Anastasia was scrutinising me with the sort of thousand-yard stare that probably had half the club bouncers in London petrified, and Clemmy was just looking bored, twisting her nose-ring around in a manner that made my own nostrils twitch in sympathy.

"Really, it's nothing so formal as that!" I protested, but Miss Thorne hadn't finished.

"That goes for you too, Divinity. I don't care how famous the discotheque is, or which *Big Brother* star you're supposed to be seeing there, you're both on warnings for late attendance," Miss Thorne reminded her in a stern undertone, then turned to me. "Clementine is one of the few three-term girls we've had in recent years."

"Oh?" I said. "How long are the terms now?"

"Eight weeks," said Miss McGregor. "Although, in some cases, it can feel like a lot longer."

"Tsk. God. Tell me about it," moaned Clemmy. "People get less for nicking cars than I've had stuck here. It's like community service, but with *quails' eggs*." She rolled her eyes within the thick black kohl, but the effect was more "spooky toddler" than "girl gone wild". It was hard, I thought, to give it the full street routine when you sounded exactly like Nigella Lawson. I admired her for trying, though.

Miss Thorne didn't, from the acid glare she directed towards Clemmy. "Believe me, Clementine, we would like nothing more than to see you transformed into the charming young lady we all know you to be . . . underneath. But your father insists you're not leaving until there's no danger of a repeat of that unfortunate moment at your brother's passing out parade. At Sandhurst." Her voice went up into a scandalised hiss. "In front of the *Duke of York*."

"Nothing he hadn't seen before," observed Divinity. "He was, like, *in the Navy*."

"Buckle down, ditch the pentangles, and you can ship out, is the message," added Miss McGregor.

Clemmy set her jaw at the pair of them. "I don't have pentangles. I have Wiccan symbols. There's a difference?"

"Pardon me?" Divinity waved her hand at me, and pointed at my feet. "Where did you get your shoes? I *soo* want them! Are they Fiona Flemings? I saw them in *Elle*. They're *soo* shiny!"

"Miss Thorne told us that only tarts wear patent leather, since you can see your knickers in them!" added Anastasia, conversationally. "Is that true for you?"

"Um, I . . ." I couldn't think what to say.

Fortunately for us all, at that point there was a knock on the door and Paulette's head appeared. Then disappeared as she remembered some distant order about knocking and waiting.

"Oh, come in, Paulette," said Miss Thorne, crossly. "You're in now."

Paulette reappeared, with a big smile at me and a more nervous one at Miss Thorne. "Miss Thorne? The bursar needs to see you urgently upstairs." She consulted her notebook. "Apparently the bank's going spare about some unpaid bills, and he wants to know why we haven't paid the electricity. Could we get a treadmill in the cellar for the girls to power, or something . . ." She paused. "Actually, that might have been a joke. Mark says, can you remind everyone to switch off the lights after they leave the room, please. And if they're cold to wear an extra jumper. Oh, and there's been a delivery from the wine place — ten cases of sherry, right?"

"*Ten cases*?" I said, automatically.

"*Thank* you, Paulette!" Miss Thorne looked furious, then her eyes narrowed as she tried to work out how best to spin this unexpected revelation. "The sherry is for . . . parents."

"Not mine," said Divinity. "They've been clean for five years."

"Or mine," said Clemmy, with a sideways glance of pure mischief. "My mum and dad need something a lot stronger than that when they come here."

"We have to order in bulk for *economy reasons*," snapped Miss Thorne. "As Mr Montgomery is forever reminding me. Now, Elizabeth, have you seen enough to form your professional opinion? A lady never admits to being under any pressure, but I am somewhat *in demand* at the moment."

She smiled winningly at me, and I only detected a hint of gritted teeth. I had no intention of leaving though, not when things had just taken such an intriguing turn.

"I'll stay here, I think, and just observe for a while. Let you get back to the bursar. We'll save the trip to the ballroom for this afternoon, maybe?"

"Oh, jolly good idea!" said Miss McGregor, at once. "Do stay, Betsy."

"I can see how busy you are, Miss Thorne," I added. "I don't want to take up your morning when you have so much to do."

Miss Thorne looked martyred, and excused herself. I could hear her nagging at Paulette down the corridor and then down the stairs. The words, ". . . lack of breeding . . ." and ". . . *impudent* young man . . ." floated back. I assumed she meant Mark.

As her voice faded away and silence fell again in the Lady Hamilton Room, I suddenly felt conscious of the scrutiny of four forthright stares, as each girl made her own assessment of my outfit, my accent, my accessories and, most importantly, my handbag. I looked back at them, taking in their different expressions as best I could, and felt rather under-dressed, going by the Bond Street array of gold and diamond jewellery sparkling back at me.

Fiona's customers were pretty well off, and of course, I wasn't exactly on the breadline myself, but I'd forgotten just how rich you — or rather, your parents — had to be to believe that finishing school was a required addition to anyone's education. These girls were only eighteen, but between them they were probably wearing the equivalent value of my flat. Even though Clemmy was picking the black varnish off her nails and Divinity was chewing her extensions in addition to a wad of gum, they still glowed with that casual aura of serious wealth.

I reminded myself that I had practical life experience on my side, plus my own hard-earned salary and a first-class honours degree. And I knew the old social-dining lesson *backwards*.

"So," I said brightly, "how about sushi?"

Miss McGregor looked puzzled. "Sushi?"

"Yes, with the chopsticks and the bowls and all that etiquette about what you dip where." I loved sushi, but I'd had to learn how to eat it myself, via some embarrassing dry-cleaning bills. "You need to be able to handle chopsticks if you're going to eat out these days," I added, trying to get the girls' attention. "Some of the best restaurants in London are Japanese now: Nobu, Zuma . . ."

Venetia nodded in agreement.

"I had sushi once," announced Divinity. The pie-and-pint Yorkshire accent sounded weird booming out of her fragile doll's face. "Made me sick as a dog. Raw cod's balls, it was. I didn't even know cod had balls . . ."

"We don't do sushi," said Miss McGregor, and I thought I saw a flicker of something behind the half-spectacles. "Miss Thorne insists we stick to dishes the Queen might serve at Buckingham Palace. For instance, next we have . . ." She peered under a silver dish. "Artichokes."

I blinked in surprise. No sushi? "What about juggling canapés and wine glases?" I asked. "Or hot curries? Or kebabs? Or olive stones?"

Miss McGregor gave me a strange, fixed look. "Miss Thorne's rules. She doesn't think the Queen would serve olives."

"But Prince Philip's Greek!" I said, without thinking. "She must have come across an olive at *some* point."

"Oh my God!" squawked Divinity, clapping both hands to her upper chest. "We could go on a field trip to a VIP party somewhere — find out what different celebrities do with their olive stones! Oh come on," she said, as the other three groaned. "It's better than field trips to *art galleries* . . ."

"Divinity reckons we should be going round every club in London for field trips." Clemmy's startling blue eyes rolled heavenwards, then back. I wondered if she was wearing blue contact lenses, and if so, whether the constant eye rolling was a problem. "She's *desperate* to get photographed being thrown out of Raffles. We've done all the others."

"I'm a celebrity daughter," Divinity reminded her. "It's *training* for my job! I'm going to be famous and I need to know this stuff upfront, like. I need to be able to act like I'm dead *bored* with it all."

"Well, the way you dress, they'd throw you out in seconds." Venetia folded her arms, which were tanned and toned and bare beneath her sleeveless cashmere top. Like Victoria Beckham, she didn't seem to have enough body fat to wear so little in the depths of January, but even in the chilly house somehow there wasn't a goosebump on her. "The fashion police are on standby for you, and the *real* police are on standby for the Vampire Bride there."

Clemmy spun furiously in her seat. "Whereas you've got the St John's Ambulance on standby for *your* dates, in case their pacemakers pack in while you're unloading their wallets!"

"And me?" demanded Anastasia, proudly. "I have Interpol waiting for me, no?"

No one bothered to answer that. It was too, too obvious.

"Girls!" I could see weariness in Miss McGregor's dignified face. "You're not giving Betsy here a very good impression of our class," she tried, with a wintry smile.

"No, we're not," said Divinity, who seemed the only one of the four who'd noticed Miss McGregor's despair. "Let's crack on. Jesus. This is a globe artichoke?" She held up the offending vegetable. "I give up. It's a trick, right? How bored would you have to be to eat this at a dinner party?"

She looked at Miss McGregor's notes on how to dismantle one, then looked up at me in disbelief.

"Very bored," I said. "But it's a great starter for dieters. You'd be amazed how long you can spin one of those out for."

"Right," said Divinity. She sounded unconvinced, but Venetia made a note.

The rest of the lesson carried on in the same sort of vein — mussels, snails, and other foods that tasted like "phlegm", or worse — but I didn't really hear any remotely useful hints about dining in or out. When I suggested ways to attract a waiter's attention, Venetia crossed her legs in a way that made Miss McGregor cover her eyes, and Divinity banged her wine glass so hard it cracked.

It wasn't an entirely wasted hour, though, from a research point of view. I learned about Anastasia's parking offences that now ran into thousands of pounds, and Venetia's frequent invitations to yachts. She was, according to Clemmy, a "yacht whore". The girls didn't need Conversation Class: I already knew who had hair extensions, nail extensions and, if Miss McGregor hadn't pleaded with them to stop, who'd had what work done where.

We were in the middle of a discussion about what you could politely do to dispose of a mouthful of something you didn't like (Miss McGregor struggling manfully through the sniggers) when a volley of mobile phones beeps indicated the end of the lesson. The girls immediately began shoving their chairs back, grabbing for their bags, flicking open their phones to check their texts and acting as if Miss McGregor and I had vanished from sight.

I was amazed at their casual rudeness, and turned to Miss McGregor, expecting her to stop them with the icy glare that could turn champagne into sorbet at a hundred yards.

But she didn't even shout, above the high-pitched drone of *whatevers* and *hi, scarlett!*s and *ohmygod*s. She merely closed her eyes, then sighed.

"Don't they say *thank you* anymore?" I asked. "Don't they wait until you dismiss them?"

Miss McGregor pretended she didn't mind, unconvincingly, but then gave up. "Times have changed, Betsy. It's not the place you remember."

"In what way?" I asked. "I mean, I know the lessons have to move with the times, but *politeness* hasn't changed, surely? Franny used to say it's manners that matter, not etiquette. Putting people at ease, smoothing the general path, that sort of thing." I paused. "She made people feel special. That's what I think of as good manners."

When I mentioned Franny, Miss McGregor's angular face softened with affection and she leaned on her desk. "Me, too. But that's the problem, dear," she sighed. "No one comes here to learn manners. I don't know *what* they come here to learn. They're certainly not interested in any of my lessons. We've still got the half sportscar, you remember?"

I nodded. "Of course I remember."

"Well, I found the bold Divinity in that last week, demonstrating how best to get out of it without *showing off the goods* to the assembled photographers, as she put it. And then she demonstrated the more, shall we say, attention-grabbing method." Miss McGregor arched one well-plucked eyebrow. "The girl has a career in gymnastics, if the reality television career falls through."

"Well, I suppose that's useful," I hazarded. "If you're going to marry a footballer?"

I didn't say as much, but wasn't angling to marry a footballer not that different from angling to marry a minor member of the aristocracy? In which case, wasn't exiting a stretch Hummer relatively important? Divinity obviously knew her media training.

The shop manager in me wondered if half the Academy's problems could be solved simply by asking the girls what exactly they needed to know, and then supplying the lessons accordingly.

"Might you consider updating the dining lessons?" I suggested.

"I'd be happy to, dear." Miss McGregor removed her half-spectacles and polished them on the lace-edged hanky tucked up her sleeve. "We need some changes, but Geraldine Thorne is something of a traditionalist when it comes to the syllabus. We still did needlework until Clemmy had her accident — Health and Safety . . ." She put the glasses back on her long nose and smiled. "It's *lovely* to see you, Betsy. This must be very small fry for you! I hear you're running an international marketing consultancy now?"

I blushed. "Um, not quite. I should really move on to the next class," I said, before I inadvertently let her think I was being modest and was actually Trade and Industry Secretary for Scotland. "Where is it?"

"Upstairs in the Clarendon Room. Literary Discussion with Mrs Angell." Miss McGregor began to tidy up the place settings. "You'll be popping down to Kathleen's for tea at some point, won't you? I want to know what you've been up to."

"Definitely." I smiled because it really was nice to see her again. She reminded me of much happier times, with Franny. Plus, if anyone would know about the class of 1980 it would be Miss McGregor. "I'd love to have a proper chat."

"So would I," she said. "We've lots to catch up on, I'm sure."

Was that a conspiratorial wink, or a long-suffering flinch? Before I could ask, she'd stuffed her hanky back up her sleeve and begun collecting up the silver butter knives and fish forks, ready to take downstairs to the kitchens.

Fish forks, I thought. Fish forks and no chopsticks. It was like being in a timewarp.

I pulled back my shoulders and headed off to the Clarendon Room for the next lesson. Maybe things would pick up from there.

CHAPTER SIX

When someone sends you roses, bash the ends of the stems before arranging — it helps them to take up water and makes them last longer.

I used to love Literary Appreciation from my eavesdropping vantage point in the window seat. If Nancy's historical romances had taught me the theory of traditional Regency courtship, then the Lit class had filled in the real life blanks.

The class was supposed to encourage the girls to read books they could talk about while The Menfolk were hitting the port and cigars after dinner — Jane Austen, the less grisly Dickens, that sort of thing — but it always ended up being Jilly Cooper and heated debate about whether Rupert Campbell-Black was based on any of their fathers. There was usually a dog-eared Judith Krantz doing the rounds too, which bridged the gap with Biology.

I was quite pleased Literary Appreciation was still on the curriculum. Put-together girls should read more than just celebrity magazines while they were getting their roots done, I thought, slipping into the back of the room.

No one noticed me arrive — not because they were deep in heated discussion about the Orange Prize shortlist, but because a medium-sized brass band could have strolled in and not been heard over the shriek of gossip in full flow. A middle-aged woman with a mad, dehydrated bush of pre-makeover Camilla Parker Bowles ashy hair was perched on the desk, unsuccessfully cajoling them into opening up their copies of *The Time-Traveler's Wife*. Clemmy was listening, but pretending not to be interested, while Divinity carefully applied mini Post-it notes to *OK!* magazine's party pages. The main event, however, was Venetia. She filed her nails and threw out tantalising details about some new club she'd been taken to the previous evening by some lounge lizard called Milo.

Actually, I decided that he was a lounge lizard. Venetia described him merely as "loaded", and "very, *very* connected" but didn't mention an actual profession.

". . . course, I can't tell you exactly where we went," she finished, with a final flick of her hair.

"Why? Because this club is made up?" demanded Clemmy.

Venetia directed a superior look down her long, perfectly straight nose. "No, because it's members *only*, Clammy. Milo is a *member*."

"That's one way of putting it." Clemmy boggled at her, and Venetia boggled back until she realised how it was creasing her forehead, at which point she stopped and smoothed it down with a manicured hand.

"*Please* can we talk about the book?" begged Mrs Angell, taking advantage of the lull.

"Yes, can we?" said Divinity. Again, I noticed that she was the only one who felt obliged to acknowledge the actual lesson. "Because I was dead disappointed with it. It weren't about Doctor Who."

The others stared at her.

She stared back. "What? Time Traveller's *Wife*, right? Someone told me it were about Doctor Who. And, anyway, it's completely stupid. You can't, like, travel backwards and forwards in time like that. How would you know what you were meant to be wearing? Like, flares — would you be wearing them ironically, or like, for real? Or what if trousers hadn't even been invented?"

"It's not *real*, Div," said Anastasia, patiently. "It is a *story*."

I decided not to stay any longer. Maybe I was putting them off.

I meant to do some snooping around, but there was something about what I'd seen so far that drained most of my energy.

If my mother had been anything like that lot, it was amazing that I'd inherited enough brain cells to put my clothes on the right way round each morning. With the Doctor Who debate still raging behind the closed door, I went over to a window on the landing that looked out over the garden. The view didn't cheer me up. There was a takeout coffee cup stuck in the biggest rosebush and someone had put a crisp bag over the head of the stone angel.

I shut my eyes, remembering the pretty summer dresses and the inviting chink of Pimms glasses, then opened them again.

The crisp bag was still there. So was the faint sound of Venetia insisting that only wall-eyed heifers bought their own champagne in a club. One of the others was making a moo-ing noise. It sounded like Clementine.

There was a group of framed photographs on the burgundy-papered wall opposite, and as I peered at them, I had the odd sensation that any moment, someone was going to leap out and catch me at it. There were no year groups up here, just wartime Tallimore girls in uniforms, looking resourceful but glamorous on the steps. They had pearl earrings and can-do expressions; the sort of girls who delivered unexpected babies before heading to the Cuckoo Club for gin slings, not dropped them off and scarpered.

This was hopeless. What I needed was to find Nell Howard's number from the records. Get some proper information, instead of hunting through the history of deportment in pictures . . .

"Can I help you?" asked a man's voice and I jumped and spun round.

It was the man from the reception — the bursar. Mark Montgomery.

I only recognised him from the dark-rimmed glasses and tense expression. Instead of the formal suit he'd had on at the memorial, today he was wearing a tweedy jacket with a grey jumper underneath and a pair of dark green cords, and he looked much more comfortable. All he needed was a faithful spaniel by his side and he'd be the perfect country vet.

Stop imagining, I told myself. I'd spent so long filling in my own possible past that it was hard not to do it for other people.

I spotted a sheaf of papers in his hand, some of them red bills, and my own stomach tensed. Mark seemed agitated too — his dark hair was ruffled, as if he'd been rummaging his hands through it. Now I looked more closely, I could see it was thick, and wiry. He must have made quite an effort to get it so flat for the memorial.

"Sorry, have we met?" he asked, peering at me. "I feel like we've met somewhere before."

Jamie would have made that sound like the cheesiest chat-up line ever, and probably used the opportunity to lean up against the wall, but the way Mark said it, he sounded worried, as if he *should* know. His mouth twitched.

He had a good mouth for a man — quite wide, not too full, tilting down sardonically at the ends.

"Yes!" I said. "I was about to come looking for you. Betsy Tallimore? We met at the reception."

"Of course," he said, tilting his head with a brief smile that didn't quite reach his eyes. "Miss Tallimore, the famous business guru turned sandwich maker."

At once I started to feel a bit flustered. Miss Thorne wouldn't know a consultant if it bit her, but Mark Montgomery the accountant would. "Um, yes. Well, no. Not sandwiches today, I hope! I'm just here to take a look around and advise on . . ." My brain went blank as he looked at me expectantly. Again, all I could think of was Fiona's shoe shop. "Advise on getting a good fit between customer and curriculum. Polish everything up. Weatherproof it for this tricky . . . season."

Mark raised his eyebrows as if I were a bit mad. "Season?"

"I mean, financial climate."

There was a distinctly unladylike cackle of laughter from the direction of the Literary Appreciation class.

"Oh my God, I'll kill that tattooist! I said a porpoise! Not a tortoise!" Divinity's anguished howl was probably audible back in Leeds.

"Shall we go to my office?" Mark sighed. "You can only hear a delightfully dull roar from the girls up there."

I followed him up the back stairs to the second floor, where the offices were — Nancy's old matron's san and the other secretary's office, now empty, of course. In fact, it seemed that only Mark ever came up here from the way it had been left to return to nature. By the time we reached the upper landing, the wrought-iron pansies in the banisters were grey with dust, not gold gilt, and the cobwebs draped over the portraits were like something from a Hallowe'en shop. I half expected to find crows perching on the banisters.

"When was the last time this place was spring-cleaned?" I asked, unable to stop myself. "Or are you running some kind of spider sanctuary?"

"Ha ha," said Mark. He pushed open his office door, which still had "Col. J. C. P. Montgomery, Bursar" on it, left over from his father's time, and let me go through first. "If I had money for cleaners, do you think I'd have just spent the last hour debating with Miss Thorne about whether to pay the electricity bill or the lawyers?"

"And which did she choose?" I hoped my voice didn't sound too ironic.

His dark eyes met mine over the edge of his glasses and his mouth turned up at one corner, as if he wouldn't normally be sharing this particular information. "Neither, since you ask. She'd already spent the money paying the taxi company. But she's made a list of things we can sell, so that's OK."

"Oh, really?" I said. "Is that up to her?"

"No." Mark closed the door behind him, and shrugged off his tweed jacket. I realised why he was wearing such an outdoor selection of clothes: though the classrooms were warm, it was virtually sub-zero up here. "So you want to stick your nose in the books, do you?"

"Please." I tried to sound cheerful. "I always say, get the worst thing over first and everything else is easy."

He slung his jacket over a chair, started rummaging in the filing cabinet, and said, over his shoulder. "I should warn you, it's not a pretty sight."

I wondered whether he was talking about his office or the accounts. If Miss Thorne's study was an essay in hothouse elegance, no such expense had been lavished on the Bursar's office. Files and papers were stacked on every available surface, apart from the large oak desk, which was perfectly clear, with only a thin laptop, a silver vase of scarlet tulips and a calculator on the red leather top. It gave the impression that someone had just shoved everything off with one furious sweep of the arm.

"They're not my tulips," he said, catching me looking. "Someone puts them there every morning I come in. Tells you everything you need to know about this school's away-with-the-fairies attitude to economy, if you ask me."

I wondered who was putting flowers on his desk. Then I wondered why he didn't wonder. What sort of man didn't wonder that? Well, maybe men didn't.

"Oh, I disagree," I said. "You only need three or four, they look cheerful and last for ages. Good value for money, for flowers." I thought of the enormous display of fake lilies downstairs in the foyer — and the air freshener. "Better to have nice plants though. They last longer."

Mark snorted. "Would you like to tell Miss Thorne that? When the flower budget's bigger than the insurance budget and no one will listen to a word a qualified accountant says, you have to wonder what the hell's going on." He stopped rifling through papers, and looked at me. There was a directness about his expression that made me feel oddly warm in the chilly room. "Please, sit down. I think you'll need to, if we're going to be talking about the finances."

He gestured towards the library chair opposite his, and I dusted it with my hand before perching on the edge and getting my notebook out to buy myself a moment to compose myself — *again*.

"So," I said, clicking my pen. "What's the situation? Be honest."

Mark took off his glasses and squeezed the bridge of his nose. "In layman's terms?"

I bristled at that. I'd already had my outfit and my manners assessed today. My brain wasn't something I was worried about, though.

"If it makes it easier for you," I said. "But I've got a Maths degree. I can do really hard sums. Often without using my fingers."

Mark had the grace to look apologetic. More surprised than apologetic, actually.

"Sorry," he said, with a remorseful smile. "I've got rather used to talking to Miss Thorne. She doesn't think nice girls sully themselves discussing money."

"This one does," I said. "And I reckon the girls downstairs aren't afraid to, either."

"Fine. I won't sugar coat it: the Academy's on the last lap," he said, rustling through some papers. "There's no money coming in for the next year, because for some inexplicable reason, we have absolutely no takers for the Running a Stately Home course, and the trust is down to loose change. I've advised Lord Tallimore that it would make sense to sell the house, and, if they absolutely have to carry on with this finishing school, buy somewhere smaller. In — I don't know — in the suburbs or somewhere." He found the document he was looking for and pushed it across the desk.

I picked it up, and my fingertips brushed against his. They were short and had traces of oil or something in the cuticles. Mark pulled his hand away quickly. "But, if you want my professional opinion, and it's amazing how little anyone cares about *that* round here, I think he should sell, full stop. Finishing schools have been a ridiculous anachronism since before the war."

My attention was immediately distracted from the faint tingle in my fingertips and the beginnings of a blush on his cheek.

Sell the house? Give up the Academy, just like that? It sounded so much more real, coming from a complete stranger. And if it was sold, that was the end of my investigations, even before they'd begun! I couldn't stop a huff of shock escaping my nose, and he spotted it at once.

"You don't think Lord Tallimore should sell?" He looked at me in a direct way. "Or you think we should still be teaching flower arranging to grown women?"

I tried to keep my face neutral. I didn't want him to think I was letting my emotional connection to the place cloud my professional judgement.

Supposed professional judgement.

"Well, surely there are things we could try before selling up or moving?" I suggested. "The location is what makes a place like this. It's *part* of old London. I bet Anastasia's dad wouldn't have sent her if the Tallimore Academy was in Streatham."

Mark swung in his chair, and avoided my gaze. "Listen, I understand. It's always hard when a property like this goes out of the family. But we won't undersell it, if that's what you're worried about. I'll make sure you're not done out of your inheritance."

Was he suggesting that I was in this for *the house*? My neutral expression started to melt.

"This isn't about any *inheritance*," I said, hotly, putting my hands on the desk so he turned back to face me. When our eyes met, I flinched at how challenging his expression was, but I held my ground. "It's not about money for me. It's about keeping something alive that's been in the Tallimore family for years. Something that my . . . my mother cared deeply about. I know it's got its problems, but I'm sure we can put our heads together and come up with new measures to . . ."

Mark raised a hand and interrupted me. He seemed more weary than cross. "Betsy, I appreciate what you're saying, but if you're trying to tell me that there's a market for finishing schools in this day and age, you're talking to the wrong man." He folded his arms over his chest, and tipped his head on one side. "Shall we put our cards on the table here? I think it's *terrible*. *Insulting*. Encouraging girls to think there's nothing more to life than folding napkins and making themselves pretty, for God's sake! What next? Spinnet lessons?"

"I'm not saying things have to stay exactly as they are . . ." I began, but he hadn't finished.

"I've tried to suggest updated courses, like house buying or managing their not inconsiderable allowances, for instance, but Miss Thorne insists that it's not what they're here to learn."

"And what are they here for?" I asked. "I wish someone would tell me."

"To turn into the ideal wee wifey? But what would I know? I mean, I'm just a man." He lifted his palms and I got the feeling we were actually agreeing, not arguing at all. "That's what we should be looking for in a girl: napkin-folding. Not smart budgeting, or funny conversation." Mark stopped, self-consciously, as if he'd said too much. "Anyway, I don't know if it's worth it anyway — not a single one of those girls downstairs has the first idea what goes on in the real world," he went on, pushing a hand into his dark hair and making it stick up even further. "Forgive me if I'm being tactless here, but I'm amazed at just how normal you are. I was expecting Management Barbie, but you're the first Academy graduate I've met that makes any sense at all."

"I didn't *go*!" I nearly yelled, almost missing the cack-handed compliment. "You must be the only person here who doesn't know that!"

"Oh." He looked surprised. "I assumed . . ."

Maybe I over-reacted, but he'd touched a raw nerve. "What? You assumed I'd just waltz in here and start telling you what to do? No!" I snapped. "I've got real business experience, and I want to do everything I can to keep this place open, because I promised Lord Tallimore that I would try. I'm not here to catch you out or take over, I'm just here to help him. If I can't think of anything, *then* we can discuss selling the house. But not until I've tried."

Up to that moment, I hadn't properly understood how strongly I wanted to do just that, and I realised I was prodding the desk for emphasis. Mark was looking at me rather differently. He sat back in his office chair and folded his arms, waiting to see what I would say next.

It occurred to me that experienced management consultants probably didn't prod the desk in meetings. Not so soon, anyway.

"Have you got a brochure there?" I asked, trying to modulate my voice. "I think I should have a look at how the Academy's marketing itself. And last year's accounts too."

I watched him as he opened and closed drawers, pushing up the sleeves of his grey sweater as he muttered to himself about filing. There was a different atmosphere in the room now — as if we'd edged tentatively into each other's confidence. He'd been a bit too honest with me; I'd been a bit too honest with him. But it felt all right, as if we might actually be on the same wavelength.

At least this was one man who wouldn't be put off by my geeky Maths degree, I thought, noticing the frayed collar of his checked shirt. Mark didn't seem like a man who bothered too much with clothes. That sweater looked more like a Christmas present from a girlfriend.

"Here." I jolted back to attention as he passed a glossy brochure over the desk, along with a clear plastic file of neatly typed figures. "Don't read it while you're drinking coffee."

Now that he wasn't looking cross, Mark really wasn't bad-looking, in a bookish way. The glasses were cute, and I admired the way he was more concerned about Lord T than upsetting Miss Thorne, who he clearly didn't have much time for. We had that in common too. He just seemed quite . . . exasperated about things.

"Why not?" I asked.

"Because you might find yourself spitting it all over the place." The corner of his sardonic mouth lifted. It was a smile you couldn't help returning. "I understand that's terrible table manners."

Mark had been right to warn me about the coffee. I read the brochure over lunch, in the Pret A Manger round the corner, and I nearly scalded my tongue on my cappuccino with shock.

The brochure was unbelievably awful. I stopped being surprised at the paltry four students enrolled, because frankly I was amazed they'd even got that many. It was expensively printed on glossy paper, with no vulgar mention of prices, but the text was weird and dated, as if it hadn't been changed since Franny's day. Since *before* then, even. Under Miss Thorne's new management, the Academy seemed to have gone backwards into the England that existed only in period dramas where everyone talked in tebbly, tebbly, clipped eccents and had impassioned clinches next to steam locomotives.

No manners are more prized than those of the English lady, someone (Miss Thorne, presumably) had written beneath a photograph of a girl in three strands of pearls trying to choose between hats — one like a loo roll cover with frills and a larger one that looked more like a flattened cabbage, while Miss Thorne lurked instructively in the background. I think they were hats, anyway. *The Tallimore Academy prides itself on taking the girl and handing back a lady who can comport herself with style and grace in the highest echelons of society.*

I wasn't sure how that related to the awkward photographs of more pearled-up girls sharing some hilarious joke over a porcelain tea service while Miss Thorne looked on with approval and a very smooth brow. They were all sitting with their knees super-glued together in a Las Vegas hotel version of the Palace of Versailles. Or possibly teatime at Madame Tussauds.

We will endeavour to equip our students with every charm necessary for a challenging and socially inspiring life, it went on, underneath a picture of a model pretending to read *Madame Bovary* as if she'd never actually held a book before, while another model pretended to talk on an old telephone that wasn't connected to anything. I didn't know who she was talking to. Dame Barbara Cartland in the afterlife?

The courses, when they were finally listed, were infuriatingly vague. "Everything a lady might need to know"? In 1980, maybe, if she lived in a Bavarian castle surrounded only by bishops, with nothing to do all day but arrange après ski parties and make needlepoint cushions. Formal dinner settings, engaging household staff, "chalet cuisine" . . . There was some vague reference to "life presentation" and "letter writing", but otherwise it was as if email, female emancipation and budget air travel hadn't been invented.

I'd solved Maths equations comprised solely of numbers and Greek squiggles, but I couldn't make head nor tail of the Academy's prospectus. What *was* protocol? What did personal ethics *mean*? Why did Miss Thorne think that hovering in the back of each shot like an etiquette policeman was anything but sinister?

I sat back in my chair and stared in dismay at the brochure propped up against my sandwich. To think I'd spent the best part of my adult life feeling swizzed that I hadn't been allowed to take lessons in how to drink a cup of tea. At least, I think that's what the assembled etiquette-bots were doing in the illustration.

Had it always been like this, I wondered glumly. The fascinating secrets I remembered Franny dishing out like sweets, things that made me long to be grown-up enough to test them out . . . was it really just this? I wouldn't have wanted *this*.

I binned my empty cup and sandwich box, and walked back down Piccadilly. The sun had gone in but I hardly noticed.

I couldn't even sneak back up to the bursar's office to go through the files, because Miss Thorne grabbed me as I came in, and insisted that I attend her own personal class: Conversation.

Conversation wasn't really the point, it seemed — well, not as I knew it. Miss Thorne's tactic was to teach the girls how to stop any conversation dead in its tracks if it started to veer off the appropriate lines, whereas the girls only wanted to discuss topics that made Miss

Thorne's plump little hands flap up and down like air traffic control paddles. But she'd had thirty years' experience and all they had was sheer determination to wind her up. It was like watching a team of pub league strikers fire shots towards an England goalie.

"So, Anastasia, how are you?" she was saying when I slipped in.

"Very poorly," said Anastasia, with a pretend hacking cough, "I have a terrible hangover from the bar I went to last night. They add something to my drink, I know, because this morning my stomach makes a noise like my father's tank and . . ."

"No!" Miss Thorne's hands flew up. "We never discuss physical symptoms! Or violent behaviour! Stick to something pleasant about the venue!"

"But it was a sheethole," said Anastasia, opening her eyes wide. "I thought it was a transvestite bar but apparently not. You ought to know these things before you go."

"Tizzy Barber should have *said*," added Clemmy. "It was her stupid party. If we'd *known* the waitress wasn't a bloke, then Anna wouldn't have punched the . . ."

"Say you enjoyed an interesting new experience," said Miss Thorne, through gritted teeth. "And move on."

"What good is that to anyone?" demanded Anastasia and I had to agree with her. But unlike Miss McGregor, Miss Thorne wasn't about to let me start making suggestions, so I sat, listening to her block any comments about gossip, celebs, illness, politics, television and tattoos — on which the girls were surprisingly entertaining — and counting down the minutes until I could drop in on Kathleen and Nancy for some moral support and a dose of reality.

At four o'clock on the dot the girls bailed out as if the place were on fire. I was in dire need of a cup of tea, possibly fortified with a shot of whisky. I didn't drink whisky, but there was something about Miss Thorne's uptight conversation class that made me want it. Just for the sake of being unladylike.

I made my way through the neglected garden towards the mews cottage, which was, in contrast, neatly kept; the brass knocker gleamed out of the dusk on the front door. Before I'd even lifted it, the door had swung open and there was Nancy, welcoming me in as if I'd just crossed the Arctic which, in a way, it felt like I had.

She rushed me inside, and settled me in the chair by the Aga while Kathleen piled up my plate in the manner of someone constructing a dry stone wall of sponge cake.

"So, how did it go?" Kathleen asked, when I'd downed my tea and held out my cup for a refill.

I hesitated, trying to think of something positive to balance out the negatives, but she caught me. "Be honest, Betsy," she said, sternly. "Tell the truth and shame the devil."

"It's . . . in need of a spring clean," I said.

"What's to be done?" asked Nancy. "Do they need some new teachers? Miss Thorne did make a lot of them redundant last year." She frowned, worried, but then smiled. "I expect you can think of some clever things to do. You'll make one of your lists, I expect."

I looked at them, the kindest, sweetest, most honest old ladies, and struggled. They'd been here nearly all their lives, and adored everything Franny had stood for — kindness, manners, decency. How could I tell them things were so bad that I almost agreed with the bursar about closing down?

But they'd also brought me up to be honest, so I made myself meet their expectant gazes.

"I don't know what to do," I confessed. "It's going to be very hard to persuade new students to come here, unless a lot of things change. The bursar thinks we might have to advise Lord Tallimore to sell."

"Sell?" gasped Nancy and her china cup rattled on its saucer.

"Now, Nan, we knew that was on the cards." Kathleen gave me a stout look.

"Well, what if he does sell?" I said, trying to sound cheerful. "It just means you'll get some squillionaire non-dom businessman next door — they'll only be there twenty days a year!"

At that, Kathleen's face took on a shadow, and Nancy pressed her lips together. The lines deepened around their eyes, and I was painfully reminded of just how old the two of them were getting. I wanted to hug them both to me, just like they'd once crushed me to their mighty bosoms, but my bosom was nowhere near so comforting.

"What?" I asked, and for once neither of them corrected me.

"Well, it's not just the house that'd go on the market, is it?" said Kathleen. "There's not many properties round here come with their own three-car garage and staff quarters. He'd put the lot up for sale. The mews too. We're tenants, you see, Betsy. Always have been. Part of our retirement package, this."

My mouth dropped open, and I could have slapped myself for being so slow. It had never even occurred to me that selling the Academy would make Kathleen and Nancy homeless.

"But surely Lord T would find somewhere for you in the country," I stammered. "At Bellingham Manor — there must be some room . . ."

Kathleen folded her arms. "Live in the country? At our age? I don't think so, dear. Dreadful place. Smelly. And dark. Not like London."

"No, we don't want to be moving out of London, not now. I suppose the new owners might want some staff," said Nancy, her brave smile wobbling. "I hear you can get vacuum cleaners that go up stairs these days, save my old back. And Kathleen's still a dab hand —"

"No!" I said, pushing back my chair. "That's not going to happen! Do you think Franny would allow anyone to throw you out of your own home? She'd be furious!" I blinked, because I was very near crying now, and I knew Nancy was too, and I didn't want to set her off.

"The Tallimore Academy is *not* going to close, and it's *not* going to be sold," I said, and grabbed my notebook. "There must be something we can do. I've got the brochure, and it's mad. Flower arranging, dinner parties, dealing with staff . . . Aren't there *any* teachers under fifty?"

Nancy and Kathleen exchanged looks.

"Well, there's always Adele," said Nancy.

"Who's Adele?" I asked. I hated the name Adele. I couldn't hear it without thinking of the only Academy girl I'd ever really disliked. But then no one liked Adele Buchanan, and she didn't care. She wasn't what you'd call a girls' girl, even at eighteen. Her nose had been like a spring onion at the beginning of the year, and then she "went skiing" and came back with a teeny button nose and new teeth.

"Adele Buchanan," said Kathleen, as she got up to put the kettle on. "Do you remember her? Bottle blonde, never bothered with the regulation skirt. Or regulation knickers, come to that. She's very thick with Miss Thorne — flounces in now and again to 'mentor' the girls. Whatever that means."

"Really?" I couldn't imagine Adele teaching. "Isn't she married and running some huge estate somewhere? That was what she said she was going to do. She wanted a helicopter pad. I remember her saying."

"Recently widowed," said Nancy, meaningfully. "She married the Duke of Pertonshire. Rather tragic — they were playing tennis one night, and a bolt of lightning hit his pacemaker and struck him stone dead. Still, he was over eighty. Fancy him being so active! I suppose it must have been a floodlit court . . ."

Kathleen met my eye, and pursed her lips. Neither of us needed to say any more, although Nancy was still musing on the oddness of it.

"If you ask me," said Kathleen, "that one's got her eye on Lord Tallimore. Always manages to be here in a tight skirt whenever he pays a visit, and makes a big thing about her husband's only just dead. She's giving him *grief counselling*, Geraldine Thorne says."

"Oh, no, Kathleen," said Nancy, looking at me quickly. "I'm sure she wouldn't be so bold."

"I'm sure she would," retorted Kathleen.

I felt something twist inside my chest. The Tallimores had had the perfect, supportive marriage I dreamed of — the kind of breakfast-in-bed, nights-by-the-fireside security I was still holding out hope of finding somewhere. You couldn't replace that overnight! Not with someone like Adele Buchanan.

I didn't mean to say anything, but it burst out of me anyway. "But they were married for forty years! He still has her breakfast tray set up by the kettle in the butler's pantry — I saw it at Christmas! And you know what he's like about *ladies*, he's got no idea that women like Adele even exist!"

"Pay no attention to Kathleen, Betsy!" said Nancy, tucking her little hand around mine. "I'm sure it's never even crossed his mind, even if the silly girl is setting her cap at him. *No one* could replace Lady Frances. Don't you go worrying yourself! You've quite enough to think about!"

As I squeezed back, I felt a sudden jolt of fear at how fragile her hand, once so firm, seemed.

Franny had already gone, and when Nancy and Kathleen went, who would there be to tell me who I was? If I couldn't find my mother, there'd be nobody.

Kathleen, though, was still gnashing her teeth about Adele. There was obviously a raw nerve there.

"Lord alone knows what she's teaching those girls. She's just as hard-faced as she ever was," she snapped. "And she's got one of those shih-tzu things, brings it in with her in its own little handbag. Its own handbag, if you don't mind! Can you *imagine* anything less sanitary?"

Well, she couldn't have designs on Lord T, I thought, with relief. He was a Great Dane man, through and through. The Tallimore Great Danes ate lapdogs for a mid-morning snack, between cats and pheasants.

CHAPTER SEVEN

Find your stopcock and your fusebox and tape the number of your nearest plumber and electrician to them before you have an emergency.

By the time I arrived on Liv's doorstep at seven, I felt like I'd been up for about three days straight, even though that morning I'd been up in Edinburgh and in a whole different world. A world where Raffles was something you did at church fairs.

My legs ached from marching around in my high consultant heels, my head was pounding from my early flight, and my mind was going round and round in ever-tightening circles as I turned over my stupid promise to Lord T and the Academy. I knew I had to do something, but what? I didn't even know where to begin.

If I told Lord T to sell the Academy because it was a money-sapping, feminist-enraging dinosaur, Nancy and Kathleen would be out on their ears, Franny would turn in her grave, and I'd never find out who'd left me there. On the other hand, if I encouraged him to keep it open, I'd have to find a way to make it work, and I had more chance of bringing Jane Austen back to life to teach a bridge class than pulling that off. Plus, I'd have to keep up my impression of Sir Alan Sugar for another fortnight and persuade Fiona not to sack me for deserting my post.

I swung my leather carry-on bag over the other shoulder, and pressed the doorbell. Maybe something would come to me when I tried to explain it to Liv. I never had to pretend anything with her: we had no secrets. I knew she dyed her eyelashes. She knew I didn't really pass my driving test first time.

I closed my eyes and wished really hard for some divine bolt of inspiration.

Inside the house, footsteps thundered towards the door, which swung open with some force, to reveal Liv, her blond hair soaked and plastered over her face. In the background, I could hear a thudding sound.

"Betsy!" she gasped, grabbing my hand. "Quick! Help!"

"What?" I dumped my bag as she dragged me down the hall towards the kitchen. "What's happened?"

"I've flooded the house!" she wailed. "And I can't find the cat! And . . ."

"Deep breaths," I said firmly. "Take a deep breath and tell me what's happened."

She took a deep, shuddering breath. "I thought I ought to wash the sheets before you came. I used the last clean ones, and didn't have time to buy any more so I put them in the wash."

"And?"

"And . . ." Liv blinked and raised her hands. "And I don't know after that!"

I rushed past her to survey the chaos in the kitchen. Soapy water was creeping across the tiles, with a pretty pink froth on top, and it seemed to be coming from the washing machine, which was making weird banging, grinding noises.

The washing machine door was partly open and a slimy pile of pink sheets had disgorged on to the floor in the manner of a gruesome birthing scene from a vet drama. Worryingly near the puddle of standing water was an ironing board, with an iron laid flat on a wet sheet, and a . . .

I didn't waste time asking. I bounded across the kitchen, unplugged the iron, yanked it off the sheet just as smoke was beginning to rise from the scorchmark, and then, twirling round for somewhere to put the iron, turned the washing machine off at the mains for good measure.

Then I turned the radio off too, just to give myself a clear head, at which point the sound of a cat throwing up could be made out in the sitting room.

At the door, Liv burst into tears. "Sorry!" she howled. "Sorry!"

"Liv, it's fine," I said, scooping up the soggy sheets and dumping them in the sink. "Everyone has a washing machine disaster at some point. Think of it as a . . . painless floor wash."

But Liv had sunk to a chair and was burying her face in her arms.

"I've had such a shit da-a-a-ay!" she howled. "Everything's going wro-o-o-ong!"

I tried to keep calm, and picked out a rogue red hand-dyed T-shirt, the source of the pink.

"Look, at least you *tried* to wash the sheets," I said, looking under the sink to see if she had any colour run remover, but finding only an empty can of fly spray and a used J-cloth. "That's much more sensible than just going to buy a new set."

Liv made a terrible gurgling sound, much worse than the washing machine. "I *couldn't* get new sheets! My card got refused! I've got twenty-three quid left in the world and Dad's on the run! From the law!"

"What?" My head bounced up so rapidly I almost hit it on the ironing board.

"Dad's gone to Spain and he hasn't paid my allowance and he can't help me because he can't move any money out of his accounts!" Liv dragged her hair back off her face, and I could see the whites around her eyes. She looked a bit mad. "I mean, he's not acting worried, but he won't say what's up, just that his assets are freezing or something and I . . ." She clapped her hand over her mouth and squeezed her eyes shut. "What if the bailiffs kick down my doors?"

I started running hot water over the sheets. "Liv, that only happens on telly. Calm down. Deep breaths. Tell me properly. What's happened?"

She wiped the mascara under her eyes, and fought to stop her sobs, staring at the mess between hiccups, as if she couldn't believe how it had got there. "I wanted to get the house nice for you coming to stay," she hiccupped. "I put everything in together, and it took me ages to work out which liquid was which, and . . ."

"Forget the washing machine, this is soon cleared up. I mean, what's happened to *Ken*?" I asked. "Look, we need tea. You put the kettle on, and I'll start on the flood. Did he say when he'd be back?" I dragged the squeezy mop out of the cupboard and began squidging.

"No. But now that wad of cash he gave me last week makes sense . . . Oh," she said, peering at my rapid mop action, "is that what you're meant to do? Push, then squeeze? I've never used that. It's clever, isn't it?"

"Easy when you know how. Keep taking deep breaths." The water was receding and so were Liv's hiccups. But that only gave her more breath to panic with.

"What am I going to do? No Erin, no Jean, no Dad . . . I can't even put a *wash* on without flooding the house," she said, following the mop, hypnotised. "And I've got a whole bunch of letters from the bank and the mortgage people and I don't understand them because Dad always takes care of stuff like that . . ."

Liv stopped suddenly and looked me in the eye. "Tell me honestly, Betsy, I need to learn. That washing machine. The door's meant to open, right? If you press the emergency stop button?"

"Olivia," I said. "I'll be frank with you. There isn't an emergency stop button on a washing machine. That's the on/off switch."

"Really?" she said. "And do you put the liquid bag things in the . . . drawer part?"

"You really don't know how to work your washing machine?"

"No," she said, in a small voice.

I opened my mouth, then closed it again.

I'd always known Liv was one of those lovably ditsy types whom people rushed to bail out; I'd been explaining everything from bicycle locks to the Euro to her since we were at school. But I had no *idea* she'd managed to arrange a whole wall of people to shield her from the grim reality of washing machines. If she couldn't wash her own pants, what was going on in her brain about mortgages? Liv wasn't stupid, far from it. She had, after all, managed to line up five fiancés, one of whom had his own plane, and keep all the engagement presents afterwards.

She *does* know about wine, I told myself. And she has basic French, her hair's immaculate, and she always looks like she has a live-in stylist.

"You are OK to make the tea, aren't you?" I asked, hesitantly.

"Of course!" Liv pouted, then undermined herself by having to check all the cupboards before she located the teabags.

I shook the last drops off the mop into the bucket, and pointed to the kitchen table, which was, I noticed, covered in the same piles of paperwork I'd sorted when I was last there. "We'll sit down, open *all* those letters, and get things straightened out. I'll help. It's not that hard."

Liv had one final hiccup. "God, Betsy, you make it sound so easy. How come you always know what to do?"

"I don't," I said, simply. "I just deal with things one at a time. Now, from the start. Ken called you to say that he's not on holiday, but on the run . . ."

It took a while to extract the details, since it hadn't occurred to Liv to ask certain key questions (like, why? Or, for how long?) but reading between the lines, it seemed that certain officers of Her Majesty's Inland Revenue Collection Agency had sniffed fruity accounting, and now investigations were afoot into Ken's empire. Consequently, Liv would no longer be receiving her monthly allowance — the proceeds from certain rental properties.

"It's a nightmare!" she wailed. "He kept saying, it's better if you don't know! And I don't *mind* not knowing, so long as I know roughly what it is he's not telling me! I mean, is it better not to know he's going to prison? Or that he's remarried and doesn't want to tell me? Or what?"

Much as I liked Ken, if he'd been there, I'd have kicked his sweet-talking arse right over Clapham Common and into Wandsworth Town. It was one thing, treating your little girl like a princess, but leaving her in the lurch with a mortgage that she didn't even know how to pay wasn't fair at all. Up until now, Liv's part-time job in a Scottish-themed wine bar run by her friend Igor, plus Erin's rent, had been keeping her in takeaway and shoe money while the "house account" took care of the serious expense of living in London.

The house account currently had fifty-three pounds and ten pence in it, and Liv's *heat* subscription was due to go through any moment — which could wipe out the lot, since Liv couldn't recall how much the direct debit was for.

"Calm down," I said, "we can work this out. It's just a case of adding things up." I automatically arranged the various bills into priority order. In this case, from black, to very black, to red, to — oh my God — a court summons. I slipped that out and sat on it, just for the time being. "You know roughly how much you need to cover utilities and the mortgage and stuff?"

Silence. I looked up to see Liv chewing her lip and looking ashamed.

"Liv?" I prompted. "How much is the monthly mortgage?"

"I don't know!" she squeaked. "Erin worked everything out on her spreadsheet and I paid my half. Come on, she was good at it!" Liv helped herself to another organic triple chocolate cookie — we'd cracked open the emergency chocolate supplies. "I'm sorry, Betsy. I feel so stupid. I didn't ask you down here to sort out my life." Pause. She gave me an appealing blue-eyed peek through the lashes. "Unless you could . . ."

I forced myself to be firm with her for her own sake. "Olivia, you've got to do this," I said. "It's not your fault you haven't done this before, but soonest started, soonest over, as Nancy says. You've got to open these letters. All of them. I'll help you, I promise."

She stared into her cup of tea. "I suppose you're right." Then she put the whole cookie into her mouth, as if she didn't know when her next organic bakery trip might be.

I decided not to push it. I didn't want Liv bolting for Spain too. So I made a proper pot of tea this time, and to make her feel like she wasn't the only one in over her head, I told her about my rollercoaster day, starting with Miss Thorne informing me that I had a parlourmaid name, and finishing with Kathleen and Nancy's impending eviction, with a bit of Mark the Bursar's sell-sell-sell spiel inbetween.

". . . And when Nancy looked at me like one of those abandoned old mutts you see at Battersea Dogs Home and said, 'I suppose the new owners might need someone to hoover the stairs . . .' " I spread my hands wide and blinked, half-laughing, half-crying, at Liv. Tears were coursing down our faces. "What could I say?"

"Nothing, it's too horrible." She rubbed her eyes with the back of her hand. "Poor Nancy and Kathleen. What are you going to do?"

I sighed and shook the last cookie out of the packet. "Well, that's the thing. What *is* there to save now? It's pretty hard to argue with Tightwad Mark when he says we should just tell Lord T to sell up and get out. I mean, obviously I don't want to do that, but I just don't remember it being so . . ." I struggled to find words to sum up how weirdly let down I felt by the ramshackle, dated mess I'd found.

"So what?" prompted Liv. "So big? So posh?"

"No, so *irrelevant*!" I dug the brochure out of my bag and slid it across the table. Liv's eyes widened when she saw the photograph of the girl in white gloves shaking hands with a vicar, under the heading "Making the Right Connections". "It's all meaningless etiquette stuff about . . . butlers! Who in their right mind cares about butlers any more? Apart from maybe Paul Burrell?"

"Betsy, people do! You can't *move* for etiquette guides in WHSmiths!" Liv flipped through the pages, frowning. "You only say that because you already *know* it. Everyone else is like, this is a *minefield*! I mean, weddings." She pulled a "save me from this horror" face. "Remember when I nearly got married to Charlie Palmerston and you helped me work out what to do with the divorced bits of the family so no one was offended — I hadn't got a clue, but I knew *they* did." Her expression darkened. "And if you hadn't given me that wake-up call about his mummy complex . . . well, that was even more helpful. Believe me, if there's an accepted formula when it comes to breaking off an engagement, people want to know."

"Maybe *that's* what they should be teaching the girls," I suggested, drily. "Arranging a wedding, and then getting out of one, if necessary."

"Well, yes — exactly!" Olivia nodded, ignoring the fact that I was joking. "Mothers aren't what they used to be when it comes to advice like that. I mean, look at us. Rina bunked off before I even had a boyfriend to ask her about. Didn't Franny give you that big Things

You Should Know talk, remember, when we were in the fourth form? What to do about Wandering Hand Taxi Man? And Lend Me a Tenner Boy? You had it all in that notebook."

I knew exactly what she meant: the notebook and the advice. All the Tallimore girls had lilac leather books that they were supposed to jot down the lessons in, and I'd always had them at school. They made me feel extremely sophisticated, even if I was just scribbling down addresses. Franny's "things you should know" advice had been delivered over a series of girls-only teas at the Ritz the summer I was fifteen, and I'd felt deliciously grown-up as we sat there, sipping tea while Franny reeled off all the different men who'd apparently be queuing up to take me out for dinner — their good points, bad points and "things to watch out for".

"Course I remember that," I said. "Shoes are still the first thing I look at on a date."

"Where are those notebooks?" asked Liv. "God, the hours we spent, going over and over them . . . They were like *Cosmo*, but better. More ladylike. You should publish them, you'd make a fortune."

"They're in my old wardrobe at Kathleen's. I haven't seen them since . . . since I went to university." I blinked away the memory of shoving them in and slamming the door shut, in a fit of humiliation at the thought of not being allowed to compile official ones. "But I don't think they're teaching anything like that now. It's all snobbery and globe artichokes."

Liv pointed at the brochure. "But it says here there's a course on putting clothes together — isn't that useful?"

"There is, but it's all '*tell your dressmaker*' yadda yadda yadda. Girls need to know about sales shopping, and how to buy a perfect little black dress, not *hats*!" It made me cross, the brochure's assumption that normal women had the time or the money to *have* half the "little social worries" the Academy would fix. "Now, if they were going to teach you how to do a salon-perfect blow-dry at home . . . How much money could a girl save if she knew how to do her own nails, for instance?" I gave Liv's glossy merlot manicure a pointed look, in light of her own personal Credit Crunch. "How much money are you spending a month on your nails, for a start?"

"I don't want to think," she said, then, under my gaze, conceded, "A lot. I mean, I *used* to."

"Well, think how much money you could save if you could do it yourself? It's Budget Day, Olivia O'Hare." I wagged my finger at her, with a pretend stern expression. "You don't have to dry-clean jeans, you know, they go in the wash. I can't believe the stuff no one's told you over the years. And how to set up your direct debits so they don't crash your bank account . . ."

My finger wagging slowed down, as the faint shape of an idea began to take form in my mind. The Academy used to teach girls skills for marriage, why couldn't it now teach them skills for independent life? Could DIY be the new interior decoration?

Could professional blow-drying be the new flower arranging?

"Steady on, Betsy!" Liv gasped, but I wasn't hearing anything. There was no point trying to recreate the Academy's former glories — we had to reinvent the finishing school for the twenty-first century! Even Mark Montgomery had to agree that had potential *and* post-feminist credibility. I reached for the notebook in my handbag, and started to scribble.

"Basic household stuff — I wish I knew more about that. I spent a fortune on calling out plumbers last year, and I never know if decorators are ripping me off. Do you know where your stopcock is?"

"I didn't know I had one," said Liv faintly.

"And mortgages," I looked up. "I'm assuming your dad didn't explain the difference between fixed rate and trackers?"

Liv shook her head.

"And wouldn't you love to know, without having to have some mouth-breather from the bank tell you?"

She nodded obediently, then asked, "Um, why?"

"Because . . ." I searched around for a better reason than "because"; it had never occurred to me, growing up with no dad to fix my taps or set up my Internet access, that anyone *wouldn't* want to know. "Because . . . then no one can patronise you! Or take advantage!"

"Right," said Liv, unconvinced.

I was on a roll. "This is what the Academy needs to offer! Short courses in making a woman's life as stylish as possible. What's more stylish than knowing you're in control of your destiny? It doesn't have to be for rich girls — it's for anyone who wants to feel more in *charge* of their lives!" I tapped my silver fountain pen against my lips, then pointed it at Liv. "What else makes you feel inadequate because you don't know how to do it?"

"Parking," she said at once. "How to reverse park in one go so those evil taxi drivers don't honk and put you off. God, I hate that. Why don't they realise it *makes* me hit things?"

I wrote down "London driving". If you could drive in London, you could drive anywhere. "Exactly! And something about wine — I always wish I knew more about wine. Um . . . What else do you really wish someone had told you when you were eighteen?"

"That the bars of London are paved with divorced men? And some who aren't quite divorced but tragically saddled with wives who *just don't understand them?*"

"*That* is a great idea . . ."

"And stepchildren," she added. "There's something no one tells you about in *Brides* magazine."

"Great . . . And alimony?"

"Yes, alimony. And pre-nups. What about breaking off engagements? Someone should teach that. And turning down proposals."

"Oh, they do that," I said. "They work on the principle that once you're a Tallimore girl you're turning titled suitors down left, right and centre. What they don't tell you is how to decide *who* to marry." Another light bulb lit up in my head. "Does your friend

Beattie still work for that matrimonial law specialist? Would she come in and talk about pre-nups?"

"If the new Director of Studies at the Tallimore Academy asked her, how could she say no?" asked Liv, only half-jokingly.

"But I'm not going to be in *charge* of this, I'm just . . ." I began, and ground to a halt. Would Miss Thorne take me seriously? Would any of this even make sense outside Liv's kitchen?

Liv spotted my wobbling confidence and leaped in, as she always did. "It's a really great idea, Betsy," she said, reaching over the table to grab my hand before I could start chewing my nails. "I can't believe they haven't thought of it before! It's a *brilliant* idea. Even if that toxic old cow hates it, I bet the *girls* will love new lessons about beating the sales and dumping a loverat!"

I thought of Anastasia. She probably had her own methods for dealing with loverats. None of them needed to economise on manicures, but in the few hours I'd been there, I'd noticed that Divinity, for one, seemed eager — paranoid, even — about doing the "right" thing. And Clemmy struck me as being deeply insecure, rather than genuinely angry. Maybe they would get something out of real-life lessons.

"I suppose so," I said slowly. "I guess everyone needs to spot a good man and a classic coat."

"Exactly! What have you got to lose?" said Liv. "If it keeps the place open for another few months, it gives you more time to do some hunting around for potential parents. If it closes tomorrow, that's it. The files are shut." She slapped her hands together dramatically. "You'll be reduced to going on one of those daytime DNA shows if you really want to track her down."

My stomach plunged. I'd had that selfish thought niggling at the back of my mind the whole day, but hadn't liked to acknowledge it. It was true though. If Mark had his way, the house would be on the market in a matter of days, and I'd only have myself to blame for not looking earlier.

"You know, you're the only person insensitive enough to put it like that," I said, with a crooked smile.

"Yes, but I'm the only person who knows how much you want to find her. Deep down, when you're not worried about hurting anyone's feelings. It's about time, Betsy. You've done so much on your own, and you've been the best daughter the Tallimores could have had, but you've got to move on with your life."

"By going backwards?"

"No, by finding out for definite, so you can make some decisions about who you are, instead of worrying that deep down you're not good enough!"

"Is this about those application forms again?" I said, but it didn't come out as lightly as I'd hoped it would.

Liv shoved back her chair, got up, and gave me a tight hug, in a gangling rush of long arms and blond hair. She smelled of fresh white flowers, as she had done for years. We'd picked our signature fragrance at thirteen, on Franny's recommendation: hers was Pleasures, mine was Chanel No. 5.

"I know you can do it," she said, squeezing me. "You just have to work out what you think *I* ought to know, what Franny told you, and what you've learned. Listen, if you can teach me to be half as capable as you, I'll be fine. And I'd pay to learn that."

"Liv, that's really sweet," I said, but already my brain was whirring with possibilities, and calamities.

CHAPTER EIGHT

Don't save your best underwear for special occasions — wearing it might create one!

The Practical Reinvention of Olivia O'Hare began the next morning, with a proper breakfast, of the sort Kathleen would approve.

I had to nip out myself to the local supermarket to get the actual food, but by eight the porridge was on the stove, the toast was in the toaster, and I was head-deep in the fridge, wiping down the sticky marks, when Liv came stumbling blearily into the kitchen in her dressing gown. This was one she'd nicked from The Ritz in Paris.

"Breakfast?" she said, yawning. Even yawning, Liv didn't have a double chin, the lucky mare. She looked pretty the same when she'd just woken up as she did in full going-out mode. "I just have coffee in the mornings, generally."

"The Book of Kathleen says an empty stomach is a false economy," I said, moving wizened-up bits of ginger and nail varnishes round the shelves. "What you need is a bowl of porridge first thing — it wakes up your brain for work, and stops you grazing all morning. And then blowing a fortune on nibbly things for lunch."

"God, yeah. Igor might as well give my pay cheque to Fresh and Wild." Liv sighed. "There's one opposite the bar; I must have spent half my take-home pay on organic salad."

"Yes, well, that's the first thing we're going to tackle," I said. "Your take-home pay and where it's going."

"Ha ha ha," said Liv. "Before nine o'clock? You're funny!" She looked at me. "You're not joking, are you?"

"No," I said. "Sorry."

"I'll put some coffee on," she said, shuffling towards her shiny espresso machine — one of the happier relics of an abandoned engagement that had reached the giftlist stage.

"Now, are those *all* your bills on the table?" I asked, stirring the porridge. "Or just the most recent ones?"

I heard the sound of a cup being dropped in panic. "I don't know!"

"Well, that's this morning's job," I said, carrying on stirring, calmly. "Find them and file them. Even the ones you've hidden in the biscuit jar."

Liv made a strangled noise. "How do you know about those?"

"First place I looked. Are you working at Igor's today?"

"No, I don't have a shift until tomorrow afternoon."

"But you've asked for some more shifts, to cover Erin's share of the bills?"

"Er, no. Ooh! Can I have some porridge now, Goldilocks?" she asked, hopefully.

"Have you got a calculator?" I said, firmly. "We need to work out whether more shifts are going to cut it, or whether you might need to rethink the whole part-time bar girl, part-time art photographer thing."

"Really?" Her hand inched closer to the magazine that had arrived in the morning's post. Liv had subscriptions to everything; a weekend with her was worth three hair appointments.

"It'll take five minutes to do, compared with days dreading doing it," I said bossily, then realised to my horror that I sounded just like Kathleen. "It's not as bad as you think," I added, in a consoling voice. "You'll have some rent from me coming in for the next fortnight — no," I added, as she tried to protest, "fair's fair. I insist."

Liv sighed. "That's really kind of you. But we can save on some supper tonight. Jamie's going to take us out. He was just going to take me for a pizza round the corner, but then I told him you were here, and he upgraded us to a steak in Chelsea. Must be trying to impress you, eh? Either that or he's checking it out for some work reason."

My wooden spoon slipped on a rogue bit of porridge at the thought of Jamie impressing me, but I don't think Liv spotted it.

"Don't look a gift steak in the mouth," I said, then turned round to see if she had any other Jamie details to add. But she was already checking her stars in the magazine.

"Ooh, Saturn's bringing me an exciting new business opportunity," she mused. "And you're . . . following your heart until the end of Feb." She looked up. "We're going to be fine."

"Liv, you can't take Saturn to the bank when your card gets stopped," I urged. "Either we add up your budget now, together, before I leave or you can get your financial advice from Mr International Party Machine. You know what happened last time you asked his advice . . ."

Liv slapped *Red* magazine shut. "OK," she conceded, "when you put it like that . . . I'll get some paper."

The coffee and porridge made the maths go down much better, and before half eight we'd covered two sides of paper. Even I felt reassured, seeing the figures written down, even if they were kind of terrifying on the "out" side.

"Oh my God," said Liv. "Oh my God! I had no idea electricity cost that much! I thought it just . . . flowed. What am I going to do?"

"Economise."

Liv looked at me as if I'd just suggested she levitate.

"You need fashion maths," I suggested. "It helps if you imagine how much worse it could be. Always add the money you *could* be spending but aren't to the total you're actively saving. Like, I could be driving into work this morning, which would be congestion charge, plus petrol, plus parking." I scribbled. "That's nearly twenty quid. If I go on the bus, it's cheaper, but if I *cycle*, using that mountain bike gathering dust in the cellar, it's free. Five times a week saves . . .?"

"Over a hundred pounds!" said Liv immediately.

"Exactly," I said. "Isn't that more satisfying than saving twenty? Now work out how much you could be spending getting to work in a cab, and eating out, then how much it'll cost to walk with a packed lunch. Just don't add it to your spending budget," I added hastily. "It's not real money."

And having left Liv with a calculator and her bills, I dragged the bike out of the cellar and set off to the Academy. It was partly to show willing — who enjoys saving on their own? It's worse than solo dieting — but I didn't mind cycling the few miles from her house to Mayfair. It gave me a chance to examine my brainwave from every possible angle, before I mentioned it to anyone else.

I cycled over Chelsea Bridge and down past the smart riverside houses of Cheyne Walk. I didn't have to go round by Buckingham Palace, but I did, just for the nostalgia of seeing the big golden queen, surrounded by tourists even at this hour. After I'd weaved my way down Piccadilly, I wheeled the bicycle into the empty garage behind the main building, where the Academy Bentley was once parked. The oily smell took me right back to when I used to practise royal waves from the car, my chubby legs dangling off the bucket seats, breathing in warm red leather and polished wood. The car was long gone, like the Court Presentations it had once ferried Tallimoras to at the Palace.

Using the spotted old mirror on the door (no surface went unmirrored in the Academy) I did my best to remedy the chronic hat-hair caused by the cycle helmet, and did my BLT checks.

Buttons, fastened; red lipstick, unsmeared; teeth, fresh. Hair, flat.

Ready.

Paulette was ready to greet me with a wooden hanger when I went to hang up my coat in the hall.

"You've got pink cheeks!" she said, by way of hello. "Been up to something, have you? Eh?" She added a wink, in case I hadn't got it.

"I cycled in," I explained. "It was a bit further than I thought. But good exercise! And green!"

"That's what Mark says — he cycles in too." Paulette winked again, this time so hard her earring nearly caught in her cardigan. "Though in his case it'll be to save money, I reckon. He's one of those types who recycles his own —"

"Good morning!" I said loudly, as the front door was flung open and two girls slouched in.

I tried to remember which two they were. They weren't easy to make out, being wrapped up head to toe in Manhattan duvet coats, fur hats and Ugg boots, topped off with bug-eye shades. The only difference was that one of them had a fiercely studded black leather tote, and the other had long caramel extensions spilling out from under her fur hood.

From those small clues, I guessed it was Divinity and Clemmy.

"By 'eck. It's cold enough to freeze a girl's implants out there!" announced Divinity.

"Really? Have you got implants, Divinity? I thought you might have, because — Ow!" Paulette rubbed her ankle where I'd kicked it, then looked at me. "What? I was only asking."

"Yes, but then she might tell you. Far be it from me to step on Miss Thorne's teaching toes," I said, "but I think for everyone's sake, let's leave body parts out of conversation at least until lunch."

"Right," said Paulette. "I'll just . . . Make some coffee, shall I?"

"Lovely. Thank you! Now, good morning, you two!" I held out my hand to the girls, and made a snap decision not to tell them I was related to the owners. I wanted them to think I knew what I was doing, at least to start with. I could use my middle name; the one Franny had given me, in tribute to the marmalade box.

"I'm Betsy Cooper!" I said, gripping the floppy hand Divinity half-offered to me in surprise. "I don't think we were properly introduced yesterday. It's lovely to meet you. I'm here to look around the Academy and see what's what."

Divinity's hand remained limply in mine. It felt as if I'd picked up a chicken fillet. Not very nice.

Introductions had been a day one lesson in the old days. Franny hadn't taught an official class, but she made a point of ensuring that each student left the Academy "capable of helping everyone remember her name, from the prime minister to the coat check girl". She had me coming up with three conversation starters when I was only five — not to show off, but to help other people fix your name in their heads, in the confusion of a party. It was old-fashioned, maybe, but helpful to me when I was a nervous fresher. Nothing disguised my nerves better than a conversation about what your secret super power would be.

Divinity's hand still wasn't moving in mine. I squeezed it, and gave three firm shakes, smiling as I did it.

"Sorry, I didn't catch your name," I prompted her.

Clemmy snorted and rolled her eye skywards.

Divinity looked surprised that I didn't know who she was. "I'm Divinity Hogg? With two gs." She added a camera-ready smile that revealed the gum behind her sparkling teeth. "Lee Hogg's daughter?" she added, when my face didn't register sufficient amazement. "He's a footballer. Ex-England and Manchester United."

"He's a player-manager now? For, like, one of the biggest teams in Italy?" Clemmy elaborated as if I had some kind of hearing impediment.

"He's on telly all the time," said Divinity. "As a pundit. Do you not have a television?"

"Wow! I didn't realise, how exciting!" I said. "But *you're* the person I'm meeting — I'd rather know something about you, not your dad."

Divinity looked blank, and moved her gum from one side of her mouth to the other.

"Pretend you're at a party," I suggested. "How would you introduce yourself there, if we met?"

She gave me a funny look. "What? If they didn't already know me?"

"Yes," I said. "Try to include an icebreaker, so we can start chatting at once. Something interesting about yourself? Something you like?"

Divinity frowned, but then said, "Hiya, I'm Divinity and I like cheese." She glanced over at Clementine and made a tiny "wackadoo" gesture with her eyes.

"Really? Me too!" I exclaimed, as if she'd just invented Dairylea. "You'll have to tell me more about that, Divinity."

"Will do!" she bellowed, and winked.

"Hello," I held out my hand to Clementine with a fresh smile. "Betsy Cooper."

"You said that already," she said, with an equally limp grip, which tightened up noticeably when I increased the pressure from my side and inclined my head, in anticipation of her name. I could feel all her many rings digging into my hand, which served me right.

"Clementine Worthington," she added, reluctantly.

"Call her Clemmy, everyone does," said Divinity. "When we're not calling her Clammy. Or Glumentine. Or . . ."

"Watch it, Div," Clementine snapped. "I've got those camera-phone photos, don't forget."

"Hello, Clementine," I said. "It's lovely to meet you too. Are you enjoying your term here?"

"No. But I've been expelled from three schools, and my parents have," she hooked her fingers in the air, " 'run out of options'." Clemmy tossed her fringe out of her eyes as if she didn't care either way. Her hair was even more blue-black than it had been yesterday, and now I looked closer, she had a swallow tattooed between her thumb and first finger. Only a very small one, though, and it looked suspiciously smudged. Almost as if it was drawn on in biro.

"Her dad's a bishop," explained Divinity. "Brother's one of the Vicars to Watch for 2009. They've got enough bats knocking around the belfry without her turning up at confirmations dressed like that. What is it your mum does, Clemmy? Spiritual healing with blessed twigs?"

Clemmy gave her a warning glare, and Divinity raised her hands. "Just saying."

"I'm a disgrace," she informed me, staring up from under her fringe, challenging me to be shocked. "Not like my sister, who's married with about a hundred kids, and my brother who's, like Div says, a *career* vicar. I'm the black sheep of the family. I have parishioners praying for me on an hourly basis," she added, looking almost gratified.

With her sleepy kohl-ringed eyes, Clemmy reminded me more and more of a grumpy raccoon.

"Three schools?" I tried to look impressed, not disgusted. "Wow. For the same offence each time? Or did you develop a range? All the best people have been expelled from somewhere. My best friend's brother was expelled for running a profit on the school disco. He does it for a living now, so you never know."

Clementine's mouth drooped, as if that wasn't the reaction she'd hoped for.

"Do tell me more later, I'd love to hear the gory details. Anyway!" I said brightly. "Now we've been introduced, shouldn't you be in a class? What's your first lesson? I don't want to hold you back."

"Cordon Bleu cookery," said Divinity. She'd turned quite matey and offered me some gum, which I turned down, on account of a spearmint allergy I'd just made up. "We call it Cordon Bleeeeuurgh because half the class throws up whatever we make. It's all like, brandy snaps and crème brûlée and bits of stuff in gelatine."

"The kind of thing that your granny serves at Christmas parties," said Clemmy. "On paper doilies."

"OK. So what would you prefer to be making in cookery lessons?" I asked, getting my notebook out.

"Cocktails!" squealed Divinity.

"Anything vegetarian," said Clemmy.

"And organic," added Divinity, more piously. "Detoxs would be good."

I liked Divinity's cocktails *and* detox attitude.

"But food you can cook yourself?" I suggested. "And a seduction supper if you want to win a man through his stomach? And something for when you're on a diet, or needing cheering up? What about a simple dinner party you can throw together for some friends, or for when you get back from a club and you're starving?"

"What? You mean if your mobile's dead and you can't get the delivery number?" suggested Clemmy, sarcastically.

"Exactly," I said, ignoring the sarcasm.

"I'd like to be able to do a Sunday roast like my other nanna does," said Divinity wistfully. "Yorkshire puddings and gravy and that. All the trimmings."

"That's a great suggestion," I said, scribbling. I'd have to hold Kathleen back from teaching a Sunday Roast. And what was more sociable or sexy than a girl who could whip up a dish of crisp roast potatoes? "I need lots of feedback from you, so tell me everything you'd like to know, OK?"

I smiled and without thinking, Divinity and Clemmy smiled back. For a second, they looked like a perfectly charming pair of girls, not scary fashionista rich kids at all.

Then Clemmy looked shocked at the strange sensation in her facial muscles, and reverted to scowling like she was concealing a bat under her puffa coat, prior to biting its head off at the first opportunity.

The cookery class was held downstairs in the house, in a side room off from the old kitchens that took up most of the basement. When the house was the first Tallimores' London residence, there'd been marble-lined ice-rooms and game cupboards and tens of kitchenmaids and cooks in various ranks, all slaving to turn out elaborate dinner parties, and more skivvies to wash it all up afterwards.

Two hundred years later, the high-ceilinged rooms echoed sadly, and the huge ovens sat silent and cold. I peered into one of the kitchens, where big Kitchenaid mixers were enveloped in plastic covers. I used to love watching the goings-on in the Cordon Bleu classes, where the girls learned lumpy cheddar cheese straws in preparation for jolly chalet girl jobs, and gossiped about their dates . . .

"Are you all right?" said Divinity, and I realised I'd stopped in the doorway.

I gave myself a good shake.

"I'm fine, thank you!" I said. "Just thinking what a shame it is, not to be using these facilities. There must be something Miss Thorne could be doing with the space."

"Sunbeds? Or a hair salon?" suggested Divinity. "I want to be a top stylist when I leave here. You get to fly on private jets, and get free stuff from designers? And I want to get my own perfume range too!"

At least Divinity had an ambition, I thought. That was a start. On the way downstairs, we'd established that her mother had sent her to the Academy to learn how to behave nicely in case her dad was made a UN Goodwill Ambassador when he retired from international football and she wanted to be a celebrity in her own right too. Clemmy chewed her lip and remained silent.

"Have you had any lessons about styling?" I asked. "Advice about what to wear, when, that sort of thing? Dressing up your good points, hiding anything you don't like?"

Clemmy gave me yet another pitying look from her vast range of withering expressions as she pushed open the door to the Cordon Bleu kitchen. "Yeah. If you want to go around looking like some old granny. But then what do I know? *Nothing* I wear's ever right."

"Unless you're going to a wake," added Divinity helpfully.

I ushered them into the class.

The cookery class involved the creation of meringue swans, which, Mrs Angell insisted with diminishing conviction, could be used to carry placecards at dinner parties.

Venetia made some perfunctory efforts, but Clemmy decided to pipe gruesome meringue rats, and Anastasia finished early and spent the remainder of the lesson selecting a new ringtone for her mobile.

It wasn't remotely useful — apart from the hour it gave me to make notes and sketch out ideas for new lessons.

When the girls stampeded from the building for coffee and cigarettes, I took the opportunity to slip up the stairs to the bursar's office, in search of more covert information. If anyone asked, I was looking for details of any marketing the Academy had done recently, but what I really wanted to get my hands on were Nell Howard's contact details, and, ideally, the missing photograph.

Climbing up three flights of stairs all day was certainly going to get me fit, I thought, pausing to catch my breath at the top of the moth-eaten landing. Mark Montgomery's office door was closed and I knocked, though I didn't expect a reply — if Mark only came in once in a blue moon, thanks to that full-time job in the City he was so keen for me to know about, it would be ages before he reappeared.

Hearing nothing, I slipped in and shuddered as the fine hairs sprang to attention along my arm. I'd been in fridges warmer than the upper floors of this house, and Mark clearly turned off every radiator as he left the room, along with the lights and possibly even the spare oxygen. I pulled my green cardigan tighter around me and headed to the filing cabinets, which I was relieved to find weren't locked.

To be honest, I wasn't really sure what I was looking for as I rifled through the manilla folders, or, indeed what I would say to Nell Howard once I did find her details and ring her for a cosy chat about illegitimate children and sex scandals. But if Mark Montgomery was planning to advise Lord Tallimore to sell up, I didn't really have time to worry about the polite way of doing things.

My fingers flicked through files marked "Floral Decoration", "Ski trips/Austria", "Ski trips/France" and "Guidelines for Divorced Parents". Some of the files were so old they were written in copperplate, and most of them contained ancient heating bills in pounds, shillings and pence, or typewritten letters about overdue fees. Nothing remotely scandalous or interesting — although what did I expect in the bursar's office? Presumably anything juicy would be in Miss Thorne's files; and I didn't want to ask *her*.

Frustrated, and with time ticking away until Miss McGregor's napkin-folding class began downstairs, I chewed my lip, then had a flash of inspiration. The invitation list for the memorial service — Nell Howard would be on that! And I'd seen something about that with the unpaid bills on Mark's desk the previous day . . .

I was over by his chair in an instant. His desk was clear, apart from the red tulips and some unopened post in the letter tray. Mark obviously wasn't the sort to leave an in-tray unfiled, but maybe, if he was anything like me, he sometimes dumped the unsorted work into his top drawer if he ran out of time . . .

I couldn't believe I was rooting through the drawers, yet I was. And there was the green file. "Tallimore Memorial: bills and admin".

Bingo.

I shuffled through the pages of notes and letters until I found what I was looking for: the list of guests, neatly ticked for invites, and ticked off again for RSVPs by Miss McGregor. She was right in the middle: Eleanor Howard, Westbourne Grove, Notting Hill; and three phone numbers, two mobiles, one home.

I jotted them down, with one ear cocked towards the door for footsteps, then slid the file back in the drawer. My heart was thumping with nerves and I felt weirdly elated. Twenty years of deliberately not thinking about how easy or hard it would be to trace my mother, and here I was, taking the first tiny steps.

Towards what, though? It was like applying for a Proper Job. I might actually find out what I was — definitively. I'd be set in stone, at last. My days of tragic ballerinas and TV detectives might soon be coming to an end, and there was no guarantee that I'd like what I found. What if Hector had skedaddled because my mother's father had come after him with a shotgun?

What if she turned out to be a silly, selfish Sloane Ranger who didn't want any reminder of her youthful mistake? What then?

My stomach fluttered. Still holding the piece of paper, I rested on the edge of Mark's desk, and gazed out of the window at the street below. It was washed with rain and the cars glistened.

I'd forgotten how much I missed London, and its many subtle shades of grey. The pigeons, the pavements, the stone facades, the January sky — a whole *palette* of grey, livened up with bright red splashes of buses and postboxes. Very chic. I had to admit I loved it. I'd tried to prefer Edinburgh, and even persuaded myself that all that granite was more elegant, but there was something about London's cheerful grime that I secretly loved more. It was *home*. And someone had chosen to make this my home.

My eye was drawn by a commotion unfolding on the opposite side of the street. A small figure in a huge fur coat and blond hair was arguing furiously with someone in a uniform next to a silver Porsche. From the way the arms were windmilling and the traffic warden was taking nervous steps backwards, it could only be Anastasia. Divinity was next to her, pointing everywhere — at the car, at Anastasia, at her own head, at the sky. Even though the windows were shut, I knew the language would probably make Miss Thorne's cashmere go bobbly.

Lesson four. Diplomatic situations and their solutions, I thought, reaching for my notebook. How to handle being arrested, being overdrawn, being in court and generally being a lady under pressure.

Suddenly, I heard feet and the sound of whistling on the stairs, and I bounced off the desk just in time for Mark Montgomery to push the door open.

He was wearing his tweedy jacket again, but this time it was accessorised with a battered brown briefcase and neon-blue cycle helmet. His thick black hair stuck through the spaces and he was still pink with the effort of cycling in the freezing January air. He clearly wasn't expecting to see me.

"Oh, er, hello," he said, yanking off the helmet, embarrassed. "Didn't think anyone would be up here."

"Sorry, I needed some quiet. To make notes. About the Academy. And the lessons. I've been sitting in. Didn't have you down for a cyclist!" I gabbled, unexpectedly flustered. "I thought City types like you roared round in Maseratis and damn the congestion charge. Are you one of those responsible car-free types?"

"Just during the week," he said, removing his jacket. It needed patching inside; clearly he could afford a new one, so it had to be an old favourite, I reckoned. I rather liked men who clung doggedly to their favourite jackets. It boded well for girlfriends. "I've got a Jaguar, but it's forty years old, covered in dents, and I race it at weekends, so it doesn't score many points with the hedge-fund boys. What I save on the congestion charge goes straight into the petrol tank, along with pretty much every penny I earn. If you ask me, cars are even more expensive to run than Tallimore girls." He ruffled his hair back up, and looked over at me, as if he was waiting for a snappy comeback. "It doesn't even have a passenger seat, so I'm afraid I can't offer you a lift."

"Shame," I said. "I'm very good at getting out of sports cars. It's something I learned here, you know."

"Again, you amaze me with this endlessly useful knowledge," he asked. "Learned anything else today?"

"Oh, yes. Meringue swans and how easy they are to scorch if you're not *meticulous* with your oven timer. Also, you are *so* not supposed to let your mum go on Facebook. You might as well . . ." I pretended to check my notebook. "Totally *die*."

Mark half-smiled, half-frowned, his eyes creasing at the edges. It was a frustratingly unreadable expression.

"There you go, your education is complete," he said, hanging the helmet on the back of his chair and opening his briefcase.

"Not until I've added strawberry lilypads," I said, trying to match his deadpan look, and failing. "But that's next week. I thought I might suggest a vodka jelly pond for the week after."

He snorted — with amusement? I hoped so.

"I was going to ask you, actually," he said, pausing to flick a silver letter opener through the first envelope. "Is there a firm of surveyors you could recommend? I suppose you must come across some, in your line of work."

"Sorry?" The only surveyor I'd met was the one who told me my flat had damp and a strange smell in the bathroom that even he couldn't explain.

"A surveyor." He looked at me more closely. "You know, for checking over business premises?"

"Oh, no," I said, confidently. "No, no. Fiona deals with all that sort of thing."

Mark raised an eyebrow. "And Fiona is?"

Oops. Wrong job.

"My assistant," I fibbed, quickly. "She sometimes . . . fills my shoes for me."

He seemed impressed.

"What do you need a surveyor for?" I asked.

"Thought it might be a good idea to find out the worst, before the estate agents move in. Forewarned is forearmed and all that." He carried on opening the envelope and I spotted a familiar estate agent's logo on the back. My heart sank. He really did want to sell.

"Lord Tallimore's away until the end of the month as you know," he went on, "but we have a regular meeting to discuss matters arising. I thought it would be less painful for him if I could put together various options."

"But I thought we were going to try to come up with some ideas!" I blurted out, filling with panic. He couldn't close it yet. I hadn't even found the missing year photograph, let alone any other details!

"Betsy, apart from the fact that we just don't have the money to carry on much longer, I've got to be honest with you — the whole finishing-school concept . . ." Mark began, and I knew from the pained expression on his face that he was going to start his "etiquette is a form of social apartheid" routine again.

I'd have preferred some time to think about this, maybe even write some key phrases on those little cards you were supposed to have for speeches, but I had no choice. I leaped in before he could get on his high horse.

"I know! It's out of date — but that's the whole point. Let's bring it *up* to date! I've been thinking about new lessons, new approaches. We really can make the Academy appeal to normal, everyday girls," I said, aware that my "confident" grin was turning a little manic round the edges. Fake it till you make it, I reminded myself. "I've had a brilliant idea to drag it into the twenty-first century!"

"After *one* day?" Mark abandoned the wryness and stared at me with naked cynicism. "Either you really are the most genius business brain since the man who bottled water or the sherry fumes have gone to your head."

"No, I just know what *I'd* like to have been told at eighteen!" I insisted. "You're right about social rules being outdated and snobbish — we should be tailoring everything to what girls need to know *now*. Take my best friend, for instance. Liv's twenty-six, but she thinks cash machines print the money from inside and she can't dump a man without getting engaged to him first, because she only knows how to break off an engagement, not call a halt after three dates. She's *desperate* for someone to tell her how to deal with the small stuff. How to get an upgrade on a plane. How to get a date. How to play poker."

Liv was forever being taken advantage of there.

I could see from Mark's dubious expression that I was losing him, so I played my financial trump card.

"It's got a much broader appeal, for a start. Think of all the girls out there who'd love to have their lives sorted out in ten easy lessons! And short courses means higher turnover, quicker cashflow."

"Go on," he said, folding his arms and looking at me expectantly.

That was about as far as I'd got with Liv the previous evening. I swallowed, and tried to look as if I wasn't just making it up as I went along. But Mark's dark eyebrows weren't quite as tightly clenched as they had been a moment ago. And, I encouraged myself, he was a proper, qualified financial expert. If *he* bought this idea, he could sell it to Miss Thorne and I wouldn't be risking making a fool of myself.

"Well, I hadn't got as far as planning actual lessons," I admitted, "but it wouldn't take us long to brainstorm a timetable. What have we got to lose? We could try it for a week or two, to see how the girls respond, then, when we have this meeting with Lord Tallimore, we can offer him this solution, as well as the sale option."

Two weeks. That ought to give me enough time to meet Nell and snoop around, I reckoned.

Mark sat down at the desk and steepled his hands, so he could rest his chin on them and stare at me. His brown eyes were sharp, even through his glasses. He didn't mince his words. "And you think the girls won't mind getting an entirely different set of lessons to the ones their parents signed them up for?"

"Do they even *know* what they were signed up for?" I bluffed. "Is there anything in that prospectus that actually confirms lesson plans?"

"No," said Mark. "And you're pre-supposing that they've read it."

We looked at each other, and I tried to make my face as hard to read as his. I don't think I managed. My mouth was twitching. "Come on. The Secrets of Life in Six Weeks. A User's Guide to everything from Toxic Exes to Spanx. How easy would that be to market?"

"And you're the woman to teach this brave new syllabus?" Mark tipped his head on one side. "Because I don't see Miss McGregor taking a toxic-ex class. And I don't even know what Spanx are."

I blushed. "Well, I'm not saying I know *everything*. But I've been independent since I left school, and I can find experts for the rest. We can hire them by the hour, instead of keeping them on the pay roll."

Mark pressed his lips together and nodded. "And, of course, you are a business owner," he added. "You can maybe drill some sense into them about budgets and the boring side of life."

I blinked, then nodded. "Yes. Yes, of course."

Mark carried on looking at me, but now there was a sort of gleam beneath the stern banking expression.

"Miss Thorne won't like this," he said, but he didn't sound disappointed. Far from it, in fact.

We stared at each other for a moment, like co-conspirators, and I was convinced he was going to say, "Fine! But let's drop the consultant routine." He didn't, though.

"Why don't you put something down on paper tonight and we'll go and see The Thorne tomorrow morning," he suggested. "She can hardly say no, if we both suggest it's in the Academy's best interests. It's only for a fortnight, after all."

I couldn't stop myself grinning. "Brilliant. Thanks! But," I added, "shouldn't you be in work? Are you taking time off for all this?"

"Annual leave," he replied, going back to his post. "I'm going away this weekend. Racing the car."

"Oh, really?" I began, but then the phone on his desk rang, and he pulled a quick apologetic grimace, and answered it.

"Mark Montgomery," he said, in a brisk, businesslike tone, quite different from the one he'd just been using. I pretended I wasn't listening, but secretly I was ticking off another box. I liked a man with a businesslike phone manner.

I leaned back on the desk again, and watched him concentrate on the call, turning a pen round and round in his fingers. OK, so Mark wasn't a shameless charmer like Jamie, but it wasn't all about sexy eyes and expensive clothes and flirty conversation . . .

Mark's impassive business face collapsed and he squeezed his nose wearily. "Paulette, for the millionth time, you can't possibly know that the caller is dodgy, just from the way he pronounces his name. There are *lots* of reasons why he might be breathing heavily. Well, a cold, perhaps? Or a medical condition?"

He scribbled something on the back of an envelope and shoved it across the desk at me.

I noticed with some curiosity that Mark's nails were much rougher than the City boys I knew. He had nice cufflinks, in the shape of red enamel elephants.

He'd written "COURSE ON PHONE MANNERS" in very neat capital letters, underlined twice, and as I read it, he widened his eyes and drew a spiral in the air next to his ear.

I nodded, and wrote COFFEE? underneath it.

Mark gave me the thumbs up, and I went downstairs to find some, feeling about a hundred per cent more positive about everything.

CHAPTER NINE

Store facial wipes upside down to stop them drying out.

Liv texted me as I was cycling back across Chelsea Bridge: "Don't forget Jamie taking us out for dinner!!!!"

As if I could forget. I'd raced through my to-do list at the Academy — speak to Miss McGregor, teach Paulette how to put a caller on hold properly, not by covering her end of the phone with her hand and yelling, etc — so I could be back at Liv's in time for a shower, two outfit changes and a serious session with my hairdryer. Dinners with Jamie needed a lot of preparation in order to achieve that critical "this old thing?" effect.

The front door was ajar as I walked in, and to my horror, I could hear the sounds of an O'Hare sibling squabble in full effect. There were probably people in the next postcode who could hear it.

". . . don't need *any* help from *you*!" Liv was insisting, at the top of her lungs. "Coming here, patronising me like that! Betsy and I are managing fine . . ."

Jamie retorted something I didn't catch, to which Liv roared, "Jamie, that is out of order!"

If Liv's besotted older-man fan club ever saw her rowing with Jamie, I thought, they'd wonder how the Face of the Upper East Side could have the Voice of *EastEnders*.

While they were still bickering (about what? I couldn't quite make it out even though my ears were twisting round like radar dishes) I pushed my cycle helmet off and stared into the hall mirror, trying to effect what damage limitation I could. My hair was flat on the top of my head and frizzy underneath — I knew from experience that my industrial-strength serum wore off in about five minutes, at which point I'd look like something from the more exotic toy classes at Crufts. Added to that, my nose had gone red with cold and my freckles were showing through my end-of-the-day make-up.

Oh God, I thought. After my dismal showing at the memorial service I'd wanted to make a better impression this time round. I'd planned the perfect outfit and everything and now he was going to think I'd turned into a troll.

I yanked at my hair with a comb, and wondered if I had time to sneak upstairs and down again before Liv and Jamie reached the "I'm leaving!/No, *I'm* leaving!" stage, but before I could even get my red lipstick twisted up, the kitchen door flew open and Liv rushed out, followed by Jamie.

"I will *show* you the bloody stupid bloody note he left me . . . Oh, Bets, you're back," said Liv, pulling up short. Jamie pulled up behind her, nearly knocking her over. Together, they made a ridiculously attractive jumble of long legs, and geometric cheekbones. Genetics, I thought. All right for some.

"Hey, Betsy!" said Jamie, with a broad smile that lit up his handsome face. "I heard you were here!"

"Hargh," I said, as my brain went limp.

Jamie pushed Liv out of the way — he was the only man who didn't treat her like a china doll — and opened his arms, clasping me in a big hug.

"It's good to see you," he went on, as my nose went into his shoulder. Behind him, I could see Liv pulling a "yeah, yeah" face, but I wasn't really concentrating. I was wallowing in Jamie's sexy expensive cologne — a sort of limey, fresh smell — and his soft green shirt and the skin on the side of his neck, of which I had a great view. I could see where he'd had his hair cut recently, because there was a tiny line of paler skin next to the winter tan.

"Ngh, cold?" I managed.

"How's things up in Edinburgh? Has Fiona opened a London branch?" he said, holding me at arm's length now, and giving my outfit an approving onceover. "You look really smart!"

"This? Oh, it's just a sale bargain," I heard myself mumble. "Hobbs, seventy per cent off." What was he talking about? Apart from the fact that I'd just cycled across town and was on the rumpled side of dishevelled, my A-line skirt was creased like a concertina and I'd got meringue on my shirt from where Clemmy's piping bag had exploded under fierce pressure during the Corden Bleu course. It had dried unpleasantly.

"Well, it looks very Miss Moneypenny," said Jamie with an appreciative look. I tried to think of something offhand but flirtatious to say, like the hundreds of glossy-shinned socialites he hung out with would, but — no, nothing.

"Mmnngh," I said instead.

"Oh, for God's sake!" Liv tossed her head so hard she flicked hair in my eyes as well as her own. "It's *Betsy*! There's no need to go into chat-up mode! She's just come back from Full Moon Street like I told you — I told you, didn't I, that she's pretending to be a management consultant? I *did*, Jamie, you weren't listening as usual. That's why she looks like that."

I nodded, geekily.

Jamie nodded too, expecting me to elaborate. He smiled encouragingly, showing his lovely white teeth and the dimple on his chin.

"It's . . ." I struggled to put the bizarre last few days into words that would make sense. Any sentence containing the words finishing and school were hard to set in a reasonable context, and my brain was already flagging after eight hours listening to the girls' relentless excitement over everything from the new Gucci collection to Ped Eggs. "It's . . . complicated."

Liv looked between me and Jamie, and interpreted my inability to speak as professional discretion. "She's had a long day at work, Jamie, she doesn't want to talk about it now, can't you see that? Betsy, there's been a change of plan, *again*." She shot a disparaging glance at her brother. "Some *ex* of Jamie's has opened a bar down the road, so we're going to try that out, if that's OK with you."

My spirits sank. Jamie seemed to know every blonde in London, all of whom he claimed to be "great friends with", which Liv and I privately agreed was a euphemism for two-night-stands upwards. Plus, I hadn't brought the outfit for an evening out, even if I did have the energy.

"She's not an ex," said Jamie, patiently, checking his phone. "She's Kirstie, an old friend, and I said I'd call in and support her new project. Is that so awful? I'm a professional event planner, I need to know about new venues. Whereas you just research them on an amateur basis. With your team of *fiancés*. Sorry, dinner dates."

"Is that supposed to mean something?" demanded Liv.

"Not really," said Jamie, but then unable to stop himself, he looked up from his mobile. "Any weddings coming up this month that I ought to know about? Now Dad's probably not going to be available to give you away, I suppose I'll be the one marching you down the aisle."

Liv put her hands on her hips and looked at me for support. "See? He's been back in this house about ten minutes and already he's winding me up. For your information, *Jamie*, I'm having a complete man detox for the foreseeable. Dad's really dumped me in it, and from now on, I am all about being a strong, independent female. I don't need *you* patronising me about how I . . . how I pay my whatsits."

Jamie turned to me. "What can I say? Apart from good luck, Betsy. If Liv wants to join you and me in the big bad real world of work, then who am I to stop her?"

Liv started to make noises about the nature of Jamie's "work" but I was too delighted by the way he'd bracketed us together.

"You'll let me take you out tonight, won't you? At least let me do that," he went on, still looking at me in his "no one else in the room" manner. "Before Liv starts her 'I Will Survive' routine?"

"If you insist," I said, pretending to be stern. "But you have to let us choose the wine. And talk to us about mortgages over dinner."

"Deal," he said, then checked his watch. "Listen, we could go now, if you want — have a drink before we eat? Or do you want to get changed? Not that you don't look great as you are," he added, quickly.

I opened my mouth to say something, but the village idiot had regained control of my brain, and Liv had grabbed me anyway, and was pulling me towards the door.

"Oh, give it a rest, this is us you're talking to, not Tabitha Hotsy-Totsy-Plotsy," said Liv, dragging me towards the stairs. "Give us five minutes. Make yourself at home — but don't take that as permission to go through my bills, all right?"

"In five minutes? You must be joking," retorted Jamie, and this time it was me pulling Liv upstairs before the squabble could kick off again.

* * *

One of the advantages of temporarily sharing Liv's house was that I also got to share her wardrobe, which was epic and ran into two rooms. Though she was a good four inches taller than me, she tended to wear her clothes on the short side — skirts and dresses, only; she "didn't do" trousers — so it balanced out well enough, given that my legs didn't require as much showcasing as hers.

Liv dressed me up almost absent-mindedly at the same time as she changed her own outfit. "Here, wear this, it'll bring out your eyes," she said, rustling through the rails and throwing garments at me. "Honestly, Jamie! He is doing my head in. I think The Concerned Brother is the most sick-making version of Mr Social Chameleon I've seen so far. And I say that," she added, pausing only to tweak the dress I'd tugged over my head so the neckline went from eye-watering to eye-catching, "as someone who remembers his Eco-Warrior phase. When he had the dreadlocks and only drank organic vodka."

"What do you mean?" I pulled out the only jewellery I had — my gold bee necklace — and added some of Liv's "polishing cream" to my re-straightened hair. I didn't see any point in trying to compete with her; better women than me had tried and failed.

"Oh, he's flown back to bail me out, apparently, but he's only saying that because he's furious with Dad. Although you know what Dad and Jamie are like — if they weren't so identical they might actually get on." Liv pulled her hair into a bun, stuck a gold hair pin in it and added some nude gloss to her full lips. In her smock and big purple bead necklace she looked like she'd just slouched out of David Bailey's studio in 1968. "Not just that though — when he wasn't giving me a hard time about my *financial dyslexia*, as he kept calling it, he was going on about changing his life and settling down, and how Dad skipping off has been a wake-up call for him." She turned round and slackened her jaw. It wasn't pretty but it conveyed her feelings more than eloquently. "Settling down! The man who keeps a toothbrush in his laptop bag."

"Blimey," I said. "Won't there be a lot of disappointed ladeez out there?"

"Depends what he terms settling down. I wouldn't put it past him to have found a religion where he could keep a fully stocked harem just off the King's Road." Liv added a final swipe of blusher to my face, almost in passing, and cheekbones sprang out of nowhere. "If you ask me, it's all an act. He perked up and started being his usual self the moment you arrived, you notice."

"Should I take that as a compliment?" I asked, transfixed by my reflection in her ornate boudoir mirror. Liv's hours loitering in Harvey Nichols' cosmetics hall hadn't been in vain. I normally only went for red lips, and jetblack eyelashes, but now I was beginning to think I should invest in blusher.

"I don't know," said Liv. "But just brace yourself for a smug-arse lecture about how turning thirty changes your perspective on everything. I've had about as much as I can take from a man who spends more on novelty Martinis than I do on the mortgage."

* * *

There was no sign of the lecture over the first round of drinks we had at Kirstie's new bar, though, or the second, which were brought over by Kirstie herself, who was as gorgeous and giggly and "thrilled to see you, darling" as I thought she'd be.

"Definitely an ex," muttered Liv in my ear as Kirstie tousled his hair, more than affectionately. I wouldn't have minded tousling it myself — Jamie's hair was a dirtier blond than Liv's, but it had a very touchable softness to it, even though it didn't fall as far into his eyes as it used to.

He spotted Liv's tense expression and finished up his chat quickly. "So," he said to me, as Kirstie wiggled away, his business card in her pocket, "what's this about curtseying lessons?"

We ate olives and bread while I told Jamie about the piles of yellowing placecards I'd found, pre-prepared for a test on seating four Royal Families and the Dalai Lama, and the catwalk left over from the sixties.

"Divinity and Anastasia have been using it to choreograph their acceptance speech for when they win *The X Factor*," I told them. "I found them up there with a karaoke machine, weeping into microphones and thanking their mothers. Not doing any singing, mind you. They're getting someone else to do that for them, apparently. Miss McGregor's popping Nurofen like M&Ms."

"But tell him about your new plans," Liv prompted, as our starters arrived on strange black plates. "That's the really amazing part. The part that *I'm going to be helping with*," she added, waving her fork at Jamie, against all Academy rules. "My ignorance is going to be their gain, or something."

"So it's a three-year course now, is it?" Jamie enquired.

I reeled off my ideas before they could start squabbling again, with Liv chipping in whenever I paused for breath. Jamie seemed impressed, especially by my Modern Social Minefields strategy class. He even suggested some Minefields I'd never considered before.

"I can't believe there isn't something like this already — it's a great idea!" he said. "What you really need, though, is an Insider's Guide to Men. Explain the mysteries of life from the poor, misunderstood male perspective."

"*Oh* my God," moaned Liv, but Jamie ignored her.

"How to break it off without destroying his ego," he went on, "what a guy means when he says . . ."

". . . the sexy blonde wearing your dressing gown is just a friend?" Liv interrupted. "And/or his sister?"

". . . he values your friendship too much to start a relationship?" I added.

". . . you remind him of his mother, 'in a good way'?" Liv was only just warming up, I could tell.

". . . when he suddenly switches from thinking marriage is the devil's own community service to hustling the next woman he dates down the aisle?" I said, thinking only slightly bitterly of my last miserable break-up.

Jamie held up his hands. "I said I'd do a lesson, not explain every reason you two have ever been dumped. But, since you're asking," he went on, holding up his fingers to mark off the questions, "in order, one, she usually *is* a friend. Two, girls who make you laugh and don't play mindgames are a rare and precious thing. Three, all men marry their mothers eventually, I'm sorry to say, and four . . ." He stopped, and looked self-conscious for a split second. "Four, sometimes you just feel like moving the party back home, instead of going out every night to find it, OK? And sometimes you meet someone that you don't want to risk losing to another guy. You've got to move in quickly — it's only you women who like to spin things out."

I opened my mouth to tell him that was bollocks, and that men proposed the day they found their first nose hair, but as he lifted his wine glass to drain it, something in his body language made me stop. Jamie's default setting was tie-loosened super-confidence, but I thought I could see a flicker of vulnerability about the way he half-hid his face with the glass, and shot his cuffs slightly.

Ooh, I thought, it's personal. Maybe that was why he'd rushed home from New York with his tail between his legs. Some girl's turned *him* down, after all these years of playing the field and calling everyone babe to be on the safe side. First time for everything.

Liv glanced over at me, then looked at her brother. She was sitting between me and Jamie, and had to keep bouncing her gaze back and forth as if she was at a tennis match, and the resulting neck strain seemed to be making her grumpy.

"Sounds like you've got yourself a new teacher there," she said to me. "Well, more a professor, really. You could do a whole course on Understanding the International Playboy, just using Jamie's BlackBerry."

I nudged Liv under the table. She obviously hadn't noticed Jamie's guarded expression or else she was still stinging from his brotherly lecture earlier.

"What?" she demanded. "I'm just saying. Let Jamie into the Academy and it'd be like putting an alcoholic in a brewery and asking if he wants to test the beer. Genius — until he falls into the vat, or whatever it's called."

"Stick to uncorking wine bottles, Olivia, and leave the metaphors to the grown-ups," said Jamie, but I could tell she'd touched a nerve.

Jamie broken-hearted was a whole new concept to me — and to him, probably. I hadn't seen him dumped since we were at school, but I gave him about a fortnight to get over it. It wasn't as if he'd be short of willing nurses offering to rub his wounded pride better, not when his rejection face was almost as heart-melting as his life-and-soul-of-the-party one.

"Don't joke about teaching, because I might take you up on that," I said, trying to lift the mood again. "I need some experts. But you'd have to promise not to offer personal coaching. The current students are terribly charming and rich, and frantic to get themselves on the celeb party circuit. You're the man of their dreams, in so many ways."

Jamie was gratifyingly quick on the uptake about jokes, unlike his sister. "Oh, really?" He pretended to rub his hands like a Victorian maiden-abductor. "Tell me more. What delicious young debutantes are currently being finished?"

"Well, at the moment, there's Clementine the Goth, Divinity the footballer's daughter, Anastasia the Russian squillionaireness and Venetia, the . . ."

I wasn't sure how to describe Venetia. I suddenly realised I didn't know much about her at all, other than that she had her extensions done at Richard Ward and didn't carry cash.

"The trainee Bond girl," I finished, and as I said that, my mind made a connection with some other, older trainee Bond girls, and I remembered Nell Howard's phone numbers in my handbag.

My brain clogged up instantly with call her/don't call her arguments that had been plaguing me all day. I wanted to call her, but something in me kept putting off the moment.

"I'm going to powder my nose," Liv announced, shoving her chair back. "I mean that in the finishing school sense, not in the London members' club sense, in case you're wondering, Jamie."

"Thanks for those two delightful images," he said, and moved his chair so she could squeeze past. As he did, he leaned forward far enough to brush my hand with his arm, and an electric tingle ran right up my skin and into the inner depths of Liv's borrowed dress.

Before I could even enjoy it, the tingle was replaced with a familiar ache as Jamie gave me a brotherly grin.

Sitting here bantering with Jamie was one thing, but it was all done on the understanding that I was far too sensible to fall for his charms, and he was far too irresponsible to go for a hardworking Maths geek, who grew her own tomatoes.

We knew each other too well — in every sense. If we'd met once as kids, when he was a bit tubby and I had a ginger afro, then seen each other now, as adults, maybe it'd be OK to sweep the school years under the carpet. But I'd been best mates with his sister since I was eleven. He'd witnessed every terrible haircut I'd had, and I'd seen him date every girl with a name ending in an a between Cheltenham and Pimlico.

The killer ironic blow, of course, being that when I wasn't being a village idiot, I did make him laugh. Not always because I'd just spilled, broken or fallen over something.

"You look very stern — what are you thinking?" he asked, as he pulled his seat back in. He ended up a little nearer than he had been before. I could feel his knee very close but not quite touching mine.

I blinked. I couldn't tell him exactly what I was thinking, so I skipped back ten seconds. "Um, I was thinking about calling this woman I met at Franny's memorial tea," I said. "Nell Howard. She was a student at the Academy when I was left on the step — she thought she might have known my mother. Without realising, if you know what I mean. She knew the girls that were there then, in 1980."

Jamie opened his eyes wide, just like Liv did when she wanted to convey utter bewilderment. It was one of the few things they had in common. "What? Seriously? After all these years, and you're *thinking* of calling her? Call her! Now!"

"I will! I just . . ."

"Just what?" he demanded. "And don't give me the excuse you're thinking up."

I managed a small smile. "I *want* to, but I'm not sure what I might find out." The noise in the restaurant was getting louder as more customers drifted in from work and I had to lean forward to avoid raising my voice too loud. He leaned forward too, to hear me, and I got a distracting noseful of eau de Jamie.

"You might find out who your mother is," he observed. "Isn't that the point?"

"Yes, but what if she's . . . I don't know . . . a serial divorcée with nine other kids? Or a junkie, or a . . ." I wanted to say, *not a ballerina*, but I knew that sounded stupid.

Jamie made a tsk noise. "Listen, she can't be worse than the parents Liv and I have. A mother who cared about us so much she moved to Arizona because her new man wanted a ranch, and a father who's just skipped town to avoid a nasty tax conversation, leaving Liv trying to boil eggs in a kettle." He twisted his wry mouth up at the corner. "If I could ring someone up and have another throw of the parental dice, I'd be on that phone like a shot, believe me."

"Oh." I wasn't sure what to say. Jamie and Ken hadn't got on for a while. Ken liked to wax lyrical about how Liv was "the image of my late mother, God love her", but was furious that Jamie had inherited Rina's canapé addiction, and had no time for his "bloody pointless play-business". Coming from a man who had started his fortune selling "I shot JR" T-shirts out of the back of a Mini Metro this seemed pretty harsh, but then Ken had had high hopes for Jamie, the first one in their family to go to university. Apparently, running his own company didn't count.

"Have you got hold of Ken then?" I asked. "Liv says his mobile's off."

"No, I got hold of the next best thing: Nigel, his accountant. He filled me in, as far as he knew. Dad's fine, of course, just lying low while he liquidises some assets or something, but I don't think he realises what a mess Liv's in, the selfish old . . . I don't want to talk about Ken and spoil the evening." He tapped the table with his finger. "Where's that phone of yours? I insist you call this Nell woman right now."

I started backtracking. "But it's late. I don't want her to think . . ."

"No, it's not. It's between drinks and supper, perfect timing. What have you got to lose?" he demanded. "*She's* not your mother. It's not like you have to take it further than a chat. Ring her, meet for coffee, see what she's got to say. But don't waste any more time."

He paused, and said something quietly, so I had to lean forward. "Sorry?"

"I just said, don't put your own life on hold, worrying about what other people might think. You've got to do what you need to do. It's something I've come to realise recently."

I looked up, straight into his grey eyes, and wondered if he was talking about the girl in New York. He looked so earnest I wanted to hug him.

"Don't you want to know who you are, really?" he went on. "Aren't you curious?"

"Course I am. Sort of." I squirmed in my chair. It was easy for Jamie and Liv. They flitted easily between every sort of environment, shifting their accents as they went. Beautiful people fitted in anywhere, especially if they had plenty of money. But what sort of background created mothers who abandoned their babies? What might come out in *me*?

"I *do* want to see her and ask questions," I blurted out. "But there's no going back and I've got so much to worry about right now . . ."

"I'll come with you, if you want," Jamie said. "I'll be your moral support, ask the tricky questions, if you don't want to. But I do think you should do it, if not for yourself, then for any kids *you* might have. I'm not saying this to stir it up. I'm saying it as someone who's known you for years and years . . ."

He looked me in the eyes. "Call."

I bit my lip, and got out my phone. Immediately, I felt my fingers freeze. "It's very noisy in here," I started, but Jamie was too quick. Before I knew what he was doing, he'd shoved back his chair, taken my hand in his and was hustling us through the crowd by the bar.

His hand was dry and warm, clasping mine, and I could hear people saying, "Hi, Jamie!" as we went but he didn't stop to reply. Suddenly we were standing outside, in the street.

"Cold," I said, stalling.

He rolled his eyes, but kindly. "Excuses, excuses. I'll keep you warm, just dial the number."

I got the piece of paper with the numbers on out of my bag and began to dial. As I fumbled with the phone, I felt Jamie shrug off his jacket, and drape it over my shoulders. I was still registering the still-warm lining against my bare neck, smelling of his aftershave and warm skin, when I heard someone pick up at the other end.

My heart leaped into my mouth.

"Hello!" carolled a woman's voice. "Nell, here."

I glanced at Jamie, who nodded me on.

"Hello!" I shoved aside my nerves and switched into my polite telephone manner. "It's Betsy Tallimore, we met at Lady Tallimore's memorial and . . ."

"Betsy!" Nell sounded thrilled, although that might just have been her excellent finishing. It *was* cocktail hour, too. "Darling, I'm so glad you called, I was hoping you would. I'm such an idiot, I forgot to take your number, then I was in Morocco doing up a house for a shoot — did you want to meet up for a proper gossip?"

"Yes," I said, bravely. "I'm in London until the end of next week, and . . ."

"Cut to the chase, how about tomorrow?" she suggested. "I'm away again on Thursday, and I've dug out something for you — something that you might find rather *intriguing*."

"Oh, really?" I said. "Yes, well, tomorrow would be fine."

Jamie was leaning over my shoulder now, trying to listen in, but he was putting me off my concentration. I could feel his warm breath on my neck.

"Fabulous! Whereabouts are you lurking at the moment?"

"I'll be at the Academy," I said. "I'm working with Lord Tallimore to update it a bit."

"Rarely?" Nell was a really/rarely kind of posh woman. "Fabulous idea! Do you have a local? Last time I was there all the pubs were full of prostitutes and dukes, and Miss Vanderbilt wouldn't even let us stop outside them, let alone go in! Probably all tarted up now, I expect." She cackled. "As it were!"

I thought quickly. "Do you know Igor's? In Chelsea?" I gave her directions to the bar where Liv worked. She'd be able to get us a nice quiet booth.

"Sounds extraordinary! Five-ish suit you?" she went on.

"Yes, fine," I said, amazed at how easy this was turning out to be.

"Darling, no — not the *rhino* head! The other one . . . yes, that's the fellow!" she yelled, then said to me, "So I'll see you there then."

I hung up. One phone call and all the little cogs had started to move. My hands trembled — with excitement or cold, or maybe both.

Jamie raised an eyebrow. "So?"

"I'm seeing her tomorrow, for a drink. And something intriguing. Here." I offered him his jacket. It was a nicely heavy jacket, and the lining was a flamboyant gold. "We should rescue Liv. She's probably being chatted up by a waiter as we speak, and you know how keen she is to stay on her man detox."

"Indeed." Jamie put a hand on my back as he pushed his way gently through the crowded bar area. "Want me to come with you?"

I stopped and looked at him, to see if he was being serious.

"For moral support?" he went on. "I can imagine it might be a bit weird. I don't mind pretending to be a boyfriend, give you a second opinion?"

"I should be fine," I heard myself say. "But thanks."

Damn! Why did my brain take over like that? Was it like a safety switch, or something? I'd have *loved* Jamie to pretend to be my boyfriend.

"I guess one O'Hare is more than enough to deal with at any one time," he said, tilting his head on one side. "But I meant it about the classes. Sounds like a great idea. If you need any help, advice, PR, you know . . . Call me."

He said it really sweetly, but then he made a phone gesture with his thumb and little finger that was so cheesy I couldn't stop myself.

"But you're so busy with work," I reminded him. "Weren't you telling Liv ten minutes ago that Party Animals isn't just an excuse to test champagne and meet every gorgeous woman in London throwing a twenty-first? That some nights you barely sleep for worrying about the world's caviar stocks?"

Jamie pretended to look affronted. "The only reason I set up my own business was so that I could be in charge of the days off." He patted me on the arm and winked. An old friend gesture. "You work out what your girls need to know about men and I'll fill them in. So to speak."

"Thanks," I said. I wanted to tell him that he could start with me, but I didn't.

CHAPTER TEN

The right bra transforms your whole wardrobe: book a fitting every year along with your dental check up and eye test.

Before I strode consultant-ly into the Academy on Wednesday morning, dressed in my Proper Job suit and yet another designer blouse that Liv hadn't even taken the tag off, I did something I should have done right at the beginning of the week: I went to have breakfast with Nancy and Kathleen.

I knocked on the mews cottage door at ten past eight, and Nancy let me in, cooing, "Guess who's here?" to Kathleen in the kitchen. Kathleen's voice bellowed back, "If it's that George Clooney again, tell him to bugger off."

"No, it's *Betsy*!" said Nancy, who had years of training in tuning-out sarcasm. She ushered me through to the kitchen. "Come on in, we've just made you a little snack, to set you up for the day . . ."

As usual, the table resembled the breakfast buffet at a country house hotel. There was a vast dish of scrambled eggs on her hostess warmer with bacon sizzling alongside bulging Cumberland sausages and a massive pot of tea and coffee and orange juice on the table.

"But I told you not to go to any bother," I said weakly.

"This? Oh, I whipped up an extra egg," Kathleen insisted from the hob, where she was frying half a sliced loaf of bread. "What did I tell you? Breakfast like kings, dine like paupers — healthiest way."

"Tuck in, Betsy," Nancy urged, pouring the tea. "You're skin and bone since you moved up to Scotland. You need some feeding up."

That was hardly true, but I began heaping a plate with golden scrambled eggs, speckled with pepper and made with more butter than I'd normally use in a week. I tried to resist seconds, but I couldn't.

"Is my stuff still upstairs?" I asked Nancy, to stop her piling thirds on to my plate and to stop myself eating it. "Last night I suddenly thought, I should have a look at my old notebooks."

"Everything's exactly as it was when you left it, petal," she said, fondly. "We didn't move a thing."

"Except to tidy up." Kathleen gave me a much less starry-eyed look. "It was like a charity bazaar in there. After all Nancy taught you about a place for everything and . . ."

"Everything in its place. I *know*. I'm a model housekeeper these days!" I protested, and put my knife and fork neatly together on the clean plate. "And I'm trying to teach Liv how to cope with domesticity."

"Ooh, Betsy, that's a job and a half," said Kathleen.

"God bless her," added Nancy.

"Well, that's why I want my notebooks," I said. "I reckon everything she needs to know is in there." I didn't add that I wanted the extra little confidence boost of hearing Franny's voice in the scribbled ideas; or that I was equally nervous about opening up a Pandora's Box I'd deliberately ignored for ten years.

"Can I tempt you to a tiny bit more bacon?" asked Kathleen, wafting the plate near mine.

"No," I said, and I had to push myself away from the table as I said it, because my stomach was saying, oh go on then. Delicious as Kathleen's cooking was, you needed the eating stamina of a cow to cope with her Hansel and Gretel complex.

"I'll make you some sandwiches," Kathleen shouted after me, as I headed for the stairs. "You can share them with that nice young bursar. I bet he'd not say no to an egg roll . . ."

I made my way carefully up the stairs, trying not to knock off any of the assorted framed samplers or baby photos, and opened the door to the little room where I'd grown up.

It was, as Nancy had said, just as I'd left it, right down to the hair ribbons on the dressing table, and the magazine pages of famous redheads — and potential mothers — that I'd used to paper the inside of the wardrobe: Fergie, Gillian Anderson, Nicole Kidman, Rita Hayworth (bit of a long shot, that one). Feeling a bit like an intruder, I dropped to my knees and reached into the back, between the slithers of winter coats and long skirts, my hands groping for the shoebox I kept my treasures in.

My hands met something box-shaped, but much bigger than I was expecting. I drew it out, and when I saw what it was I sat back on my heels with a thud.

An old Cooper's marmalade box.

My heart seemed to stop beating. This had to be *the* marmalade box, the one Nancy insisted had been thrown away for hygiene reasons, every time I asked where it was. They hadn't thrown it away. They'd kept it.

My throat tightened as I lifted it up, turning it in my hands so I wouldn't miss a single scuff or crease. I'd never seen this before. Someone had put me in this, and then walked away.

Now I had it in my hands, my old daydreams sagged. What would a ballerina be doing with a gross of marmalade? It wasn't exactly something *normal* people had knocking around the house. Only the Academy took marmalade in quantities like that — they'd started taking Cooper's as a tribute to me, Franny had said.

Suddenly, in adult hindsight, that sounded like Franny being nice. They'd probably *always* taken Cooper's. Was that where the box had come from, the Academy kitchens? Surely that meant my mother *had* to be an Academy girl. The fact that she'd chosen a box with a Royal crest sounded like the kind of thing Miss Thorne would recommend for the appropriate disposal of unwanted babies.

But she could just as easily have found the box round the back, where the bins were. Or got it from the hotel where she worked. There were plenty of hotels around Mayfair, plenty of chambermaids — and plenty of dubious ladies in paid-for flats . . .

I put it to one side, and lifted out the box inside it: my own Chinese box of treasures.

In 1999 I'd slammed this box into the back of the wardrobe and sworn never to open it again. I hadn't actually thrown it away — I didn't have enough history to make grandiose gestures, but I'd hoarded everything that had the tiniest significance to me: gummed-up nail varnishes, notes that Liv and I had passed in class, plane tickets, goofy passport photos of us before our school trip to Boulogne, Valentine's cards. I wanted to inspect them all, but I made myself put them to one side until I'd found what I came for.

At the bottom was the stack of lilac-coloured leatherbound notebooks, the ones handed out to the Academy girls each term: Franny had given me one as soon as I was old enough to write my own name, and after that, I dutifully wrote down everything, even when I didn't really understand. It made for some confused scrawls about Tenshun Headakes and Marritul Relashuns, but I kept the notebook with me in my pocket, even when Franny and I were out shopping or in a car. She always had something worth noting down.

I wrote down Kathleen and Nancy's tips too, but they tended to be the "use hairspray on ink stains" and "iron + brown paper removes candlewax" variety, and they went in the back of the book. Even my notebooks had a dual personality.

As I read through the spider diagrams illustrating the Ten Steps to The Perfect Party, I could hear Franny's voice — calm, but confident, because her parties were never less than perfect.

"Water and a slice of lemon looks like a gin and tonic if you can't drink but don't want to be a party pooper."

"Give the plate of canapes to the shyest guest."

"Wear white things near your face — the light's more flattering."

My writing grew up as I turned the pages, and I felt a sudden yearning for that time in my life when Franny's tips had made grown-up life seem so gorgeous. You'd never think I was a normal child with scabby knees, the notes I had on stopping roses dropping their petals and how to get a tiara to stay on. All I really had to bother about, according to these books, at least, was whether I'd ever find a boyfriend who wore the right shoes with country attire.

A couple of photographs fell out of one book — me and Liv just after our final exam, in our shades, hers, Kate Moss Aviators and mine, retro cat's eyes above red lips, very Audrey Hepburn. It dawned on me just how much I'd changed when I'd stormed up to Scotland. I'd been a girl's girl in those days, more like an old-fashioned Tallimora, with my tumbling copper curls and pretty sundress. And my eyebrows . . . I'd forgotten how into eyebrow pencils I was at sixteen, but it did make my pale face seem more together.

I also seemed to laugh a lot more. I turned the photo but there was no date. I thought Jamie must have taken it. That was probably why I was smiling in that half-pouty, half-nervous manner.

I put the snap to one side to show Liv later, and carried on reading the notes I'd made. It *was* going to be useful: I just had to adapt it. That tiara tip — it'd work for hair pieces now or those tiny fascinators. And men always needed telling which shoes to wear with what. My spirits started to lift as I read on through to the scrawls at the back — the goodbye notes from leavers, bouncing out of there to go on to run ski companies or take jobs at Christie's.

"I'll miss you SO MUCH, Betsy, PLEASE stay in touch, THERE'S A HOT TODDY WAITING FOR YOU IN VERBIERS!!! xoxoxox!" Charlotte Prior-Yardley had scribbled, along with several phone numbers (London/Bucks/Scotland/France). They were always *devastated* to leave, and *compleeeetley* dying to meet up again "as soon as". Charlotte's sidekick, Tilly Tarrington, had rebelliously drawn hearts over all her "i"s (one of Miss Vanderbilt's pet hates) and written "See you at my wedding to Tom Cruise!" which even then I'd thought was hopeful.

Something about their sweetness made me melt nostalgically inside. God knows where they were now, these girls, but the hot toddy would definitely still be on offer. There had been reasons I'd wanted to go to the Academy. It hadn't all been snobbery and . . .

My eye fell on the last signature as I turned the page and my stomach contracted automatically at the superneat writing.

"The best of luck to you in wherever life takes you next. Best wishes, Adele Yvonne Buchanan."

Adele Buchanan. Seeing her writing brought her to life at once in my head. Blonde, perfect, and so icy she could chill your gin and tonic at ten paces — unless you were a man. Adele hadn't offered anyone her phone number on Lady Tallimore Leavers' Day. In fact, according to Kathleen who told Nancy when she thought I was safely washing up, the only phone number she was interested in was Charlotte's recently divorced father. He had a helicopter — Kathleen's undertones were quite carrying — and she'd told someone she wanted a rich man, then a titled man and then a rock star "before my tits go and I hit the cruise liner circuit".

"Betsy! Oh, fiddlesticks!"

I spun round to see Nancy standing at the door, a cup of tea in her hand and a worried expression on her round face.

"I thought you might like some tea . . ." she began unconvincingly, then put down the cup so she could wring her hands in dismay. "You've found the box! Oh, I *told* Kathleen not to put it in your wardrobe, but she was having one of her tidying fits, you know what she's like."

"Where's it been until now?" I asked.

"Frances had it, at home, in her room. Wouldn't throw it away. When she died, Lord Tallimore thought we might like it. I didn't know what to do with it, but Kathleen put it in here, evidently."

I couldn't imagine Lord T transporting an old cardboard box down to London, just for Kathleen. It was an unexpectedly gentle thing for a man like him to do.

"Why did you always tell me it had been thrown out?" I asked.

Nancy squeezed her Russian doll frame past the bed, and with a series of painful clicks, sat herself down next to me so she could put her arm around me, just like she had when I was small. I let her, even though I towered over her.

"Look at it," she said. "Tatty old thing. Would you want to know someone had left you in that?"

I shook my head.

"No, I shouldn't think so. She should have put you in a Moses basket, precious gift that you were. I'll never forget that morning. 'Look what the milkman's left,' Kathleen says to me . . . But you don't need to hear that again." She stopped and looked embarrassed. "You need to be getting away. Keeping you back, gassing like this."

"No," I said, and squeezed her. "It's been like old times, having breakfast here with you two."

"Did you find what you wanted?" she asked, anxiously.

"Yes." I picked up the notebooks and put them in my red handbag. "I did."

Kathleen pressed a Tupperware box of sandwiches into my hand as I left, and by nine, I was in Mark's office, trying to type up my ideas into a presentation.

I'd never given a presentation, or even listened to one, unless you counted the desperate sales pitch I endured every year from the man who made organic suede protector in Glasgow — Fiona had only made me manager so she could shunt the polite sales pitch suffering on to me. Still, I made a list of BBC news-type phrases starting with "maximise demographic" and tried to shoehorn in one per sentence.

Paulette stomped up the stairs with the post at half past nine, and nearly dropped the wrap of tulips she was carrying when she saw me at Mark's desk.

"Jeez! What are you doing here?" she yelped. "I thought you were in the pheasant-plucking class."

"Pheasant plucking?" Somehow I couldn't imagine Venetia up to her false nails in a pheasant. Well, I could see Anastasia making short work of one, but Divinity and Clemmy would surely boycott it on animal rights' grounds.

"Yeah, makes a right mess. They watch mainly because they can only afford one pheasant at a time. Plucking ridiculous." Paulette grinned cheerfully. "The jokes are the best thing about that class."

Eyebrow plucking though — not a bad idea. I jotted it down underneath the Modern Grooming section.

"Nope, I gave it a miss," I said. "I already know all I need to about plucking pheasants. Which is absolutely nothing. Are those for me?"

"What? These? Um, yes," she said. "No. They're for Mark. Well, for anyone really. I like putting flowers round the place, and Miss Thorne gives me the flower budget. It's only a tenner a week so I've got to make it stretch, and tulips are cheap."

The flower budget wasn't a tenner a week, I thought, outraged. It was more like fifty quid a week — I'd seen the accounts! That meant Miss Thorne was pocketing, what, a hundred and sixty pounds a month?

But I didn't let on to Paulette. "I love tulips," I said. "Are you pricking them, just under the heads, so they last longer?"

"Yeah . . ." said Paulette evasively. "I am now."

"Morning!" Mark strode into the office, bike helmet under his arm. "Ready to face trial by extreme politeness? What do you reckon, white gloves on or off for a spot of Headmistress-Throttling?"

Paulette giggled. "Ooh, Mark, I'll tell her you said that."

"Don't!" I said, then said, "Don't!" again, more seriously, because I now knew Paulette was a human parrot: she repeated everything, to anyone, at any time. "I mean it, Paulette."

Mark coughed into his hand, although there might have been a "sherry-holic" in there too. "Absolutely. I was speaking figuratively, of course. White gloves would be absolutely *de rigeur*, and I think Her Majesty's Police will back me up on that . . ."

"Paulette," I said over him, "we've got an appointment with Miss Thorne this morning to discuss some new ideas for the Academy. Can you make sure no one comes in to interrupt us, until we come out?"

She nodded, eyes wide. "Even if it's life or death? Or her dermatologist?"

"Even if it's the Queen Mother calling from the other side with advice about ducal proposals," said Mark.

"What if it's Lord Tallimore?" she asked.

I looked, guiltily, at Mark. "What do you reckon?"

"You haven't managed to get hold of him?" he asked, removing his overcoat. He was wearing a suit today — not as formal as the memorial one, but definitely something that said, "My proper job's in the City." I sensed he'd smartened up a notch from yesterday: the shirt was blue and sober, the hair was tamed, and he was freshly shaved. Maybe he felt the need to dress up against Miss Thorne too.

"What? Overnight? I haven't had time," I protested. "I was out late last night — I mean, I was working on this proposal, and I know he's up in Scotland shooting this month so he won't have his mobile with him. If he's even got one. I think his housekeeper looks after it for him."

Mark twisted his mouth, and slipped into what I suspected was school cadet-corps mode. "Might give Thorne an opening. We'll have to play it by ear. See how the land lies once we're in there. Leave it with me."

"Ooh," Paulette giggled again. "Leave it with him, Betsy. You don't hear many men say that these days."

"They wouldn't dare," I said, and I hoped Mark noticed my arched eyebrow as I said it.

"Fearless, that's me," he said, then tapped the desk in front of me, where my notes and papers were strewn around. His eyes were questioning but not unfriendly. "So, where's this troubleshooting proposal of yours? We have manicure classes to discuss . . ."

Miss Thorne made me and Mark wait for five minutes outside her office while she "attended to some urgent calls".

We knew she wasn't attending to urgent calls because Paulette popped out with some coffee and pink wafer biscuits and informed us that Miss Thorne was on hold to the cattery where she was trying to book her Persian cats in for her fortnight in Le Touquet.

"Pink wafer biscuits," I said, turning one over curiously. "I haven't seen these in years. You know there are hostess trolleys and coffee percolators downstairs?"

"You'll probably find Florence Nightingale if you look hard enough . . . Ah, Miss Thorne!" Mark leaped to his feet.

"Mark, Elizabeth, *so* sorry to keep you waiting." Miss Thorne stood at the door of her office, her small hands open in apology. She was wearing a bobbly collarless jacket that was probably Chanel, or at the very least, something her "little woman behind Harrods" had run up to look like Chanel. It was in the same colour scheme as the pink wafer biscuits. "Do come in."

Mark and I followed her across the thick pile carpet, and I tried my hardest not to feel as if I'd done something wrong. Mark didn't seem to be suffering from the same mindset, though, as he settled himself in the chair nearest her desk, and crossed his long legs.

I noticed he was wearing brown suede brogues with his suit, and hoped Miss Thorne wouldn't spot them.

She did, of course.

"Brown in town, Mark?" she trilled, girlishly.

Mark affected not to know what she was talking about. "I'm sorry?"

"Brown in town? Your shoes, dear!"

He looked at me, for clarification.

"What Miss Thorne means," I said, trying to keep my face straight as Mark's brow creased theatrically, "is that one isn't supposed to wear brown shoes in town. And not with a grey suit."

"Really? And why's that?" He turned back to her. "Is this to do with stagecoaches?"

She flapped her hands. "It's just . . . taste, dear. A matter of taste. Your dear father would never have worn anything but highly polished Oxfords. It was a matter of pride for an Army man."

"Was he supposed to carry his sword around with him too?" Mark enquired.

"So long as you're not wearing trainers," I said, "that's fine with me."

"Yes, well . . ." Miss Thorne gave me a sympathetic "you wouldn't know any better" look. "That does seem to be the modern way."

"Can we get on?" Mark looked in pain.

"Yes," she said, clasping her hands and resting them in front of her. "Quite. I understand you have a little proposal for me, Elizabeth?"

The hot room turned a degree or two hotter, and I drew a deep breath. Think confidence, I told myself. I could hear Franny saying, *Smile and you're halfway there*.

"Yes! I've been *tremendously* inspired in the last few days," I said. My voice had gone very SW1 all of a sudden, possibly because I was trying harder than ever to channel the spirit of my notebooks. "I remembered *everything* I loved about growing up here — the elegance, the magic of adult life, the sense of style — and I'm absolutely determined that the Academy must carry on."

"Marvellous!" Miss Thorne paused in her rummaging of the Limoges mint imperial bowl and looked up. "This *is* going to be a quick meeting."

"But to do that," I ploughed on, glancing at my notes, "we need to distil that essence of classic Tallimore elegance into a modern, accessible version — like a diffusion line, if you know what I mean."

"I'm not sure I do, Elizabeth," Miss Thorne replaced the mint in the bowl.

"We need to let in some fresh air," I said.

"Literally," she enquired, "or metaphorically?"

"Both," I replied, firmly. "It's basic business sense. We have to put ourselves in the shoes of our potential customer, work out what they want to buy then offer it. And make sure they know where to get it."

"This isn't Marks and Spencer's, Elizabeth," Miss Thorne reminded me.

"No," said Mark. "And good job it isn't, otherwise the refunds desk would be queueing down the stairs."

"But we should offer that quality department-store experience," I said hurriedly. "Fabulous, useful lessons in everyday elegance, tailored to what a modern girl needs to know. It's not about social cachet any more, it's about knowing how to be stylish. People will always want that."

Mark slid the pages of my proposal over the desk to her. "What Betsy has suggested adds up. It's a toolkit for life — everything from handling difficult conversations to ending relationships to getting a pay rise to choosing diamonds."

"For yourself," I added. "Not waiting for a man to present you with one."

We'd thrown that last one in for Anastasia's benefit more than anything else. I quite fancied a field trip to Tiffany's, just to watch her shopping. I was fairly confident her negotiation skills would be an education to us all.

"And who is to teach these marvellous lessons in . . ." She peered at my notes. "How to stay chic at an open-air festival? Do you mean Glyndebourne, dear?"

"Glastonbury, Miss Thorne. I've recruited a number of volunteers," I said, crossing my fingers. I hadn't yet, but I would.

"Experts in their field? As knowledgeable about . . ." Miss Thorne glanced back down at the paper. " 'Minibreaks without Tears', as Mrs Angell is about spun sugar baskets?"

I had Liv lined up to teach that, though she didn't know it yet.

"Even more so," I said, confidently this time. "What my Minibreak expert doesn't know about the ins and outs of romantic weekends isn't worth knowing."

"I've gone through the accounts every way I can think of, and there's just about enough money left to cover this term," Mark interjected. He seemed keen to get the meeting over and done with. "For next term to happen at all, we need to sign up about ten new students with deposits, before the end of *this* term. What Betsy has proposed, and I fully support her suggestion, is that we trial these new classes right now, advertise an Open Day to be held in about three weeks' time — the middle of February — to relaunch the Academy for a new generation, and take it from there."

I looked at my hands. I had an ulterior motive for the Open Day that I hadn't confessed to Mark. Holding an Open Day meant inviting as many people as we could think of: journalists, estate agencies and offices whose staff needed people skills, sixth formers heading off to university, and of course Old Girls who might want to give a Secret Weapons of Womanhood course to their god-daughters.

Old Girls who might then turn up, and reveal themselves for subtle interrogation.

"I see," said Miss Thorne. She turned the pages of my proposal very carefully, holding the pages between her fingers as if the ink might come off on her hands. "Oh, how sweet! How to buy a house! I suppose some people have to do that. But I have two problems, Mark. Firstly, I don't think I'd be doing my duty as principal if I let you throw out every tradition we've worked hard to establish here, on a whim! Have you spoken to Lord Tallimore, for a start?"

"No," I said, bravely, as Mark began to cover for me. I was too bad at lying to try. "No, I haven't. He's away and I didn't want to disturb him with this until I knew what your feelings were. I don't think it would be easy to get hold of him this week, in any case, he always goes up to a friend's in Scotland this time of year."

"Hmm." Miss Thorne made a small but meaningful pout with her pink lips.

"It's something we were going to raise at the end of month meeting," I added. "If it hasn't worked by then, then . . ."

Mark coughed. "I'm confident it will work, and I know Lord Tallimore supports any initiatives to keep the Academy afloat."

"I appreciate that, Mark," said Miss Thorne, condescendingly. "But we are bound to offer those girls upstairs the courses on which their parents enrolled them. We have legal obligations."

"I don't think any of them would . . ." Mark began.

"We can split it, mornings and afternoons," I said. I didn't want to horsetrade with Miss Thorne, but if we didn't get a handle on the new classes, the Open Day would be a shambles, or worse, not be allowed to happen.

"The second problem?" Mark recrossed his legs. His socks were *red*. I really hoped Miss Thorne didn't see those.

She smiled, cat-like in her Chanelique jacket, and I knew she had a trump card to deliver. I half-expected our seats to hinge and slide us down to the piranha pit beneath. "Well, the second problem is that we already offer classes very similar to these."

"You do?" I couldn't help it. "Where? I haven't seen any."

"Haven't you? Well, they are more seminars than classes. It's a form of mentoring." Miss Thorne was looking positively delighted now. "It's fairly new so it isn't on the brochure and — this is very much between us, Elizabeth — it isn't on offer to every girl, only those who we feel will benefit from it."

"What is it?" I demanded.

"We call it Personal Development," said Miss Thorne. She looked so smug her eyes nearly disappeared into her cheeks. "It's designed around preparing a very specific type of girl for entering society at the very highest international level."

"*Entering society?*" said Mark. "What does that even *mean* — outside the nineteenth century?"

"Who teaches this?" I asked. I had a sinking feeling that I already knew the answer. How could I have forgotten?

"Actually, it's one of our old girls!" said Miss Thorne. "You might remember her — Adele Buchanan. We're very lucky that she agreed to come and share her considerable knowledge . . ."

Of course it was Adele Buchanan. Presumably she was sharing her specialist subjects: Social Leapfrog, and How to Make Friends and Marry Their Fathers.

I could see my own face in the mirror behind Miss Thorne's desk, and the reflection was not an attractive one. I also spotted, too late, that I had a coffee blotch on the shirt I'd borrowed from Liv that morning, and while I was trying to manoeuvre my scarf over it, somehow I missed the gentle hush of study door being forced over thick pile carpet.

"Hello, Geraldine . . . Oh, am I interrupting?"

I looked up again into the mirror and this time saw someone I hadn't seen for fifteen years.

Adele must have been in her mid-thirties, but she looked younger than me. Still baby-blonde, still dressed in head-to-toe camel. Still looking through me with the kind of eyes that read everyone's social standing like a barcode. She was the only Academy girl who didn't join in the "ooh, you could be a princess!" chorus, preferring to look sad and murmur things about being kind to girls who "fell on hard times".

I knew it would be very hard to persuade *this* one that I was a management consultant. She could probably tell how much I earned just from looking at my earrings.

Adele opened her mouth and smiled with enormous delight.

"Oh my God, it's little orphan Annie!" she cooed and looked as if she'd been waiting fifteen years to see me again. In turn, I managed to choke out a smile.

I had to hand it to the Tallimore Academy — they certainly taught cast-iron social skills.

CHAPTER ELEVEN

If you wouldn't say it to someone's face, don't risk it in writing.

"Adele, what perfect timing — come and join us!" cooed Miss Thorne as if we were just having a spot of afternoon tea, not discussing the imminent financial collapse of the only place in the world that she'd ever be able to work. "I was just telling Elizabeth about your wonderful new mentoring programme."

"Oh, don't!" Adele pretended to blush modestly as she sashayed across the room and took the seat next to Mark. It was tricky to sashay across pile carpet in three-inch stilettos and a tight camel skirt, but Adele gave it her best finishing-school shot. "You make it sound so serious, when it's really just me trying to help the girls out as best I can, in my own way!" She turned to Mark. "Hello, Mr Montgomery!" she said, putting a teasing hand on his knee. "How good of the world of finance to spare you!"

Mark uncrossed his legs and regressed in front of my very eyes to awkward adolescence.

Miss Thorne beamed at Adele across the desk. I'd forgotten how the pair of them were a mutual appreciation society. Adele had won the Lady Tallimore

Prize in her year, technically for being the most poised and promising, but, Kathleen reckoned, for sucking up harder than a vacuum cleaner in French Sole pumps.

"How was your trip, dear?" she asked, as if Mark and I weren't there.

"Oh, amazing. Such fun!" Adele's eyebrows flickered, as if she'd like to say more, but couldn't possibly (yet).

"Have you been away?" I asked, to be polite.

"Adele has been up in Scotland," said Miss Thorne, then waited a beat and added, "With Lord Tallimore."

What? I could feel my mouth start to drop open and had to stop myself. Lord T's January shooting trip was strictly old boys only — The Young Guns, as they called themselves, even though half of them were on their third hips. "But he never takes *anyone* up there!"

I almost added, not even Franny, and had to gulp. It really was hard to remember she was gone sometimes.

Adele giggled and flapped her hands. "Oh, I'm sure he would, if you *asked*, Betsy! I just mentioned to Pelham before Christmas that I'd never been shooting — poor Edgar had an allergy to tweed, made him *swell* — so he invited me up to Scotland for a day or two before the season finished. I could hardly say no, could I?"

You bloody well could, I thought. It was only a few weeks after his wife's memorial service!

"Did you manage to bag anything?" I asked crossly.

"Isn't it mainly ropey old birds at this time of year?" asked Mark, turning to look at me with an innocent expression.

“It depends how high you’re aiming,” I said.

Miss Thorne gave me a piercing look over her glasses.

Either Adele was oblivious, or she was pretending not to notice the barbed words clattering around her.

“And how are you, Betsy?” she asked, swivelling towards me, keeping her knees demurely locked. She wore very glossy tights, I noticed, reluctantly conceding that she had the legs of a teenager. An athletic teenager. Her eyes were still a bit close together but everything else was polished into the sort of sheen that comes from letting someone else take over your basic maintenance. She’d worked on her elocution, too, because her voice was now so low and velvety she could have done voiceovers for men’s razors.

“I heard you were here . . . helping out,” she went on. “Pelham said I might bump into you. Anything you need to discuss, you’re very welcome to run by me, you know.” She waited a moment until I was about to speak, then added, “Don’t take this the wrong way, Betsy, but I do think I’m a teensy bit more qualified to advise them on the realities of weddings and marriage and so on. Although I’m sure you’re doing your best.”

Rise above it, I told myself. You’re a successful, fulfilled, taxpaying graduate. All she’s done is persuade old men she’s interested in golf.

“Well, it’s not all going to be about weddings and marriage. Mark and I were just discussing the new direction,” I said. “We think there should be a fresh approach, with more emphasis on independence.”

"Elizabeth thinks we should be teaching girls how to change tyres and apply for bank loans," Miss Thorne confided over her desk.

Adele laughed, right on cue. "Isn't that what husbands are for?"

"And when your husband's laid up in hospital?" I asked, before I could stop myself. This was exactly the sort of enraging "who needs the vote when you've got lipstick?" attitude that was all over the prospectus. "Or bankrupt? Or not there?"

Miss Thorne shot me a look. "*Not* very sensitive, Elizabeth, considering Adele's recent bereavement."

"Of course, I'm so sorry," I began, mortified, as Adele looked tragic but courageous as she waved away my apologies.

"I think everything you need to know is in that outline," said Mark, leaping into the growing tension, with a little show of impatience. "Betsy's laid it out perfectly. I was very impressed. We'd offer five basic courses: Home Life, Work Life, Social Life, Love Life and Family Life, each lasting a week. Clients can mix and match which courses they want. Lots of role play, lots of lectures from experts, lots of practical discussion."

His body language had turned brisk, and I caught a glimpse of what City Mark must be like, when he was doing that "Buy! Sell!" thing, or whatever they did. It was quite steely and impressive, and not very bookish at all. I rather liked it.

So did Adele, from the shameless way she crossed her shiny calves and put her chin on her hand to listen to him.

It was as if her whole body was miming, ooh, you're so clever and manly, I thought, crossly. And her calves didn't spread, either.

I noticed Mark was deliberately not responding to her gaze.

"I'll read the proposal," said Miss Thorne, in a regal manner. "And we can discuss it further when Pelham joins us for the January meeting. In the meantime, I give you my *temporary* approval."

I glanced at Mark. "But the Open Day . . . I know it's after the meeting, but I really think we should go ahead and start planning."

"I agree," he said at once. "Geraldine?"

"An Open Day? What a gorgeous idea!" trilled Adele. "*Do* let me know if I can help."

"Perfect. I'll put you on the bread knife and sandwich-filling rota, Adele," said Mark. "I hear the Party Catering maths lessons were excellent here in your day." He got up. "If you'd excuse me, ladies, I should really make a move. Give me a ring if there are any financial matters arising, otherwise Betsy's really the mastermind behind this."

With a quick nod to me, and a neat body swerve of Paulette, who was entering with coffee and more pink wafers, Mark slipped out of the room, and I was left very much on my own.

"So!" said Adele, turning to me.

"So!" echoed Miss Thorne. "I want to hear all about your shooting holiday! Was it your first time?"

I couldn't bear to sit through a discussion of Adele's Highland fling with Lord T. It was buttock-clenching enough just imagining her in her Hunter Barbie outfit, sneakily interrogating his red-cheeked friends about their acreage.

"I should really make a move too," I said, hoping I sounded brisk like Mark. "There's so much to do! Letters, and so on."

"Oh, must you dash off?" Adele pouted unconvincingly. "I've only just got here. I haven't even asked you about my little surprise present for Pelham."

I didn't want to think about that. "I have to talk to Mrs Angell," I said, gesturing upstairs. Which was true enough — I needed to know whether she was on for teaching a class on Pet Etiquette. "I'm sure we'll have a chance to catch up soon."

"Far be it from me to blow my own trumpet . . ." Adele raised a self-effacing hand, "but I've *quite* a reputation for throwing parties that are talked about afterwards. I'm sure it's down to the training I had here."

As Miss Thorne simpered and Adele simpered back, in a slightly higher register, something occurred to me: this was a golden opportunity for some detective work.

"Miss Thorne," I began, "I was thinking that it might be rather fun to have some Then and Now photographs dotted around the Open Day, to show we're keeping the style but updating the teaching? Could I have a look in the archive? I'm sure Miss Vanderbilt kept some fascinating bits and pieces in her bureau."

The simpering abruptly stopped. Miss Thorne's eyes shifted from left to right as if she'd spotted a mouse running under the cupboard. "The archive? Oh, we threw a lot of things away, after that terrible . . ." She cleared her throat. "Let me know what you need and I'll sift through for you. It'll save you time, when you're so busy."

I got the distinct impression I was being fobbed off. "Some photographs from, say . . ." I pretended to think. "How about 1980-ish? The year I arrived?"

"I'll see what I can find," she said, tersely.

"Thank you!" I hesitated, but her mouth clamped shut and I could tell I wasn't going to get much more. "I'll leave you to it then!"

"Oh dear!" said Adele, in a "surprised" tone worthy of a village panto. "I think I've left my mobile phone upstairs. Would you excuse me, Geraldine, while I go and have a look? Come on, Betsy — we can have a girlie natter on the way . . ."

She was next to me at the door before I knew what was going on, and I found myself being swept out into the hall on Adele's arm. Beneath the silky blouse were biceps of pure steel.

Her heels click-clacked next to mine on the tiles as she powered me towards the stairs, and I racked my brains for something polite to say to her. As it turned out, I didn't need to, because I barely got a chance to breathe, let alone contribute to any conversation.

"So how are you getting on with the girls? They're so funny, aren't they? Don't you find Venetia a sweetie-pie? She's extraordinary — she and I have an absolute riot in our lessons together, well, I say lessons, it's more of a chat with an older sister. I'm merely passing on my experience, because God knows you learn a thing or two when you're out there in the big wide world; I'm sure you're just the same. Although it's such a different view of life they'll be getting from you," she babbled. "Working, I mean. Having to come home to an empty flat and putting out your own bins or whatever it is you dynamic career types have to do for yourself. Have you had your hair Yuko'd, by the way? It's looking very . . . tamed."

"No," I said. Yuko'd? What was that? I'd have to check with Liv.

"I'm sorry to hear about your recent bereavement," I said, desperate to make my apology before it went on the slate that I hadn't. "It must have been an awful shock."

"Well, he *would* play tennis at all hours of the day, and after a wee dram too," sighed Adele. "I did tell him, Edgar, watch your heart, but . . ." She lifted her shoulders. "*What* can you do with these outdoorsy men? I still think of him, every time I smell cherry brandy. And Deep Heat."

"It takes a while to get used to it," I said, thinking of Franny as we swept past her old rosebowl. "I know I still pick up the phone to call Franny — Lord T does too. They spent their whole lives together, you know."

"*Did* they? Although not their *whole* lives," Adele corrected me, with a gentle squeeze of the arm as we started up the staircase. "Pelham has many happy years ahead of him."

"I meant they spent nearly every minute together," I said, determined not to fall into her trap. "They were *devoted* to one another."

"Yes, we were talking about that this weekend," said Adele. "That man is *so brave*. But I said to him, Pelham, you *must* keep busy. You *have* to get out there and live the rest of your life. It's what Frances would *want* you to do. As I'm always telling Venetia, it's no good thinking life is a fairy tale and that Prince Harry will come and rescue you. They need broader horizons. International aspirations."

I stopped on the landing, amazed that Adele and I had a single thought in common. "Do you think so?"

"Absolutely! Why restrict yourself to Englishmen? You've got to *research* your prince, there are plenty of them about these days, with the strong Euro," Adele went on, walking again. "Have a *plan* — a nice little starter marriage, and then something challenging, and then a longer term companionship deal, so you don't spend your fifties trailing around IVF clinics. I'm still very young, of course, but not so young that I've got time to hang around looking miserable. Edgar would have wanted me to be happy. My next husband would ideally be titled, and still fertile, because I plan to have children at thirty-seven and thirty-nine. Then I hope to meet a lovely American chap — I'm saving Americans until I'm a little older and more in need of their excellent private health care."

I stared at her to see if she was joking, but I didn't think she was.

"So what's held *you* back?" Adele asked, suddenly solicitous. "Don't tell me — you were the other woman? Waiting for him to leave his wife, but he never would?" She made a "so sorry" face. "Darling, it happens. Move on."

"No!" I stammered. "I was *not*!"

"Or are you one of those girls who makes out that she doesn't want to be looked after but secretly has a crush on her gay best friend?" Adele wagged a finger at me. "Because that's fine for a few years, but you're not getting any younger — and I say that as a friend, Betsy."

I couldn't imagine a parallel universe in which Adele Buchanan would be a friend of mine, but I controlled myself, under the gaze of several previous Lady Tallimores. Besides, we were outside the Lady Hamilton room now, with the girls waiting for Mrs Angell to get out the old Sliding Scale of Tips chart. They could probably hear everything.

"I've got more ambitions for myself than just getting married and having children," I managed.

Adele grabbed my forearm with both hands. "God, I'm *so* insensitive! It's because you're worried about what inherited conditions you might pass on, isn't it? It must be *terrible*, not knowing your own medical history. You're *so* responsible. And *so* right. Are you teaching this class?"

I nodded, dumbly. I'd never really thought of that before. What inherited conditions *might* I have? She didn't mean Charmer Addiction or Lack of Willpower — I honestly didn't know what there was, running through my veins.

No, I reminded myself, I *did* know. There's more than likely fifty per cent of Hector Tallimore in my make up. And that's something I could find out about, albeit via an embarrassing conversation with Lord T. It was something I should have done years ago.

And I ought to do it, before someone like Adele decided to winkle it out of him. She was the *last* person I wanted to hear anything like that from.

"We must get together and have a chat about Pelham," she gushed. "I'm dying to give him a thank you present to let him know what a special weekend I had, and I'm sure you can give me some wonderful hints as to what his secret weaknesses are. But I musn't keep you from your class! Toodles, darling!" With that she pressed her fingertips against her lips, waved them at me, and shimmered off.

I blinked to recover myself, but I was trembling. I pulled my sleeves down and hoped Adele's words hadn't travelled. Stupid cow.

"I'm totally going to start saying 'Toodles, darling'," said Divinity admiringly as I walked in, and I knew they'd heard everything.

CHAPTER TWELVE

The moment you can't balance in your party heels, call a taxi.

Igor's, where Liv worked part-time uncorking wine and fending off proposals, was technically called The Soho Typesetters and Darkroom Association, but it was years since anyone had actually called it that. The new crowd of trustafarians with "creative aspirations" and media types who frequented its murky booths referred to it as Igor's, and the old guard of artists and semi-professional drunks who knew the full name were too addled to remember what order it went in anyway.

It was one of those bars that was always cropping up in "10 Places You're Not Cool Enough to Know About" lists, because you had to have been before, sober, just to be able to find it. For a start, it wasn't anywhere near Soho. Igor's was practically in Westminster, down a side street near the Thames, and I walked past the plain black door at least twice every time. Inside wasn't much better: like all good dives, it looked significantly better after half a bottle of wine at eight o'clock than it did during daylight hours, but Igor's had a passionate following and if you could get in, you were guaranteed a good time and at least three globs of juicy gossip.

Liv had got her bar job there because Igor was an old drinking buddy of Ken's. Ken knew everyone, and so did Liv, which gave her the ideal lack of interest when otherwise scandalous shenanigans took place under her nose. As I kept telling her, Liv could easily have been running the place, if she wanted to: the other bar staff were gorgeously vacant Chelsea girls, and she was the only one who could understand what Igor was saying through his thick Glaswegian accent. The fact that she couldn't summon up the energy to demand a promotion was partly down to her easy-going nature, and partly down to the pleasantly half-asleep atmosphere that pervaded the place like a mild anaesthetic.

When I shoved open the door at half five, Liv was behind the oak bar drying glasses like a patient angel while Igor waved his beringed hands around and gabbled in tongues.

"I know!" she was saying. "Oh dear. I know! Really? *Dame* Judi Dench? Wow. Betsy!" She made a weird drama pointing into the furthest booth, the one usually reserved for VIPs and PRs cutting deals with each other.

I assumed she meant that Nell Howard had arrived, and had been whisked into the most private seat in the house. "Thanks!" I mouthed.

"Barg," grunted Igor. "Snot tae scunner, barg, Olivia!"

"Mm," she said, nodding meaningfully over his greasy head towards the back of the bar.

I swallowed, and picked my way around the tables, trying to ignore the butterflies rising up in my stomach.

I spotted Nell Howard before she spotted me, when the top of a feathery fascinator bounced over the wooden partition. I could see a petrol-blue patent leather boot too, sticking out, as she crossed her legs, breaking about three Academy rules in one go. They had failed to beige Nell up and it made me warm to her even more.

She popped her head round the booth. It really did take a certain personality to turn a hair feather into daywear, I thought, impressed. She was wearing a long black jumper dress, with a big jewelled belt over the top, and the boots were perfect.

"Darling! *Here* you *are!*" she cried, conspiratorially. "What an extraordinary place — I love it! Love it! I had an old date who used to come here, passed out in those very lavatories, if I remember correctly, with the Secretary of State for Wales's girlfriend . . ."

Most people had a story like that about Igor's.

Liv appeared out of nowhere with a tray. "Gin and tonic for you, and one for you too. And nuts, courtesy of the management." She set the huge tumblers in front of us. "Let me know if you need anything else."

"Thank you, darling," said Nell, flashing her a brilliant smile. "Perfect!"

I hadn't actually ordered anything, and was about to tell Liv that I really only wanted a cup of tea, then decided that when it came to drinks, she probably knew best. I needed some Dutch courage.

Liv crossed her fingers at me, and retreated to the nearest bit of the bar, where she started polishing more glasses in a too-casual fashion.

"So, without further ado, I found you this," said Nell, reaching into her vast, embroidered handbag. "Thought I should let you have it, after leaving you dangling like that at the memorial, with just half a tale. It's a piccy of that year above mine. It's the only one I could find with everyone on."

She slid an old photograph across the table. I picked it up eagerly, and Nell sank her nose into the gin and tonic, watching my reactions over the top.

"Wow," I said, as my eyes scanned it greedily. It must have been taken before some formal party or other: there were thirteen, no, fourteen girls grouped around two couches, with Miss Vanderbilt in the centre of one and Franny in the other, and the oil painting of the first Lady Tallimore billowing blowsily in the background. All the girls had mushroom-clouds of curls and tight, practised smiles, and they were sporting the sort of ballgowns that pinned the photograph firmly around 1980: off-the-shoulder flounces the size of valances, tiny pintuck ruffles, black velvet bodices over taffeta skirts in royal blue, magenta and bright green.

Well, nearly all the girls were. Two had very non-regulation gowns. Leaning on the back of the sofa, where Miss Vanderbilt couldn't see her sultry camera expression was a stunning blonde in a full-length black jersey halterdress, with a silver snake slithering up the side in multicoloured sequins. Next to her, on the other side and equally out of eyeshot was a mischievous brunette in shoestring straps and a tigerlily stuck in her bobbed hair.

"I mentioned that there were some wild girls in that year — well, that's Coralie, for a start," said Nell, pointing to the brunette. "She was *terrible*. We were always being told not to be like Coralie Hendricks, but we all had raging crushes on her. She had a bonkers dachshund called Mitzi that she trained to attack the art teacher and she smoked Marlboro Reds out of the loo windows." She sighed. "Of course the boys *loved* her."

Was that like me? I wondered. Was I naughty? Was that the sort of thing that you could inherit?

"And that's Sophie. Sophie Townend," Nell went on, pointing at the blonde. "She was what we called a ten-pointer. Got herself a small part in a Bond film, can't remember which one, doing something mysterious and sexy with a deck of tarot cards — after she left here, of course. Not on old Vander's curriculum, being shagged to death by a secret agent."

"And Hector dated her?" I asked. She looked like the prize pick: the man-eating model in a garden of sweet nannies-to-be. I didn't feel drawn to her much, but then — would I? Should I? My eye jumped from one face to another, while I monitored myself for any telltale flashes of recognition.

"No, Hector went out with Emma-Jane." Nell moved her red nail across to the girl sitting next to Franny, who sat with her hands folded on her pink taffeta lap and her eyes cast down beneath a heavy blond fringe. "Don't let that shy look fool you. Lady Frances had her sitting there for a reason."

"Which was?"

"So she could keep an eye on her. Emma-Jane *never knew when to stop*," said Nell, darkly, and tapped the side of her nose.

I stared hard at Emma-Jane, searching for any vague familial resemblances, but couldn't see any: she had a long nose, where mine was turned up, and she was a pink-and-white blonde, no sign of redhead genes at all. But if she was Hector's girlfriend, she was my best bet — unless he'd had an away day with one of his other roaring mates?

"Did Hector . . . just date Emma-Jane?" I asked, carefully.

"More or less," said Nell. She took another sip of her gin and tonic and the ice clinked. "He didn't like to show favouritism, did Hector. I think everyone had a spin in his Golf GTi at some point, in a manner of speaking. But Emma-Jane was his favourite. He went seriously off the rails when she got engaged to Charlie Cato. Everyone thought that was what caused the Great Bunking Off to Argentina."

"Emma-Jane got engaged to someone else, just before Hector left, which was just before I was born?" I felt like I should be taking notes. All these names — would I have to google everyone in London over the age of fifty?

"Yes, I suppose that's right. Her first of four. As I say, never knew when to stop . . ." Nell clucked and raised her eyes to the ceiling. "Like I can talk. Three down, and counting myself! Never let it be said that the Tallimore Academy didn't prepare you for marriage!"

There were two redheads in the photograph, as far as I could see — one plump-shouldered strawberry blonde and one with long, Irish-red curls, tumbling down her back.

"Who are these two?" I asked, though neither of them looked particularly inspiring.

"Caroline de la Grange and Bumps Fitzroy. Caroline's married to Mr Tin Foil, can't remember his real name, Sir Tin Foil it might be by now, actually — and I think Bumps is a nun, somewhere in the wilds of Ireland. Convent education followed by Coralie Hendricks can do that to a girl's nerves." Nell looked at me. "Is this helping, or am I just making it worse?"

"I don't know," I said, honestly.

A silence fell between us, as I studied the photograph and Nell drank her gin and tonic. In the background, I could hear Igor gargling at a customer, while Liv translated — it was the available single malts list.

"'Scuse the nosiness, but do you want to *find* your mother?" Nell asked, without warning. "Or just know who she was? I mean, what would you say to her if she walked in right now? Would you be thrilled? Or bloody furious?"

I opened my mouth, but stopped before the usual answer could tumble out. I'd rehearsed various dramatic reunions over the years — weeping, clutching of clothes, curls of baby hair produced from matching lockets, etc — yet faced with someone who might actually have *known* my mother, and might hazard a good guess at where she'd be now, that all seemed a bit, well, fake. I wasn't actually sure what I'd say.

"I'd say . . . hello."

Nell squinted at me. "That it? I think I'd jolly well want to give her a piece of my mind."

"No," I said, slowly. Somehow it was easier to be honest with this stranger. "I don't think I'd be *angry* with her for leaving me, because I had a wonderful childhood. I couldn't have *been* happier, or more loved. I guess I'd want to know *why* she couldn't keep me. If it was circumstances, or . . ." I hesitated. I hadn't said this aloud to anyone before. "Or if I was a mistake that she couldn't bear to see. If my father had been . . . you know, the wrong sort of man." I took a gulp of my gin and tonic. "If she'd been well, *forced* into —"

"Oh, I don't think that would be the case!" said Nell, quickly.

"How do you know?" I replied, anguished by the images now occurring to me. "I mean, we're assuming she was rich, from a smart background — but it might not be any of these girls! It might have been one of the *cleaners*' daughters! It doesn't sound like Hector operated much of a door policy on his bedroom antics."

"But there was the little bee in your box," Nell pointed out. "That was a big craze that summer — all the Academy girls had them. They were from a little jeweller's in Bond Street. We said that at the time, it must be one of us."

I fingered the bee on the gold chain round my neck, and slowly brought it out from under my sweater.

Nell's face lit up as soon as she saw it, her eyes creasing up in delight.

"Gosh, that brings back memories! Oh, look, it's one of the ones with diamond stripes — how swanky!"

"Do you recognise it?" I asked hopefully, but she shook her head.

"Yes, but I couldn't say whose it was, darling. We all had them. Sophie had five, all on a gold chain, from different chaps. Worker bees, she called them. But I do think it points to one of these girls." She nodded towards the photograph again. "Not that it narrows it down much for you."

I stared at the round-faced girls, and Franny in her special occasion diamond collar, and Miss Vanderbilt looking like someone had shoved a broom handle down the back of her dress, and naughty Coralie and vampish Sophie and Bumps the nun. My mother did not spring out at me as a tiny part of me had hoped she would. But surely she was there? One of them?

Franny must have known, I thought. She *must* have recognised the bee, and the handwriting, even though she always batted my questions away by swearing she didn't. But then maybe she just chose not to ask: the art of never asking direct questions was an Academy speciality, after all.

"Well, did any of them go away? Suspiciously?"

"Hard to say," sighed Nell. "We didn't all do a year, you know. Some people had a term at the Tallimore, then a term at a Cordon Bleu school, then a term in Switzerland . . . People came and went. But I'll dig out my diaries."

I blinked in the low light. I felt much nearer and yet further away from the truth, all at the same time.

"Can you write down the names, please?" I asked, offering her my lilac notebook.

"Of course. So, what's your next move, if I might be so nosy?" Nell reached into her bag for a pen and began scrawling a list in handwriting that rambled over the lines.

"I'm not sure," I admitted. I mean, I couldn't exactly ring these women up and ask them if they'd got any illegitimate children they might have left in Full Moon Street, could I? Or could I? Desperate times and all that.

"There. That's everyone who was at the Academy, in the autumn of 1980 which is when, if my maths is still up to snuff, you were the twinkle in someone's eye." She passed my notebook back.

"Course, she might not want to see me." I hadn't said that aloud before, either, and it came out in quite a small voice.

"Oh, darling!" Nell seemed shocked. "I'm sure she'd love to see you now! What an extraordinary young woman you've turned out to be!"

"How do you know that?" I asked, and held her gaze. Nell didn't look away.

"I just know," she said, simply.

When I didn't reply, she added, "Don't be too hard on them. Coralie and Sophie might have been a bit silly, but we were all just babies, really, and totally romantic about everything — no one worried about ghastly diseases or mortgages. We didn't know *anything*, we just spent all week planning the weekend and the dates and the castles we were going to marry into. Poor Lady Fran tried her best to knock some common sense into us, but we all knew Diana Spencer, through friends of friends, and we just wanted to meet our prince too, and be swept off in that carriage in a compleeetly enormous frock! Marriage junkies, the lot of us! That's why we've racked up so many between us!"

I managed a weak smile. "I'm afraid I've gone the other way. I don't believe in fairy-tale weddings, just finding a reliable man. Boring, I know."

"God, probably much more sensible," sighed Nell. "But whatever your mother was, she honestly believed in a fairy-tale ending. And in the end, she did what she could for you, by giving you to the one person we thought could deal with all life's dramas: Lady Frances. I'm sure if you wanted to meet her now, she'd *love* to see you. Just to explain."

Nell's jaunty expression was strained, as if she was trying to hold something in. I felt a tiny prickle of something in the pit of my stomach. *How* did she know that? Was there something she wasn't telling me — something really quite important?

Before I could frame the question, she picked up her drink and drained it with that quick practised gesture I'd seen at the reception. The ice clacked back into the empty glass. "Darling, I'm terribly sorry to dash off, but I have to fly to Ibiza tonight. Got to turn some client's house into a Raj paradise by the weekend. It's what I do, before you ask, interior decoration."

"Wow," I said. "How glamorous!"

"Not really." Nell winked again. "When you've got married and moved as many times as I have, you get used to tarting up new places. Plenty of friends downsizing, upsizing, nothing wrong with making your hobby into your business. Means you're always dying to get to the office!"

I thought of Jamie. That was something he'd say. Something he'd done, in fact.

"Is there anything else I can tell you, before I go?" she asked.

It popped out of my mouth before I could really think what I was saying. "Who was the nicest?"

"The nicest?"

"Yes." I pulled the photograph back out of my notebook and put it on the table in front of her. "Not the cleverest, or the most popular — who was the nicest girl? Was there one who you'd consider a friend? Still?"

Nell fell quiet for a moment, and when she spoke, it wasn't with the wildly exaggerated Sloane tone she'd used before. "Well, darling, I'm in touch with all of them, at Christmas and birthday — it's just what you do, isn't it? But . . ." She touched the photo gently. "Rosalind, she was the sweetest, no doubt about it. Look, you can tell what a poppet she was, just from her face. She let Coralie wear her pearl choker, never said a mean word to Sophie, even when she nicked her date for this dance."

Rosalind, in a floral strapless gown, was sitting on Franny's other side, and only giving the camera a brief glance. She had a thick fringe of mousy highlighted hair that hung in her eyes like a pony, and barely stood out at all, apart from her beautiful white shoulders. They were like marble.

"She's looking like that because Miss Vanderbilt made her take her glasses off for the photo," explained Nell, affectionately. "Poor Rosie. Blind as a bat, but absolutely adorable."

Sadly for me, Rosalind had as many ginger genes as Nell did. Still, it proved that the possible mother pool wasn't all rip-roaring totty.

"Oh, balls, look, my phone's ringing. I have to go, that's my driver, going potty outside." Nell was gathering her bag together, and arranging a huge black throw around herself. "You've got my numbers, haven't you, darling!" she said, fastening it with a giant diamante cobweb which somehow looked like the only thing to fasten a huge black throw with. "Call me if anything springs to mind? And thank you so much for bringing me to this fabulous place — I love it!"

She gave me a swooping kiss on the cheek and then she was weaving through the small tables as if operating an invisible hula hoop. "Bye, Igor! Bye, Olivia!" she called towards the bar.

Of *course* she'd discovered and remembered their names. She was a Tallimore girl.

Then she was gone and Igor's seemed a slightly gloomier place again.

Liv was over at my table before the door stopped swinging, with fresh drinks for us both, which was technically against Igor's rules, but if anyone could bend Igor's rules it was Liv, since she was the only one who could understand them.

"So? Who is it? Did she tell you?"

I shook my head and passed her the photo. "It's one of them, she reckons, plus Hector, I guess."

Liv moved a candle closer so she could inspect the faces. "Did she confirm Hooray Hector as your father? Didn't you ask about the other chinless wonders he ran around with?"

"No, but it's obvious, isn't it?" I felt I could say that now, now I was officially on the trail. It didn't seem so presumptuous any more. "Anyway, I'm not so bothered about my father. If he was worth bothering about, he'd be in the same place as my mother, wouldn't he? Standing by her."

"Good point, Sherlock. Blimey, you can tell how posh this lot are, can't you?" she said, pointing to Bumps Fitzroy the nun-in-waiting. "You can smell the Diorissima and saddle polish from here. Look at her eyes! It's like she's staring at her own nose. That is *not* your mother, Betsy."

"Thank you, Watson." I sipped my drink. Liv made very strong gin and tonics, to Ken's recipe, which started, "half fill your glass with gin".

"Is that her there?"

"Is that who where?"

"Her. Nell. There." Liv was pointing at the photo, but I didn't bother to look up. I was staring at the names and thinking about what I could do next.

"No, Nell's not in the photo. She was in the year below."

"Oh," said Liv, thoughtfully. "OK."

"I've got the names, so now I suppose, *if* I wanted to, I could invite them to this Open Day." I looked up. "Did I tell you we're full steam ahead on Operation Sinking Ship?"

"Brilliant!" Liv clapped her hands. "And then what?"

"Well . . . I don't know," I admitted. "It'll come to me."

I sipped my gin thoughtfully and hoped something would.

CHAPTER THIRTEEN

Keep the safety pins off your drycleaning in your handbag — you never know when something might snap.

The new curriculum began at half ten the next morning, and I felt I should lead from the front and take the first lesson myself.

I'd made a list of useful ideas, but I decided to start at the very beginning, with the one thing that kept me going from bleary morning to stumbling-in night, as well as cheering me up on the bus and making me feel like a proper woman.

My big red investment handbag, and its family of tiny subsidiary baglets that held my life together in easy-to-reach pockets.

Handbag Love was about the only thing the girls and I had in common, and I hoped it might result in some more enthusiastic audience participation than I'd seen so far for Miss McGregor and her globe artichokes.

As per notebook recommendations, I didn't give myself time to be nervous outside the Lady Hamilton

Room. I thought of Franny, pulled my shoulders back and my spine straight then breezed straight in, with a cheerful smile masking my nerves.

"Good morning, girls," I said, making my way to the desk at the front.

To my surprise, they were all there, surrounded by Starbucks venti takeaway cups and muffins. But instead of lounging at their desks texting, they were gathered around one desk, from which I could make out an impassioned wailing. It sounded like Anastasia, from the violent untranslatable bursts of fury punctuating the yowls.

"What's the matter?" I asked, hurrying over to the source of the drama. "Are you all right, Anastasia? Is she hurt?"

I directed this question to Clemmy, one step back from the scrum of concern shielding Anastasia from view. She was opportunistically hoovering up the remains of a muffin with a wet finger.

"Her Porsche's been towed," she explained, crumbily. "Left it on a red route once too often. Now it's in Colliers Wood and we're not even sure if that's in London. Dad's gone berserk — and he's in Moscow."

"My father!" sobbed Anastasia, one arm thrown dramatically over her face. "If it happened again he said he would keel me! And I will keel the parking warden . . ." The rest was lost as Divinity and Venetia administered scandalised hugs.

"Why doesn't she just get a parking permit?" I asked Clemmy. "Surely it's not that hard, outside her own house?"

Clemmy hoiked up her eyebrows which she seemed to have stencilled in with charcoal. "Complicated. For legal reasons."

For a small woman, Anastasia could make a truly bloodcurdling noise. You could have heard her on the Steppes.

I thought quickly. "Ana," I said, raising my voice over the din. "Ana, stop crying. I'm sure we can come to some arrangement about getting you a parking permit registered to this address. There may even be space in the garage for you to park there."

Instantly the howling stopped, the crowds parted, and Anastasia's sharp face appeared from under her mane of streaky hair. "Really? You could do that for me?"

"Er, yes," I said. Mark looked like the sort of man who knew about London parking permits, and the garage had been empty since the Academy Rolls-Royce had been sold. "We might make a small . . . administration charge," I added, thinking about champagne for the Open Day.

Relief swept over Anastasia's face. "Votever you want," she said happily. "Thank you so much!"

"No problem," I said. "Happy to help."

The other girls boggled at me, as if it was weird to have anyone listen to one of their problems, much less help them out. I took advantage of their momentary silence to get the first lesson underway before I had time to think about what I'd just promised to do.

"Now then, change of plan," I said, heaving my handbag on to the desk. "From today, morning sessions are going to be with me, or with my team of specialist tutors. We're going to focus on some more modern skills. Things you need to know when you're out there, living on your own and fending for yourself."

"Oh my God!" said Divinity, clapping her hand across her mouth. Her nails were gold and long, and she nearly took her own eye out. "I am so not going to be able to feed myself! My mam has to come down every weekend and start my dishwasher for me!"

"You're *so* lucky," said Clementine. "I can't wait to get out of my stupid parents' stupid house and their stupid rules. Bring it on."

"Good! That's really positive, Clemmy. So, first things first!" I said. "Could you put your bags on your desks, please?"

They didn't need asking twice, and laid their bags reverentially in front of them, tweaking the straps and buckles to their best advantage, and casting competitive sideways glances.

Venetia's was a tiny underarm clutch for credit cards only, whereas Divinity had a Chloe Paddington with a massive lock. Clemmy's patent leather bag was pocked with chains and studs, and Anastasia's classic tote seemed to be made from some endangered species. Swan skin, possibly.

"Oh," said Venetia, in a syrupy tone of fake approval, "your Chloe Paddington again, Divinity. It's so *sweet* the way you're such a one-bag girl."

Divinity beamed, but Clemmy gave Venetia a dirty look. "Better a one-bag girl than a ten-man *bag*, Venetia."

I stepped in, terrified that the fragile mood of positivity would vanish before I could start. "They're all gorgeous! I'm very envious! Now, could you tip them out?"

"What?" laughed Venetia, then her voice turned hard. "No."

"I ken't," said Anastasia. "Not without my lawyer." And she clamped her lips shut.

"Why not, Ana?" asked Divinity. "What have you got in there? A gun?"

"Not in this bag, no," said Anastasia. "But I have a . . ." She whispered something into Divinity's ear, and from the way her eyebrows shot up into her hairline, I decided not to make her share it with the class.

"OK," I said, trying to sound confident. I didn't want to lose momentum. "Let's start with *my* bag. This morning, we're going to talk about editing down, so you don't end up giving yourselves back problems."

I undid the zip with a flourish and opened it up like a flower. "As you can see, it's not as big as Divinity's, but I bet it's got more in it."

Venetia's perfect eyebrow hooked sarcastically. "Oh, who's that by?" she asked, faking confusion. "I don't recognise it."

"The label doesn't matter, it's what's inside that counts," I said. "Now, the trick is to have bags inside bags, so it's easy to see what you need straight away."

One by one, I unpacked my essentials: silver make-up pouch, mobile bag, notebook, mini-umbrella, painkiller-and-breathmints bag, gold change purse, lilac pencil case, and so on and so on, until the desk was covered with a surprising amount of stuff.

I felt a bit as if I were undressing in front of them — a woman's bag is, after all, the inside of her brain in portable form — but it seemed to have got their attention.

"Oh my God," breathed Clemmy when I'd put the final handkerchief down. "It's like that Mary Poppins job, with the hatstand."

Spooky Clemmy's Disney-watching habits was an unexpected treat, and the girls' impressed expressions did boost my confidence. For a moment, I felt like a real teacher.

"I'll be honest," I admitted. "I took out a whole bag's worth of receipts and manky paper tissues before I came."

"And your spare knickers?" Divinity winked. "Eh? Eh?"

"We'll come to that," I said. "Right — let's make a list of what every girl needs in her bag! What are your must haves?"

"Shades," said Venetia and Anastasia at the same time.

"Yes!" I said. "They stop crow's feet, hold your hair back, and also disguise hangovers and end-of-the-day make-up."

"And to stop guys eyeing you up in clubs," giggled Divinity.

"And to stop guys eyeing you up in clubs." I went back to the board and wrote down "shades". "What else?"

"Phone?" said Venetia. "The right phone, of course." She cast a sideways look at Clemmy, which I guessed was pointed. "If you only have one, it's much easier."

I ignored that. I wasn't going to get into a "how many phones have you got?" discussion with Venetia. "Of course, phone. Has everyone got a taxi number saved in their phone? And two contacts saved under ICE?"

They looked blank, so I added, "In Case of Emergency, if you're hit by a car? Or if you pass out in a club?"

Anastasia and Divinity started to scribble.

"Who else should you have in your phone?" I was on a roll now, drawing arrows on the whiteboard. There had been two pages on this in my notebook: Franny had been very thorough in Crisis Prevention. "Your dentist — I can't even think with toothache let alone find old appointment cards — your doctor's surgery, your local police station, and perhaps the number of the local car pound, too, in case your car mysteriously disappears?"

I glanced at Anastasia as I said that, with a hopeful smile. I was relieved to see her grin back.

"Ebsolutely," she nodded. "Also AA, in case of . . . emergencies."

"Very good." I wasn't sure whether she meant *the* AA or just AA, but didn't think it was the moment to go into it.

"And one of those crack spring-cleaning squads," cackled Divinity. "If your parties are anything like mine. Remember the last one, Clemmy? When that friend of yours sledged down my stairs on a suitcase and took out the whole banister and we thought the house was going to collapse? Clemmy? Oi!"

I noticed Clemmy was looking mutinous, and tried to involve her.

"Clemmy? What are the essential numbers in your phone?"

She tossed her black hair. "My therapist. And my life coach. And my dad's Diosces exorcist. She's pretty cool."

"Therapist," I said, writing it down as if it were normal. Poor Clemmy, I thought. Even if she's making it up, that's pretty sad.

"Everyone needs a few celebrity numbers," announced Venetia while my back was turned. "To avoid queues."

"You *have not . . . shut* up . . ." chorused the other girls.

"OK, this is one of my own secret lifesavers," I interrupted, swiftly. "If you're a terrible drink-dialler and you've got an ex whose number you can't quite bring yourself to delete, save him under "Are you sure?" or "Trouble" or something to remind yourself why it's not a good idea."

The raucous teasing stopped, and they regarded me with curiosity for a moment. Even Clemmy forgot to sulk.

"That is the first useful thing anyone's told me since I came here," said Venetia.

"How old are you?" asked Divinity. "If you don't mind me asking, like."

"Twenty-seven," I said. Ten years older than them, nearly. And didn't I feel it.

"And you have a lot of exes?" asked Venetia.

"No," I said. "But I think we've all got one problem ex, haven't we?"

"*Divinity*," said Clemmy, meaningfully.

"*Clemmy*," retorted Divinity.

"What else?" said Anastasia, clicking her pen impatiently. "I terminate my exes. Move on. What's in that pink bag?"

"Minimalist make-up," I said. "Skip mascara, tint your eyelashes. One less thing to worry about when you wake up after a heavy night."

"*Divinity*," Clemmy started again, but the others shushed her quiet.

After half an hour the whiteboard was crammed with arrows and items. We'd talked about:

Multi-purpose blusher for disguising hangover skin

Keys, ideally on chain attached to bag to avoid snatching

Purse, also ideally on chain, ditto

Emergency bag: to contain selection of Sellotape, Vaseline for sore heels and cracked lips, gum to prevent snacking

Powder compact for checking teeth and tables behind you

A-Z to "assist" attractive tourists

Diary and/or notebook for ideas and for leaving notes for parking wardens

Two man's hankies for emergencies (emotional/practical)

Hand cream (for hands and flyaways)

Spare pair of pants, rolled very small

Spare plastic carrier bag rolled even smaller (multiple uses)

It quickly became plain that there was a certain gap between my needs, and the girls'.

When I produced my hand sanitiser — "You know that yucky feeling you get on your hands when you've been on the Tube in summer?" — I could see them trying to imagine.

"I *don't* know that yucky feeling," said Divinity. "The yucky feeling is the reason I don't go on the Tube."

"Um, what if you've had sushi for lunch and there was no miniwipe?" I suggested, and they chorused, "Oh yeaaaah," and wrote it down.

They didn't get my brilliant suggestion about saving up the minis from "gifts with purchase" to downsize their travelling make-up bag either (they weren't the sort of girls who only shopped when there was an offer), and when I asked what they'd do if they ripped their skirt, the baffled consensus was that they'd go and buy a new one.

But apart from that, it went a lot better than I'd expected. And then it was time for lunch.

"Lunch is going to be in the kitchens today!" I announced, as the girls scraped their chairs back and started chatting. "So if you want to make your way downstairs . . ."

I noticed that Venetia had swanned over to the other side of the room, where she seemed to be checking her immaculate make-up in the reflective glass of a gloomy oil of some Victorian widow at the same time as she was deftly pulling her butterscotch mane into a messy updo. To my surprise, she then added a pair of spectacles — the type you see secretaries removing, prior to untumbling their hair and revealing themselves to be office foxes.

I could tell from the acidic glances Clemmy and Anastasia exchanged that this wasn't new behaviour.

"Going somewhere, Venetia?" asked Clemmy. "Or are you tarting yourself up for our benefit?"

She snorted. "Don't be ridiculous. I have a . . . lesson with Miss Buchanan at twelve thirty."

Adele hadn't said anything about it to me, and there was no note on the timetable Miss McGregor had thoughtfully provided.

"I don't think you are," I said, pleasantly. "This is the new timetable. This lunchtime, we're all going to learn how to make omelettes!"

"Omelettes! Ace!" said Divinity. "I love an omelette, me."

"That's because your mother keeps chickens in your backyard — or whatever it is you call your garden up north," said Venetia, as she shoved some diamante clips into her hair.

"Shut up," snapped Clemmy. "Divinity's mother's got her own llamas. For *fun*."

"Forget it, Clem. I'm ignoring her," said Divinity. "I'm rising above it, like Mrs Angell says." She made a "nose in the air" gesture that Venetia couldn't see. Or maybe she could. Maybe that was the point.

"Venetia, I'll have a word with Miss Buchanan to see if she can rearrange your lesson, but I'd really like you to join us for our lunch so we can all chat and discuss what new topics are coming up." I paused. "What exactly is it she's teaching you, anyway?"

Venetia turned round with a flick of her fringe, and looked me up and down as if she wasn't sure how much she had to tell me.

"It's a Personal Development class," she said. "And it's only me taking it, because . . ." She paused for maximum disdain. "Because Miss Buchanan doesn't feel that there's anyone else here who'd appreciate the lesson."

"Ooohh!" said Divinity, with scary dead eyes. The other two didn't seem to be taking it lightly either. Forget omelettes, I could have scrambled eggs on the resentment radiating from Clemmy alone. Anastasia had gone scarily still.

I smiled as nicely as I could, and said, "It's not up to Miss Buchanan to decide who she teaches. She should be offering the same class to everyone. I'll see if it can be rearranged for this afternoon," I said. "In the meantime I'll see you in the kitchens in five minutes, with everyone else."

"Yeah, right." Venetia turned her back on me and started glossing over her lipstick with a lip brush, although from the amount she was applying a spatula would have been more appropriate.

"Rise above it," whispered Divinity. I had to stop myself doing the snooty nose gesture, but I managed it, somehow.

CHAPTER FOURTEEN

If you can't afford a new party outfit, invest in a salon blowdry & a red lipstick for an instant glamour upgrade.

Venetia did not appear for Kathleen's lesson in whipping up a healthy fridge lunch, and Paulette didn't know where she'd gone.

"Lunchtime's a funny time to go for a lesson though, innit?" she mused from behind her novelty desk tidy, full of pencils with fluffy ends. "Unless it was social dining or something? They did get into a car with some bloke in a hat, could have been a chauffeur or it could just have been a bloke that enjoys wearing uniforms, I suppose. You read about men like that. Not that I was spying out of the window or anything."

"Thanks, Paulette," I said, grateful for once for her total lack of discretion.

I went back upstairs to make some lists for the Open Day, and got as far as the database of Old Girls who'd been invited for Franny's reception. This time my heartbeat raced as I checked the names Nell had given me against the names on the database and found that though all had been invited, only half had RSVP'd, and there was no record of who'd actually been there. Sophie had been there, and Caroline, Lady Tin Foil, and several others but not Rosalind or Coralie.

I filed my nails thoughtfully: it always helped me think. There were loads of reasons my mother might not have wanted to come back, if indeed she hadn't. She could have been ill. Not everyone enjoyed memorials. She might have worried that I'd be there, waiting. I'd have to think of a really great reason for them to come back to support an Open Day — something that would tug at the Tallimore strings of duty.

I had to do it quickly, too. According to the large calendar Paulette had put on my desk, I had about ten working days to arrange the whole bash. I could rely on Kathleen to handle the food, and Mark to sort out wine or something, but everything else would have to come from me, otherwise Miss Thorne would make it look like her awful brochure, and there'd be flirting with fans going on in the foyer.

I started drafting a letter but soon realised I couldn't concentrate without more coffee and headed downstairs to get some refreshments. The noise in the Lady Hamilton Room stopped me in my tracks.

Mrs Angell was supposed to be teaching Miss Thorne's traditional syllabus, but the yelling was audible outside the room. I put my head around the door, in case Mrs Angell had thrown in the towel and left them to fend for themselves with a copy of *Debrett's* and the works of Nancy Mitford.

"Ah, Betsy!" said Mrs Angell, her glazed eyes latching on to me gratefully. "You can settle an argument for us. Is it, or is it not, appropriate for a first date to take place in the most expensive restaurant you can find these days?"

"No!" I said, shocked. "Of course not! Who ever says that?"

"Adele," said Venetia, at once. "She says it's important to assess your date's commitment to the future of your relationship."

"That's rubbish," I said. "It makes you look as if you're putting a price on your company! Besides, you should *always* offer to split the bill, just so he can say no, but what if he says yes? What then?"

Venetia's expression conveyed that this was beyond her sphere of experience.

"Why would you do that?" asked Anastasia.

"Because . . ." I looked round the class at Mrs Angell for help, but her frizz suggested she'd spent much of the lesson with her hands either clawing at her face, or raking through her hair.

"Well," I said, "you should *offer*, he'll say, no really, and that's that, but sometimes, if the date isn't going well, and you have no intention of seeing him again, offering to pay half is a better way of making that clear than ignoring his calls for the next month. It's a polite way of saying, I had a nice evening *as friends* but let's not do this again."

"What if it's a crap date and you feel like he owes you?" asked Clemmy.

"Only you can decide how much you're worth in oysters," I said.

"You must have been on some terrible dates," said Divinity, sympathetically. "You're an expert on exes." Her face brightened. "An ex-pert!"

I felt my face go red, then tried to rally. They didn't know about my rogue's gallery of first dates. "Why are you discussing this?" I asked. "Is it part of the lesson?"

"Divinity has a date," said Clemmy. "We're helping her organise it."

Mrs Angell's eyes bulged in appeal. "We were talking about how to announce one's engagement. Divinity suggested *heat* magazine."

"So you've gone back to basics with some Date Management discussion! That's a great idea!" I said, reaching for my notebook and struggling for the confidence I'd felt earlier. "So, who's your date with, Divinity?"

Divinity's face was glowing. "Don't ask," she said. "I don't want to jinx it!"

"Matthew Hartley," said Venetia, sounding bored. "He has no money, stupid long hair, and a junkheap of a car, and he bailed out on her the last two times. I'd go for sushi, Div — you can eat on your own then, and you won't look as if you've been stood up."

Divinity spun in her chair. "Shut your head. He couldn't come. He's an artist, he had a deadline."

"Had no cash, more like," replied Venetia, scornfully.

"Then you should suggest somewhere he can afford," I said, ignoring her and making for the blackboard. I found a pen and wrote: Location. "The more informal the better. Which do you want, after all — great conversation or lobster?"

"Lobster," said Venetia and Anastasia at the same time as Clemmy and Divinity said "Conversation."

"Where should I go?" Divinity's pen was poised and she had a familiar, paranoid expression on her face. "Name names!"

It was a while since I'd eaten out in London, and my mind went blank. All I could remember was La Poule au Pot in Chelsea, where Jamie had taken me once when I was down visiting Liv and she'd been called away by an urgent fiancé. It had been all those things: cosy tables, delicious food, free-flowing wine, although I hadn't really noticed at the time, thanks to the outrageous gossip he was telling me. I didn't even know the gossipees and it was still hilarious. If I'd ever had a date with Jamie, it was definitely where I'd want to be taken.

"La Poule au Pot is . . ." My voice went funny and the girls stared. "Very good. Or Le Boudin Blanc round the corner from us here? Bistro food, quite romantic, easy to get home from if it's gone badly, or easy to go for a stroll if it's gone well . . ."

That had been another one. When I thought about it, I could remember pretty much every restaurant Jamie had taken me to — he knew all the nicest places and insisted on paying because it was "good research for Party Animals". Our dinners did linger in the memory, despite not complying with my usual rules for successful dates. I usually had at least one glass of wine too many, stayed until the poor waiters were sweeping under our table, and ended up falling a tiny bit more in love with him, as he put me in a taxi home — alone.

They weren't dates, I reminded myself. That was the whole point.

"You've gone very red," Anastasia observed. "Are you having a hot flush?"

"Anastasia!" gasped Mrs Angell. "Medical symptoms! And how old do you think Betsy is, anyway?"

"She's twenty-seven," said Divinity, helpfully.

"She's bright red," Anastasia repeated. "Look at her."

"Dates in restaurants are a nightmare," groaned Clemmy, ignoring my confusion. "I always worry about how much to tip and then if he doesn't tip enough I get embarrassed and feel like I should add something but I never know how much that should be."

"Tipping is a good litmus test, though," I agreed. "Tight wallet, tight heart, as they say."

Mrs Angell seemed relieved the lesson had got back on to safer ground. "Tipping! Yes, good! Fifteen per cent! And a pound for the coat girls! What other tricky moments can we encounter when we're dining out, and how might we rise above them? Have you had a tricky moment?"

"Oh my God, yes!" agreed Divinity. "What should you choose so you don't look like a pig? I always worry about that. Is it, like, still really bad to have the bread?"

"No," I said. Where did they learn this stuff? "Always eat exactly what you like. My friend Jamie says that nothing puts a man off more than a girl who orders mineral water and a green salad and then won't add dressing. And he's dated more girls than you've had hot dinners."

Looking at them, maybe that wasn't the best choice of expression.

"Anyway," I hurried on, "who wants to look like a high-maintenance control freak on a first date?"

"That's not what Miss Buchanan says," said Anastasia. "She says men find control an aphrodisiac."

She said aphrodisiac with dramatic relish.

"Adele says we should regard a first dinner date just like other girls might approach a job interview," said Venetia. "The right clothes, the right questions, the right background reading." She curved one corner of her lusciously glossed mouth into a superior smile. "The trick is to make them think *they're* doing the interviewing."

"And the metaphorical position you'd be applying for?" I demanded.

"Any position they'd like to offer," muttered Clemmy.

"Wife," said Venetia, surprised I was asking. "If you want to marry well, you have to apply yourself. It's no use imagining that the right man will just fall into your lap." She cast a sympathetic look over at Divinity. "Unless they're the type to fall off the career ladder for you."

"You're here to learn more than just how to be a wife," I pointed out. "You're here to learn how to be *yourself.* The best version of yourself you can be."

"Of course you're here to learn more than just how to be a wife," said Mrs Angell, hurriedly. "Adele would tell you that herself. She has many other accomplishments that . . ."

"No, she wouldn't," said Venetia, quite confidently. "She says marriage is like a merger. You have to get your assets in order and be prepared to negotiate hard if you want to secure a decent pension."

I'd heard enough. It was bad enough knowing Adele was peddling her own brand of matrimonial carpetbagging while I was trying to suggest there might be more to a girl's horizons, but the merest thought that Lord T was the next in line for her acquisitions board was just too much.

"It depends what you want from your dinner then, doesn't it?" I said, quite vehemently. "Do you want an evening out, getting to know someone and enjoying yourself, or do you want to sit through an expensive power struggle for three hours?"

Venetia didn't even bother to reply.

Divinity put her hand up. "What am I supposed to wear? Should I wear high heels? I'm always falling off them after I've got a few on board but my legs are dead stumpy otherwise."

I turned back to the board and wrote "outfit?". Might as well make a lesson of it, I thought.

"Liv," I asked when I got in that evening. "What *are* you supposed to wear on a first date?"

Liv was in the kitchen, watching *Judge Judy* on the breakfast bar TV while she ironed some crisp white sheets. Her face was wreathed with steam and the blissed-out expression she used to save for her Pilates class. I'd taught her how to use the iron, mainly by calculating the Fashion Maths incurred by not sending everything to the dry cleaners, and now she was ironing everything in sight. I suspected I'd replaced one addiction with another, but at least it was keeping her out of TopShop.

"Depends where you're going, but you can't go wrong with a black dress and boots," she said. "Stuff some accessories in your bag and dress up or down when you get there." She held up a perfectly flat T-shirt and gazed lovingly at it. "You know I'd forgotten I'd got this? Ironing is just so cool! It's amazing what I've been finding in my laundry basket — it's like free shopping."

"How much have you ironed?" I stared at the pile. "That can't all be yours, surely."

"Oh, Jamie dropped a bag of his round, in exchange for some wine," said Liv, beatifically. "He wanted me to do it for a bottle, but I beat him up to a case. He said Dad would be proud."

I put my handbag down on the table and removed my shoes so I could massage the balls of my aching feet. "I could have done with you today. I just can't *talk* clothes like you do, not in front of that lot."

"Oh, you can," said Liv, kindly. "You've got your own style. It's . . . classic."

"You mean boring."

"No, I mean classic." She started on one of Jamie's handmade shirts — black, with purple paisley inside the collar and cuffs. "Not everyone needs to be a slave to fashion. You have a classic separates look. Pared down, simple. You use your hair as your accessory, which is . . . elegant."

I still suspected she meant boring, but didn't rise to it. I stopped massaging my feet and moved on to massaging my temples, elbows on the table, eyes closed as the smell of the fresh ironing calmed me down. It reminded me of growing up next to Nancy's never-decreasing stack of tablecloths and girls' shirts.

"You know you said you'd help me teach a lesson?" I asked.

"Mmm." The iron hissed.

"How about tomorrow?"

There was another hissing noise that might have been Liv, not the iron.

"How about that black dress?" I suggested. "Take one black dress and change it round. From work to party to nightclub — that's really useful."

"Isn't it more from party to nightclub to party to your mum's affair flat in Knightsbridge with that lot?"

"Well, yeah. But it's for the Open Day more than anything," I explained. "I need to have something useful to show people when they come to look round."

"I suppose I could," she said, dubiously. "But I'd have to practise. How about next week?"

"Practice is fine." I hauled myself up to a sitting position. "No time like the present. I'll make a pot of tea and you can use me as your dummy."

Liv shot a burst of steam at me. "Betsy, there's only one dummy round here, and it's not you."

* * *

One pot of tea later, I was standing in the sitting room on the coffee table in one of Liv's nineteen "definitive" LBDs, surrounded by a sea of scarves, shoes, jewellery, hats and fake-furry bits and pieces.

She'd picked a stretchy knee-length dress from Banana Republic, with a deep V-neck and three-quarter-length sleeves, and for my office look, she had added a cardigan and a shiny belt, and my patent Fiona Flemings, and twisted my hair up into a neat half bun, ignoring my pleas that it was about to frizz.

"Stop faffing about your bloody hair," she'd said. "It looks fine."

I'd made her take a photo, so we could create a workbook, and now we'd moved on to "the bar for a quick one after work" version.

I have to admit, I was secretly enjoying the experience. Liv had a real knack for pulling out the best features and blurring the rest. My reflection was looking gratifyingly unlike me: taller, curvier, much sexier and accessorised like the sort of woman who bought cruise collections.

"I just think of a sentence in my head, that I want the outfit to say, and go for it. This is saying, I have a great figure but I don't need to prove anything with it," she explained, pushing the sleeves up a little, and wriggling the dress just above my knee. "I don't know why you don't make more of your figure, Betsy. You should have men falling at your feet with knees like that."

"I work in a shoe shop," I reminded her. "The only men I meet who appreciate a good ankle tend to be ordering the larger sizes, if you know what I mean."

"That's no excuse." She hovered between two long strands of beads. "You've got to *invite* romance into your life, instead of expecting it to appear from nowhere. You've got to look. Sometimes it's there under your nose."

I thought this was pretty rich coming from a woman who worked in a veritable supermarket of available, well-connected fashionable types, most of whom were already fairly uninhibited, thanks to Igor's bohemian attitude to closing time.

"It's not like I don't have dates . . ." I began.

"Oh yeah, you're great at *dates*," she said. "You're almost as good as Jamie when it comes to dates."

"Sorry, Liv!" I pretended to clean out my ear with a finger. "It's just that I thought you said Mr Lover Lover and I were on the same sort of level there."

Liv put her hands on her hips, still holding a chain belt and a bolero. "Actually, you know what? I take that back. I think Jamie might have moved ahead of you on that. I think he's having some kind of early mid-life crisis. You know he came into Igor's this lunchtime, and asked if I wanted to spend an evening this week sorting out some bills?"

"And?"

"And he got his diary out, and apart from work, there were no dates in there at all."

"Blimey." My mouth fell open. "Not even on Friday?"

Liv shook her head. "He had a fancy dress party to check in on at ten, and then a personal trainer session first thing Saturday. And he told me he's thinking of buying a house with a *garden.* For a dog! I'm starting to think he actually means it about settling down. You might be right about there being some bird in New York. He's been really cagey about why he's back." She unclipped my hair and rearranged it over my shoulders, doing something to it with her fingers that separated the curls into thicker waves. "Good for her if she's given him a taste of his own medicine. Last time he was single for this long he had that funny rash on his . . ."

"I don't want to know," I said hastily. There were very good reasons for Jamie's playboy reputation.

"Mind you, that was five years ago," said Liv. "Things change. People change."

"No, they don't," I said. "That's just something marriage counsellors say, to drum up business."

"But they do. When they have shocks, like Dad disappearing. Would you like Jamie more . . . if he got a bit more responsible?" Liv asked, casually. She wasn't very good at casual.

"Isn't that like asking me if I'd like him more if he got a bit more Danish?"

"No." She swatted me with the chain belt. "Be serious, will you? I think you two would really balance each other out — if he stopped acting like he's God's gift, and you stopped thinking there's only one man in the world who's perfect for you, and that everyone else will mess you around and leave you up the duff."

"I do *not* think that!"

"Oh, come on, Betsy, you do. Some people, not me, obviously, might think that the only reason you're so fussy about Mr Ideal is just so you'll never have to find him, and he won't let you down." Liv fixed me with the sort of firm stare only a very, very best friend could. "But what if Jamie turned out to be sensible underneath it all? What if he got a briefcase, and stopped wearing shiny suits?"

"I think you've gone mad," I said, feeling my face go hot. "In that case, he'd stop being Jamie. Jamie *is* irresponsible, and outrageous. It's what makes him so horribly sexy and absolutely wrong for anyone with a brain in their head and . . ."

Liv's mouth twitched into a smile. "*Oh, really*?"

I realised what I'd just said, and hurried to correct myself. "I'm not saying *I* find him horribly sexy, I'm just speaking as an impartial observer of . . ."

"Do me a favour!" She dropped everything to gesture wildly with both hands. "I saw you over dinner the other night — you couldn't keep your eyes off each other! You go red when he talks to you, and I've never seen you do that for any other bloke. And the other night? You drank my wine twice and dropped nuts all over yourself when he laughed at your stupid jokes. Of *course* you fancy him. I'd have to be blind not to notice."

I looked down at my feet. How long had Liv thought that? Was it that obvious? I wondered if Jamie had noticed too. I wondered if Liv had any thoughts on how *he* felt about *me*, and immediately felt mortified. How old were we? Fifteen?

"I don't mind," she insisted. "I'd mind more if you carried on pretending you didn't. So long as you can still see what a *knocker* he can be and you don't mind me whining about what a bossy arse he's turned into. Go ahead and fancy him, please — you'd be the best thing to happen to him in years! In fact, I don't even mind you getting together." She paused. "So long as it didn't happen here. That would be too weird."

"Liv, there's no chance of that happening," I said hurriedly. "OK, so I have a bit of a crush, but it's not going to happen — it would be a disaster. For him as well as me. I need someone a bit calmer, more reliable, and he's after an heiress, isn't he?"

"But this is the thing," Liv looked tortured, as if it was killing her inside to admit it, "he's offered to help me change my mortgage! And explained home insurance! That is not the Jamie O'Hare I know!"

"Liv," I said firmly. "It's just shock, about Ken. It'll pass. He'll be caught red-handed with twin Tatlerettes by next week, don't worry. I'm happy to wait for the right man — I've said it before."

She sighed, and passed me a pair of diamante chandelier earrings. "Why are you still single? You'd make some lucky sod a wonderful girlfriend. Can't you start jogging in Green Park at lunchtime and bump into a banker?"

"Actually, there is someone nearer than that," I said. "The bursar, Mark. It turns out he's not quite as prematurely Dad-like as we thought."

I ignored the fact that Mark was still a bit touchy about lights being turned off, and had told me to bring in extra cardigans for the end of the week when, "according to his home weather forecasting kit", there'd be a nip in the air and no increase in the heating facilities upstairs. I liked a touch of grumpy charm, but I didn't think Liv would get it.

She didn't. Her expression struggled between encouragement and horror. "Not Mark Montgomery the Sandwich Rationer?"

"Yes . . ." I began, but she hadn't finished.

"Mark D'Arsey? Mark who put the Mean into Mean Average?"

These were just some of the names we'd come up with after the incident at the memorial. They were, I realised now, something of an over-reaction to his wine measuring cup.

"OK, but that aside . . ."

Liv peered at me. "Have you been sniffing furniture polish again?"

"So he's got a lot to learn about first impressions," I conceded. "But he's taller than me, he's not divorced or covertly married, he rides a bike, he's got a job, he isn't fussy about his fingernails, like some men who have manicures . . ."

"Leave Jamie out of this for the moment," said Liv, conveniently forgetting she was the one who'd brought him up in the first place. "That all sounds great from the point of view of your famous checklist, but, important question: is there a tingle? And I don't mean from the static in his bicycle clips."

Tingles were important to Liv. She had a Richter Scale of tingles, from passing attraction to full-on obsession.

I thought about Mark and the dry way he sometimes glanced at me, when he thought I wasn't looking.

"Yeeees," I said, trying to remember if it had been a tingle or just a chill. We'd definitely had a conspiratorial chuckle about Miss Thorne's Bond-villain cats, and I'd felt a promisingly warm glow when Mark complimented me on my lesson proposal. "I think there could be a tingle. He's the kind of man who needs a little defrosting, but you know I *prefer* that to the type who hit you with the charm and flattering comments about your hair straight away. It's not very English."

"Quite Danish, in fact," said Liv, archly.

"What's Danish?"

Liv and I turned to see Jamie strolling through the hall towards us, and I felt a definite tingle run simultaneously down from the top of my head and up from my toes, to meet in the middle of my stomach where it rippled out in delicious minitingles to all my extremities.

"Did you let yourself in?" demanded Liv. "Where did you get those keys? Do I have no privacy any more?"

Jamie jangled the offending keys. "Sorry, I've always had them, just in case you burned the house down making toast. Joan made me a set," he said, not looking at her but staring directly at me in my cocktail outfit on the coffee table. My knees felt hot all of a sudden. "Hello, Betsy? Is this the new table dancing course?"

I knew there was a witty retort in my brain somewhere, but it disappeared like a donkey sinking into quicksand as soon as he winked at me.

"Nurgh," I said brilliantly, and pulling the dress back down over my knees I wondered if I could step down without falling headfirst into the sofa or crashing into the television.

"You're interrupting my first lesson," said Liv, with a cross huff.

"And what's that?" Jamie settled himself on the sofa opposite and slung one long leg over his knee. He carried on beaming at me, and I tried to imagine if someone with eyes that outrageously suggestive could ever be sensible in a recognisable sense of the word.

"I'm going to show the girls how to make three outfits out of one dress using only different tights and simple accessories!" announced Liv. "This is the evening-wear section."

"And very good it looks too," said Jamie. "Ten out of ten. Can you make the skirt a bit shorter though?"

"Jamie!" Liv snapped.

"Well, if you've got it . . . You should be teaching the girls to maximise their assets, Miss O'Hare. Or should I call you ma'am?"

I felt too self-conscious to carry on standing on the table, but also too self-conscious to move in my current clumsy condition.

"Oh, Liv!" I said, as if I'd just remembered. "I found something at Kathleen's — Jamie, would you get my bag out of the kitchen for me?"

"And bring us a drink at the same time?" added Liv.

Jamie raised his eyebrow but got up anyway, with a sarcastic salute.

Gratefully, I scrambled down off the coffee table and slipped on a stray scarf as I did, stumbling towards

Barry the cat, who leaped backwards behind the sofa. It could have been worse.

"See?" said Liv, while I tried to disentangle the scarf from my heel. "You're a mess. And he's doing sensible fetching and carrying. You have a magical effect on each other."

"Shh," I hissed, "he's coming back."

Jamie returned with my handbag and a bottle of wine and some glasses expertly hooked beneath his fingers. "So when do I get to do my lesson?" he asked, peeling off the foil.

"Oh, here we go," said Liv. "What lesson's that going to be?"

"Something very useful to the modern girl and related to my area of expertise."

Liv cast a despairing look in my direction. "I swear to you, Betsy, what I was saying earlier? I wasn't making it up. I know it looks like I was . . ."

I opened my notebook and found the old snap of me and Liv outside our GCSE exams. "See, I used to be able to accessorise. Have you ever seen so many bows?"

Liv took it from me, as if it was an antique. "Oh, Betsy, you look so pretty! Look at you — I'd forgotten . . ." Her voice trailed away and she sounded quite choked for a moment.

"Forgotten what? Liv, are you OK?"

"Yeah, fine." She smiled, and I could see her eyes had filled up. "We just look so *young*, and you look so *pretty*. With your hair nice and curly and those old-fashioned dresses you used to wear, you know, before you went all . . .” She stopped herself and looked rather guilty.

“All what?” I asked her, but she fiddled with the belt she was holding.

“Before you went off to university and started dressing like a grunge librarian,” Jamie finished for her. “What was it you said? Alice bands were for girls who needed their brains holding in? Here, let me see.”

I looked at Liv. “A grunge librarian?” I mouthed. OK, so I’d dumped the prom dress and pearls look I’d had at school, but surely it hadn’t been *that* bad.

Liv carried on fiddling with the belt, as Jamie crossed the room and leaned between us to get a good look at the photo. My nose filled up with the smell of his cologne and warm skin.

“Oh, that photo! I had a copy of that,” he said, chuckling. “You’d never know what a pain the pair of you were at the time. Windy day, was it? Ah, my sister the toy poodle.”

Liv shoved him. “You were no better. You had spots and a Madchester bowl haircut. Anyway, what were you doing with a photograph of us?”

“Just to make me look popular, why else?” Jamie nudged her back. “Two more girls on my wall — swelled the numbers, helped the reputation. Anyway, this leads me nicely on to what I wanted to talk to you about, Betsy. My lesson.”

I glanced quickly at Liv. I’d almost forgotten Jamie’s offer of help; I hadn’t realised he meant it. “Um, right. You know, we do have a lot of party experts on the staff already and I don't want to make it *all* about socialising. And I know you're very busy . . ."

"Not too busy to help you out! And don't worry, this is going to be very useful *and* practical."

"OK," I said, warily. I wasn't sure that the girls would be listening to Jamie's actual words. Not if he turned up in full charm mode. "What is it? A guide to New York? That would be helpful . . ."

"No, How to Look Good in Photographs," he said, with a ta-da flourish. "I've been giving it some thought, and I reckon it's something everyone needs to know. As you can see," he waggled the photo, "it's not something that comes naturally, but who wouldn't like some top tips? We can mock up a "welcome to my lovely home!" *Hello!*-style shoot in the ballroom if you want. They can take turns to pose by the grand piano and practise looking modest."

Liv covered her face. "Oh God, Jamie, don't you listen to anything? Betsy's trying to make this course look approachable, not some It girl fantasy."

"No," I said slowly, "that's a genius idea. People never stop being photographed these days — weren't you moaning just the other night about how someone put the New Year photos from Igor's online and you look like . . ."

". . . the Ghost of Christmas Pissed, yes, yes." She scowled. "You don't know fashion critiques until you've worked in a bar full of theatrical gentlemen."

"Well, then!" I smiled at Jamie, nervously at first, because he smiled back and the flash in his eyes put me off my stride. "Your driving licence and your passport are just as important as a photospread in *Hello!* And who better to coach the girls than the son of a top model and star of more party photographs than Sienna Miller?"

"Exactly," Jamie began, then stopped, his face abruptly sober. "No, don't you mean, the owner and CEO of Party Animals, the highly regarded and very exclusive events management company?"

"Oh, yes," I said.

"I want them to take me seriously as a teacher, you know," he said, with a touching air of wounded pride.

"Well, quite," I sounded more brisk than I meant, because he'd started loosening the top button of his shirt as he made himself comfortable in Liv's huge white leather armchair. "I don't want Miss Thorne thinking I'm just hitting up my friends and flatmates for replacement staff. It's not like *I'm* a qualified teacher."

"I'm sure you're teaching them more than you think," he replied, with another teasing wink.

I opened my mouth to make some obvious retort about what he could teach them, fnar, fnar, but I couldn't. My mind had vanished into the quicksand again.

He *was* looking at me differently, I thought. That wasn't his normal, friendly expression. There was something almost challenging in it.

Was that what Liv had meant, I wondered? Did he want me to take him more seriously?

Or was he seeing *me* differently, in this clinging dress, with Liv's expert smoky eyes and my hair all over the place instead of neatly smoothed back?

A delicious tickle spread over the deep V of my little black dress. The bits that were covered in Liv's dramatic jewellery, anyway.

"Olivia," he said, without taking his grey eyes off me, "will you tell Betsy to stop ironing her hair flat and wear it like that more often? It's much more the Betsy I remember."

"Tell her yourself." Liv held out her empty glass. "Are you going to pour that wine, or do we need to teach you some manners?"

Jamie got up, but saw me blush, and as he got up to retrieve the bottle from the chiller, he smiled at me, a long, eye-contacty smile that warmed me from the inside out.

Thank God I wasn't standing on anything because I'd have fallen off it.

CHAPTER FIFTEEN

If you can't remember your godchildren's birthdays, give them presents on your birthday instead.

Between Liv's How to Dress lesson and Jamie's Image Management tutorial, the new timetable was starting to come together even more quickly than I'd hoped.

To be honest, it was leaping out of my notebooks, which were stuffed full of surprisingly relevant advice. Most of Franny's advice wasn't etiquette but simple good manners — it was still important to be nice to shop assistants and not talk about your diet over dinner. I just had to tweak it for the world of emails and iPhones.

I began to fall in love a little with the new Academy I was creating, as it came to life in my mind's eye. Every time I opened the thick creamy pages of my notebooks, I could hear Franny's voice, and I felt some of her elegance returning to the way I did things: I made more effort to stand up straight, and remembered to use handcream. But I was determined that my own more boring life experience was going to be useful too, and I outlined lessons in all the things I'd had to pick up the hard way: managing money, and knowing how to set about finding a job.

Just because Clemmy and the rest had lots of money didn't mean they shouldn't know how to look after it. The trick, I decided, was to present financial savvy as being as cool as knowing how to mix a good Martini. Mark — after some persuasion — agreed to take a class in Credit Cards without Tears, to be followed by How to Live a Million-Pound Life on a Credit-Crunch Budget.

We sat upstairs in his office on Friday lunchtime, almost out of earshot of Mrs Angell's Literary Appreciation class (this week: *Sex and the City*), eating sandwiches and exchanging competitively miserable stories about our student cheapskatedness.

"Kathleen used to tell me that money was an umbrella. That it couldn't stop a rainy day, but it kept your head dry," I said, swinging on my chair. "And Franny used to say a clever girl kept enough cash secreted away to pay two months' rent or buy an emergency killer outfit."

"And which would you pick?"

"Both," I said. "I was the only student I knew with Premium Bonds."

"Why? I can't imagine the Tallimores kept you short." He raised an eyebrow as he fished the tomato out of his sandwich and dropped it in the bin.

I flushed. "They didn't. I just liked . . . having my own money."

I'd actually had a *very* generous allowance, which I'd put away every month. I preferred spending the money I'd earned, and I supposed I had an irrational fear that one day, when my mother turned up to claim me, I might have to give it back.

Now, in my new Nancy Drew frame of mind, I was starting to think their generosity made sense, if it was really *Hector's* allowance they'd been giving me . . .

"So, you were telling me about your flatmate," said Mark, cutting into my thought. "The one whose life you're auditing? Do you make a habit of taking your work home with you?"

"God, no, she doesn't need my advice about *shoes*, she's a shopaholic," I started, then remembered he meant was I troubleshooting Liv's personal life in my Proper Job capacity, not was I road-testing stilettos. "Oh, um, no," I flustered as he looked at me oddly. "No, I just helped her . . . isolate her parameters. And identify areas of operational weakness."

Viz, I explained how to use the loo brush.

The phone rang on his desk, but for once Mark didn't grab it. Instead he nodded, encouraging me to go on.

"I'm agog," he said. "I'd love to know how you've turned the housework into fun little seminars with *heat* magazine titles. OMG, it's DIYSOS, right?"

"Are you trying to suggest I think of the titles then invent the seminars?" I demanded, feigning outrage. Well, half-feigning.

"I wouldn't dream of it," Mark replied. His face was so straight I knew he was joking.

We'd moved into non-Academy conversational waters. This was definitely a non-work chat, and the phone was still ringing. He swung on his chair and looked at me over his glasses and I was distinctly reminded of why I liked men in cashmere jumpers who made jokes about ISAs. There was a comforting solidity about them.

"Maybe you should answer that," I said. "Could be your secretary."

"Or yours?" He raised an eyebrow.

"I don't think so," I replied, with some confidence.

He picked up the Bakelite phone, but carried on looking amused — straight at me. "Mark Montgomery," he began, in his office tone, and then suddenly sat up in his chair. "What? Now? But it's in my diary for the end of next week. No, I'm *not* raising my voice."

He caught my eye and pulled the pinchy, Persian cat licking a nettle face we'd mutually agreed was Miss Thorne.

"Yes, she's here. I'll let her know. Absolutely, ten minutes." And he put down the receiver, looking grim. "I mentioned the termly meeting between me, Miss Thorne and Lord Tallimore?"

"Yes?" I said, hoping he was about to tell me it was cancelled.

"Well, we're having it right now. Lord Tallimore finds himself in London and thinks it would be a good time to discuss your ideas."

The sandwich stuck in my throat and I coughed. "But we can't! We've barely started the new lessons!

Miss Thorne will talk him out of it." I had a terrible thought. "We haven't warned the girls!"

Mark had put away his lunch and was sorting through papers on his desk, obviously used to emergency meetings. "Don't panic. It's better this way — she can hardly complain that it's not working if she hasn't seen them in action."

"But why's he back so soon?" I wondered aloud.

"Maybe he wants to see you." Mark handed me some papers. "There are some projections I did. Wave those at her, and I'll back you up."

I hesitated. "Are you going to go in there with your estate agency details? You might at least tell me now."

Mark drummed his fingers on the desk for a long moment, and said, "Not this time. I think it's only fair to give you a decent shot at making something of this place. And anyway," he looked up, and his face was more relaxed than mine, "I'm starting to be persuaded that it's not such a bad business idea, after all."

My tense expression was swept away by the smile breaking over my face. "It's a gentleman's prerogative to have his mind changed," I said, and swept out to the bathroom to smarten myself up.

Once I'd established that my buttons, lipstick and teeth were in sparkling order, I leaned over the top stair rails to the black and white hall two storeys down, and saw Lord T standing by the trailing ivy jardinière.

Excellent, I thought, and I rushed down the stairs, not quite as elegantly as Miss McGregor would have liked, eager to see him and to fill him in on what I'd started, before Miss Thorne got there first.

But as I got to the bottom, I realised I was too late: I could hear his familiar deep voice patiently trying to get a word in edgeways between another, more silky female voice.

I hated myself for eavesdropping but I couldn't resist.

". . . it's what Lady Frances would have wanted. You must have that break — I'll come with you if you need some company. Of *course* you're not too old for skiing! You're still a young man, Pelham!" The girlish giggle gave it away.

Adele. My teeth set on edge.

I wondered if Lord T knew that taking up sport with Adele was a risky business.

I listened, my hand tightening on the banister as she went on. Her voice was dripping in sympathy and was pitched at a level that suggested she was standing *very* close to him.

". . . *anything* I can do. I mean, if *anyone* understands what it means to lose a loved one suddenly, it's me, Pelham . . ."

". . . you're most kind . . ."

I marched down the rest of the stairs before I heard any more.

Lord T looked pleased to see me, but a brief flash of something crossed Adele's face before she replaced it with delight. As I suspected, she was virtually leaning on him, with her arm through his where she'd been patting the sleeve of his dark cashmere overcoat. She didn't remove the hand, though the patting had ceased.

"Here's Betsy!" she cried. "Darling, that's a very sweet little suit. I love the way you're showing the girls how they can dress for the Credit Crunch. There are some *gems* on the high street."

The closest Adele came to the high street was Sloane Street, going by the outfit she had on.

"Thanks!" I said, pretending not to have noticed the barb. "Franny always said that good shoes were the key to any outfit."

"Then you obviously get your sense of style from her," said Adele graciously, and then spoiled it by adding, "In a manner of speaking, of course."

Lord T seemed oblivious to any verbal karate, and carried on smiling.

"I understand we've got a meeting to go to," I said to him.

"Marvellous, yes." He nodded, happily. "Good timing, as it turned out. Adele here needed a spot of advice about a painting she'd seen, so I popped into Christie's with her, and suddenly thought, better to make a day of it, see you, catch up with Montgomery junior, have a chinwag with Miss Thorne about how things are shaping up . . ."

He did sound cheery, I had to give Adele that.

Adele touched his arm. "Would you two excuse me? I must go and prepare a lesson."

What? I thought.

"Marvellous," said Lord T while I was still open-mouthed at Adele's shamelessness. "*So* glad to see everyone pulling together in this hour of crisis."

"I try!" she said, and waved her French-manicured fingertips at us. "Toodles, darlings!"

I almost raised my fingertips back but managed to stop myself in time. There was something awful but hypnotic about Adele. Like a really well-polished king cobra.

The meeting, such as it was, took less than ten minutes.

I outlined my ideas, Mark backed them up, Miss Thorne made sad noises about "losing our precious exclusivity" and Lord T told me to carry on the good work and see what happened after the Open Day.

And that was it.

"Do you have time for a cup of tea?" he said, as we got up to leave. "I've been going through some of Frances's things — got one or two things for you at my club, thought you'd like them."

"I'd love that!" I said, eagerly, and we strolled across the bustle of Piccadilly down St James's, into the serene hushed world of the gentlemen's clubs, towards the Athenaeum, where Lord T stayed now when he came to London.

He settled me in a quiet corner with a tray of tea then disappeared, and returned with a sequinned clutch, which I recognised as Franny's vintage evening bag, the one her mother had had in India and which only came out on special occasions.

"Few things in there," he said, and I took his sudden awkwardness to mean they were of sentimental value. "Thought you'd like them. Tea?"

He poured from the silver pot, taking his time as I unpacked the bag slowly, seeing fragments of my childhood pile up in my lap. He'd jumbled everything together, like a man would: there was a pair of earrings I'd always coveted, very old ones with sapphire flowers, and Franny's pearl necklace, the one she'd worn every single day, with tweeds, sweaters, sundresses or swimsuits. A leather photo wallet with pictures of me on a pony, fat legs sticking out, while Franny held the reins, and Nancy and Kathleen hovered behind, in Barbour jackets. Another photograph, of Franny holding me, at about a year old, in front of the rosebushes at Full Moon Street. I was wearing tiny green velvet knickerbockers.

Lord T's voice cut in. "First photograph she ever took of you," he said. "She was too worried someone would come and take you away before then."

I looked up in surprise. "Really?" She'd never let that show. I thought *I* was the one who worried about being taken away from *her*.

"Was she expecting someone to come back for me? Someone in particular?" I'd never asked that before. "She must have had some idea, deep down."

Lord T passed me a teacup, and his face tightened. His natural reluctance to wade into the unknown waters of Emotion was battling with his equally natural instinct to do his duty. "Neither of us had the first clue who had left you. We made enquiries, naturally, but . . .

we were so happy to have you that it didn't seem to matter."

"But didn't you have your suspicions?" I pressed on. "Didn't Franny guess from the gold bee I had in the box?"

"The bee? Well, if she did, she never mentioned it to me," he said, bewildered. "Is it relevant?"

"All the Academy girls had them," I said. "I met someone at the memorial who recognised it immediately. She thought it was a sign that my mother was there, just before I was born. Surely Franny would have known that?"

Lord T looked absolutely horrified. "Who on earth said that to you?"

"Oh, an old girl," I hedged, not wanting to drop Nell in it. Just yet, anyway.

"And what did she say about . . ." He looked a bit sick.

"Just that they socialised a lot with a gang of Hooray Henrys who were rather notorious in their day. You know, rich and badly behaved and, um," I used one of Nancy's words, "colourful." I gazed with concern at Lord T. His face had gone the colour of cold rice pudding. I almost didn't like to add, "She said that Hector was one of them?" but I had to.

I managed to stop myself adding, *so was he my father? Was that why I was left with you*?

The question seemed to be asking itself, from the way he closed his eyes and let out a long breath. "That wasn't the Academy's finest hour," he said, eventually.

"Apart from your arrival, obviously. But I have no reason to believe that there's any connection."

It sounded like someone sticking their fingers in their ears and going lalalala to me.

"What was Hector like?" I asked instead. "I mean, what *is* he like?"

"He's the sort of man who didn't come back to his mother's funeral, for a start," said Lord T, shortly.

"Why not?" I found that extraordinary. Women had flown from all over the world to Franny's memorial service — and yet her only son had sent a pathetic circlet of white roses to the tiny family funeral. "He must have done something really bad not to be able to come back for that," I went on. "I mean, just what did he do? Was he *banned* from the funeral?" An awful thought struck me. "Is he in *prison*?"

"No! No, he's not in prison." Lord T rubbed his nose. "Betsy, it's very hard to explain . . ."

Because he's my father, I thought. Why doesn't he just *say* it?

The fire crackled as Lord T gathered his thoughts together, clearly uncomfortable. "Frances used to insist that Hector wasn't a bad person, just a very weak one. Not enough stuffing. Always was easily led, from the time he was at school, liked to do exactly what everyone else did. Those boys he hung around with — Frances and I weren't keen, not the sort of men she wanted for her girls, let alone her own son to be going round with. One chap was a racing driver, quite a good sort, but careless. Another was the son of some of our friends, who'd gone off the rails. Hector was perfectly charming, but he lacked much moral compass and I'm afraid to say when he really needed these so-called friends they let him down rather badly."

He stared into the middle distance and his voice trailed off. It was clearly causing him some pain, but I really needed to know. Even if it was terrible.

"You don't want to think that any child of yours could be rotten," he said, eventually. "But I fear Hector was, and probably still is."

I was beginning to realise how astonishingly good the Tallimores were at ignoring unpleasant details. This wasn't the handsome, amusing boy on Franny's bedside table.

"What happened?" I asked. "Why did he run away?"

"There was a car crash, involving some of his friends. Not his fault." Lord T let out a long breath. "It emerged that it wasn't *unconnected* with some gambling debts with some shady types that *were* his fault, and the same morning, instead of being a man about it, he upped and left. Left a note that broke his mother's heart, saying he'd done something he was too ashamed to admit to her face, and until he'd put it right, he couldn't face her."

I was holding the evening bag so tightly the sequins were cutting into my skin. "Was that when he went to Argentina? Did you find him?"

"After several years of searching for the little sod, yes. I had detectives on the case, combing everywhere I could think of. He'd gone to Buenos Aires, but before I could get there, he'd vanished again." Lord T looked furious but almost impressed. "First time I'd seen the lad show any initiative in his life. I kept trying to track him down, even went out there myself a few times, but it's not so hard to go missing in a country like that, if you've got the money."

He looked up and met my worried gaze. "And I must confess, Betsy, after a while, I decided that I didn't want to keep looking. Frances kept writing to him, to the last address she had, but he never replied. I didn't reckon much to that. I thought that if he wanted to be in touch with us, when he sorted out whatever it was that was so important, he would be in touch. I tried to find him when she fell ill, but . . ." He raised his hands. "Clearly, he didn't want to be found. The last thing she said to me was that she'd have forgiven him anything, anything at all, if he'd only come back. But I don't think I can forgive him for letting Frances spend her last moments blaming herself."

Hot tears were prickling at my lashes, burning my throat like mustard.

"But she had you," he said, reaching for my hand and squeezing it. "She had you, and you brought her so much happiness."

He smiled at me with those familiar baggy blue eyes and I felt a jolt of understanding. It was all falling into place in my head. Hector must have got some Academy girl pregnant, and gambled money to run away with her — and then got into trouble with moneylenders, and fled the country. She'd been kicked out by her horrified parents, dumped me with the Tallimores, and he'd vowed never to come back until he'd managed to put things right. Maybe she'd fled to Argentina too? Maybe they were out there together and that's why she hadn't been at the memorial either?

No wonder Franny and Lord T looked after me like their own — I *obviously* was. Lord T clearly wanted me to save the Academy, so she and Hector would have some reason to come back. Maybe I could bring things full circle, not just for myself, but for Hector and Franny and my mother.

I gulped down the lump in my throat. I'd been the cause of all this! I'd been the reason Hector had run off and Franny had died heartbroken. "I'm so sorry," I said.

"Don't be sorry," insisted Lord T, fishing in his pocket for a handkerchief. "Don't be sorry! You were the one good thing that came out of that hideous business!" He flapped open his hanky and offered it to me. "I'm just sorry I have to be telling you such a ghastly tale." He looked rueful. "God knows I'd love to be able to say, yes, my son Hector's a successful management consultant, with a degree from a good university. But I can say it about my girl, can't I? And it makes me very proud."

My girl.

I smiled through my tears and felt happy and guilty at the same time.

It was only when I was at home later, unpacking the evening bag again, that I found something at the back, hidden in the zipped compartment next to an old Estee Lauder lipstick, in Franny's signature scarlet red.

It was a folded piece of writing paper, with a short note scrawled in the middle, in round cursive hand.

"*Please look after my baby. I want her to grow up to be a proper lady. Thank you.*"

I stared at it, amazed. The note my mother had left with me. I'd never seen it before, just like I'd never seen the marmalade box.

There was something quite perfunctory about it, no kisses or explanations or even a name. Maybe that was why Franny hadn't wanted me to see it. But she'd said "my baby". I was someone's baby, and she'd wanted more for me than she felt she could give me.

And the writing was so young, just like the bobbly fat style Divinity and Clemmy had. Whoever wrote this hadn't been much older than them. My heart cracked for the teenager who had scrawled this, because it looked exactly like the jolly messages in the back of my notebooks — "See you in Val d'Isere!" "Caroline 4 Hugo 4 eva 2 gether!!!!"

Franny had kept it, hidden with her own treasures, and then made sure I had it, along with her pearls and her earrings and her art deco evening watch.

She must have wanted me to find my mother now, I thought, staring at the girlish writing. Because if I find my mother, then I'll find my father too. I'll find Hector for her.

I got my phone out of my bag and dialled Nell Howard's number with shaking fingers, unable to tear my eyes from the words. Nell would recognise the handwriting, wouldn't she? I knew it was a pretty standard Sloaney style, but even so . . .

"Darling, it's Nell!"

I started to speak, words tumbling over each other. "Nell! It's Betsy! I wonder if . . ."

"I can't take your call right now, too boring of me, I know, sorry, but leave a number and I'll call you as soon as poss! Thanks!"

I stared at the wall, as the phone beeped in my ear, and then hung up.

Then I made a new list in my notebook.

Open Day: things to do.

1. invite every old girl from 1980.

CHAPTER SIXTEEN

Conkers keep moths out of your cashmere, and spiders out of your rooms.

I had to hand it to Jamie — he certainly took his new responsibilities as an educator of young ladies very seriously.

For his lesson in looking fabulous in photographs, he would, he said, require the assistance not only of me, but of Liv also.

"I need you in a professional capacity, Olivia," he informed us, coming by the night before en route to an engagement party themed around *The Godfather.*

"You think they'll need a stiff drink before you start teaching?" I asked from my comfortable position wedged into the sofa with Barry the cat and a bowl of chicken soup.

"No, she'll have to wield that camera she's always going on about." He looked over to Liv. "You are still considering yourself a part-time art photographer, aren't you?"

"Yes," she said. "And move, you're blocking the Nazis."

Instead of going out, Liv and I had been engrossed in a money-saving showing of *The Sound of Music* — she was taking the male singing roles, and I was doing the nun stuff — and neither of us were really prepared for the sight of Jamie in full gangster mode. He suited the Don Corleone look more than you expect a blond half-Irishman to, with his hair slicked back and his strong jawline freshly shaved.

I felt very conscious of our money-saving hair treatments and hoped Jamie couldn't tell we had money-saving home pedicure socks on under Liv's Ugg boots.

"Great! Well, bring your camera and your laptop and I'll see you there at eleven," he said. "I'll need you too, Betsy," he added.

I slid down in my seat and wished Jamie had come round *after* the party, not before it. We had *Pretty Woman* lined up next, by which time our nails would be gorgeous. "Fine," I said, moving a cushion over the soup stain on my sweatpants. "I'll be there from nine. Don't use me as an example, please."

"Certainly not. Anyway, got to dash. People to see, parties to start. I'm pleased to see that giving up men hasn't led you to letting yourself go," he observed, as a parting shot.

Liv threw her cushion at his back as he left, then passed me the paper tissues, so we could have a good cry at the nuns foiling the Nazis as Julie Andrews ran up the mountain.

* * *

When Jamie swung into the Lady Hamilton Room at dead on eleven the next morning, less Don Corleone and more Don Draper, I saw a dramatic change come across the girls' faces. Their shining eyes followed him as he strode confidently towards the desk and slung his laptop on the table.

It was a bit like the moment when the keeper walks past the leopard enclosure with a side of raw beef.

Liv and I trailed in after him, but the girls didn't seem to notice we were even there.

"Good morning, ladies!" said Jamie, and I could tell his accent had shifted down a gear, to a trendy East London drawl. Jamie's accent was, like him, constantly changing to fit his surroundings. He was a natural at fitting in, and sensing what would go over best.

"Good morrrrrning," purred Anastasia, and the others murmured behind her.

"Today, we're going to do something very practical. I hope none of you are camera shy?" he went on. "Betsy, could you adjust the curtains, please?"

"Sorry?"

"The curtains." He nodded towards the dusty green velvet curtains. "I need to cut the lights."

I wasn't sure that the curtains wouldn't collapse in a shower of mould and moths, but I walked over to the windows anyway.

"Oh my God!" squeaked Divinity. "Is this like . . . Introduction to Glamour Modelling?" She looked more thrilled than horrified. "I don't mind doing a bikini calendar, but anything else has to be tasteful!"

"No!" I said, coughing as ten-year-old dust puffed straight down my throat. "No, it is not." I gave Jamie a nervous look. He hadn't quite explained what it was he was going to teach, just that it was "useful party skills".

"How's my technical expert getting on?" He glanced over to Liv, who was trying to plug her digital camera into his laptop. I went over to help her. Jamie had requested an improbable amount of technology for his lesson, including a projector that he'd "borrowed" from work, and, fortunately for Liv, insisted on setting up himself.

"Fine," said Liv. "Just don't go too quickly."

"I never go too quickly," said Jamie, with a grin and my heart sank. I really didn't want him to tease the girls. They were already cackling like a bunch of over-sexed geese.

"Are we ready?" he asked, and the girls squealed, "Yeeeesss!" as if they were in some cheesy Ibiza club.

"Oh God," Liv moaned under her breath. "Brace yourself."

"OK. Recognise *this*?" Jamie demanded and clicked the mouse on his laptop.

A huge blow-up of Catherine Zeta-Jones stuffing wedding cake in her mouth appeared on the white wall.

The girls gasped in shock.

So did I. "Where did you get that?" I demanded. "Wasn't that under injunction?"

"Private collection," said Jamie smoothly. "Or how about this?"

He clicked again, and this time Britney Spears and her knickerless undercarriage emerging from the back of a car filled the wall. The girls shrieked.

"Oh my God," I said. I'd never seen that without the black squares.

"Blimey," said Liv. "Shouldn't that be in the personal grooming class?"

"Or this?" A quick sequence of Paris Hilton, Tony Blair, and Beyoncé Knowles flashed up at a variety of parties. All three were frozen in that peculiar "my leg's gone to sleep and I'm playing an invisible trumpet" pose that happens when you're letting your hair down on the dance floor, unaware that someone is standing by with a camera.

I felt my stomach clench in recognition. I was a terrible "pointer" after a few beers. Most New Year's Eve photo albums featured me directing invisible Italian traffic. I sincerely hoped Jamie wasn't going to start fishing through my laptop for examples.

"The camera is like that best friend you can't quite trust," Jamie said, in a deep movie trailer tone. "Handle her right and she will reward you with flattering images you can use for up to ten years. Treat her recklessly, and you will forever be known as 'the girl with all the chins'. Everyone, whether they're appearing in *Hello!* magazine with their new nose, or just appearing in their own passport, needs to know how to look good in photographs."

Even in the dim light, I could see Divinity's face register shock, then intense desire to learn.

"Do you think this is Jamie's ultimate fantasy?" Liv murmured. "Telling socialites what to think, in a darkened room, while they stare at him like he's the second coming?"

"Of course, you can go too far the other way," Jamie went on, and clicked again on his laptop. "You work out what suits you and then you do it again, and again and again until it looks like you've got some kind of photographic paralysis . . ." As he spoke, a series of identikit images of Liz Hurley at Premieres Through the Ages whizzed past, in which she was doing the same left leg forward, chest out, hand on hip, dress slashed to the thigh pose. Even at someone else's *wedding*, for God's sake.

"That's a classic pose," said Venetia. "It makes your leg look longer and thinner."

"It makes her look like she's dying for the loo, more like," said Clemmy.

"What we need to achieve is something in between," said Jamie. "Something that looks natural, but in fact is totally rehearsed from every angle, and something you can do the second you see a camera. You want to walk into a party, throw your pose at the snappers at exactly the same time as you say, 'OK, that's your lot', and move on before they work out who you are. Gets you snapped every time."

"Oh my God, this is so useful!" breathed Divinity.

"The best way to look good in photos is to be *in* photos, and that's what we're going to work on today, with the help of Olivia O'Hare, top fashion photographer."

The girls swivelled to stare at me and Liv. I could see their teeth and diamonds shining in the semi-darkness, and in Divinity's case, a flash of white gum.

"Hey! Gum out," said Jamie. "Bit of flash on that and you'll look like you're wearing a mouth guard."

She had it out and stuck under the desk in an instant, which was quite impressive since she'd resisted all my attempts to remove it on human rights' grounds.

"Can we have some light, please?" Jamie asked, waving at me and beckoning at Liv.

I made a sarcastic aye aye salute and opened a curtain. Liv moved nervously to the front of the class with her camera, but at least she looked like a fashion photographer, in head to toe black and silver.

"Before we start, some dos and don'ts for party pics," he said. "*Do* delete any photo of yourself with a double chin, red eyes or sweat stains — takes a second, and it builds a reputation for being photogenic. Do assume that where there are people, there are cameras."

"And don't we know *that*, Anastasia," muttered Clemmy.

"You say press intrusion, I say five grand from the *News of the World*," said Anastasia. "Those loos were in a public area."

"Do powder your nose and your forehead unless you want to look like Shrek, and by that I don't mean any *other* kind of powder," he went on, with an arch look. "If you needed any other reason to say no, you might want to consider *this*."

He added a brief and possibly libellous flurry of celebrity shots on the projector, featuring gurning, bad dancing, coked-up pointing and several nosebleeds. "As someone very famous assured me just last night, you can't take it back to the stylist once you've bled on it. Never let anyone photograph you from below, never do a full-on face shot if you can help it, and, as you can see here, when people tell you to dance as if no one is looking, ignore them. There is *always* someone looking, and they usually have a camera. Now, shall we make a start?"

Jamie's advice turned out to be surprisingly practical. "Put tin foil on your knee for passport photos so you've got your own reflector" was just one tip I found myself sneaking into my notebook. He also made the girls take it in turns to be photographed by Liv, in "a variety of event situations", which they rehearsed with glee, and then critiqued freely on the projector.

Venetia excelled at the red-carpet poses, being very good at sticking out her long legs and feigning open-mouthed excitement.

Clemmy was less good at the wedding-style shots but that might have been because the mere thought of a cathedral made her scowl. ("Remember to aim for *serene* at weddings," said Jamie. "You don't want to upstage the bride, but don't let yourself be caught looking miserable, or else everyone'll think you've got a Bridget Jones complex.")

Divinity was a natural in front of Liv's camera, which she modestly put down to her existing celebrity lifestyle. By way of demonstration, she ran through her range of expressions. "When we had our new pool put in, we sold the photos to *OK!*" she confided in us. "I did 'thrilled with my new life in Madrid', and 'proud of my superstar dad' and 'having fun with my sister, Peace'." She demonstrated, and even Jamie had to agree, you could definitely see the different emotions there.

Anastasia was "fierce". Not so much in the Tyra Banks sense of the word, but just . . . scary. Liv photographed her around the ballroom, trying to make her seem soft and romantic, but she just looked as if she was about to tie someone to a chair and cut off their ear in every single one.

I had worried that Jamie's advice would be a bit, well, leery, but he was kind and honest. All those years of picking through party photos had obviously armed him with more knowledge than I gave him credit for, and he was gentle about the girls' pictures, concentrating on their good points, and ignoring the fact that Clemmy's nose stud looked like a giant spot, and Divinity had a thing about the left side of her face that made her contort herself into grotesque shapes to avoid it being photographed.

"How do you know all this stuff?" Anastasia demanded while Venetia was posing for "a very upmarket newspaper interview about my life" (hand on chin, eyes focused on the middle distance, knees together). I could tell Liv was only pretending to take photos now. "You are very expert."

"Oh, just experience," said Jamie. "My company organises a lot of private parties, and I like to make sure that if someone's paying me to throw the night of their lives, they've got fabulous photos to show for it. All part of the service." He grinned and I saw Divinity melt in her seat. "And if that means manoeuvring the hostess into more flattering lighting, then yes, I have been known to pick her up and carry her three feet to the left."

"Do you do celeb parties?" asked Divinity. "I would *love* to see your address book."

"Well, play your cards right, I could get you on a guest list or two . . ." He looked at me. "How about a field trip? I could throw in some wine-tasting, Olivia here could advise you on making sure your underwear's invisible, Betsy could offer her inimitable take on brushing off unsuitable men . . ."

"When can we go?" demanded Anastasia. "Dates!"

"Yes! Can we bring dates?" asked Divinity.

"I'm not sure Miss Thorne would run to that . . ." I said faintly.

Jamie carried on looking at me very seriously, although his twinkling eyes undermined whatever credible expert look he was going for. "You can't beat practical experience in being unimpressed by parties. I could arrange something, no problem. I mean, I know it's tempting but you've got to avoid being photographed with a star, even for your Facebook page," he said to Divinity. "They're always going to be thinner than you, and they're always going to have more make-up. Even the men. The trick is to be having such a great time in your own corner that *they* want to get over *there*. Then be photographed with them from afar."

"Can we?" Anastasia's eyes were pleading, like a very wealthy puppy. "Please?"

A field trip to the next vodka launch under the care of me and Jamie. I could see it all going horribly, horribly wrong.

"If the Open Day goes well," I said, feeling like someone's mum.

I'd never seen the girls so rapt or quiet, and their pens were positively flying over their notebooks.

Jamie left just before one, promising to return the following week with tips on getting a party going, but not so much that it went over the top and turned into a riot.

Hormonal twittering broke out as soon as he and Liv were out of the door, and I was glad, for his ego's sake, that he wasn't there to hear it.

"Ohmigod, ohmigod, ohmiGOD!" squawked Divinity, flapping her hands as if her sleeves were on fire. "He is like, the cutest man I have ever, ever seen! He is totally hot!"

"Jamie is verr hendsome," agreed Anastasia. She looked flushed, and uncharacteristically distracted. "And very knowledgeable."

"He's quite hot," said Venetia. "For a young guy."

Clementine nodded furiously. "Yeah. He's hot for any kind of guy."

"Oh come on," I said. "That was *appalling*! I mean, the lesson was great, but he was being a terrible flirt!"

"No, he wasn't! He was just being nice." Divinity's eyes were wide with adoration. "He said I had a *gorgeously expressive face*. He does proper compliments, that one."

"He *does* that!" I said, forgetting I wasn't really meant to know him. "You should see him at parties — he's always being followed around by adoring women. It's like he's leading his own conga line."

They all turned to look at me and I detected a new emotion in the air. Was that . . . admiration?

"Is he your ex?" asked Clementine.

"Jamie? I mean, Mr O'Hare?" I said. "No, he's not."

"Bit quick?" said Clementine. "Are you sure?"

"Yes, I am." I could feel the colour flooding my cheeks; even the slightest blush made me look like a Victorian maiden who'd accidentally walked into a nudist colony. I was about to tell the girls that Jamie was my best friend's brother when I realised that advertising the fact that proper teachers were now a bit thin on the ground and they were paying for the thoughts of random friends probably wasn't the best look.

"Mouth is speaking, eyes are lying," observed Anastasia. "As we say in the old country."

"So you do know him then?" Divinity persisted, her eyes sparkling with gossip. "How? Where from?"

The girls might have been a bit slow on the uptake with basic housekeeping, but when it came to potential gossip, they were a bunch of police sniffer dogs.

"He's . . . he's a business associate," I said. Near enough.

"He's far too cute to be a businessman," scoffed Venetia. "And he was wearing a really nice watch."

"Watches aren't everything," I said, trying to change the subject. "You're better off judging a man by his shoes than his watch."

"Why?" demanded Divinity.

"Isn't it time for lunch?" I tried, suddenly keen for the lesson to end.

Venetia and Anastasia immediately snapped their mobiles open and headed for the door, but Divinity and Clemmy hung back.

"What can I do for you two?" I asked. "Please don't tell me you want homework from Mr O'Hare." He'd be too flattered for words.

Divinity gave Clemmy a shove. "Go on. I told you, she'll know what to do. She sorted out my date with Matt, didn't she?"

"Did it go OK?" I asked, pleased. I'd been wondering how things had worked out but not known how to ask.

Divinity said nothing, but shyly showed me a new Tiffany heart, amongst the three she already wore.

Clemmy rolled her eyes and made a puking noise.

"Oh, don't be so mean." Divinity put her hands on her hips. "Right. Clem's got a problem. She's homeless. She's not talking to her mam. What can she do?"

"Homeless?" I feet guilty for assuming Clemmy's recent moodiness was just stylish gloom. "Clemmy, why didn't you say?"

"I'm not . . ." Clemmy glowered at Divinity, then said to me, in a sulky monotone. "I had a party, right, while my parents were at some *synod*, and I put it on my website? And more people came than I invited, like, only about fifty more, or something, and . . . OK, a few things got smashed. But nothing, like, *historical* or anything."

"They've got a posting to Namibia, and they've banned her from coming with them!" Divinity blurted out.

"I didn't want to go anyway!"

"And they won't talk to her! Or let her stay in their flat on her own! What's she meant to do?" Divinity spread her hands dramatically, as if she was acting out Clemmy's dilemma for a West End musical.

"She finds a flatshare," I said. "Doesn't she?"

"How?" muttered Clemmy. "I've never . . . I've never had to do anything like that. What if I don't like the people? What if I get, like, ripped off?"

She was staring at the floor, but I could see she wasn't quite as belligerent as before. Under all the eyeliner she looked scared and I felt rather sorry for her, even if she had just trashed her poor mum and dad's house. People just turned up at parties, you couldn't stop them. Especially when you were eighteen. There was a fine line between looking popular and calling the police from the loo.

"It's not so hard," I said, soothingly. "You just need to go through the papers and talk to some flatshare agencies about houses in the areas you like, and . . ." I stopped, as the incomprehension turned into plain fear on her face. "Would you like some help?"

Clemmy nodded, then remembered to look surly.

"But what about her mum?" Divinity went on, with another dramatic jazz hands gesture. "She's grounded her! And banned her from wearing make-up within a mile of the diocese! Which is, like, against her human rights! Even for a bishop's daughter!"

"Clemmy, I've had disaster parties, and this is what I'd do, if I were you," I said. "First, I'd write your mum a letter, on proper notepaper, and say you're really sorry. Over and over again. It'll mean more than flowers. And then I'd find a cleaning company and book them to do a blitz on the place. Then I'd look on the bright side: living on your own's fantastic!"

I patted her arm. "Bring me the evening paper and *Time Out* after this afternoon's lesson and I'll give you a hand. I bet you a tenner she'll beg you to come home the moment she thinks you're actually moving out. Then you can choose!"

"See? Easy." Divinity folded a new stick of gum into her mouth. "Cheers, Betsy. That's ace."

"Yeah, cheers. Got to go," said Clemmy. They slunk towards the door, but after Divinity went through, Clemmy turned back and gave me a quick, shy smile. It changed her face entirely, showing her white teeth and crinkling her eyes up.

"Thank you very much," she said, just like the polite bishop's daughter she was underneath, then slid out.

I felt something warm spreading through my chest and I realised it might actually be job satisfaction.

CHAPTER SEVENTEEN

Pop a Nurofen an hour before your waxing appointment and the whole experience will be a lot less agonizing.

It was too good to last, of course.

I woke up too early on Friday morning, with a banging headache, bathed in a cold sweat. I'd been dreaming that I'd gone back to Bellingham Manor, only to find Adele, in a wedding dress, at the front door welcoming guests, none of whom I recognised. She was ticking them off a clipboard, and when I got nearer I realised that not only wasn't I on the list, but I'd forgotten to make the three thousand meringue swans for the wedding cake.

Downstairs, last night's plates were still on the table. The drizzle began as I wheeled my bike out, and my phone rang in my pocket all the way. When I got to the Academy, I stomped upstairs to the bursar's office. The chilly office wasn't the best place for a girl with a sore head. My tulips had wilted in the Siberian cold, and I could see a pile of bills on Mark's desk that filled me with fresh dread. I'd barely got my coat off when my mobile rang and added another layer of gloom to the situation: it was Fiona.

My heart sank. I knew it had to be urgent. She normally didn't get into the shop before ten, let alone start making calls. I grabbed it and answered in a cheerful, reassuring manner.

"Hello, Fiona!" I began. "How are things in . . ."

"You've got to come back this afternoon," she howled, without preamble. "I'm sorry, but I need you up here. The stockroom's got mice and I can't work this stupid, *sodding till*!" I heard a muffled *thud*, followed by a mournful bleep.

"Don't worry about the till!" I said, calmly. "It's very simple. You need . . ."

"No, it's not simple!" She sounded hysterical. "It's *not* simple. It's new season time and Maria's sick and that new girl is pinching stuff and the mice are ruining my spring stock, and I'm here on my own and my kids need me and *I need you here*! Today!"

I swallowed. Fiona wasn't great in a crisis; I'd had to talk her down from several threatened shop closures, and spur-of-the-moment sackings before.

"I'm really, *really* sorry," I pleaded, "but I can't leave yet. I'll be back as soon as I . . ."

Fiona made a scary growling noise, and said, "Betsy, if you're not back here first thing tomorrow morning, then don't bother coming back at all."

"What?" I felt sick. "Fiona, you can't just sack me! I've worked for you for four years!"

"You're meant to be my rock! I need a manager I can rely on!" she yelled. "Consider this your notice period! You've seriously let me down!"

And she hung up.

The blood banged in my ears as I tried to take in what had just happened. It felt too surreal. Fiona had *sacked* me. I didn't have a job to go back to in Edinburgh. I was *unemployed.*

Oh my God. I went hot and cold and a wave of nausea rose up my throat. After everything I'd done for Fiona over the last few years — all right, so I'd abandoned her during the busiest time, and I didn't know when I was going to be able to go back, but this was important too!

I hated letting people down, but it was like being torn in four different directions — I couldn't not let *someone* down.

My eye fell on the desk, where I'd made a list of tips the girls needed to know — facialist, housekeeper, maitre d'.

Suddenly I couldn't bear to be in the Academy, a veritable temple to women who didn't *need* to get a job or worry about money unless it was how much to tip their manicurist. I grabbed my coat and ran out to Green Park where I sat for twenty numb minutes, trying to call Fiona back and failing to make a list of what I could do next.

I sat for as long as I could, but vanity eventually overcame my inertia: the drizzle was turning my hair into a ginger Shirley Temple nightmare.

It was the end of January and it was absolutely freezing, and I could hear Kathleen's voice reminding me that a problem faced is a solution started. I knew I had to go back and face the music, so I did, but unfortunately, the first person I ran into on my way back was Mark, on his way to teach the girls Budgets for Beginners. Being Mark, and fired up with the prospect of passing on his many hints on economising, he didn't notice my poleaxed expression, but insisted I come with him to his class for moral support, since my "history of gainful employment" was worth a thousand pie charts.

The irony of the situation wasn't lost on me.

"I'm going to give them both barrels on how they need to get real about money," he said, clearly relishing the challenge. He'd put on his work suit, to psych himself up, I guessed, although his socks were real "bottom of the laundry" specials. "You set them a good example — you don't mind if I refer to your job in the class, do you? The Maths degree is great on its own, but the fact that you've turned it into a practical career . . ."

"I'd rather you didn't," I said painfully.

"You're too modest," Mark replied, and gave me a smile that I'd have enjoyed on any other day, but today, it made me feel even more fraudulent than I already was.

He pushed open the door for me, so I could go in first and the girls looked hopeful that the male voice might belong to someone more exciting than the bursar.

"Oh, it's just you," said Clemmy, looking disappointed.

"Yes, just us," said Mark, not rising to the bait.

"No Mr O'Hare today?" asked Anastasia.

"No," I said, more tetchily than I meant to. I dragged up my last remaining shreds of self-control. "Today we're going to talk about how to be smart about money, which is a surprisingly attractive and useful skill to have these days."

"Indeed it is," said Mark. He slipped off his jacket and took out some notes from his briefcase. "Speaking as a man, what really gets my pulse racing is a woman who understands cars, the LBW rule and how to make her money work for her."

He looked up. "I think you'll find most hedgefund managers and millionaires are the same, so you might want to pin your ears back."

Venetia took out her silver pen and clicked it, deliberately. It was the first time I'd ever seen her attentive since Liv revealed her secret sample sale mailing lists in her Guerilla Shopping seminar.

"Now, contrary to what you might think, the Bank of Daddy isn't funded by central government," said Mark seriously, handing out his preprepared sheets. "And one day, you might find the cash machines don't work."

Divinity looked stunned and scribbled.

"Divinity, that's not literally what might happen," I said. "Don't panic."

Venetia cast a sly look across the desk to Anastasia, but Anastasia was fiddling with her phone, presumably checking that the International Bank of Daddy was still open.

"Are you two listening?" I said, and their heads jerked up. "Because this has just happened to a friend of mine, and it wasn't very funny."

"Venetia was probably wondering if that includes sugar daddies?" suggested Clemmy.

"Sugar daddies are the first to economise in an economic downturn," said Mark. "Take it from someone who manages private portfolios. You don't want to be the economy some married man is making."

"Smart girls need a rainy day account for emergencies," I said, hurriedly, before we could get sidetracked on to the career prospects of Other Women. "What sort of emergencies might you want to save up for?"

"An elopement," said Divinity. "Or a boob job."

"Or a boob job repair job," added Clemmy.

"Or a hitman," said Anastasia.

"I was thinking more of house repairs, or an operation or something," I said, feeling the yawning social gap between us yet again. "But it's always good to have some money in case you find yourself out of work or . . ."

It tripped off my tongue, after years of repetition, but suddenly I was talking about myself and I felt sick. Of course I had the recommended two months' salary in the bank, but that wasn't going to make me feel less angry or humiliated.

Mark spotted my choked expression, and raised his eyebrows.

I tried to hide my churning feelings. "The first thing to do," I said, "is to add up everything you spend — rent, food, entertainment, everything — and then see what you can save on, to put into your rainy day fund."

There was a general groan, and Mark added, "It's not *hard*. I've made these budget sheets for you — you just have to fill them in. We'll go through it together. Who wants to volunteer to come up here and be the example?"

Four pairs of eyes immediately glued themselves to the desk, as I could have predicted. Mark, who clearly wasn't an expert on the female mind, ignored the warning signs. "OK, I'll pick," he said, and pointed to the nearest girl, Venetia. "Would you mind?"

She tried to protest, but the girls bayed their encouragement and she found herself standing by the board, marker in hand.

"You'll all be doing this alongside, so concentrate!" he warned. "Now . . . How much is your rent, Venetia?"

"I don't pay rent." She tossed her head.

"Really? Where do you live?" demanded Clemmy.

"None of your business."

"You don't still live with your mum and dad, do you?" Divinity persisted. "Why didn't you say? I'd love to live with my mum still. Wouldn't have to worry about washing or owt."

"I *don't* live with my mum and dad!" said Venetia, turning red.

"Morden, isn't it?" said Clemmy, slyly. "One of those stops right at the end of the Northern Line?"

I was about to help her by suggesting she made up an amount, knowing how competitive the girls were about things like this, but it was too late: Clemmy had hit a nerve and the girls were on it like scent hounds.

"My parents live in *Wimbledon*!" snapped Venetia. She swallowed and pushed her hand into her mane of tawny extensions. "I spend *some* of the week there. And it's just temporary . . ."

"Let's say six hundred a month for rent," I said, quickly. "For the sake of argument."

"What was it you said to me about living at home . . . ?" mused Clemmy. "Lack of . . . what was it?"

Venetia clenched and unclenched her hands. "Can we move on?"

"Yes, let's," agreed Mark. "Now, utilities, by which I mean, heating, lighting, gas, that sort of thing. How much, roughly, do you think you need to set aside for that?"

"Three thousand pounds?" suggested Divinity, trying to be helpful.

"No idea!" said Venetia, defensively. "What sort of *normal* person knows that?"

Even though I could tell she was overplaying it, I still felt annoyed. "All normal people know how much their utilities cost!"

"I'm not a normal person," said Venetia and tossed her head. "And I don't want to be either."

"No," said Clemmy. "You're an It Girl who lives at home with her mum and dad. In Zone 6."

"Shut it, Batgirl!" snapped Venetia, and although my annoyance was building, I was curious at the glimpse of something darker beneath Venetia's smooth expression. She seemed very jumpy all of a sudden. She'd been happy enough to go on about her thousand-pound hair extensions and her waxing regime costing more than Clemmy's driving lessons — why was she being so defensive now?

"Am I misunderstanding," mused Anastasia, "or did I overhear Miss Buchanan say it was better to pretend your family were tragically diseased if they lived outside an Ocado delivery zone?"

"Deceased," Clemmy corrected her. "She said to pretend they're *deceased*."

"Ladies! Can we concentrate?" demanded Mark.

I thought that was unlikely, given the electric mood now crackling back and forth between Venetia and the others. Mark's determination to wring actual figures out of them was only going to end with some teeth-grinding competition about who spent the most on nothing, and I didn't think I could face that, not with Fiona's sacking ringing in my ears.

"This is intrusion!" Venetia slammed down the pen and stormed back to her seat.

"Right," I said, grabbing the marker myself. "We'll come back to budgets in a minute. Let's go back to basics. Fashion Maths. Pay attention. This is how you work out the difference between the cost of something and its value to your wardrobe. That one classic LBD you buy at full price for five hundred pounds seems like a lot, but divide it by one wear per month over, say, three years, and suddenly it's just . . . thirteen pounds per wear! That's a low CPW!"

"So long as you don't mind wearing the same drrrress so much," said Anastasia. I think she was trying to be funny, but I wasn't in the mood.

"You accessorise." I clenched my teeth and turned to Mark for support. He was frowning, his arms crossed.

"You've lost me," he said. "LBD? CPW?" He looked blank. "Is this advanced maths?"

"Little black dress," explained Divinity. "Cost per wear."

"Ah," said Mark. "Not really my forte, fashion."

"We know," said Venetia, with a sympathetic glance, which I took exception to, on Mark's behalf, though he remained oblivious.

But at least they seemed to be awake now.

"Don't forget the HFC: hidden fashion costs. That sequin dress you snap up in the sale for a hundred quid, reduced from a thousand," I went on. "Looks like a bargain — or is it? It's probably been dumped in the sale because the trend's over, so you have to wear it a lot while it's still in fashion. First time out, someone spills something on it, you have to take it to a specialist dry cleaner, it costs thirty pounds. You wear it again, someone says, 'Oh, it's your signature dress!' you feel embarrassed, you drink too much, you rip a section of sequins off, more dry cleaning, more repairs, suddenly it's cost you *two* hundred pounds . . ."

"I had no idea shopping was so complicated," said Mark.

"Sequins, cashmere, anything dry-clean only: high HFCs," I said, scribbling on the board. "Now, imagine your dad's stopped your allowance — how can you save up some money to spend in the sales?"

"I'd hold my mother to ransom," said Anastasia. "And get a pigs' ear from the butchers, and . . ."

"I'd go to *OK!* magazine and do a spread," added Divinity, thinking we were embarking on another role-playing sort of game. "Or go on a reality game show."

"I'm not joking," I said, firmly. "Serious now. Any suggestions?"

There was silence.

Mark and I exchanged a brief, pained look.

"Right," I said. "This is the simple way to save up for your . . . your boob job. You all bring skinny soya lattes in for breakfast, don't you? Call it two fifty per day, multiply it by five, that's twelve fifty, times fifty-two . . ." The pen squeaked on the whiteboard as I added up.

"Why fifty-two?" asked Divinity.

"Weeks of the year," muttered Clemmy. "On our planet, anyway."

"And that's six hundred and fifty pounds a year," I finished, circling the total. "That's without the muffins. Double it for muffins." I paused, as the penny — or rather, pennies — started to drop.

"Who here gets charged for late payments on their credit cards?" Mark asked. "That's at least twelve pounds a time, plus the interest . . ."

Fifteen minutes later, we stared at the whiteboard, which bore the Possible Painless Savings for disposable umbrellas left in taxis, manicures, and, specially for

Anastasia, parking fines. Her parking fines could pay for a whole second car.

"You see?" I said, rather pleased at the results. "You could have a holiday for that, just by doing your own nails and going into three more shops before you make that impulse buy!"

"I'm depressed just thinking about how much I've spent on taxis," said Clemmy. "I feel like I've got a hangover."

"Just think how much your hangovers have been costing you," said Venetia, sardonically. "You could have been investing that in some decent skincare and saving up for your old age."

I looked round at their faces and was dismayed to see how blasé they were. This wasn't the effect I'd been aiming for: I wanted them to feel the buzz I got from being in control of my cash, making it beat the budget every month, and knowing I had something to fall back on in an emergency. The buzz I'd managed to share with Liv, who virtually had a Children in Need-style totaliser of the money she was saving.

It wasn't about being *mean*, it was about being independent.

"Don't be depressed! It's smart to have back-up cash!" I said. "You think all those millionaires got rich by frittering money away?"

"Write it down then!" said Clemmy, in a snippy voice. She wagged her finger and tightened up her face, as she blinked to emphasise her words. "Quick, it's useful! For *real* life!"

The girls burst out laughing, then tried to hide their sniggers, and I realised Clemmy was doing one of her wicked impressions.

Then I realised she was doing *me.*

"Pennies make pounds!" she went on, getting more pinched in the face. "Oh no, wait!" And she flattened her hair down round her cheeks, then whined, "Ask yourself, do I *need* this bag? How much does it *cost,* versus how much is it *worth*?"

I felt myself go chilly, then hot. Was that how they saw me? Mean and lecturing? And someone to make fun of?

"You're not taking any of this seriously, are you?" I asked, and my voice sounded wobbly, even to me.

No one replied. Venetia and Divinity had the grace to look embarrassed and started fiddling with their notebooks, but Clemmy rolled her eyes defensively and glanced at Anastasia, a familiar gesture which I regret to say only stoked the flames of my temper.

They might not care where the next venti soya cappuccino had come from, but I'd just lost my job, trying to keep this place open! I'd done my best to make these lessons interesting for them, persuaded my friends to help, swallowed my pride and gone back to a place that I'd promised myself I didn't need.

Mark had been right from the start. It was all a total waste of energy.

They didn't want to learn any of the things I thought were useful for life. Girls like Divinity or Clemmy didn't buy houses, they *inherited* them. They didn't have to apply for jobs or worry about being sacked.

They just wanted to have a good time, all the time. And normal girls, well, weren't they too busy *working* to sign up for classes like these? Like I should be?

I had a sudden, heart-breaking insight: I couldn't ever make this work because I wasn't Franny. She was the real deal, a truly confident, socially assured lady, whereas I was a shoe-shop manager trying to recreate something that only really existed in my notebooks, in my child's-eye view of how lovely it would be to be grown-up. I couldn't bring Franny back by teaching modern girls old tricks, and if my mother was anything like these spoiled brats, with no idea of what it meant to do a day's work, did I really want to find her?

A dull ache spread through my chest and up into my stomach as every reason for being here slithered between my fingers and trickled away.

I put the cap back on the board marker and clicked it shut with the palm of my hand. "Over to you, Mark," I said. "I think you can take things from here."

I passed Paulette's office on the way out, and barely registered that she was on the phone, being massively indiscreet about the Academy's alumnae.

I just wanted to be out of the stifling, airless museum and back into a world I understood.

CHAPTER EIGHTEEN

Turn off your phone: passive conversation is as annoying as second-hand smoke.

The air outside was damp, and I pulled my collar up around my neck and set off with my head down against the chill.

I'd no sooner taken five steps than I bumped into someone heading towards the Academy.

"So sorry!" I began, stumbling back in full apology mode. "I wasn't looking . . . Oh."

It was Jamie, standing there in a double-breasted black coat that made him look like he was about to star in a Guy Ritchie film about an old Etonian bank robber.

"No need to apologise!" he said, throwing his hands in the air in fake surprise. "This is a top street for bumping into well-mannered ladies. I come here a lot."

I wasn't feeling very smiley, but one crept out.

"Lovely! I was on my way to see you, actually," he went on.

I didn't think I could summon up the necessary lightness of heart to flirt with Jamie right now. "I was just going out for a coffee," I said.

"Then let me join you. Do you mind?"

I shook my head, and we started walking down towards Shepherd's Market.

"I've been thinking about this Open Day of yours, and what you could do to get bodies through the door," he said, conversationally. "I reckon that's your main challenge — once they're in, and you explain it all, they'll sign up in droves. You've left it too late to advertise, but my old flatmate Charlie runs some listings websites, and a daily shopping blog. Huge mailing list, lots of different sorts of people. I know he'd give you a bit of a plug, if you wanted. If you give me the details, I'll give him a ring."

"Thanks," I said, surprised and rather touched. I had been worried about how we'd get the word out, and hadn't even mentioned it to Liv yet. "That would be great."

"And I had lunch the other day with a friend of mine who works on a features desk. Have you met Imogen? She *loves* the idea of a modern finishing school, and I sort of gave her the idea of writing something about it, my how-to boot camp kind of thing. Imogen's a real sucker for hints and tips and stuff. Always going on about how to get stains out of shirts. Wine stains, usually. But not always. Quite a fun girl, Imo . . ."

"A friend, eh?" I said, out of habit.

"From university," said Jamie, turning his coat collar up so it framed his square cheekbones. "Anyway, I thought you girls were meant to approve of men with lots of friends. Shows we're not total bastards." He looked at me, over the collar, and just his eyes were visible. They twinkled at me. "Should I be insulted or flattered that you think every woman I bump into is an ex?"

"Well, if they're not already, they will be before long," I said, resorting to a bantering tone. "It's just a matter of time and three dinners."

I don't know why I said that. I didn't really mean it, but we seemed to slip into those roles so easily, and Jamie didn't seem to mind. In fact, he seemed pretty amused to me.

"Maybe it's just sensible girls I have no effect on," he mused. "You've managed to resist." Theatrical pause. "So far."

"Ah, but I've seen the photo of you in your page-boy outfit at your auntie Breda's wedding," I retorted, smartly. But my cheeks went hot and I was glad we were walking side by side.

"So, can I give Imogen your number?" Jamie went on. "I thought you could set up a good photo-op, like How to Dress For Your Ex-Boyfriend's Wedding, or something. You could show them the good manners' outfit, and the get your own back outfit. Ask Liv, she's done both often enough. The girls could help there — bet they've got some stories about pulling focus at the reception . . ."

I groaned inwardly. The thought of persuading the girls to cooperate in front of a journalist made me feel ill — and that was if it was still worth doing.

"What now?" Light drops of rain had begun to fall, and Jamie had to increase his pace to keep up with my cross fast walk.

"Bad morning," I said. "I think I might have reached my limit."

"With what?"

"With the girls. With everything." I stopped walking, suddenly right out of energy. We were in the middle of the street, and Jamie pulled me into a doorway to avoid being crashed into by the pedestrians walking quickly to avoid the drizzle. "They don't care about what I'm trying to do. They don't understand about real life, or real problems. And I've been sacked."

"You? Sacked? By who?"

"By Fiona, my boss. In Edinburgh." I leaned my head back against the red brick wall and closed my eyes. Telling Jamie finally made it real. "She told me to get back today to deal with her crisis, I told her I couldn't, she told me not to come back at all."

"Oh, bad luck," said Jamie. "But everyone gets sacked at some point. It's character-building."

"I've never been sacked," I said, sorrowfully.

"Then you probably weren't having enough fun at work." He nudged my arm. "Anyway, haven't you been bellyaching to Liv for months about getting a new job?"

"Well . . ." Had Liv been discussing my moans with Jamie? And had he been interested? "Yes."

"So there you go. You don't have to worry about resigning. And you've got another job lined up already," he said, reasonably.

"Where?"

"Here, you plum! Lord Tallimore's paying you the going rate for your consultancy, isn't he? You could either take that cash and go back to Edinburgh and overhaul finishing schools on a professional basis, or you could stay here and teach at the one you're successfully overhauling now."

"If it stays open."

Jamie pretended to slap his own head. "Well, what better incentive have you got to make it work?" he demanded. "This is *business*, Betsy. This is what it's like. You think that Douglas and I didn't spend a fortune hiring our friends to pretend to make our first twenty-four parties look overbooked? You think we started out experts in the art of high class entertainment?" He paused. "Well, obviously, I did, but it took a while to bring Dougie up to speed. The coaching I had to do to get him to stop dancing like his dad . . . You should see him now, though. He dances like *my* dad."

He waved his hand in front of my face so I had to look at him instead of gazing gloomily at the pavement.

"Sorry," I said. "It's just getting . . . I don't know. I feel out of my depth."

"Really? That's not the impression I get." Jamie seemed genuinely surprised. "You've got everything up and running in what, a few days? And I love your lesson ideas; I was telling Imogen and she couldn't wait to get her name down for next term."

"It's not just the lessons." I threw up my hands, not sure if I could put it into words. "It's everything *else*. I mean, just going back there's bringing up all sorts of things I haven't thought about in years. How bad I felt when I wasn't allowed to go as a student, because it wasn't for the likes of me. Having to think about my mother. Wondering who I really am. I mean, I'm not *like* those girls in there."

"Of course you're not. You've got drive and purpose. And determination. And of course you're about a million times more sensible . . ."

"That wasn't what I meant." I didn't want Jamie to tell me how sensible I was. The girls had already made me feel like the dullest woman in the world this morning, and to make it worse, sensible women didn't get sacked. Or seduced in nightclubs. Or flown to Venice. Or snogged by Jamie O'Hare. Or anything. We just paid our tax on time and knew how to change fuses.

I pushed myself away from the wall and started walking again. "I need coffee."

"No, you need a walk and a change of air. Weren't you brought up by a proper nanny? Come on, let's go to the park."

Jamie steered me away from Berkeley Square, over the solid traffic on Piccadilly and into the peaceful stretch of Green Park. The grey skies and bitter weather had kept most of the office workers inside for lunch and we strolled down the tree-lined avenue almost on our own. I felt better, walking along in silence together. There was something about the orderly trees, and the sight of Buckingham Palace and the London Eye rising up over the skyline that distracted me nicely.

Jamie bought us hot coffee from a stall and I wrapped my cold fingers around it to keep warm as we headed towards the huge golden statue of Queen

Victoria where tourists were taking holiday photos of the Guards stamping around inside the palace gates.

"Last time I watched the changing of the guards at Buckingham Palace, I was five years old and had mittens on a string," I said as we leaned companionably against a pillar.

I thought Jamie was going to joke back with some gag about his East End upbringing, but he didn't. Instead, he turned and looked at me, and his eyes made me melt, despite the cold.

"Don't give up on this, just because you've had one bad day. What you're doing is genius," he said. "I wish I'd thought of it myself. You're selling something everyone wants: secrets to a good life. That's what makes you confident, feeling like you're in the know. You've always had it. Mum taught Liv how to walk like a model but you were always the one who looked like you were on a catwalk." He paused. "You can't see it yet, because you want everything to be exactly like some vision you've got in your head, but give them a few weeks and I bet those girls will surprise you." He looked meaningfully at me. "They'll want to be like you."

My heart bumped, and I noticed how each grey iris had a bright ring of amber around the outside. Was that what made Jamie's eyes so piercing? Or maybe it was just the way he was looking at me, as if there were no one else around.

"Your problem is that you set incredibly high standards," he went on. "Not for other people — you're *great* at helping other people — but for yourself.

There's no point me telling you it'll work, you've got to believe it, instead of assuming the worst." He prodded my shoulder, playfully. "It's going to be amazing. Stop thinking it won't."

"You're making it sound so *easy*." I hoped I sounded casual, as if I wasn't buying this flattery, but my voice was unsteady. So were my knees. I groped for something clever to say but all I could think of were the guards behind the gate, going through their drill, pitch perfect and absolutely on time, their uniforms glowing in the winter sunshine.

"Why are you so hung up on being perfect," he said, still giving me that disconcerting twinkly look, "when actually, a little imperfection is the most attractive thing in a woman? If she doesn't mind it. I'm sure Franny would have told you that, if you'd asked." He nodded towards the palace. "I liked the Queen a bit more when I read about the Tupperware cereal boxes."

I still couldn't think of the right thing to say. I didn't want to be flippant; I didn't want to be sensible. Maybe that was a bit too ambitious, in my current state of mind, so I said nothing, which seemed like the best option.

"Do you want to carry on walking?" he asked, as if he was asking me to dance, and I nodded.

We strolled back through the deserted park and around the cigars-and-tailors heart of St James, past more shiny-booted guards outside Clarence House, then past Nell Gwynne's old residence, a royal gold-digger even Adele would be proud of. We'd started back towards Full Moon Street, through the tall townhouses of Mayfair which hid their modern offices behind graceful balconied facades when I finally worked out what I wanted to say to Jamie.

I touched his sleeve, and he stopped walking. "Thanks," I said. "For listening. And for all your help with lessons and the Open Day and everything. I'm grateful. Really, I am. I couldn't have got going without you and Liv, and . . . it means a lot to me that you think it'll work." I corrected myself, trying to be positive. "That it *can* work."

"You're welcome. I think it *is* working. I wish I could make you believe it."

We both looked at my fingers, long and white against the navy wool of his overcoat. My red varnish, done the evening Liv and I watched *Pretty Woman* was still unchipped and, thanks to the oil I'd dropped on it, shone like wet ladybirds. Without thinking, I moved my hand up to Jamie's shoulder, and squeezed, and then, when that suddenly didn't feel like enough, I lifted my head and pressed my lips against his cheek.

I don't know where it came from. It certainly wasn't very sensible.

Jamie's skin had a faint chill, from the rain in the air, but it was smooth against my lips, and without thinking I kissed him again, just to feel it a second time. It was only his cheek, and only a friendly kiss. The rain was falling more heavily now, but I could sense the warmth between our faces, as we leaned together for a moment.

Then I stepped back, surprised at what I'd just done. "Um . . ."

"Um?" he repeated. I thought he might arch his eyebrow and make a joke of it, but he didn't — his expression was less certain than before.

"Sorry, I . . ." I stammered. My mind went blank, apart from a little voice saying that this would be an excellent Awkward Moment to discuss.

Jamie broke the tension by reaching into his laptop bag and bringing out a collapsible black umbrella, which he shook out and held over my head.

"Where's your umbrella?" he asked. "I thought you carried everything in that bag?"

"Normally, yes," I said, flustered. "I must be losing my touch."

"Sorry, this isn't a very big one, if you'll pardon the expression. Do you mind?" He put his arm around my waist so we could huddle closer together. "I don't want to get my hair wet, you see. And I'm sure you don't want to ruin your lovely hairdo either."

My hair! I clapped a hand to my head and felt the familiar crunch of frizz. I'd just about calmed it down with a dab of handcream — top emergency measure — but this rain was more serious. I started scrabbling in an inner side pocket of my bag for the emergency plastic rainhood. It was revolting and looked like something Kathleen might wear, but the alternative was too grim to contemplate.

My fingers closed on the rainhood and I yanked it out. Clear plastic with big white spots on. I hesitated. There was a time when I'd have had a *silk* scarf in my handbag for this very eventuality, damn it. My life really had gone too practical.

"If you're worried about what you look like, it's only me," said Jamie, good-humouredly. "Don't forget I've seen you tie yourself up in your own wrap dress after a couple of bottles of champagne. Do you remember Liv's eighteenth?"

"No," I said, tying the hood furiously under my chin. "That wasn't me. You're confusing me with another redhead who had an allergic reaction to the canapés."

"*An allergic reaction to canapés*, I'd forgotten." Jamie put his arm round my waist and hurried me along under the umbrella. "That was a very good night," he went on, nostalgically. "Do you remember lying on the boat deck after everyone had gone? And how you tried to tell me that the Chelsea and Westminster air ambulance was a shooting star?"

I did remember. I'd re-enacted it nightly in my brain for months after: Ken had hired a boat on the Thames and right at the end, when we were cruising back toward the dock, Jamie, Liv and I had crashed out with a bottle of champagne, gazing up at the ink-blue night sky, until Jamie's girlfriend at the time had arrived to drag him to the next party. My replay focused on the feeling of Jamie's hair very close to my cheek, the smell of his breath. Liv had fallen asleep, or passed out, for ten crucial minutes, in which Jamie and I were technically lying there together, talking rubbish in whispers so as not to wake her.

We'd stopped walking again.

"Yes," I said. "I do remember. You tried to tell *me* that we were looking up at The Great Typewriter and Orion's Dustbin."

The rain drummed on the umbrella above our heads. It was so small that we were standing almost toe-to-toe. I felt very conscious of my crackling rainhood, and of Jamie's wet woollen coat, and his breath mingling with mine.

I loved that memory because it had been the closest I'd got to being one of those lucky girls whom Jamie swept off their feet. I could feel the wooden deck shifting beneath me as we'd leaned closer to catch each other's whispers, but even as my fingers were twitching to touch his, a cool voice had warned me that this was how girls went wrong, that this was probably how my father had tumbled my mother into some romantic clinch that had ended up with me, and all my messy life-ruining consequences. I'd been eighteen — a very young eighteen, still living my life through the elegant rose-tinted world of Franny's notebooks and Nancy's breeches-strewn romances.

I'd never know whether Jamie really did try to kiss me, or if it was just the boat catching a swell, but I moved anyway, and the moment had gone, along with the ducks floating past in the dark.

"I like to think I'm older and wiser now," he said. I couldn't quite meet his eye. "If I ever get to lie on a deck on a warm summer night, half-cut, with a beautiful woman suffering from a canapé allergy, I'll come up with much better made-up constellations." He paused. "Or not bother with the constellations at all."

I couldn't deal with the sudden change in mood. Was this flirting? Or just friendly teasing? "And if your sister was there?" I asked, and my voice squeaked at the end.

"I'd chuck her overboard."

The rain seemed to be easing up, and for the first time in my life, I wished it rained more in London.

"Can I take you out for supper?" asked Jamie. "Liv's working on Thursday. I don't know whether you're also boycotting men buying you dinner in your campaign to emancipate her."

"Um . . ."

I wanted to say yes, but something held me back. I knew technically what the notebooks would tell me to do — suggest somewhere matey, not datey, to put temptation out of the way — but I was scared that it would live up to my expectations. Scared and a bit thrilled.

Come *on*, Betsy, I told myself, you never have a problem fixing dates with anyone else. You're *teaching* it now, for crying out loud. You're twenty-seven.

Jamie wasn't put off by my wavering. "You could add it to the syllabus?" His eyes glinted with amusement. "Just don't tell me what lesson you're extrapolating from it."

I didn't know what to say. I smiled goofily instead.

"I'll take that as a yes," said Jamie. "Now, can I put you in a taxi back to the Academy? Don't want you to be late for Deportment."

"Yes," I said. "And it's not Deportment, it's What Every Chic Woman Needs In Her Drinks Cabinet. With our very own Mark Montgomery, who is, I believe, an expert on single malts."

Jamie rolled his eyes in horror. "Let me get you a taxi as soon as possible. You won't want to miss a minute of that one!"

I smiled, and squeezed his arm again.

I was going to go back. And I was going to make it work.

CHAPTER NINETEEN

Don't lend money to friends, it's the fastest way to break up a friendship (after sleeping with their husbands). Only lend what you can afford to give.

There were some silver linings to my suddenly unemployed status. Or, as Kathleen put it, when I popped in to tell them I'd be staying in London a little while longer, "It's an ill wind that closes a door and doesn't open a window."

I didn't have to lie to them about the shoe shop/management consultancy thing, for a start. From now on, as Liv reminded me constantly, I really *was* a consultant.

"Sometimes a total disaster is the best thing that could happen to you," she insisted cheerfully, as we made supper that night. "I mean, look at me. This time last month, I was doing my head in about Finn Crozier, and I thought an ISA was some kind of pudding. Now, I'm getting paid to talk about how to buy the right shoes! And you're living here with me! And even my brother is taking me seriously!" She beamed with delight. "Result!"

"He is?"

"Yes," said Liv. "He said it's about time I followed your example. He came into the bar this afternoon, and told Igor he should consider making me manager. Igor's giving me some extra evening shifts to try me out. So that's great, isn't it? It's like Jamie said, if I'm working, I can't be going out on dates with the wrong man *and* I'm paying off my credit cards faster."

I stopped, halfway through making a cup of tea. Was that my example? Working and not going on dates? "Jamie said that?"

Liv looked up from her computer, where she was compiling a fantasy shopping basket at Net A Porter. I'd changed two digits in her auto-input credit card, so there was no danger of it going through but she still got the shopping hit; we agreed fantasy outfits was a good way of soothing her tissue-paper cravings, a bit like Nicorette patches.

"I don't think he meant it in a bad way. He's being very helpful at the moment," she observed. "With the Academy, and that. He said he saw you this lunchtime too. That's twice this week. He's spending more time there than he is at his own business." She added a meaningful eyebrow raise.

"Oh, he's not daft — probably scoping for new customers," I said airily, though inside I let myself hope there might be another reason. "Four twenty-first birthday parties, four engagement parties, four 'look at my new teacup Chihuahua parties' . . ."

"Well, you think that if you want to. I say different. Is he giving you the benefit of his publicity-generating skills for this Open Day?" said Liv, clicking a pair of terrifying high heels into her basket.

"Mmm." I started hunting in the cupboards for supper and found a jar of black truffles, left over from some Fortnum & Mason food parcel. "He's set up a journalist to come in next week and do a nice puff piece about being finished, twenty-first-century-style." I paused, jar in hand, as I suddenly saw a new angle. Imogen was a journalist: wouldn't she check up on my qualifications? What if she found out I'd just been sacked — from a shoe shop?

I looked over at Liv, blissfully adding handbags to her look. "Will you come in too? For some moral support?" I asked.

"Yeah, right, tower of academic strength, that's me!" said Liv, and then realised I was serious. "Why? You're not *worried*, are you? It'll be fine . . . Jamie's hardly likely to send some hard-nosed war correspondent."

"I know, but . . . I just think we need to *keep an eye* on it. Miss Thorne's somehow convinced herself there'll be photographers crawling over the place, 'taking advantage of the girls' natural exuberance'," I said, flinching again at the mere memory of the glass-cutting glare she'd given me. "She started going on about discretion and the *need to remain exclusive.* She just doesn't get the fact that we have to make people come to this event, to get them to sign up."

"*You're* going to be in the feature though, aren't you?" Liv paused on the jewellery page. "Because, God bless Miss McGregor but she's not your cutting-edge life-coach type. You need to be in there, looking all dynamic but normal. Kirstie Allsopp Lite."

I ignored the last bit. "Well, that's the other thing . . . I thought that if my mother was somewhere in London still, she might read the feature and recognise me. Then come to the Open Day! I've invited all the old girls I could find, but the letter didn't come from me, of course, it came from the desk of Miss Geraldine Thorne. And it's not like I can enclose a photo of myself in that, is it?"

"Genius!" Liv tipped her head on one side. "You've got to let me dress you. Because — and I say this as a friend, Bets — any old girl's going to take one look at you in that suit and think, ooh no, that can't be my baby. I left a child in colour, not black and white."

"And what's wrong with this suit?" I spluttered, but I knew what she meant. I'd been trying to add some more colour recently, and my old style was slowly coming back, but I was still miles off the beribboned, becurled, bewilderingly girly girl I'd been at school. I couldn't throw off ten years' simmering identity crisis just like that.

Liv swivelled the computer round to show me. "This is the kind of thing I had in mind. It'll make you stand out. Show off your hair."

She had picked out a bright blue Marni dress, with a full skirt and neat jacket, finished with killer heels and a clutch bag.

I gulped. It was gorgeous. Was that me? Could I be that colourful?

"That's an outfit that says, I'm in charge but you're going to like it," said Liv, confidently. "And that, in my opinion, is you all over."

"Maybe for the Open Day," I said.

Imogen the journalist rang me in the morning to confirm that she'd be "popping in" for a day's tuition at the Academy on Thursday, and I sprang into action to make sure it would be memorable for the right reasons, and not because Anastasia chose that morning to be busted by the Red Route police.

Mark called round at lunchtime the day before, to go through my final plans, and also to calm me down with a series of questions about money-saving tips we could be implementing.

". . . and don't take her up to the top floor because I'm trialling some eco light bulbs that mean you can't see the dust but you can't see the stairs that well either," he finished. "So, run her itinerary by me again?"

"Ten o'clock, Imogen arrives. Ten ten, coffee and biscuits, and compliments in library, ten thirty, chat with Divinity and Clemmy in ballroom about their take on modern elegance. Photos."

"Divinity and *Clemmy?*" He raised his eyebrows. "You're sure Clemmy can be photographed in daylight? She won't be invisible?"

"Of course she can. She's a perfectly charming girl," I said. "Once you get past the attitude. Did I tell you I've found a flatshare off Brompton Road for her to move into with Divinity next month?"

Mark put a finger on his chin. "Near the cemetery?"

"No, near . . . Oh, stop it." I flapped my hand at him. "She's lacking confidence, that's why she's so narky all the time. I want to show her that I trust her. That's why I've asked her to do this."

"Well, it's a risk," said Mark. "You're sure you don't want someone to sit in on them and remind Divinity to take her shades off and her gum out?"

"No! She'll do both. Jamie told her to — she listens to him. Moving on. Eleven thirty, walking in high heels, in the garden."

"What?" Mark covered his face. "Now you really are kidding me. Walking in high heels? Seriously? Isn't there an EU law banning that in finishing schools?"

I lowered my notes. "I know it sounds bad, but I think it's a post-feminist skill. No one can do it any more, because everyone wears Uggs and flats, and it's something all women should be able to do. You should be able to *run* in high heels. I learned when I was a teenager. Came in very useful for work, as it turned out," I added without thinking.

Mark frowned, trying to see what on earth that had to do with business management, and I changed the subject quickly. "I learned here, in fact. In that garden. Franny taught me, when I was sixteen."

"Didn't have you down as an expert," he said. "I haven't seen you wearing high heels much."

"I didn't realise you noticed that sort of thing," I said, surprised. Surprised and slightly flattered. "I used to wear them all the time. You don't lose the knack. It's like riding a bike — all about balance and momentum and proper weight distribution. The right shoes can transform the way you walk."

"You're making it sound like a matter of engineering," said Mark, his mouth curling up at the edges. "I had no idea it was so scientific."

"Well, it is," I said. "And for the summer, we'll be doing how to walk in flip-flops without the waddle. Anyway, after that, it's reverse parking in the mews." I looked up at him hopefully. "I need a favour — from you? I'm short of a car for reversing around. Anastasia's going to let us use her Porsche, and Miss McGregor's got her Morris Minor, but I don't want to risk a random stranger's vehicle. Not with Divinity on the loose."

He looked at me with something approaching horror on his face. "You're asking me to lend you my pride and joy, the reason I slave away at the coal face of banking every day, for the girls to crash into?"

"Ah!" I waved my finger at him. "Except they won't! Because *you'll* be in Ana's car, teaching them not to!"

"Oh, that's very good," said Mark, leaning back and folding his arms. "That's very good, Miss Macchiavelli."

"Then lunch, then two o'clock, Worst Case Dress Disasters with Liv. It'll be, what to do if you're wearing the same as someone else or if you snap a heel, that sort of thing, finishing with a class on putting together a simple kitchen supper for friends with Kathleen, if Imogen hasn't run for the hills by then. What do you think? Be honest."

I leaned back in my chair too and held my breath, waiting for Mark's reaction. I knew I'd get a genuine response from him. Unlike Jamie, Mark wasn't good at positive spins — unless they were on a race track, I supposed.

"Betsy," he said, after a minute's agonising pause, "you know what?"

"What?"

He pushed his glasses up his long nose. "If it wasn't for the high heels thing, I'd be writing you a cheque and signing up for next term myself. Actually . . ." He tilted his head enquiringly. "How big are your shoes?"

I nearly burst out laughing. It was the kind of thing Jamie would say, but it wouldn't be as funny as it sounded coming from Mark, in his checked shirt and cords.

"Sorry," I said, and pointed to Franny's notebook. "A lady never lends her shoes."

The next morning, while Imogen interviewed Clemmy and Divinity in the library, Anastasia and I sat in the Lady Hamilton Room with Jamie, trying to imagine what they were saying.

We were supposed to be having a role-playing lesson about how to get out of a bad date with good grace — starring Jamie as the date from hell, which I could tell Anastasia regarded as something of a stretch — but since Venetia hadn't turned up, it felt more like sitting in on someone's disintegrating relationship, and we'd given up.

Well, Jamie and I had. Anastasia was still quite keen.

"Where is Venetia?" he asked.

"Venetia, Venetia," snarled Anastasia, throwing up her hands. "Must you talk about your ex the whole time we are eating? It is so rrude."

"We're taking a break, Ana," I said, and sighed. "I hope she does turn up today — it's important."

Just then Divinity reappeared through the door, her eyes wide. She was wearing a lot of make-up "for the photoshoot", and had had about six new inches added to her hair. It nearly touched her tiny bottom.

"Oh, my God, that Imogen is so *nice*," she screeched. "I told her everything you said to — about our flatshare and about how we're stylish but savvy, and she's just photographing Clemmy by the grand piano in the ballroom."

I checked my watch. I needed to get the walking-in-heels lesson underway soon, but without Venetia, the only one of them who ever wore heeled footwear, it could easily go wrong. "Divinity, do you have any idea where Venetia might have got to?" I asked. "It looks pretty bad if there are just the three of you here."

Divinity looked a bit embarrassed. "She said she were going out for lunch. With Miss Buchanan. She's maybe gone early."

I glanced at Jamie. "Why've they gone out for lunch? Is it a lesson?"

Anastasia's eyes widened. "I doubt it. Unless it's about how *not* to eat anything."

"No," said Divinity, "it's a date-coaching thing."

"What?"

"Venetia's got some rich bloke on the go and Miss Buchanan's giving her tips on what she'll have to do when she gets married to him. Parties and social life and that."

"But I thought that was something you actually learned with Miss Thorne?" I asked, curiously. "On the old syllabus."

"No, he's foreign, and political — it's dead complicated, apparently," said Divinity. "I don't know any more than that. Venetia's right coy about it. Apart from his cash. She's not coy about that. He's rolling in it."

"We're not offered this advice," said Anastasia. "Even though my dad is foreign and *very* political. And he is *spinning* in it."

"I wouldn't want those lessons, any road." Divinity chewed her upper lip. "In fact, she told me I should get rid of Matt. Said he'd never have the earning potential for a proper springboard husband."

"And a springboard husband is . . . ?" asked Jamie.

"A man who launches you into the right kind of circles," said Divinity. "He's your first one. Then you need a concrete husband. To cement you into place."

"I have a friend who married a man like that," agreed Anastasia. "Or at least, he was, by the time her father . . ." She trailed off, seeing my dismayed expression.

"Well, I thought it was stupid!" Divinity said. "I told her what you said about company being the important thing, and she said that was why you were still on the shelf." She looked horrified. "Sorry."

"I'm *not* on the shelf," I interrupted, very conscious of Jamie sitting next to me. "I'm an independent woman, who doesn't need a man to springboard me anywhere! There's no such *thing* as a shelf any more, for God's sake! And . . ."

"Moving on," said Jamie, smoothly. "Divinity, I've taken you out for a drink but I've brought my mother along with me to check you out. What are you going to do about it?"

"Your *mother*?" said Anastasia, leaping in and feigning bewilderment. "You are his mother? But you are so young! Surely you are his older sister? You must tell me where you got your marrrvellous skincare routine."

Jamie turned to me. "You really are teaching them fast."

Jamie had a meeting in town at twelve, so I gave Venetia another ten minutes and then herded the girls into the back garden, leaving Paulette with strict instructions to call my mobile when Imogen and the photographer were on their way down.

"We're going back to basics," I told them, unlocking the garage. The old Silver Cross pram was right at the back, looming under a huge dustsheet where it had been since I'd last taken my heel wearing lessons, about ten years ago.

"God. That's like something out of the ark," breathed Anastasia as I struggled to get it out. "My *car's* smaller than that."

"Were you, like, one of those huge babies you see on telly?" marvelled Divinity. "*Help: my tot's a ten-ton toddler?* That kind of thing?"

"No! It's just been in the family since about 1950. Everything was bigger in the old days. Are you going to give me a hand?" I gasped, dragging it into the garden.

We stood round it and stared as dust rose from the ancient cloth hood. I gave the handle a tentative shove. It came up to Divinity's chest, practically, and creaked like the Mary Rose in a high wind.

"Right, girls," I said, pushing up the sleeves of my cardigan. "Watch this."

I wheeled it to the end of the path, threw my flats into the pram, slipped on my killer heels and proceeded to push it towards the house.

"Shoulders back, hips forward, bosom out," I yelled over my shoulder. "Your hips should be making a figure of eight — put one foot in front of the other! Weight on the ball of the foot, not the heel!"

The pram made it much easier, but I could have done it without. I'd forgotten how much I enjoyed wearing heels. I felt lighter, and flirtier, and longer, as if someone was pulling me up through a string attached to my head. My walk bounced. I was facing away from the girls, so they couldn't see the smile that crept over my face as I lifted my face to the February sunshine.

At the end of the path, up by the house, I did a neat three-point turn, spun round on one foot and started back, this time slightly quicker with even more wiggle in my walk.

Anastasia put two fingers in her mouth and gave a deafening whistle, just as my mobile started ringing in my pocket.

"The eagle is landing!" yelled Paulette. "I said, the. Eagle. Has. Landed!" Unfortunately, she was standing by an open window, right above us, so not only did I hear her without answering the phone, so did Imogen, returning with Clemmy.

Imogen was staring at the pram with a quizzical expression on her face, and I suddenly realised that I had to get this right, or else it would look very *very* bad. It made perfect sense to me, because it was how I'd learned, but to an outsider . . .

Eek.

"Stay there," I muttered to Divinity and Clemmy, parking the pram next to them.

"Is this supposed to be ironic?" asked Imogen, getting her notebook out. "Preparing them for a life of looking glamorous while child-rearing?"

"No, they're learning to walk in high heels," I said, confidently. "Some people recommend using shopping trolleys in supermarkets, but that's rather public, I think, whereas this not only balances you better, but gives the biceps a work out too."

"But walking in high heels?" Imogen didn't sound totally convinced. "Isn't that just walking with a book on your head by any other name?"

"Not really. Heels are a fact of life, but no one tells you there's an art to walking in them, like driving. I think there are lots of skills that our generation aren't taught any more, but we're still expected to know, somehow," I said. "And when we don't know how to walk in heels, or write a letter of condolence, or make a birthday cake we feel stupid, when all it takes is someone telling you how. That's what we're trying to do here — filling in the blanks like a stylish godmother might. My mother was such a graceful inspirational role model for me, and I'm really just trying to teach the girls what she taught me, starting with this very pram. It's just like she told me at the time, there's something about being able to carry off a pair of heels that makes men take you very seriously. It's when you *can't* that they assume you're a bimbo."

I had no idea where the words came from, but they streamed out effortlessly, and to my huge relief, I saw Imogen nod.

"Can you really teach it in a morning, though?" she asked. "I haven't worn heels since I nearly broke my ankle at fifteen on a pair of wedges."

"It's just balance. Imogen," I said, mock-seriously, "would you like a go on the Pram of Deportment?"

She hesitated, with a longing look at my shiny ruby stilettos. "You're sure I won't break anything?"

"Absolutely! Divinity, do you want to demonstrate?" I asked.

Dutifully, Divinity braced herself, and lurched down the path in her new Louboutins.

"Ohmigod, it's getting away!" she shrieked. "I'm going to fall over . . ."

"Head up!" I shouted. "Keep your weight back!"

"Ooooooh!" Divinity's legs were buckling like a newborn calf's, but she kept going, gripping the handle for dear life as the pram picked up momentum. After a scary pause, Imogen let out a shriek of laughter, and followed her up the path, roaring encouragement.

"That's amazing!" Divinity gasped. "I want to go again. But quicker!"

"Give Clemmy a go," I said, in my best pretend management consultant voice, then turned to Imogen with a bright smile, trying to visualise exactly what I wanted to appear in the paper.

Not just a glowing new Academy. I wanted my mother to see what a smart lady I'd turned into, with or without the Academy's help.

". . . And she ended up staying for tea," I told Liv as we walked back from the supermarket, carrying the week's shopping. "I took the high heels class up the stairs, over the polished hall tiles and off-road on the grass, so we covered all hazards. I put music on so we could dance. By the end we were like something out of a Girls Aloud video."

"Wow. Did you get a deposit cheque off of this Imogen bird?" said Liv.

"No, but she's coming to the Open Day," I said happily. "She wants to see your class on smartening up a guy on a date without him realising."

Liv bent to scoop the post off the mat, while I stepped past her into the kitchen.

"I thought we could use Jamie and Mark as examples?" I yelled, getting the biscuits out. Deli cookies, my treat. "You might have to desmarten Jamie first a bit."

There was no response from the hall.

"Liv?" I paused. "Liv, if that's a big red bill, just open it right now, OK? Don't try and hide it. It's not going away."

Still nothing.

I made the tea and went to see what was up.

Liv was standing stockstill in the hallway. There were three opened letters on the table, but it was the postcard in her hand that seemed to be causing the problem. Tears were streaming down her lovely face, and when she opened her mouth, nothing came out. She did it twice, and just when I thought my hearing had gone, she managed a horrible sob, like a crow.

"What is it?" I said, alarmed.

"My subscriptions have all run out!" she howled. "*Vogue, Glamour, Elle, Red* — all on the same day! And the cable TV package has been cut off too!" She hiccupped in distress and pointed at the letter which I now saw Erin had forwarded from her new address. "I couldn't work out why there were only five channels on the telly last night . . . And now, like I didn't have enough on my plate, bloody Dad's telling me not to worry! I *wasn't* until he told me not to! He's not on holiday, is he? He's in some kind of tro-hu-hu-ouble!"

I grabbed the postcard out of her hands.

It was from Ken. *Just to say I'm thinking of you, princess, and not to worry about your old dad. Don't tell your mother where I am, or the police. Jamie will give you anything you need. Love, Dad xx*

I turned it over. It had a flamenco dancer on it but no location, which I assumed was Ken's cunning idea of not revealing his whereabouts to anyone who couldn't read a postmark.

"Liv, don't," I said. "He'll roll up in a few months' time and it'll turn out he's bought a casino or something." I rubbed her heaving shoulders. "You don't need Sky, and you can read the magazines in the hairdresser. Come on, you're coping fine on your own!"

Liv's reply was salty, and lost in my hair. Then she pulled herself away, and said, with her huge, wounded puppy eyes glistening with tears, "I hate men. They're *all* thoughtless, selfish bastards. Did you know Finn was married? I found that out today — he came into Igor's with his wife and he wouldn't even look at me! I felt so *stupid*! I wish I was more like you," she hiccupped. "You don't let yourself get taken for a ride by anyone. You always end up coping *fine* on your own."

I held her at arm's length. I knew the relapse had to come at some point: it had been going so well. "Olivia. Look at me. You're well out of it with Finn. And don't worry about Ken — he's *more* than capable of getting himself out of whatever fix he's in. And *you're* doing fine!"

"Yeah, right . . ." She looked wobbly, and her eyes slid sideways to the phone, and her massive address book. I knew what she was thinking, and it involved a lot of cocktails paid for by someone else.

"Stop right there — we're staying in tonight," I said, getting into my Independent Woman stride. "We'll put a film on, I'll make a shepherd's pie, and a nice pot of tea, and we can do intensive pedicures with that mad foot cheese-grater thing you got in America."

Liv narrowed her eyes. "This isn't some kind of test run for a lesson, is it?"

"No! Course not!" I looked affronted. "It's you and me time. No Academy, no budget lectures, no stressing about work — just lots of compliments about how great we both are. And chocolates. And a crap film with a happy ending that doesn't involve getting married in any shape or form."

She sniffed. "Can we watch *Titanic* again? All the blokes drown in that."

"Good choice," I said. "I'll get the tea."

We were sitting on the sofa, halfway down the second bottle of wine and twenty minutes into *Titanic*, when Jamie let himself in.

"Hang on, I think there must be a time shift going on here," he said, and pretended to back out and in again.

"What?" demanded Liv. She couldn't turn her head all the way, thanks to her aspirin face mask caking her face like a medieval skin complaint.

"You two. It's like stepping back into our house ten years ago. *Titanic*, face packs, cheap wine . . . *Anyway*, I'm delighted you're putting so much effort into our dinner date, Betsy, but you'll have to hurry up, I've booked a table for eight and I'd like a cocktail first."

"What?" My heart sank. In the flurry of work, I'd forgotten all about agreeing to have dinner with Jamie. "Was that tonight? Did we actually make a date? In our diaries?"

I knew I sounded as if I was talking about a business meeting but I couldn't stop myself. I turned to Liv as another thought dawned on me. "Weren't you supposed to be out this evening?"

"No," she said. "Oh, yes, I was going to do a shift. But then Igor had one of his strange turns this morning and decided he'd be holding his annual séance in the cellar, so we're shut."

"It's fine," said Jamie. "Just wash off whatever you've got on your face and we'll go in ten."

I didn't point out that it was Liv who had the mask on: I had a foot treatment instead.

"Um . . ." Which was worse manners — blowing out an unconfirmed date, or abandoning a distressed friend? Franny's notebook probably wouldn't help.

I looked at Liv, who glared through her peeling aspirin mask and said, "Mates before men. Isn't that what you're always telling me?"

I looked back at Jamie. He said nothing, but raised an eyebrow, which made my stomach flip.

"Well, the thing is, Jamie," I started, very reluctantly, "I'd love to go out, but Liv's had some . . . bad news and I thought . . ."

"I slipped your mind. Betsy, I'm hurt."

"Girls' night in, wasn't it?" demanded Liv, rapping the remote against the sofa. "We don't need men to take us out for dinner, wasn't it?"

"But . . ."

"But nothing." She reached out for the bottle and refilled her glass.

"You can join us, if you want?" I offered, feeling horribly torn. It was easy to say no, I need to be with Liv, but I felt a weird sense of disappointment — with myself. "I've made shepherd's pie? With lots of tomato sauce and peas?"

"No!" Liv turned up the television. "Not unless he's going to put on a hair mask and talk about how unreliable men are."

I gave Jamie a pleading glance, but he just looked back at me with amusement in his face.

"No, sorry. I can't watch *Titanic,* it'll make my testosterone dry up," he said. "I'll just have to find another dinner date. No big deal, I just thought you might be at a loose end."

He turned to go, and suddenly I found myself leaping to my feet and squelching across the room in my cling film socks.

"Hang on!" I gasped, and caught up with him by the door.

"Look, I'm sorry," I said, under my breath, "I didn't mean to blow you out, but this came today." I showed him the postcard, which Liv had jammed angrily behind the telephone. "And it turns out that her last admirer has just got married to someone else. If he wasn't married to her before. Which I suspect might be the case."

Jamie's face darkened as he read the card, and he looked as if he were about to say something, but then changed his mind.

"Bloody Ken. I suppose I'll just have to sort it out, like I always do," he said. "Course I don't have a proper job, which makes it so much easier." He tapped the card against his hand. "You're sure you can't just leave her to Leo and come out? She'd be happy enough."

"Mates before men," I said apologetically. "Honour before thieves, etc."

"Are you *ever* going to come out for dinner with me?" he asked, crossing his arms. "I don't want to know what your next excuse is going to be. A superhero secret identity? A hermaphrodite appendage?" He widened his eyes. "You don't think we're . . . secretly related?"

I laughed. "No!" I said, "no, I'm just . . ."

Our eyes locked for a moment or two, and Jamie tipped his head, enquiringly.

"It's the scene where she pretends to do Irish dancing!" roared Liv from the sitting room. "Come and see the pretend Oirish people!"

"What were you going to say there?" he said, softly. "Go on."

I let his grey eyes search my face, but I couldn't admit it. I almost preferred this tingling flirtation, when I could imagine what it would be like, to actually being there, and it maybe going wrong, or falling short of my years of imagining. At least this way, there would always be a dinner on offer.

He'd be going back to Manhattan soon. I was going back to Edinburgh. It would fizzle out. He'd move on, I . . . wouldn't.

"Betsy?" he said, and pretended to check his watch. "My other dinner dates are stacking up like planes at Heathrow — are you coming out or not?"

He was joking, I think, but it made me decide.

"I have to get back to the ship," I apologised.

"Another night?" he said, casually. "You're here for a while now, aren't you?"

"Yeah, another night."

We smiled nervously, at each other.

"Betsy!" yelled Liv. "I know you're both talking about me but I need you on this sofa *now*!"

Jamie raised a finger. "I'll hold you to that," he said. "The dinner, not the sofa."

"OK," I said, and felt a shiver run across my skin.

CHAPTER TWENTY

Never ask a man his starsign, his salary or his age.

Friday's Field Trip was supposed to be The National Gallery, but instead we went to Selfridges with Miss O'Hare, Personal Style teacher, to investigate "classic but creative interview outfits".

I had to explain to Divinity that these were outfits for attending job interviews, as opposed to interviews you might conduct on the acquisition of a new swimming pool or nose.

"It's always best to shop with someone who doesn't know you very well," I explained as we marshalled them outside Full Moon Street like ducklings in their big coats and shades. "They don't have the same hang-ups as you do, and they'll make you try new things."

"Absolutely," nodded Liv, who'd dressed the part in a fashionable display of statement necklaces and layers that I wouldn't know where to start assembling. "Now, remember we're looking for classic pieces — that perfect black skirt we talked about, and the Versatile White Shirt — but with twists. So, you've all got to find a handbag that sums you up, just so they know you're not a robot, OK? Prize for the best shoes under fifty quid."

I'd thought styling the girls would be a logical extension of Liv's online shopping fix with the bonus of actually drilling some useful fashion advice into them. She and Ken's credit card had been on first-name terms with all the best in-store shoppers in London, and we were soon ensconced in the biggest personal shopping suite while Liv marched round the store, pulling various Jackie O suits and crisp pinafores off the rails and steering them away from glitz and towards tailoring. We then had to try on our finds while Liv stood on a chair and critiqued us, starting with me.

She didn't hold back.

"Now do you see what I mean about how pretty Miss Cooper looks when she colours herself in?" Liv said, when I pulled back the curtain in the clothes she'd picked out for my own "creative interview" Open Day outfit: viz, a silky Miu Miu skirt printed with huge blue cornflowers, teamed with a bracelet-sleeved cardigan. "See how the blue makes her hair shine, and her eyes pop?"

"What do you mean, pop?" I demanded. "Like a fish?"

Liv ignored me. "And see how we've emphasised her waist, with the patent leather belt? Clemmy, put Anastasia's belt over that jacket of yours — a thinner belt's more flattering . . . There! You see? Gorgeous!"

"Your waist's really tiny," said Clemmy, with a covetous sigh. "Lucky you."

Liv had charmed Clemmy out of her usual greys and blacks and now the transformed Clementine was sitting on a footstool in a tomato-red dress that made her skin adorably creamy. Liv had twisted her dark hair up in a neat chignon to demonstrate necklines, and the result was a Clemmy-on-her-way-to-Ascot, not Glastonbury. She was sitting with her knees and ankles together, and Miss McGregor wasn't even in sight.

"Write this down," said Liv. "Thin belts for thick waists, thick belts for thin ones. Betsy, stop looking for problems in that mirror — you look great."

"You don't think this blue clashes with my hair?" I asked, doubtfully. Black might have been boring but at least it wasn't competing with the riot of colour that was my red hair and green eyes. My notebooks had always said, *three colours maximum per outfit, and red hair counts as one.*

"No," said Liv.

I twisted round. "You don't think the belt just makes my bum look bigger?"

"No," said Liv. "Shut up."

I had to admit it, Liv knew what suited me better than I did. I would never have bought such a strikingly printed skirt — I mean, it didn't go with a thing I owned — but she somehow produced the pointy-toed shoes, and then fiddled with my hair until it was a whole outfit, and I looked so amazingly fresh and bright in the mirror that I hardly recognised myself. I wasn't blending in, or looking discreet: I was me, but at the same time, not.

I tried to pinpoint what it was that was so weird, then it struck me: I looked like I used to imagine I would when I daydreamed about being twenty-something as a little girl. Elegant, grown up, with shoes that meant business.

"Buy it," urged Liv. "Buy it and wear it for the Open Day. Go on, you need a new outfit."

I started to protest that I didn't need any new clothes, but something stopped me.

I wanted to *be* this person — bright and colourful and confident.

Maybe it was the gorgeous swish of the skirt. Maybe it was the growing camaraderie between me and the girls, and the sense that maybe I could pull the Academy through into the twenty-first century after all. Maybe it was the something bubbling between me and Jamie.

Whatever it was, I felt better about myself than I had done in years and years.

I did a little half turn, and smiled. The Betsy in the mirror twinkled back.

"Go on," urged Clemmy. "You have to."

I bought the lot. On my credit card.

The fruits of our efforts with Imogen came on Tuesday afternoon, in perfect time for the Open Day on Saturday.

We were in the middle of a role-playing class about Worst Case Scenario: Very Public Disasters when there was a knock on the door, and Mark put his head around the door of the Lady Hamilton Room.

"Sorry to interrupt," he said, "but I've got something for you." He waved a copy of the evening paper at me.

"Ah ha!" I said, as my butterflies fluttered up into my stomach. "Shall we take a break, girls?"

"No!" said Clemmy. She glared at Mark. "Mr Montgomery can help."

"Help with what?" he asked, pleasantly.

"What you would do if you'd got to the church and decided that you didn't want to marry your fiancé after all." She paused. "We wanted it to be because the groom was sleeping with a bridesmaid and two of the ushers, but Betsy made us stick with 'because he's not Mr Right'."

Mark took an unsteady step backwards. "Sorry, I hoped it was going to be something about tax relief."

"Well?" demanded Divinity. "What's the best thing to do?"

"Whatever . . . Betsy's said? Which is?" He looked at me, with hilarious desperation, but I was eagerly eyeing the newspaper in his hand.

"I said it's never too late to call off a wedding if you realise you can't go through with it and will be ruining his life as well as yours, but it's better to pretend that you've had some kind of massive allergic reaction and/or fake a kidnapping on the way to the church."

"Isn't that a bit melodramatic?" Mark asked, surprised. "Shouldn't you just be honest about it?"

"Well, normally, I'd say honesty is best," I admitted. "But weddings are different. People talk about jiltings for the rest of your *life*. You should create some kind of drama to distract people's attention from the fact that you're standing up your fiancé. And then get your bridesmaid to redirect everyone to the reception, to tuck into the food and drink while you go off on the honeymoon and return, 'unkidnapped' a few months later."

"You seem to have given this some thought," he said, with a dry smile. "Do all women have this planned out?"

"All women worry about being jilted," said Venetia. "It's good to have a Plan B."

I didn't have Venetia down as a wedding worrier. Personally, I'd sometimes dreamed about marrying Jamie, only to get to the altar to find another woman standing in my place, or my mother turning up and revealing herself in mortifying fashion. It would be complex enough, just working out where to sit everyone, when there were only four people on the bride's side and technically no family at all.

"What would a man do?" the girls demanded. "What would you do?"

"I would try to speak with my fiancée and get the ushers to clear the church," Mark said solidly. "In instances like this, guests don't want to poke their noses into other people's distress."

"You've never been to a celebrity wedding," observed Divinity.

"And vot about the reception?" Anastasia tapped the table. I think she was still playing the part of the outraged mother-in-law, as per the role play earlier. "Is all paid for!"

"I'd have got sale or return on the drinks, and I'd send the food to a homeless shelter and the flowers to a hospital," said Mark.

"But vhy?" she wailed, rending her hair. "How could you treat my daughter so badly? My husband knows people . . . you vill never work in Hempstead again . . ."

"Ana," I said hurriedly, as Mark edged towards the door, still holding the paper. "That's enough. Mark, can I see the paper . . . ?"

"Your daughter were shagging an usher too," said Divinity, wagging her finger. "*And* she's maxed out my son's credit cards with her online bingo habit!"

"He drrove her to the bingo!" Anastasia snarled back at her.

Mark regarded me nervously from the door. "Um, should I come back later?"

I held my hand out for the paper. "No," I said, "you're being a great help! Now, what was the . . . ?"

"What are you meant to do as a guest?" Venetia buttonholed him with a direct look. "If you think something's going on backstage, as it were?"

"Get your camera phone out," said Clemmy. "And get it on to YouTube."

"No!" I said. "Just . . ." I wasn't sure what you *were* meant to do, actually. "Mark?"

He shook his head. "Offer to arrange a game of charades to pass the time?"

"Is that our interview?" yelled Divinity and had the newspaper off him faster than you could say pre-nup, her fingers flipping through the pages to the centre.

"Did they use the picture of me in my car?" demanded Anastasia. "Or Clemmy pushing the pram?"

"No, she said she had some beautiful photographs of you in the ballroom with . . ."

We all fell silent as I reached the page in question. Under the headline "Practically Perfect", was an enormous colour photograph of Adele and Venetia, sitting on the grand piano in the old ballroom, looking "like sisters" with their long blond hair, ankles glued together, and spectacles perched on their noses.

"But Adele doesn't even *wear* glasses," snorted Clemmy. "She's wearing Miss Thorne's!"

"Oh, look, we are in it," offered Anastasia, pointing at a tiny picture of her, Clemmy and Divinity posing in the mews on her Porsche.

My eyes were skimming through the copy, with mounting disbelief. After a brief mention of visiting us in our car-parking class, and chatting with "two refreshingly normal graduates of the new-look Tallimore Academy," — Clemmy and Divinity — Imogen's feature was hijacked by an interview with Miss Adele Buchanan, and her protégée, Venetia Knight, in which Adele outlined her own take on the female graces, which seemed to comprise exfoliation, depilation, pre-nuptial agreements and breath mints.

I couldn't tell, from reading it, whether it was meant to be tongue-in-cheek. Venetia, I discovered, "makes any party feel like a premiere" and "hides a razor-sharp mind behind her razor-sharp cheekbones". She also enjoyed "playing the stock market and polo". Adele, meanwhile, had been "the most fun hostess in London since she arrived in town in the early nineties" and was now "passing on her little black book of social secrets to a new generation of girls". "It's the least I can do!" she was quoted as cooing.

I strongly suspected Adele's own hand in most of that.

"Oh, look," said Clemmy, pointing. "You're in it too."

I'd missed it, being dazed by Adele's shiny legs, but there *was* a small but quite flattering photograph of me, taken during our procession round the house in our heels. I was kicking away at the front of the shoe conga, and my hair was coming down from the neat bun Liv had put it in, but at least I looked like I was enjoying myself.

" 'The fresh direction is the brainchild of twenty-seven-year-old Betsy Cooper," Anastasia read aloud, "who is pretty nimble on her stilettos, and also pretty nimble when it comes to advising on tactful ways to bail out of dates, and where to stick your savings. If anyone could teach me how to park with panache, or rustle up a dinner to win any man's heart, it would be polished, unpretentious Betsy, and I'll be seeing her at the weekend, to sign up for a course in making the most of myself. Because if I don't sign myself up, my mother certainly will.' "

"Ker-ching," said Divinity, looking at Mark. "Gotta be pleased with that, haven't you?"

"Yes," he said. "Although obviously I'm crushed that she didn't mention the parking instructor by name."

"She said you were a racing driver, not an accountant," Divinity pointed out. "That's pretty flattering."

"And come on," said Clemmy. "She didn't mention Mr O'Hare either, and she used to go out with him. She told me so, in our interview."

"That'll be why she didn't mention him!" I laughed, although I felt a twinge of disappointment. Why had he said she was just a friend? Just goes to show, I thought. Leopards don't change their spots. They just cover them up.

"You're very photogenic, though," said Divinity, generously. "You look like you're having a whale of a time."

I stared at the small photograph of myself. I wished my hair was neater, and that I'd maybe worn more lipstick, but it wasn't a bad photo. Liv's portrait practice must have paid off. But was it enough for my mother to recognise me? Might she be sitting on the Tube this evening, or on a bus, reading the feature and thinking, yes, I'll go along on Saturday and . . .

And what? Say hello? My insides flipped over.

"Anyway, you're pleased?" said Mark.

I looked up, and saw him hovering, his eyebrows lifted hopefully.

Given that he'd virtually had estate agents measuring the place up only a few weeks ago, I reckoned that was quite a turnaround.

"Yes," I said. "I reckon it should draw the crowds, if only to meet the fabulous Venetia. You've done really well," I said, turning to them. "Well done on being such a wonderful advert."

I realised that the girls had drawn back from the table and were staring at Venetia in a hostile manner, and I wondered if they knew something they weren't telling me about her.

I remembered when I was younger I'd overheard Kathleen saying something about how some girls were born with silver spoons in their mouths and others came to the Academy to have theirs silver plated, which hadn't made much sense to me at the time. I think they'd been talking about Adele, whose father made his pile in soil diggers, but who pretended her parents lived abroad, not in Preston. I wondered if Venetia was like that. She was certainly determined to get on Adele's matrimonial springboard.

"Funny," mused Clemmy. "They don't mention anything about you living at home with your mum and dad still."

"I don't," sniffed Venetia. "I've moved out. Into Luka's penthouse. In Knightsbridge."

"Who's Luka?" demanded Anastasia.

"My *boyfriend*." Venetia smirked. "He's an entrepreneur. He has his fingers in *many* pies."

"You never said!"

"You never asked," said Venetia. "Anyway, unlike some, I don't like to bring my private life into class," she added, with a mean glance towards Divinity, who blushed.

Clemmy leaped on her. "It says in this article that you've made some lifelong friends?" she asked, pretending to be confused. "Who are those poor suckers? Is there another class we don't know about?"

"Stop it!" I said, raising my hands. "Don't spoil it! This is a wonderful advert for the Academy, better than anything I could have said, and it's going to make people rush to visit us on Saturday. I'm deeply grateful to you *all*."

I wasn't all that grateful to Venetia, letting Adele hijack it like that, making herself look as if she'd masterminded the entire redirection, but I tried to let that pass. I knew that the more little pinpricks of doubt I let Adele shove into my too-thin skin, the harder I'd find it to put on my confident front for the Open Day.

I needed all the confidence I could get, because I wasn't just pretending to be a management consultant any more. I was pretending to be an etiquette expert, and a confident woman and someone who wasn't acutely aware that she'd stirred up the past and now had to deal with whatever it decided to throw back at her.

In five days' time.

CHAPTER TWENTY-ONE

Don't bring flowers to a dinner party — it distracts the hostess from her last-minute panics — but send them the next day, and you'll be on her guest list forever!

Before I arrived at Full Moon Street first thing on Saturday morning, I did something Franny used to do for me before big occasions — I stopped at a flower stall and picked up a small bouquet for each of the girls as a thank you for helping out.

I chose the flowers carefully, out of habit. Franny and I had had a running joke, about the old-fashioned Language of Flowers that was still part of the Home Enhancement class in those days; I knew all the different messages you could make with red roses and white lilies. Unfortunately, the language of flowers was somewhat monosyllabic the week before Valentine's Day in central London, and the best I could come up with were yellow tulips ("You have sunshine in your smile!") and some pink rosebuds ("for thankfulness"). I avoided yellow carnations ("You have disappointed me!") because who wouldn't be, frankly, with petrol station flowers?

As I let myself in, I was pleased to see the lion's-head knocker was gleaming. Kathleen turned up her nose at what she called "spray and go" cleaners, and her gift to the Open Day was to arrange some "proper ladies" to blitz the place first thing. I could tell they'd been there from the crisp smell of recently polished tiles as soon as I opened the door. The florist's boxes of lilies I'd ordered had been left on the back step, and I arranged them quickly in the big urns, running through lists in my head as my fingers automatically stripped the stems and clipped off the pollen-heavy stamens, letting their heady scent fill the entrance hall.

The peaceful atmosphere in the house helped me concentrate, and I was almost startled when the silence was broken by the arrival of Clemmy, Divinity and Anastasia. I could hear a distant cackling from some way down the street, and though I hoped it wasn't them making the racket, I didn't mind so much when they crashed through the front door, and came to a halt on seeing me, their jaws flatteringly dropped.

I was wearing the outfit Liv had picked out for me, and I had to hand it to her, I *felt* amazing.

"Wow! You look hot!" said Divinity, overcome.

"That colour is so good on you," agreed Clemmy. "It's like you've had surgery or something."

"But obviously you haven't," Divinity corrected her, then looked confused. "Unless you have?"

"Always best to assume *not*, unless the person offers the information," I said. "You look pretty fantastic yourselves!"

Liv had been firm but fair about their various strengths and weaknesses, and for once they'd actually listened. Clemmy looked sophisticated in a red swing jacket and matching miniskirt, with her thick fringe cut just above her eyes, and Anastasia had dressed up her boucle shift dress with a glittery selection of paste-look brooches, which, come to think of it, probably weren't paste. Divinity, as ever, looked like a doll in a floaty black dress and cobwebby tights.

"Well, we wanted to look nice and that," said Divinity. "Seeing as how there might be cameras." She dropped her voice. "I've made sure not to wear white underwear with me black top, like you said."

"Smart move," I said. "Ooh, have you seen the special delivery?" I pointed to the hall table, where I'd put the flowers. They shrieked in delight and scrambled over to see who had what.

"Are these from Mr O'Hare?" Divinity wondered aloud. "Or Lord Tallimore?"

"You wish," snorted Clemmy, then turned to me. "It's from you, isn't it? Aw. Thanks."

"My pleasure," I said, and I meant it.

"Good morning, ladies!" Miss McGregor arrived with Mrs Angell in a cloud of hairspray, and newly set hair, with Paulette close behind. "Flowers! How delightful! Have you pricked the stems, girls? Now, what kind of vase would be best for tulips?"

"I don't think we have time for flower arranging," I said, checking my watch. "I wanted to run through a couple of things before anyone arrived. Has anyone seen Miss Thorne? Or Venetia?"

"I wouldn't wait for Venetia," said Anastasia. "I doubt if she's going to make it today. She told us she had something verrry important on last night."

"Wouldn't say what," added Divinity.

"Which means it was *nothing*," said Clemmy, sarcastically. "She's such a *fantasist*."

"It doesn't matter," I said, before they could get going.

The big clock in the hall began to chime and I was suddenly very conscious of all the things I needed to do before the Old Girls — no, before the *guests*, arrived.

"Anyway, girls, there's something I wanted to say to you before . . ." I stopped, hearing the door open.

"Sorry, am I late?" Jamie enquired. "Tell me I haven't missed the big speech!"

I had to hand it to him: he could make an entrance. The girls' heads — and Miss McGregor and Mrs Angell's — turned like a chorus line as he strode in, slipping his double-breasted coat off his shoulders and unwinding his scarf from his neck, smiling broadly at everyone. At which point they smiled one after the other, again like a chorus line.

Jamie always dressed as if he was off to, or just back from some VIP party, but this morning, he'd aimed for something more respectable than fashionable. The effect made me swallow in surprise. He'd put on his most sober grey suit, the one Liv had forced him to buy when she thought she was getting married to Lachlan the Landowning Laird, although he hadn't bothered with a tie, and his blue shirt was open at the throat, revealing a sexy tanned hollow.

What really sent my blood racing was his damp hair, teddy-bear brown where it hadn't quite dried yet into the familiar blond — there was something intimate and vulnerable about it, as if he'd been in the shower just minutes ago. It curled round his ears, just inviting someone to push it back.

"Morning, Betsy," he said, with a quick wink.

I opened my mouth, but it had gone very dry and nothing came out.

Behind Jamie, looking quietly amused, was Mark. He was wearing the suit he'd worn for the memorial service, and if Jamie hadn't been there stealing the oxygen in the room, I'd have thought Mark hadn't scrubbed up too badly. His thick black hair was maybe in need of some styling intervention and he was wearing his horrible tie again, but he was rubbing his chin with a wry Clark Kent-ishness that made up for his sartorial shortcomings.

"You've all gone very quiet," Mark observed. "Were you talking about us?"

"No. Not yet. You haven't missed anything," I said, pulling myself together. "I was just about to start. Come in and settle down."

"I'm on coat duty." Paulette pushed forward with more enthusiasm than she'd shown when I allocated her the job the previous day. "Give us your coats. Oh, this is very nice quality," she added, hanging Jamie's cashmere overcoat up. "And this one — is this your school coat, Mark? Or are you a part-time Paddington Bear impersonator? Eh?"

"There's no need to critique the guests' coats, Paulette," I warned.

"It's warm for cycling," said Mark. "I won't have a word said against it."

"You'll have to get Olivia to style you," said Divinity. "She's going to be teaching a makeover session, showing people how to update their wardrobes. I'm helping, and we need volunteers. We could workshop you this afternoon . . ." She patted his arm. "Don't worry. We'll soon have you up to scratch."

"Sorry, can I get a word in?" I asked. "Before you use up all your advice on the staff?"

"Pray silence for the Voice of Common Sense," bellowed Jamie, and everyone went quiet. He looked at me, his eyes twinkling, and my little prepared speech went out of my head. I swallowed and tried to focus. Suddenly, I felt quite emotional.

"I just wanted to say thank you," I began. "I've asked a lot of you in the last few weeks, and you've been more supportive and helpful than I could ever have . . ."

The door swung open again and I ground to a halt.

In a formation not unlike Charlie's Angels, in strode Miss Thorne, Venetia and Adele, each looking more smug than the last. They stopped just inside the foyer, Venetia in the middle. Adele had the most enormous armful of white roses under one arm, and a giant pair of D&G shades that she left on until the last moment

— the Height of Rudeness, as she ought to have known from her notebook.

Then again, maybe Adele needed them to defend her eyes against the dazzling self-satisfaction radiating from Miss Thorne. I'd never seen her looking so pleased with herself: not only was she resplendent in a black dress with a white Peter Pan collar, she was wearing four strands of pearls and matching earrings, which probably signified Grand Etiquette High Wizard status.

"Oh, I hope we're not interrupting?" she cooed, knowing from my open mouth and everyone's expression that she was.

"Not at all," I lied, politely.

"Girls," said Miss Thorne, ignoring me and clapping her plump white hands together. "I have an announcement to make. Or rather, *Venetia* has an announcement to make!"

Venetia didn't say anything but slowly removed her soft suede gloves like a very upmarket stripper — at which point her left hand spoke for itself in the international language of gigantic engagement rocks.

"Bloody hell," breathed Paulette, speaking what everyone else was only thinking. "It's enormous!"

"Mmm," murmured Venetia in modest agreement, and pushed a thick hank of hair away from her face, all the better to show off the diamond solitaire. It was roughly the size of one of Miss McGregor's quail's eggs.

"Oh my God!" shrieked Divinity, generously. "Oh my God, you've got engaged!"

Anastasia went over to Venetia, clasping her in a warm Russian hug. "Congratulations," she said. "It is beautiful diamond. Have you had it insured? I have a friend whose finger was sliced off at the traffic lights. And it was only an emerald."

"Who is it?" Clemmy demanded. "Anyone we know?"

"I shouldn't think so, Clemmy," said Adele, half-jokingly. "Venetia's not into the cider and blackcurrant circuit."

"Luka, like I told you the other day. He's a political donor and international businessman," Venetia explained. Her eyes were glittering brighter than her solitaire. "And a close friend of Adele's. We met at . . . we met at a charity dinner."

"And how did he propose?" Divinity looked ready to swoon. "Did he go down on one knee?"

"I should think that's Venetia's job," muttered Clemmy.

"Did he ask your father first?" demanded Anastasia. "Was it like in Miss McGregor's proposal lesson? Did he agree to a dowry? What did your mum and dad say?"

Venetia looked discomfited for the first time; just for a fleeting second, her hair fell over her face and I couldn't see her eyes.

"Yes, it was terribly romantic," Adele leapt in. "Venetia, tell Divinity about the proposal!"

"Luka asked me if I wanted him to put me on the insurance for his Ferrari. And I said yes."

"It was his vintage one," Adele added. "Of course, no one's allowed to drive it, but it's the principle of trust! *Quel* romance!"

"Oh, and then he put this ring in a chocolate mousse last night," Venetia added. "I almost didn't see it, because I don't eat refined sugars, and the waiter nearly walked off with a hundred grand's worth of pudding."

"That's dead romantic!" gasped Divinity.

"I can't believe you're here," said Clemmy. "I wouldn't be. Hasn't he swept you off in his private jet to celebrate?"

"Businessmen can't take time off, just like that," Adele reminded her. "And Venetia was very keen to come and help out with Betsy's Open Day. She's a perfect example of just what sort of doors can be opened to you with the right attitude."

Bedroom doors mostly, I thought, but didn't say anything. I was too busy struggling with a toxic cocktail of emotions and hoping they weren't showing on my face.

"It's a wonderful moment for the Academy," said Miss Thorne, patting Adele's hand. "Just goes to show that the traditional values of femininity are still appreciated by the men out there! I think you'll find this will have a very *positive* effect on intake for next term," she added, with a meaningful glance at me.

"We have to make some phone calls," said Adele, "so will you excuse us from your . . . whatever you're doing?" She pretended to pause. "Oh, and if Lord

Tallimore arrives, don't tell him, will you? I want it to be a surprise!"

A surprise? Why on earth would *he* care?

Then the three of them swept off to the Principal's Office, leaving the rest of us staring at our tulips, which now seemed rather underwhelming.

"Never mind," said Paulette, in an attempt at jollity. "Maybe she'll ask you to be bridesmaids!"

The three girls turned to her with looks that would have wilted the old plastic lilies in the urn.

"All I'll say," said Clemmy, holding up one finger, "is can you imagine what she'd make us wear?"

We stood imagining in silence, listening to the trio of stiletto heels clatter down the hall, then disappear in the thick pile of the study, whereupon tinkly laughter could be heard.

Mark coughed discreetly. "So what were you going to say, Betsy? Before the interruptions?"

I dragged my attention back, but the moment had totally gone.

"Oh, um, I just wanted to say thank you," I said. "And good luck with all your demonstrations." I swallowed. "Don't worry about anything other than being yourselves today, and you won't go far wrong."

"Marvellous!" said Miss McGregor, acting as if I'd just delivered the Queen's Speech. "Very wise. I'm sure everyone's going to give it their best shot, and what will be will be. Now, Paulette, you're on coats, and Divinity, I understand you're going to do the checklist for names, aren't you? Stand up straight, Clementine, you're sagging, dear."

We all stood up straight at that, and Jamie gave me a wink that set off a very different burst of fluttering in my stomach.

Ten minutes before the doors were to open, I ran down the stairs to the hall, to prepare myself.

I stopped by the large mirror and smoothed down my hair, checking my face for any tiny smudges and arranging my bee necklace so it sat right in the centre of my neckline, like a sign. Would she recognise me without it? I had a name badge pinned to my cardigan, with Betsy Cooper Tallimore printed as large as was polite, and if I stayed by the door and saw everyone who was coming in, overlooking Divinity and her checklist, I couldn't miss her.

If she came.

Nell Howard was definitely coming, she'd called me to confirm. I had my mother's letter tucked in the back of my notebook, ready for her to look at, to see if the handwriting rang a bell.

I stared into the mirror, hoping for an irrational second that I might see something in there, the ghosts of Tallimores past perhaps, offering a clue or some kind of sign. *Please let her come*, I wished. *Please let* . . .

"What do we say about looking in mirrors, Elizabeth? Once is sane, and twice is vain!"

Miss Thorne had popped up, apparently from behind the massive urn of flowers, and I nearly squeaked with shock. "Was there something you wanted?" she said, moving closer to the door, as if taking up a tactical position.

"I just thought I'd come down, in case there were any early arrivals," I explained. "We want to look welcoming, don't we?"

Her thin smile tightened. "Isn't that a job for the headmistress?"

I thought that was a bit rich, since her contribution to the planning had been limited to sending me memos about how big the sandwiches should be.

"We've had so many acceptances that I'm sure we'll both be rushed off our feet!" I said, cheerily, and turned to Divinity's crystal-encrusted iPod, hidden amongst the daffodils. Music for the Royal Fireworks began to pour out of the speakers tucked behind vases, in alcoves and up the stairs.

"Music in the hall — just like the old days!" I said with a smile.

"I fear those days are gone," sighed Miss Thorne. "Well, whatever happens today, you've done what you could, dear. And there's one bright spot, with Venetia's engagement."

I bit my lip. Was marriage really all that mattered to Miss Thorne and Adele — next to the place actually staying open or not?

"Maybe there'll be *more* good news before the end of term," she added, rather mysteriously.

"Like the next term happening?" I enquired.

There was a firm rap on the lion's-head knocker and she bustled to the door.

I bustled after her and there was a brief struggle to open the door first, which I won by dint of my superior height. I did it in one graceful but firm move, blocking her from appearing to the visitors. Those years as Goal Defence on a brutal school netball team hadn't been entirely pointless.

"Hello!" I said, extending a welcoming hand to the three women on the doorstep. "Welcome to the Tallimore Academy."

I scanned their faces nervously. Was this them? It was impossible to tell how old Tallimore Old Girls were. I stepped back, confused. Where was Divinity with her list?

Ironically, it was Miss Thorne who came to my rescue, shoving me aside with a discreet elbow.

"Yes, welcome, welcome!" she cooed, stretching out her hands. "Oh, it's Bunny, and Minty and Alexandra! How wonderful to see you again, dears!"

Bunny, Minty, Alexandra. None of those names were familiar, and they didn't seem to be inspecting me too closely either as they crowded round Miss Thorne and showered her with enthusiastic Tallimore compliments about her hair.

I could hear the tip-tap of more high heels trotting down Full Moon Street. This was just the beginning.

CHAPTER TWENTY-TWO

Everyone should have one fabulous karaoke song: practise it, so you can belt it out on demand, then retire modestly.

After that first trio, the ever-punctual Tallimore Old Girls positively streamed in, pitching up in clusters of two and three, their sweetie-coloured suits and sheepskin gilets making pastel splashes against the black-and-white tiles. They brought daughters and god-daughters and began assiduously introducing them to everyone, with hearty handshakes. It made mine and Divinity's job much easier, as I kept my ears open for the magic names. I didn't need to check with Nell's list: I knew them off by heart now.

Sophie, Coralie, Caroline, Rosalind, Emma-Jane.

The trouble was, virtually everyone who'd ever been at the Academy was called either Caroline or Sophie, so after ten minutes my ears were burning.

Hard on the kitten heels of the curious Old Girls came a stream of more regular people, attracted I hoped by the feature in the paper. There were some school-leaving teenagers in black opaques and ballet flats and huge bags; some with harassed mothers, some definitely without; a few women in their thirties with brave smiles and freshly cut divorce hairdos; and even one or two deeply reluctant lads dragged along by their sisters or mothers. Their tentative smiles at the boy/girl ratio soon turned to pure fear as Anastasia swooped on them to be guinea pigs for Liv's makeover class.

Nell Howard arrived only five minutes after the doors opened. I spotted her at once, thanks to her sheepskin hat and the dramatic full-length suede coat sweeping behind her.

"Darling!" she cried when she saw me. "Good Lord, what a throng! Ooh, and champagne!" She swooped a glass of champagne from the tray Clemmy was circulating.

"Hello, Nell!" I handed the list of names to Divinity, and muttered, "Look after this and make sure you tell me if any of the names with *stars* next to them arrive, OK? It's really important."

"Why?" asked Divinity, her face lighting up. "Are they VIPs?"

"Yes," I said. "Sort of."

"What a fabulous collection of divine classes," said Nell, peering at the day's programme and sipping from her glass. I noticed she did the Tallimore trick of discreetly licking her lips so her lipstick didn't smear on the glass. "Gosh. Dressing to Meet your Ex in the Lady Hamilton Room; eBay your way to success with Clementine; Sticky Conversations with Divinity and Anastasia — what fun! And how instructive!"

"Um, yes, I hope so. Nell, can I ask you something?" I asked in an undertone, keeping one eye on the door.

"Ooh!" she said, and let me lead her into the front drawing room. Quickly, I got the letter out of my bag, and showed it to her. "Do you recognise this writing?" I asked, my heart thumping. "It's the note my mother left in my box. I've only just come across it."

She took a pair of silver glasses out of her bag and put them on very carefully, read the paper, looked intently at it, and chewed her lip.

"Darling, I would love to say yes, but you know, *everyone* wrote like this. Those big 'a's and hearts over the 'i's." She peered again. "It does look familiar, I will say that. I think . . . I might have to ask a second opinion?"

I could feel disappointment settle in my stomach like a lead scone.

"But look, this is a page from a Tallimore notebook," she went on. "Look, you can see the hallmark." She held it up to the light and pointed between the rounded letters.

I couldn't see anything, but I made a polite mm noise, because I wanted it to be, and I could tell she was trying.

Nell didn't seem disappointed though. Her eyes sparkled with intrigue. She struck me as the sort of guest you'd love to have at house parties, if only for their boundless enthusiasm for charades and gossip. "You never know, she might be here! She might have seen that lovely photograph of you in the newspaper this week. I did — you've obviously learned some good photo tricks from somewhere!"

"Here, I hope," I said. "We have a class on it now."

"Marvellous! Am I too old to sign up?" Nell pressed the letter back into my hands, folding it over with her own. She had warm, soft hands. "I'll keep an eye out, shall I? I just know she'll be here. I can feel it!"

"Please," I said, gratefully. "I'm rather run off my feet, keeping everything on track."

Nell closed one eye heartily. "I'm on the lookout! Now, did I see some blinis go past?"

I led her back into the hall, and scanned the crowd with rising nerves.

"Don't panic, darling," murmured Nell. "I've got a good feeling about today."

I barely noticed the morning race by as I answered one question after another, about a new-look Academy that seemed increasingly real. The drop-in classes must have been going down well, because I directed more and more people towards Mark and his credit-card machine in the library, keeping one eye all the time on the crowd of curious new arrivals.

At eleven, I caught my own reflection in the big hall mirror and didn't recognise myself.

I was smiling, and my gorgeous blue skirt was swishing round my knees, and my hair was swinging and shiny like a shampoo ad. I actually looked like the confident woman I pretended to be in my head. Liv popped down between her makeover sessions to tweak me, but even she had to admit there was nothing she'd change.

"You look perfect," she said, and coming from her, that was really something.

My bubbling mood might have had something to do with the room full of flowers, and the buzz of everyone working together, for a change — and perhaps the little gestures of encouragement I kept getting from Jamie and Mark. Mark, quite subtly, with quick smiles, and Jamie, less so, with cheesy winks and thumbs up. I couldn't help winking back.

He was in his element. I saw him making conversation with a Chelsea mother, an impatient father, and their daughters outside Clemmy's eBay demonstration: the girls were giggling, obviously, but as Jamie spoke, the cynicism melted from the man's face and he laughed. Then Jamie said something, and moved on, with an amiable goodbye. I could tell by the way the ladies leaned in and whispered to each other that they were talking about him.

Jamie's got a real talent for this, I thought, suddenly. He was happy to meet new people, entertaining to be with, and skilled at putting strangers at ease — all qualities that came up time and again in the notebooks as being something to look out for in a man.

A hand tapped me on the shoulder. I spun round, a warm smile ready on my lips.

Lord Tallimore and Adele were standing behind me. Adele's slender hand was tucked into his arm, giving the outward impression that she was letting him support her, while at the same time suggesting that actually she was supporting him. I had to hand it to her, her body language was Nobel Prize-winning stuff.

I told myself not to be such a bitch and concentrated on the positive side of things. Lord T was looking so much better than he did at the memorial, in a new suit, cut narrower, and with a sparky red carnation buttonhole. His face was brighter, he stood up straighter, and his whole attitude was more involved and interested.

That's good, I thought and tried not to notice that his hair had turned a shade or two darker silver, and that Adele was patting his arm.

Patting his arm!

"Now, we're not going to monopolise you but Pelham wanted to say hello," she cooed.

"I wanted to say more than just hello! I wanted to say well *done,* Betsy," he said, his face bright with pride. "What a transformation! I can't think why we haven't had one of these Open Days before — wonderful idea! I've just been talking to Maureen McGregor and she says she can't wait to get started on these new courses of yours. 'Happy homeowning'! 'Dealing with the in-laws', indeed! Marvellous!"

"Mm," said Adele, pointedly. "Although Betsy will need a little help with the in-laws class, won't you, hon? Not having had any personal experience on that front."

"I thought *you* might have some suggestions," I replied, keeping my face neutral. Adele's marriage schedule did involve racking up about four sets of them.

"Oh, I do," Adele nodded, and glanced up at Lord T. "I'm such a great fan of marriage. It's the natural state for *everyone* to be in. Don't you think, Pelham?"

"*Absolutely.* I'm sure you ladies are all pitching in." Lord T beamed, and I wasn't sure if he'd caught her hint. "Just like the old days, seeing the place full of life. Full of laughter. Frances would be so proud."

"Oh, yes," said Adele, quickly, with a melancholy sigh. "Weren't we just saying, what a *very* special day Frances made the prize-giving? She always wore such *witty* hats, and found a prize to give to even the most *uninspiring* girls . . ."

As Lord T's eyes misted over with nostalgia, I noticed that Adele wasn't looking nearly as sharp today as she had done last time I saw her. Instead of the tight pencil skirt and skinny heels, she was wearing a softer jersey dress, with several long strands of pearls. Even her hair seemed less power-dressed than before, and was swept up into what was almost a soft bun at the back.

I watched, mesmerised, as Adele's varnished nails tapped up and down on his sleeve. They were a subtle pale pink today, and her massive sparklers had vanished, in favour of a simple signet ring. My mouth opened as the penny dropped. Adele was morphing into Franny in an attempt to bag the second engagement ring of the term!

She saw my reaction and gave me an unmistakeable filthy look that Lord T couldn't see, thanks to Paulette appearing at his side with a tray of champagne.

"Take one from the left," Paulette advised him. "That's the quality bubbly, we're running a bit short so I'm giving the cheaper stuff to people who look like they can't tell the difference."

"Paulette! Don't say that!"

"I'm sure *all* our guests can tell," said Adele with a reproachful glance.

I thought quickly. "If anyone notices, tell them it's part of a course we offer, on wine tasting or something. But don't let them take two glasses," I added, imagining Mark prising the second flute out of guests' hands.

"Not for me, Paulette," said Adele, patting her tiny stomach. "I mustn't!"

"Why? You up the duff?" she enquired.

"What? Goodness, no! I don't drink during the day!" Adele looked affronted then checked with Lord T to see if he'd noted her abstemiousness.

She was wasting her time there, I thought. He liked a woman who could hold her claret.

"Oh, right. In recovery, are you?" Paulette went on.

"Thank you, Paulette." I steered her away firmly. "I'll catch up with you later," I called to Lord T, who raised his flute to me in thanks. Adele fiddled with her unfamiliar hairpiece while she thought no one was looking and then resumed her expression of sweetness when he turned to ask her a question.

Paulette and I had barely got into the hall when Divinity came rushing up, her hair quivering with excitement.

"They're here!" whispered Divinity.

"Who?"

She waved her guest list at me. "Your VIPs! Three arrived together — I watched them getting a drink."

I grabbed the list off her, and checked: Coralie, Sophie and Emma-Jane had been grouped together by Divinity's gold pen and ostentatiously ticked off. She'd clearly learned her door policy from years of queueing outside clubs, having made her own "VIP list", which I was sure she'd be letting guests catch a glimpse of.

The breath caught in my throat.

"There was some confusion about the names," Divinity went on. "They've got, like, millions of surnames and one of them's brought her daughter, she says . . ."

"Her daughter?"

Divinity seemed puzzled. "Are you OK? You've gone dead white."

"I'm fine." I scanned the room, hoping to spot Nell so she could introduce me, but she was nowhere to be seen. "I'll . . . I'll go and say hello."

I squeezed my way through the guests, catching faint snatches of sales pitches about email etiquette from Mrs Angell and jumpstarting a flat battery from Mark, until I spotted an unlikely trio standing by the champagne table.

Nell's photo, taken in almost that very place, flashed up in my mind — languid blond Sophie, fiery Coralie and naughty Emma-Jane with the Shetland pony fringe — and I tried to overlay that with the spooky Stevie Nicks lookalike, the white-haired matron in drapey clothes, and the bouffant newsreader peering at the caviar-topped blinis Anastasia's mother had sent by the truckload as a thank you for sorting out her daughter's feud with the parking wardens.

I swallowed and counted to ten, but my heart was racing. Was one of these three women my mother? Was this it? How did I ask?

There was nothing in Franny's notebooks about how one was supposed to flush out a runaway parent, without actually asking directly. That was presumably why the upper classes invented charades: for practice.

One of them, Sophie, by the look of the blond hair, spotted me staring at them, and then I had no choice but to dive right in.

"Hello!" I held out my hand, and let my manners take over while my brain kicked into gear. "I'm Betsy," I said. "Betsy *Cooper Tallimore.* Thanks so much for coming along this morning — I hope the new ideas meet with Old Girl approval?"

If I was hoping for a Hollywood style double take of realisation and a flurry of schmaltzy strings and paper hankies, it didn't arrive.

Emma-Jane stared at me, as if she was translating what I'd said into a different language in her head, while Coralie smiled in a terrifying manner that showed expensive white teeth but no laughter lines. A creeping sensation ran over my skin; I wasn't thrilled at the prospect of any of these women revealing themselves to be my mother. I didn't really fancy any of these genes turning up in me in later life.

I pressed on, anyway.

Sophie shook my hand; it was a limp shake — what Franny used to call "a Brittle Bones Society special".

"Hi," she said. She smelled strongly of patchouli and menthol cigarettes. "Sophie Townend-Gooch. Are you Betsy *Tallimore*? As in . . ." She dropped her voice and swivelled her hooded brown eyes like a spy. "The baby we weren't supposed to know about?"

I nodded, uncertainly. As maternal opening gambits went, that wasn't very promising.

"My secret love child?" Coralie added, throwing a stray layer of greyish drape over her shoulder.

My pulse stopped for a second. Only a second, though, because Sophie gave her a ferocious nudge that sent her champagne spilling.

"*My* secret love child, you mean, you cow!" Sophie insisted.

I looked between them. "I'm sorry?"

Coralie opened her eyes so wide I could see the inner rims. She had a touching loyalty to eighties' electric blue eyeliner. "I think you'll find *I* was the bad girl of the year!"

"I *don't* think so!" retorted Sophie. "*I* was the one who led you all astray with my naughty marching powder and cheap highlighting kits!"

"Months in rehab?" demanded Coralie and put her hands on her jutting hips.

"How many husbands?"

"Mine or someone else's?"

Emma-Jane honked, but she didn't say anything.

"Are you joking?" I asked in a wobbly voice. It was so hard to tell with seriously posh people. Their sense of humour was borderline verbal assault by any normal standards.

Coralie and Sophie looked at me as if it hadn't occurred to them that I might be serious.

"Darling," said Coralie, furrowing her brow as far as it would furrow, which was not far at all, "there's no *way* Sophie's your mother, because her own dear mamma had her on the Pill at the age of fourteen after a near-miss with their gardener."

"Gardeners, thanks," Sophie corrected her. "And if Coralie here had managed to pop out a sprog in between Duran Duran videos, she'd probably have left it with the cloakroom attendant at Limelight, rather than Lady Frances."

I looked between them, bickering and shoving happily as if I wasn't there, and felt a sudden surge of relief that I didn't share a genetic link with either of them.

"Not me either," added Emma-Jane, out of nowhere, then honked again. "I'm more of a cat person."

"Would you excuse me?" I said, although they weren't listening. "I've got some other people to talk to."

I couldn't find Nell, or Divinity with the list, before another key workshop started in the Lady Hamilton Room: Liv's What To Wear When discussion.

Liv was busily transforming a nervous volunteer's jeans and top combo into a fashion forward evening look with an array of scarves and belts, while Divinity held forth in a voice that could probably be heard in the next street about the accessories she was using and in which shops "brilliant knock-offs" could be found for a fraction of the price of the designer originals.

I leaned against the door frame, finally confident that my dress wouldn't get covered in cobwebs. A lot had changed in an incredibly short space of time. The house was cleaner, the rooms seemed more alive, the girls seemed almost happy to be here . . .

But was I the same? My nerves were still jangling from seeing those faces from Nell's photograph, here, in real life. They were real women, and so was my mother, wherever she was. I wasn't sure, now, whether I wanted her to be here or not.

I felt a light touch on my shoulder and knew at once who it belonged to. The musky cologne gave it away. Mark smelled of good old-fashioned soap and second-hand tweed, not fancy scent.

Also, he didn't do light touches. He was more likely to clap me on the back.

"Hello, Jamie," I said, without turning round. "Can I help?"

"Maybe. Cup of tea?" murmured Jamie, in my ear. "Unless you've got one of your lovely charges teaching a cocktail class?"

I turned, and let him escort me down the stairs towards the tea table, where Anastasia graciously furnished me with a cup of tea and "as many biscuits as you would like within reason because they are high in *fet*", and then we went out into the garden, where a few people were milling around in the crisp February sunshine, trying to work out if they were allowed to smoke or not.

"Sorry I didn't have some flowers for you earlier. I should have thought ahead. But here you go." Jamie leaned forward to pick an early daffodil from the border. "Congratulations. That's not what it means officially, by the way. Just in my language of flowers."

"Thank you," I said, colouring as I took it. "Daffodils actually mean, 'the sun always shines when I'm with you'."

Jamie pulled an amazed face. "What do you know? I'm fluent in the language of flowers. I couldn't have chosen better," he said with a look that made my teacup rattle embarrassingly in its saucer.

"I suppose we have been lucky with the weather," I said, fumbling for words.

"That's true, but it's not what I meant."

I couldn't think of anything smart to say, so I just smiled and actually it was nicer.

"So can we take it you'll be staying on?" he asked. "Now you've sorted out the Academy for next term?"

"I suppose so," I began. "I hadn't really thought . . ."

I didn't want to think about what to do next, not when he was standing quite close to me, and I was getting an even better view of just how nice his shirt looked against his tan.

"Should I be sabotaging Liv's freezer?" he asked. "Make it seem like she needs some more intensive help so you'll move in with her permanently?"

"I hope you wouldn't sink so low . . ." My heart thumped in my chest. Jamie really had moved *very* close, and the way he was leaning on the wall meant his arm was technically behind me. In a moment, if I moved to one side, it would be *around* me.

"How low would I have to sink before you absolutely couldn't forgive me?" he enquired. His face was serious, but his eyes twinkled. "Just for future reference."

"Jamie! So glad I could catch you!"

Adele leaned over me to kiss Jamie's cheek as if I wasn't there.

I stared at her, hoping the shrieking inside my head wasn't audible to anyone else.

"Didn't want to chat while Pelham could hear — it'd totally spoil the surprise!" she gushed. "But just to touch base with you about this party — can we talk numbers?" Adele had dropped the sweet Sloane inflections and had gone back to her usual brisk rat-a-tat delivery. "I need to get the STDs out."

"STDs?" My jaw dropped.

Adele smiled sympathetically. "Save the dates, darling. You have to, when you're inviting the sort of people I'm after."

"Are you having a party?" I asked.

She rolled her eyes. "God, Betsy, Party Guest 101 — wait to be invited! Yes, I'm having a surprise birthday party for Pelham, I hear it's a 'big one' — she made the hook signs in the air — "and I want it to be special. I think I can make it memorable for him." She paused, then added, "I mean, with Jamie's help!" Adele fluttered a hand to her chest. "God! Not any other way! What do you take me for?"

Jamie suddenly found his teacup very interesting, so I turned back to Adele.

"Is Jamie organising a party for you?" I asked, rather hurt. Why hadn't he told me she was hijacking Lord T's birthday? I knew for a fact that he didn't want a fuss made.

"Betsy, darling, this isn't Cluedo! But yes, absolutely!" She bestowed a triumphant smile on me. "Who else would I get but Party Animals? Jamie," she added, "remind me to remind you about dietary requirements — Pelham tells me he's not very keen on shellfish and I want to get his cholesterol under control. It's about time someone looked after that poor man."

I glared at Jamie. "You didn't mention you were planning a party for Lord T," I said, rather pointedly. "Did it slip your mind?"

"I only really found out we were doing it today," Jamie admitted. "Douglas was the one who took the booking . . ."

"I *had* to have Jamie," Adele interrupted. "He's the best and he knows *everyone*. It'll be amazing. And if any other little announcements have to be made . . ." She let the horrendous idea hover in the air between us. I was reminded of the awkwardness that ensued when Lord T's Great Danes broke wind and no one liked to point it out in case they seemed to be making excuses.

"Shall I send you an STD, Betsy?" Adele enquired. "It'll have the dress code on, so you'll know what to wear. You can pop it in your diary."

"I think I know when his birthday is, Adele," I said, through gritted teeth. "I haven't missed one yet."

"Oh my God, you're offended!" She gasped as if it hadn't occurred to her that I might be, and turned to check that Jamie saw too. "Oh no! Betsy, sweetie! It's only because you're so busy with this place — I thought I'd be helpful and step in with my experience! I organised so many bashes for Edgar, and everyone said they were the most amazing parties they'd ever been to . . ."

Jamie hurried to smooth things over. "Betsy's probably got lots of great ideas about what would go down well, haven't you?"

"Best to leave it to the experts though, don't you think, darling?" Adele pouted her pink lips and tipped her head.

I stared at the pair of them, as Adele started wittering about how big a cake one could transport in a Range Rover. I wondered, in horror, if she planned to jump out of it.

But Jamie was nodding, politely, and my chest throbbed with disappointment. He'd gone out of his way to help me organise the day. He'd magicked up hundreds of glasses and pulled in favours and made everything sparkle, including me. But if he was doing the same for Adele — well, how special was it? It was something he was good at. Parties. People.

I looked at his handsome face, listening to Adele with all the appearance of someone listening to a rational conversation and not the drivellings of someone with peroxide poisoning.

"... Pelham through the ages, you know, with finger food from the sixties, and waitresses in hot pants, or maybe waiters in hot pants! Something for everyone! Who knows! Ha ha ha ..."

I silently handed him my daffodil back, and walked into the house. Adele lifted her fingertips without looking round, but she didn't even pause for breath before launching into her firework requirements.

"Betsy!"

Mark was waving his long arm at me over the heads of several groups of guests as I went back into the main hall. I could only assume he'd been made over by Anastasia — either that, or he was prepared for a "before" look. He'd been stripped of his sober shirt and was suffering in a fashionable purple number, and more gold jewellery than most women would pile on for New Year's Eve. But he was bearing it with surprising grace, given that his previous wardrobe colour palette was based on the shades you might paint a camouflaged battleship.

I smiled back and waved, as he pointed towards Miss Thorne's office, and gave me the thumbs up. "See you in there!" he mouthed, and mimed fighting his way through the chattering crowds.

Lord T was sitting in the small chair next to Miss Thorne's desk, oblivious to the gruesome party plans being laid for his benefit in the garden. He seemed in an excellent mood, given that Miss Thorne was clasping her hands at the desk itself, her face bright and tight with tension.

"Betsy!" He nearly leaped to his feet as I walked in. "Just the girl! I have some really wonderful news for you."

I have to admit, my heart went into my mouth. "About . . . the Academy?"

"But of course." He beamed at Miss Thorne. "Would you like to tell her, Geraldine? Or should we wait for the man of the moment?"

On cue, Mark walked in, with a bottle of champagne and four flutes.

"Is that one of the better bottles?" I asked, raising my eyebrow. "Paulette says we're running a two-tier system."

"It's better than our best," he said. "I bought it myself this morning, in anticipation." He paused, waiting for Lord T, who gave him a generous nod, then let a broad smile play across his face. "Congratulations. We've got all the deposits we need. We'll be continuing next term, and hopefully for many terms to come!"

"Really?" My voice squeaked with delight.

"There are more than enough deposits, in fact," said Lord T, happily. "I hear you're over-subscribed for the first two months. Your — what was it? — your Social Life especially seems to be particularly popular."

"I'm astounded," said Miss Thorne, as if she'd just popped a mint and discovered it was a marble.

Mark was struggling with the champagne cork. He looked up at me, and held it out with a wry smile.

"Hold the cork, twist the bottle, that's right, dear," prompted Miss Thorne, as I was doing just that. "There," she added, as the cork came out with a small hiss.

I poured out four neat glasses and Lord T raised his at once.

"Here's to you, Betsy," he said. "The new Director of Studies!"

"I'm sorry?"

"If you want it, the position's yours. Best chap for the job. Now, don't rush into a decision," he added, "I appreciate that you've got your clients and your career up in Edinburgh to think of, but if you'd like to stay here and direct the new courses . . ." His face, usually such a vision of control that it seemed to be carved from the same wood as cricket bats, was almost boyish. "We'd try to make it worth your while."

Any annoyance I'd felt about Jamie and Adele floated away as the champagne bubbles bounced around my bloodstream and the reality of what Mark said sank in. I'd done it! I'd come up with something that real people actually wanted — and I'd saved the Academy using Franny's notebooks and my own real life, "didn't go to finishing school" experience.

"When can I start?" I said, forgetting for the moment that I had an imaginary office and several imaginary employees, not to mention my imaginary clients to consider. "I'd really love to!"

I turned to Mark, who gave me a conspiratorial wink. He *suited* purple, I thought, distractedly. Whoever had made him over had done more than just change his clothes — his hair looked great, and his face was animated, and he seemed much more handsome. Much more . . . ask-out-able.

Ooh, I thought, as he tipped his champagne flute up to sip from it and I caught a glimpse of his soft inner lip. Maybe I should. Maybe this was what Liv had meant about inviting romance into my life.

"Delightful as it is to celebrate your marvellous triumph with you, Betsy dear, someone ought to be saying goodbye to our guests," said Miss Thorne, with just a hint of reproach in her voice as she pushed herself away from the desk. "We shouldn't forget our manners. Mark, perhaps you can assist me?"

Mark gave me a private look that made me feel pleasantly awkward, and then escorted Miss Thorne out in a show of gallantry. I sank into the chair opposite Lord T's and gave him a huge smile.

"Wow," I said. All I had to do now was to find the teachers, sort out the classes, check the legality of some of my ideas — but that could wait. I wanted to savour this moment, and Lord T's obvious happiness.

"I wish Frances were here to see this," he said simply. "The place is full of life. It's what she always wanted. And because of you!"

I felt my face go pink with pride.

"I, ah, I haven't mentioned this to Geraldine," Lord T went on, "but if you do decide to change horses, career-wise, I can't offer the sort of salary you're used to, but if you like, I'd hand over the ownership of the business to you. I'll just be a shareholder, you'll run the whole shooting match."

"But . . ." My mouth went dry, and I didn't know what to say. "That's too generous!"

"Not at all. It'd be yours in the end, in any case. About time I took things easier. Apparently I'm overloading myself." Lord T looked rather confused. "Thought I *was* taking things pretty easy, spot of fishing, light gardening sort of thing, but Adele reckons I need to slow down. Spend more time in the country. Foreign countries, mainly."

His face brightened at exactly the same time as mine assumed a rictus expression of horror. "She's a funny little thing, Adele. Reminds me of Frances in some ways. She thinks I ought to see the Caribbean! Can't imagine why — place is far too hot, unless you're watching the cricket." Lord T looked at me hopefully. "Do you think that might be it? Girl's a cricket fan?"

"She does seem to be well up on international matches," I said tactfully.

Lord T raised his silvery eyebrows. "Marvellous! Frances couldn't bear cricket. Still miss her grumbling away at the Test match. Knitting through the Ashes series. Knitting!" He sighed. "Adele thinks I should take up tennis — offered to book me some lessons. Never too late to learn apparently."

"Oh, I don't think there's any need for that!" I insisted so hard that Lord T nearly rocked backwards in his chair. "I mean," I added, "stick to cricket. Safety in numbers. I mean . . . it's more companionable."

"Indeed it is. Anyway," he went on, "you sleep on it, and get back to me. And in the meantime, you've made me and Frances very proud."

He raised his glass a polite two inches, being far too well brought up to chink, and nodded in a meaningful sort of way.

This must be it, I thought, dizzy with more than just champagne. The final proof. It *had* to be Hector who'd left me here — handing over the Academy kept it in the family, didn't it? Maybe Lord T had sworn some gentleman's oath not to reveal the truth to anyone in his lifetime, or something, but the pride in his eyes was enough for me for now.

I raised my glass to him, and to Franny, and to the rest of the Tallimore family. Up to and including me.

I barely had time to enjoy that heart-warming thought when it was replaced by another, much less warming one.

Mark and Miss Thorne were clearing out the guests, and I hadn't had a chance to check with Divinity whether all the 1980 girls had arrived!

I banged my glass down on a side table, missing the coaster, and leaped up. "Will you excuse me?" I gabbled, as Lord T stared in bewilderment, and rushed into the hall.

There was no one left. Only Divinity was standing by the front door, ostentatiously tallying up her guest list, while the others made desultory tidying up gestures to cover the fact they were scoffing the leftover buffet.

"Can I see that list?" I blurted out, grabbing her clipboard off her.

"Pretty good turn out. Some no shows," she said, unaware of my agitation. "I would write to them and ask why they didn't turn up. Rude, if you ask me."

My eyes scanned up and down. Rosalind and Bumps had been on the list, but hadn't showed.

"You're certain you checked everyone in?" I demanded.

"Betsy, the security was tighter than a gnat's chuff," Divinity assured me.

I stared round the hall. Had she been here? Had I got so distracted by my own business plan that I'd forgotten to look out for her?

My shoulders drooped.

"Problem?"

I could tell by the way Divinity puffed out her chest like a parakeet that it was Jamie behind me, even without recognising the voice.

He slung an arm around me. "Thought that went very well, didn't you, Divinity? Top marks for Miss Cooper, eh?"

I tried to smile, but my heart wasn't in it. I felt like I'd won one battle but lost another, without even realising.

CHAPTER TWENTY-THREE

Chic is in your own distinctive details: a signature scent, a favourite cocktail, the perfect red lipstick.

"Fruit cake doesn't stand to be cut into such small slivers," said Kathleen, inspecting the fairy-sized portions of cake on the silver stand. "You need two of these to get the taste."

"Oh, Kathleen!" said Nancy. "Stop complaining — it's not every day we come to the *Ritz* for tea." She gave me a happy pat on the knee. "It's a lovely treat, Betsy. You're far too good to us."

I could see Kathleen's point: it was a bit like taking coals to Newcastle, tormenting her with a doll's house version of her own creaking table of delights, but Nancy loved the tinkling piano and the fancy napkins and all the fuss of a proper hotel tea, and I liked seeing her enjoying herself.

We were sitting in the golden splendour of the Palm Court at a prime spot from where we could see the rest of the room and comment on the other guests as well as the lavish pastry selection. No one had dressed up as smartly as Kathleen and Nancy, who were one wicker basket short of the full Agatha Christie Sunday night special. Nancy even had a hat on. I say hat, it was almost a bonnet.

"Well, you should thank Jamie." I helped myself to a minuscule éclair. "He was the one who managed to get a table at such short notice. Normally you need to book weeks in advance for a Saturday tea."

"He must think very highly of you to arrange that," said Kathleen, inspecting a fragment of cheesecake.

"He thinks highly of you two, more like." I didn't tell Kathleen that I thought Jamie had done it by way of apology for arranging Adele's party. I'd told him he didn't need to apologise. He said he did. I hadn't meant to sound so huffy and he'd looked at me as if he wasn't sure why I was being so off, but my brain refused to cooperate and I couldn't find the words to explain why it riled me so much.

Kathleen and Nancy exchanged glances.

"There's no favour done in the day that's not collected in the dark." Kathleen popped the cheesecake into her mouth and shut it like a trap while she chewed.

"Oh, now Kathleen, don't be like that," said Nancy. "Just because he's good-looking doesn't mean to say he's *always* after something. I do think Jamie should have been born when he could have worn breeches. Will they ever come back into fashion, do you think, Betsy?" she asked hopefully.

"You'd have to ask Liv that, not me," I said. "But if they do, I'm sure Jamie will be one of the first people to be wearing them."

"I saw you talking to that Eleanor Howard yesterday," said Kathleen, in her "apropos of nothing" voice. "What did she have to say for herself?"

"Ooh, she's gone very dramatic," observed Nancy. "I remember Eleanor when she wouldn't say boo to a goose, let alone wear a fur hat during the day. Of course, she married that actor chap who didn't know whether he was Barry or Carrie, if you know what I mean . . ."

I hesitated, unsure whether to tell them about my parental investigations, but somehow it didn't seem so important, not now. I still had a snug glow of belonging from the previous day. Lord T's proud smile felt like a thermal vest around my heart.

"I've been talking to her about finding my mother," I confessed. "Nell thought she was an old girl who might have come along yesterday, but . . ." I stopped, and made my face more positive, for their benefit. "I reckon if she wants to find me, she will. And in the meantime, my family's right here."

"Ah, bless," said Nancy, patting her eyes with her napkin. "Course it is, darling. We're always here. Who'd like another sandwich? Do they still replace your empty plate? Or would that be greedy?"

Kathleen was looking at me more circumspectly, but I didn't really notice, in my general flush of goodwill.

"I know I should have spoken to Lord T years ago," I went on. "But with Franny and everything . . . Anyway, I think I know who my father is, at least. I just need him to admit it. It's not like it's going to change anything."

"What do you mean, admit it?" asked Kathleen sharply.

"That Hector is my father." I looked at them both, over the silver teapot and cake stand. "I mean, it's obvious, isn't it? I've always suspected it was, the way they took me in with no fuss, and now Lord T's given me the Academy to run, so it stays in the family! I can understand why Franny might not have wanted to talk about it, if they didn't like my mother . . ."

"Have you found your mother?" asked Kathleen, quietly.

I blinked. I wasn't so sure about this, but I was starting to have an inkling. "I think so. She hasn't actually said anything yet, but I've got my suspicions."

"And who's that, love?" Nancy looked worried.

"Well, I think it's Nell Howard." As I said it aloud, I felt sure I was right. "She was there at the memorial and she gave me a photograph of the 1980 girls, but I think it's a red herring — I think *she's* my mother. I think she's in the photograph and isn't telling me. She recognised my necklace, and I showed her the letter that came in the box — she said she didn't know the handwriting, but there was something odd about the way she said it."

"But she hasn't told you?"

"No. Not yet. I thought . . . I thought she might be waiting to see how much I wanted to find my mother."

"Oh, maybe she wants to make a declaration!" said Nancy, putting down her dessert fork. "Maybe she wants to take you back to the place where she left you . . ."

"This isn't one of your scullerymaid dramas, Miss Kirkpatrick." Kathleen beetled her brows at Nancy then turned to me. "Has Nell told you that Hector's your father? Actually told you?"

I shook my head. "But she doesn't need to. I'll ask Lord Tallimore tonight and he can . . ."

"No, you won't. Nancy?" said Kathleen and gave a very unwilling Nancy a nudge. "Speak the truth and shame the devil. I know it's not nice, but . . ."

"*Kath*-leen!"

"*Nan*-cy!"

"What?" I looked between them.

"Oh, Kathleen! Betsy, dear, Hector isn't your father," said Nancy. "He can't be anyone's father — he had a bad do with mumps. Caused all sorts of . . ." Her face went pink. "Complications . . . with his . . . you know. Hereditary parts."

I flinched in shock, as my nice comfy new world fell apart. Hector wasn't my father? So Lord T and Franny really *were* just strangers who'd taken me in? I really *could* be the child of anyone at all?

"Are you sure?" I managed.

She nodded. "Of course I am, love. I was sent back home to nurse him through it, wasn't I? I had to listen to the doctor explaining all the business to Lord Tallimore . . ."

"You didn't have to listen," Kathleen reminded her. "But your ear just happened to be pressed up against the door."

Nancy tossed her head. "It's as well to know these things. Anyway, it was a very bad do, he was warned that children weren't on the agenda. Lord Tallimore was devastated. It was bad enough Hector being the way he was, without thinking that was it, the end of the Tallimores."

Kathleen spotted my stricken expression and leaped in. "So you can imagine what a blessing it was when you arrived on their doorstep! No wonder they were so thrilled to have you!"

I barely heard a word she said for the blood roaring in my own ears. All the years I'd been imagining ballerinas and rock stars, a tiny part of me had always taken for granted that Franny and I had some link. I hadn't realised that until now. But we didn't. We couldn't. There was *nothing* binding her and Lord T to me at all. I felt as if I was cut off from everything I'd ever known.

I really was just a stranger. A nobody.

"But I thought . . . the way Franny looked at me . . ." My eyes filled up and the sandwiches blurred on the stand.

"She looked at you like that because she worshipped the ground you walked on," said Kathleen stoutly. "It didn't matter a jot to her who your father was. Or your mother, for that matter. I doubt she'd have loved you an iota more if Hector *had* been your father. So, this Nell woman — are you going to ask her what's what?"

Suddenly, I didn't know if I wanted to. Was Nell playing some game, where I had to wait before she would tell me?

"I don't know," I said in a small voice.

"It doesn't affect anything here," said Nancy, almost pleading. "We still love you, and Lord Tallimore obviously thinks the world of you if he wants you to stay on. I know it'll mean giving up that marvellous job of yours in Edinburgh, but . . ." She was bunching up her napkin in distress. "I do hope you'll give it some thought. Home's where the heart is."

I struggled inside, desperate for them not to see the shameful mess raging inside me.

Home *was* where the heart was. But I wasn't sure if that was quite enough.

I picked up some ice cream on the way back to Liv's and a DVD of *Mamma Mia,* so we could at least have a girlie night in.

But as soon as I opened the door, the smell of curling irons and perfume hit me, and the sound of Abba was already blaring from her stereo upstairs, so loud that I couldn't even hear Barry the cat mewling when I found him on the sofa in a heap of discarded clothes. The way his pink mouth was opening and closing, he looked as if he was miming along to "Dancing Queen".

This meant only one thing. Liv's man detox was at an end. She only played Abba when she was getting ready for a date. The stomping upstairs also suggested she'd reached the dance routine stage, ie, shoes on, only lip gloss to go.

"Liv!" I yelled up the stairs. "Liv!"

"I'm coming down!" she yelled, when she eventually heard me. "Two minutes!"

I went into the kitchen and was surprised to see Mark at the breakfast bar, idly going through the breadbin where Liv and I put all the bills and receipts.

He was wearing an outfit I hadn't seen before: dark jeans and a soft weekendy shirt and, blimey, indigo suede trainers. There was a black corduroy jacket hanging over a chair though, so he hadn't turned entirely fashionable without warning.

"Mark?" I said.

He spun round guiltily and rammed the council tax bill back in the breadbin. "Oh, hello, Betsy."

"Are you auditing Liv now?" I asked. "Academy not challenging enough for you?"

"Um, sort of." He gave me a nervous smile which made his face look surprisingly attractive. I wondered if the attic offices had some cruel kind of lighting flaw, because Mark looked about a hundred per cent more cute in Liv's kitchen. His hair was shinier, his expression was more confident. I took back my "porridge oat box" assessment and upgraded him to "rugged, outdoor Boden model".

He went on, "I'm taking her out to say thanks for helping me buy some new clothes."

"She helped you buy some new clothes?" I repeated, rather stupidly. I couldn't quite line up the mental images of Mark Montgomery spending actual money on clothes and Liv strolling around Selfridges with a man who wore red socks and tweed jackets. "When?"

"This afternoon." Mark looked pleased and embarrassed at the same time. "She made some rather, um, punchy observations yesterday about my wardrobe looking like someone's dad's and suggested she take me shopping and so we did, as you can see," he made a self-conscious gesture towards his outfit, "and I thought the least I could do was to take her out to say thanks."

"Right." I looked him up and down. "Well, it's definitely worth at least a burger. Those are fantastic jeans — they really suit you! Can I get you a drink?" I asked, opening the fridge. "Liv might be a while. When she says two minutes, she doesn't mean two of our earth minutes. She works on some Roman numeral system."

"Oh, er, yeah, thanks. Cup of tea would be great." I'd expected Mark to come out with some sarcastic quip about female time/space continuum, as he'd have done over sandwiches in the office, but he didn't. In fact, he seemed a lot less confident altogether out of his suit.

I put the bottle of Chardonnay back into the fridge, and stole a quick glance as I swilled the teapot with hot water. Mark was so much better-looking when he wasn't spitting feathers about Miss Thorne's expenses. It was suddenly easier to imagine him working on his car, stripping it down with oily rags and that sort of thing. That was a *good* practical hobby for a man to have. And quite a sexy one, come to think of it.

I wondered if Liv would mind me coming with them. I could help the conversation along — she was getting mildly obsessive about the change jar stacking up in the kitchen, but that didn't mean she could sustain a whole evening's chat about personal tax allowances, with a little engine chat for light relief.

Mark ran a hand through his hair, which also seemed to have been cut. Was it this light, I wondered, or was he looking more like Colin Firth by the minute? Could Liv have helpfully chipped away the outer economist to reveal the inner attractive man she kept insisting would walk into my life one day and sweep me away from . . .

The kettle boiled and I jumped, taken aback by the abrupt turn my imagination had taken into Nancy-ville.

"Great news about you staying," said Mark. "Don't suppose you'll be needing a bursar now, will you, if you're going to be in charge?"

"Sorry?"

"I mean, since you're more qualified than me, probably." He smiled wryly.

I put the teapot down in front of him. If we were going to start flirting properly, then I needed to be honest. From now on, I decided, I wasn't going to make up anything about my job, my social life, my background, anything.

"I've got a confession to make," I said.

"Go on," said Mark. "Don't make me guess. It'll only end in tears."

"I'm not really a management consultant."

"Of course you're not." He lifted the pot, and raised an eyebrow. "Milk first or second? I can't remember."

"Yes, no sugar." I realised what he'd said, and my mouth dropped open in horror. "What do you mean, of course you're not?"

"I worked that out after day two." He stirred my tea and passed me the mug. "Obvious. You didn't delegate anything to anyone. You just did it. I could understand every word you said and there were no memos, jargon or long absences while you lunched other people. The Maths degree, I could believe," he added. "Your budgets added up, at least."

"Why didn't you say?"

"Oh, stop blushing, it's fine. I didn't know what you'd told The Dragon Queen, or Lord Tallimore. And it seemed like a small price to pay for having a reasonable human being around the place for support. Anyway, it's been fun. For the first time in *years* I'm glad my dad made me promise to take over his volunteer work."

Our eyes met, and I honestly felt a small frisson run over my skin. Whatever transformation Liv had done to Mark had extended far beyond his clothes. He was positively charming tonight.

"Would you stay?" I asked. "I mean, part-time? I don't know how much money there'll be for new teachers, to begin with, so I'd need to keep you and Liv and Jamie on as . . . Mark? Mark, are you listening to me?"

He wasn't listening, and his face had gone funny. I turned to see what he was staring at.

Liv was standing in the doorway in a minidress that fell into her "restaurant dress" category: without the benefit of a tablecloth, it'd cause her serious sitting down issues, but on the all-important way to the table, it made her legs look a mile long. Her blond hair was loose around her shoulders, her make-up was invisible, and she looked as if she'd just thrown her outfit together, despite having been upstairs throwing everything else around for hours, probably.

"Hi!" she said, breathily. "Ooh, tea, fantastic!"

Mark rushed to pour her a mug and managed to slop milk all over his new jeans. "Oh, bollocks," he said, trying to mop the spillage with my Visa bill.

"Get some warm water on, from the loo — under the stairs on your left," I said, quickly.

With a shame-faced grimace at Liv, Mark rushed out, backwards.

"Doesn't he look great?" said Liv, fondly. "It only took me three hours to get him out of cords and into denim. I'm very proud."

"He looks gorgeous," I admitted. "You've really brought out the man in the management accountant."

Liv turned back to me and her face sparkled with more than just highlighter. "I know! And I take it all back — you've been right all these years! I just didn't realise how attractive a man like that can be! He's going to help me buy a car, he says. A cheap one."

"But you don't drive . . ." I began, then started again. Just to be clear. "You and Mark. Is this . . . a date?"

Liv looked coy. "I don't know. But he's lovely, isn't he?"

"But he's a man with good quality socks and a sensible job!" I hissed, in an undertone. "You said he was exactly the sort of man to steer clear of? In favour of fun? And excitement?"

"The sort of man *you* should steer clear of," Liv corrected me. "Me, on the other hand, I *need* someone who cares more about socks than, I don't know, minibreaks. As soon as I met Mark, I realised that he's the kind of guy I've been waiting for all these years." Her eyes had gone starry. "He didn't even try to chat me up! He was wearing those awful trousers and I just knew here was a man who wasn't married to anyone else!"

"OK," I said slowly, surprised at how disappointed I felt. "OK, but I thought I might . . ."

The loo flushed in the downstairs bathroom. Mark was on his way back. Liv grabbed my arm and pointed her finger at me fiercely.

"No!" she gabbled, desperate to get everything in before Mark came back. "Get it together with Jamie! I insist! I'm fed up with you two faffing around, dropping stuff and generally acting like a pair of morons when you're together, because I saw him yesterday and he does it too. He *wants* to settle down. With you! Call him tonight, have dinner, sort it out, do what you have to do, or else . . . Or else . . ."

"Or else what?" I demanded.

"Or else, *I'll* tell him you fancy him," she said.

We stared at each other in horror as her words sank in.

Liv put her hands on each side of her face. "You've turned me into a thirteen-year-old," she said. "Please, just get on with it."

Mark and Liv went out on what I now realised was their first date and I settled myself on the sofa with Barry the cat and Liv's entire selection of cheesy

DVDs, but I couldn't get past the first ten minutes of anything.

I should have been feeling on top of the world, and in some ways I did, but little things kept niggling away at me.

Adele, for a start. She couldn't seriously be making a move on Lord T, could she? Could she end up my stepmother, technically?

And Jamie. Just thinking about him working with Adele made my scalp crawl with invisible lice of mortification. That was never going to come right. And Mark! I didn't begrudge Liv a good sensible man, but it wasn't like I was inundated with candidates myself right now. I'd almost made a complete fool of myself, too — better to feel passed over than to be turned down because he fancied Liv, not me.

And Nell. What was she playing at? I'd seen her hovering around the Open Day, but then she'd disappeared before the end. Again.

I thought about my airy flat in Edinburgh and my old life that suddenly seemed very uncomplicated by comparison. Dull, but uncomplicated. I knew where I was with shoes. If I stayed in London and opened the new Academy with all the fanfare it deserved, it wouldn't be long before someone discovered that I was no etiquette expert. And what if it was my real mother who decided to turn up and expose me? She was out there somewhere, just waiting to turn up and honk at me like Emma-Jane and her farmyard animal impressions.

I opened a bottle of wine and got one of the lilac notebooks out of my bag. I held it in my hand, feeling the satisfying weight of the leather binding and the gleaming gold edgings to the paper, then opened it at random.

It was halfway through two lessons, and my writing struggled to keep up with Franny's enthusiastic advice, offered while she drifted round the class, clicking her fingers as she thought of new points to make.

I could hear her now.

". . . A Good Chap (GC) will say nothing when you're wrong, but will make a real song and dance when you're right. A GC probably won't comment on your clothes, but he'll always let you know when you've made him proud to take you out. Don't worry if he forgets flowers — only international GCs and husbands are trained in that respect, and it can be a little creepy, and make you wonder what he's hiding — just make sure he remembers to do the little things like offering to help when there's nothing in it for him, and making you tea in the morning and not criticising your parking. These are things you can't train, they're inherent, so when you find one, treasure him."

"THANK-YOU LETTERS. Always write your thank yous the same day and on good paper, or amusing postcards. Keep a stock in your desk for that reason. Don't use free ones from hotels, it's showing off . . ."

That I could do. Thank-you cards.

I poured myself a large glass of wine and got my correspondence cards out of my bag. I had a lot of people to thank, and at least I knew how to do that, even if I'd thoroughly cocked things up on the GC front.

"'*Dear Miss McGregor. Thank you so much for all your halp.* No, *help. The right fork can bring so much small happiness to*' . . . I can't read this, it's all smudgey . . ."

I opened one bleary eye. I was on the sofa, I noted, not in bed. And my head was too tight.

Liv stood over me, reading aloud mercilessly from the thank-you notes I'd started the previous night. "'*Dear Clementine. Thank you so much for all your halp.*' Again. H.A.L.P. Tsk. '*Don't let anyone tell you that you're not a strong, individual young woman because*' . . . Oh dear, anyone would think you'd been drinking when you wrote these."

"I had," I croaked, "one or two glasses."

"One or two buckets. But still writing thank-you notes! There's manners for you. '*Dear Miss Thorne, I'd like to thank you so much for all your help, but I can't because you didn't give me any, you stuck-up old* . . .' Oooh, good job that smudged."

"Stop it," I said, dragging myself to a sitting position.

"'*Dear Liv*'," she read. '"*Thank you so much for letting me share your flat and boss you around. You are the best friend a girl could want. Please tell Jamie that . . .' " She stopped. "Oh. No, I won't tell him that. You should tell him that yourself."*

I slumped back on to the sofa and waited for Liv's horrified intake of breath as she got to the end of the card.

It took longer than I'd thought — my writing *was* hard to make out.

"What do you mean, you're probably going back to Edinburgh! Why are you leaving?" demanded Liv. "You've just inherited the business of your dreams and you're going to be the first manners millionairess in London! Come on! You're making the family fortunes over again!"

"I'm not family. Hector's not my dad," I said. "Nancy told me yesterday. He had mumps that rendered him technically no danger to innocent young ladies."

"Oh." Liv pulled a "fancy that" face. "Bet that was an interesting conversation. So? You're still Lord T's family — he adopted you, for God's sake! What more do you want? And you've still got an amazing business to run."

"I *can't*," I said. "It feels wrong. Yesterday, I thought, wow, this is my destiny! I can do this because I've inherited Franny's social genes, but now . . ." I looked round the kitchen for the glass of water and Nurofen that I always left out to force down before sleeping. Typical. I forgot to take it for the first time since Freshers' Week. No wonder my head was banging.

"Now you're going to do a runner back to Edinburgh?" said Liv sarcastically. "Because doing a runner is the one genetic certainty you have? Give me a break."

"No," I started but she carried on boggling at me. "You've got very tough of late," I informed her.

"I can't think why. I've only had some first-class life coach moving in with me and kicking me up the arse and generally helping me get my act together." Liv thrust the glass of water at me. "You're not going anywhere, not just like that. Drink this, put the coffee machine on, and I'll go and get the papers. You'll feel tons better with some caffeine and a proper breakfast inside you — isn't that what you're always telling me?"

"I need to rewrite those thank-you notes, anyway," I conceded.

Liv's face brightened. "Great. Now, get in the shower and I'll be right back."

I did feel a bit better with clean hair, and significantly better with coffee flowing through my veins. Liv crashed back in while I was still in her dressing gown, making myself a second cup.

"I blew the budget and went to Paul for proper French croissants," she informed me, breezing past with several bags. "Don't even think about arguing. Mark says that you can't put a price on feeling good. And I've got a selection of papers — serious, scandalous and the one that pretends to be serious but that's just full of prurient gossip about anorexic celebrities and rich people cavorting around town."

She threw the papers down in a fan shape on the table. "You can have the pick. So long as you read the horoscopes out loud."

I managed a smile and grabbed a croissant as I pulled the nearest paper towards me.

Silence fell in the kitchen as we scoffed flaky pastry and slurped away at coffees, now no one was there to inspect our table manners.

"Would you believe Jennifer Lopez has lost weight?" I observed, turning the pages of my tabloid. "And Gwyneth Paltrow has put it on."

"Baby, or comfort eating due to secret agony?" said Liv, without looking up.

"They don't know. It looks like a bad dress to me." I bit into my croissant, and turned over.

SCANDAL. SEX. SOCIALITES.
WHEN GOOD GIRLS GO VERY VERY BAD.

She looked familiar, I thought, inspecting the blonde in question, as I reached for my coffee. In fact, she looked a lot like . . .

Venetia.

CHAPTER TWENTY-FOUR

Make sure you've got one stunning photograph of yourself ready for sending to the newspapers in case of you winning the lottery/disappearing at sea/filing a news report from some disaster zone via your mobile. The last thing you want is your moment of glory being illustrated by some hideous office party snap.

ILLICIT LIAISONS. DRUNKEN ANTICS. SEX.
THE FINISHING SCHOOL FOR SCANDAL?

My eye scanned the page up and down, unable to take all the words in at once.

The main photograph was the one of Venetia from the feature earlier in the week, but Adele had been replaced with a blurry long lens paparazzi picture of a man I assumed was Luka the fiancé with the Ferrari.

He wasn't quite the smouldering Adonis she'd made out either — from what I could see, he was about as round as he was high and Venetia would be condemned to flats for her entire married life, however long that was, according to Adele's "starter marriage" prescription.

On the other side of the double-page spread was a group shot that I hadn't seen before, but which still seemed oddly familiar. I looked closer and realised it was the missing "class of 1980", but with little "where are they now?" boxes springing from each of the girls, and photos of floppy-haired, posh heart-throbs alongside them. I didn't know any of the men, but they looked like characters from *Brideshead Revisited,* with names I vaguely recognised. Rory McAlmont, Lord Inverisle, Simon Fitzgerald, Bingo Palmer, the Hon Hector Tallimore.

My insides turned to liquid as my eye caught something in the corner of the page.

Me. There was a photograph of *me,* aged about five, sitting in the garden on Lady Tallimore Day, laughing up into Franny's face as she tugged my Pippi Longstocking plaits and looked radiant with happiness.

It was captioned, *Elizabeth "Betsy" Tallimore, adopted daughter of Lord and Lady Tallimore, owners of the notorious Tallimore Academy.*

My mouth went dry. Where did I fit into this? I forced myself to read the words though they were dancing and blurring.

"You're a billionaire businessman," the article started. "You've got friends in high places, and your fingers in many pies. The only thing you don't have is class. So where do you turn? To the last bastion of establishment, the English finishing school, where respectability and social acceptance can be bought, albeit at a price.

"Political donor and Serbian entrepreneur Luka Jankovic this week announced his engagement to society party girl Venetia Knight, a student at the establishment's favourite finishing school, the Tallimore Academy in Mayfair's exclusive Full Moon Street — and finally ended his campaign for a British passport. Leggy polo-loving Venetia appeared in this paper earlier in the week, extolling the virtues of the "new look" finishing school, which teaches its students not only the art of eating in the smartest restaurants and dressing for success, but also, it seems, making mutually beneficial marriages of convenience. New look? Or just the same as the marriage market that London's smartest heiresses were trained for a hundred years ago?"

That wasn't what the dressing for success classes were about, I thought, wildly. And the eating in restaurants thing — that was about handling your chopsticks in a sushi bar, not free-loading with rich businessmen, as the paper was suggesting!

I started to feel sick. What did they mean, the *notorious* Tallimore Academy?

"It's not the first time Tallimore girls have helped out a billionaire in need. Twenty years ago, London's out-of-control young aristocrats and playboys treated the Academy as their own private dating agency, wining and dining the privileged teens sent to learn the ins and outs of the upper classes. Rich wild girls like Coralie Hendricks (pictured left) and Sophie Townend (pictured right, as a Bond girl) cavorted in private hotel orgies and caused mayhem at high society balls, but when their moneyed indulgences tipped over from youthful exuberance into outright scandal, the establishment were swift to close ranks and hide the resulting human wreckage."

"There is nothing in the paper this weekend," moaned Liv. "Pass me the magazine section, will you? Betsy? Betsy! What's up?"

My eyes were glued to the page. "Several outrages were hushed up by the well-connected owners, including aspiring racing driver Rory McAlmont's fatal late-night Aston Martin crash on Chelsea Bridge, which killed him and his passenger, heroin addict Antonia Greene. Whispers also persisted about a newborn baby abandoned at the Academy, possibly the illegitimate child of a former student. Lord and Lady Tallimore adopted a daughter around this time, Elizabeth, now twenty-seven, though they denied any knowledge of her origins at the time and made strenuous efforts to keep the matter out of the papers."

I felt as if I were floating a foot outside my body. They were talking about *me*. Me, in the paper. Next to a heroin addict and a dead boy racer who might or might not be my parents. No, I thought, the blood draining from my face as I put two and two together. No . . .

"Elizabeth Tallimore, or Betsy, as she's now known, has taken over the mantle of the Academy, reinventing it for a new generation of party girls. Speaking to Imogen Twist this week, she joked about the importance of parties in a girl's life and revealed her vision for today's aspiring social climber: 'There's something about being able to carry off a pair of heels that makes men take you very seriously.' "

"That wasn't what I meant!" I breathed, in agony.

"Betsy, give me the paper, I want to read the morbid scandal pages in the middle," said Liv. "Ooh, let me distract you with a croissant." She dangled a pastry in front of my nose, but I was barely aware of it.

Whoever had written this sneering feature had done my detective work for me. Why had I bothered being discreet and not prying, to save people's feelings, when I could have just gone straight to Imogen and her muckraking mates, I thought bitterly.

Here they all were: Coralie Hendricks: "three times married, currently divorcing film producer, Mark Sheen." Sophie Townend: "ex-Bond girl, beat coke addiction to become Green Party activist." Simon Fitzgerald: "died in skiing accident in 1987." Bingo Palmer: "jailed for his part in an insurance scam involving his father's zoo." Hector Tallimore: "fled criminal charges by disappearing in 1980."

I squeezed my eyes shut but the words were imprinted on the inside of my eyelids: Scandal. Addict. Criminal. Betsy.

The newspaper fell from my limp fingers.

Franny and Lord T must have known what a collection of wasters were hanging around! They must have known all along that I was the result of some seedy shag at a messy party. The unwanted accident of two stupid, selfish rich kids with plenty of perfect manners but nothing decent underneath, and they'd taken me in to make sure no nasty whispers got out. It had been about protecting the Academy's reputation, not wanting me!

"Oh, thanks," said Liv, "finally!" She grabbed the paper off me and stuffed the croissant in her mouth. I couldn't move, but I heard her choking in horror.

"Oh my God!" she cried. "Have you seen this . . . Oh no. Oh, Betsy!"

I wasn't listening. Her voice sounded a long, long way away.

Liv went through several stages of fury, horror, indignation and finally fury again in the time it took me to stop feeling numb. And I'd thought my hangover was bad.

"You should sue!" she kept saying, marching up and down the kitchen, growling and throwing her hair around. "This is defamation of character! It's outrageous! I'm going to ring Dad's brief and get right on to it. We'll sue their arses off!"

She stopped, hands on hips. "Betsy, please say something. You're seriously worrying me."

I didn't know what to think first. There was just too much.

"Say something," she pleaded. "Don't make me throw water over you."

"Where's my phone?" I asked.

Liv crumpled in relief. "I don't know. I'll look." She moved stuff up and down on the counter, then grabbed something. "Here! Oh, it's out of battery. I'll plug it in, shall I?" As she did, I heard it bleep. "Oh my God, Betsy, you've got like twenty messages! Shall I play them?"

"No!" I said, and sank my head on to my hands. "They'll be people ringing to feel sorry for me. Or cancel their deposits. Or just have a good laugh."

Liv wrapped her arms round me and hugged me hard. "No one's going to be doing that! And if they do, I'm going to . . . I'm going to . . ." She buried her head in my hair. "I'm not going to let them in."

There was the sound of a key in the lock and we both froze.

"Hello?" called Jamie's voice. He didn't sound his usual flippant self. "Betsy? Liv?"

We exchanged panicked glances.

"I can pretend you're not here if you . . ." Liv began, with a worried frown, but I shook my head.

"No, it's fine," I said. "Jamie might know what to do."

We didn't even bother to joke about his experience at deflecting scandal. It didn't seem funny any more.

"Betsy, are you OK?" Jamie burst through the kitchen door without any preamble. He looked as if he'd just got back from the gym — he was unshaven, his hair was damp and he was wearing tracksuit bottoms and a hooded top under an old sweater. I'd never seen him looking so rough, but I'd never been so pleased to see him.

"I've just seen the paper. I don't know what to say. I'm disgusted. Imogen rang, she says she's been trying to get hold of you since last night. Apparently the news desk have been trailing that bloke of Venetia's for months, trying to pin something on him, and this was the best chance they've had. He's an arms dealer, been making huge donations to the Labour Party."

"And that's meant to make her feel better how, exactly?" demanded Liv.

Jamie shrugged and looked mortified. "It's not. It's just that they've twisted what they could about the Academy to make him look as bad as possible. I bet they've been sitting on that other stuff for years, waiting until the injunction ran out or something." He turned to me and put his hand on my shoulder. "You know what the press are like. It'll be nowhere near as bad as that — one of them was probably in rehab for about a month, and someone else once got a bit tipsy at a party. It's only gossip, Betsy, it'll be forgotten by the morning."

"No, it won't," I said, dully. "Not here, anyway. How can I forget *that*?" I gestured at the newspaper, lying accusingly over our breakfast things.

Liv and Jamie exchanged glares over my head and I could tell they were duelling eyebrows.

"Don't," I said, unable to tear my eyes away from the photograph of Venetia, who'd set all this in motion, the vacuous bimbo. If she hadn't grabbed centre stage at the interview, if she hadn't let Adele coach her in her stupid marriage class . . . "Don't have a row now. Please."

Liv's house phone rang on the wall and we all jumped.

"I'll get it," said Jamie, and picked up. "Hello? No. No, I think you've got the wrong number." His voice sounded harsh. "Yes, if you ring back in an hour you'll *still* have the wrong number. Goodbye." He replaced the receiver, and grabbed my coat and hat from the chair where I'd left them the previous night.

"Come on," he said, pulling the hat over my head. "We're going out."

Jamie steered me out of the house and towards his car, which he'd parked so quickly that two of the wheels were on the kerb.

He opened the door for me then went round the other side and got in, bracing himself against the steering wheel.

"So! Where do you want to go?" He turned to me, and cocked an eyebrow. He was trying to act normally, but I couldn't.

"I don't know. Anywhere. Somewhere that won't be full of people reading that paper . . ." I shuddered.

"All right," he said. "I know just the place."

We set off, and I slumped in my seat as he drove through the Sunday morning streets of Clapham. Nice couples in Barbours with their babies in pushchairs, going about their business, heading to the pub for a roast, safe in their worlds, knowing who they were, where they came from.

And me in the car, feeling like a stranger to myself.

I didn't know where Jamie was going, but he was taking the scenic route round all the London landmarks I hadn't had time to revisit in the mad few weeks I'd been back. We headed over the green common full of dog walkers, and crossed the river into Westminster, past Big Ben and the sugarcraft carving of the Houses of Parliament up towards Fleet Street where the offices were empty and the streets were deserted apart from cleaners and a few tourists making the hike to St Paul's cathedral.

As I watched the old black and white buildings turn into the glass skyscrapers of the City, Jamie kept up a soothing barrage of chat, about a new bar he'd been to here, or an interesting shop there until I felt the numbness begin to ebb away. We were deep in the oldest part of the City now, yet in the middle of the highest-tech area, and the Sunday silence was strange but soothing. It felt like we were the only people there.

"Where are we going?" I asked, as he turned away from the city streets and into a jumble of pavement stalls and Bangladeshi curry houses. Brick Lane.

"We're getting more breakfast. Isn't that one of your rules: start the day on a full stomach?" He made a sudden signal and parked neatly in a tiny space outside a sari shop. "Stay there. I'll be right back."

I sat back in my seat, and waited. There were more people around now, and the queue from the bagel bakery Jamie had headed into stretched out into the street. Some folk were carrying flowers from the nearby Columbia market; others were obviously on their way back from a night out, shivering in tiny skirts and leather jackets. There were lots of cabbies. None of them peered into the car and pointed at me.

Jamie returned surprisingly quickly with a large brown bag, and almost dragged me out of the car. "Let's go for a walk," he said, handing me a plastic cup of very hot coffee.

We set off down Brick Lane, weaving through fashion students and locals browsing the flea market. Jamie obviously knew where he was going, though I didn't, not being an East London girl, and before long, we'd got off the main street and were standing outside a huge white church, built like a wedding cake and looming up above us. Jamie herded me into the gardens, where we sat down on a bench and he dispensed breakfast: smoked salmon bagels and cheesecake.

"Right, I guarantee no one here will give a toss about Petronella Hotsy-Totsy or whatever those girls were called," he said. "You're safe. Now, eat up."

I bit into my chewy bagel. It was very good and distracted me nicely, as food always did. Kathleen hadn't been daft with her breakfast rule.

We ate in silence, watching the sun move around the white stones of the church, and a comforting peace settled on the bench between us.

"We used to live round here when it was *really* scabby, not trendy scabby," said Jamie, stretching out his long legs in a patch of light. "Before Ken's empire really got going. He wasn't always Mr Chelsea Tractor, you know. He used to be Mr Grimy Shoreditch Terrace."

"What? And look at him now?" Jamie was trying to make me feel better, I could tell, but it wasn't working. "He's on the run from the revenue in Spain."

"OK, don't look at him now," he said, changing tack. "Look at *me and Liv* now. I mean, I don't think it matters what your parents do, one way or another. It's what you do with your own life that makes you what you are. I've had no help from Ken with Party Animals — he thinks it's a total waste of my degree. As he's fond of telling me, when he makes an appearance."

I threw my empty coffee cup into a bin. "But I *want* to have that connection with someone. All right, so you're doing your own thing now, but you know you get your wheeler-dealing from Ken. You know you'll be a silver fox like his dad when you're seventy. It's like insurance, I haven't got that. I never will now, if my parents were killed in some car crash, or died in a skiing accident or whatever it is that they're hinting at in that article. You can look at Ken, even if you don't want to be him, and know that's where you came from."

"Not necessarily." Jamie crossed his leg over his knee, making a defensive block.

"All right, so you can do things differently," I conceded. "But you know what you're playing with. I just feel . . ." I looked around the churchyard, trying to find a way to express the nauseating uncertainty I felt. "I feel like I'm just veneer, not solid inside. The *outside* sounds posh and looks right, but underneath . . . I don't know who I am."

Jamie drew in a long breath through his nose and let it out again.

"I have spent years trying to live up to what my dad wants me to be. And you know what? I've come to the conclusion that he doesn't *want* me to be like him. Because he's always wanted to be someone else himself. That little gem dawned on me when I was in New York, when I'd been up thirty-one hours, putting a launch together for a new law startup. And all he could say when I told him was . . ." He paused, then said in an Irish accent, " 'Law, now that's a *real* career.' "

He turned to me, and even though I was still aching with misery, my skin prickled at the intensity of his gaze and the secrets we were sharing. "You're sure it wasn't sleep deprivation?"

Jamie said, in a quiet voice, "Dead sure. That's why I came home. I realised I was never going to impress Ken until I invented a time machine that would allow him to go back to Dublin and pass his exams to go to uni. At least you're your own person. *You* got your degree, not your parents. *You* made your choices. *You.* I don't see why you're not prouder of that. All this stuff in the paper . . . It's no reflection on *you*."

I looked down at my fingers, where I'd chewed my nails. "I work in a shoe shop, Jamie."

"You managed a very fashionable shoe shop. And now you run a life-coaching college."

"Yes, one that's about to close down through publicity that I brought on myself because I was naïve enough to allow a journalist to nose around." I was biting back tears of frustration. "Everyone's going to cancel their deposits, and demand their money back, and we won't be able to carry on! It's all over. And it's my fault because I didn't put my foot down hard enough about Adele and her stupid idea that marriage is the only thing smart girls should be doing! I should have *talked* to Venetia! I should have seen that she was only doing this for the money."

He grabbed my hand. "Betsy, people will forget! No one believes that sort of feature anyway, it's not even splashed on the front . . ."

"Get real, Jamie! It's on the Internet for ever, anytime anyone Googles Tallimore Academy! And I won't forget," I moaned. "It's only cheap gossip to anyone reading it, but for me . . ." My stomach crawled. "For *me*, it's . . ."

I couldn't hold back the tears now. I felt so small and humiliated, and angry — not just for me, and the chance I'd had to run my own business, but for Franny and her reputation and the dreams I'd had since I was a baby.

"The Academy is all I *am*," I hiccupped. "My mother left me there to be part of it, and Franny was everything it stood for. If it's cheap and tacky, then so am I."

Jamie let go of my hand and grabbed my shoulders. "Look at me," he said, and shook me when I couldn't lift my eyes from the seat.

"*Look* at me, Betsy!" he insisted, fiercely. "You are the most independent, intelligent woman I have ever met in my whole life. Everything about you is stylish. You never tried to make a sob story out of being adopted, and you were never a snob about growing up with a rich family. You were always just you. No airs or graces, no pretending to be stupid when it was obvious you were clever, no stuffing your bra or dyeing your beautiful hair. You were your own person, and I've admired that since I was fifteen years old."

"But . . ." I began.

"You can go back and find out who your real mum is if you want," he said. "Or you can think of Franny as your mother, just like you always have done. But it doesn't make a shred of difference to who *you* are, and what you've done with your life, because you're absolutely amazing, as you are." Jamie paused, and one corner of his mouth lifted in a self-deprecating twist.

"Don't take this the wrong way but I've met a lot of women over the years. Some of them very rich, some of them models, some of them bizarre, but *none* of them have stayed in the front of my mind the way you do. I go to a new bar, and I think, I wonder what Betsy would make of these high-ball glasses? Or I buy a new suit, and I think, I wonder if Betsy would say this was a bit car salesman?"

He took a loose ringlet that had escaped from the hat, and gently tucked it behind my ear. "I think the things I love about you most are the things you seem to hate. Like these gorgeous curls that you're always ironing flat. And those hilarious to-do lists that you never let yourself finish. Like you're keeping everything in check by following your rules."

His finger lingered behind my ear, sending electric sparks all the way down my bare neck. He traced a pattern in the soft skin, caressing the little hollow. "What you don't seem to realise," said Jamie slowly, holding my gaze, "is that the only person who has to make the rules for your life is you. Stop worrying about where you come from. You're you. And you're lovely."

I gazed at him, my lips opening in surprise. Had that softness in his face always been there? Hadn't I noticed the vulnerability in his eyes, or was it just that I was so much closer to him now than I'd been before?

I could smell the washing powder on his sweatpants and the coffee on his breath and I didn't want the moment to break. But still I felt that hesitation, that the anticipation might be better than the real thing . . .

But what was the point in running away from relationships, in case they turned out to be as disastrous as my mother's? I didn't even know what had happened to her. As Jamie said, I could only be myself, and right now, all I wanted was to lean forward and feel Jamie's lips against mine.

His finger traced a tender line from my ear, along my jaw, to my mouth, and across my lips. I raised my head, almost in a trance, and Jamie leaned closer so I could feel his breath.

"I know it's polite to wait to be asked," he said. "But I've been waiting all these years for you."

And suddenly I was the one leaning forward, catching the side of his mouth with my lips, until the stubble of his chin prickled against my face. We both hesitated for a microsecond, just feeling the heat of our mouths against wind-chilled skin, and then his hand tangled in my hair while his arm pulled me nearer and I felt myself being swept into the most dizzying kiss, as Jamie's lips met mine, gently parting them and sending tiny ripples of pleasure all over my skin, hot and cold at the same time.

All I could think of then was how absolutely right it was, how perfectly we fitted into each other, and how the anticipation was absolutely nothing on the real thing.

I would have stayed on the bench, lost in what Nancy's novels would call "the delicious passion of Jamie's embrace" indefinitely, if the clock in the church tower behind us hadn't struck twelve and spoiled the moment.

Three chimes you can ignore, but after five, it's impossible not to count in your head. We pulled apart, suddenly self-conscious but not, I was pleased to feel, embarrassed.

"Would you like me to help you make a list?" offered Jamie.

"I don't need to . . ." I began, eager to turn over a new leaf, but Jamie raised a forgiving hand.

"I'll let you off this time," he said. "I'd be making one, if I were you."

"OK, well, I should ring Lord Tallimore and check he's all right," I said, as my brain clicked into gear. "And Mark, to see if anyone's called to demand a refund. And the girls, in case they're mortified about . . ."

"Forget the bloody Academy!" Jamie looked aghast. "That doesn't matter now. The only person you should be thinking of is yourself, Kathleen and Nancy, and possibly Lord T. Although if he'd been a bit more open with you from the beginning . . ." He handed me my phone, which he'd helpfully charged in the car, with the ringer safely off. "Call him now."

I took it tentatively. I had another ten missed calls.

Soonest tackled, soonest finished, I reminded myself, and dialled his number.

"If I get Adele, I'm hanging up," I told Jamie as it rang at the other end. If I got Adele, I wasn't sure I could exercise politeness.

Fortunately, Lord T himself picked up on the second ring. "Betsy! I've been trying to call you all morning!" He sounded relieved but very anxious. "I'm so sorry. So very sorry. Are you all right?"

I looked at Jamie. "Yes, I'm all right. Upset, but . . . all right."

"I need to talk to you," Lord T went on. "There are some matters I absolutely must clear up, and . . ." He paused. "There's someone you need to meet. Where are you now? Can you come to Full Moon Street?"

"Full Moon Street?" I looked at Jamie, who nodded.

"I'll take you anywhere you need to go," he whispered.

"Yes," I said. "I'll see you there in half an hour."

Jamie dropped me off at the corner of Berkeley Square.

"You're sure you don't want me to come with you?" he said again as I got out of the car, knees first as always.

I shook my head. Already I was preparing myself, for what, I wasn't sure. "I need to do this on my own. I'll call you when I'm done."

He leaned over the handbrake and beckoned. "Good luck," he said, and kissed my cold nose with a tenderness that nearly made me get back inside.

I set off towards Full Moon Street, making myself swing my arms and hold my head up high, even though inside I was quivering. I even took a leaf out of the girls' book and put on my shades, so no one would see the nerves written on my face.

As I rounded the corner, my whole body flinched: there was a man with a camera and a woman hanging around outside. When they saw me, I knew they knew who I was.

The woman came haring down the street towards me. "Betsy? Betsy Tallimore? Is there anything you'd like to say for the record about the revelations in the papers?

"No," I said, politely, and kept walking.

"Are you ashamed of the way the Tallimores covered up the scandal about your birth? Don't you feel angry?"

"No," I said again. I was nearly at the door now.

"Don't you think it's morally reprehensible to set young women up for some kind of sick marriage market?" she persisted. "Isn't it like a legalised form of slavery? Don't you think you deserve to be told the truth about who your real parents are?"

"I don't want to talk about this." My voice cracked. I didn't want to talk about it. Not to her, anyway. It hadn't *been* like that.

I glanced up at the familiar sash windows where girls had once waltzed and curtseyed, and I thought of Franny and her kindness and the way she smiled at everything I did. She *had* loved me. She'd wanted the best for me, in every way. It *couldn't* just have been about guarding the Academy's reputation.

The journalist kept following me though, running to keep up with me. "Are you going to find your *real* parents?"

I turned and pulled myself up to my full height. "I don't need to find my real parents," I said. "I know who they are."

"You think your father was Hector Tallimore?" Her eyes lit up and she gestured to the photographer. "What about your mother?"

He started snapping away and I covered my face instinctively.

Then I removed my hands, and removed my shades too, for good measure.

I spoke very slowly, so she'd get every word and he'd get my best side. "My real mother was Frances Tallimore," I said. "And if I could be half the woman she was I'll be very happy."

It was then that I turned and saw Lord T standing behind me, listening to everything I'd said.

The expression on his face was so dignified and grateful and uncharacteristically emotional that I nearly wept.

Behind him, was Nell Howard. And she looked on the verge of tears too.

CHAPTER TWENTY-FIVE

All ladies need one show-stopping, spirit-lifting dress, preferably in a fabric that will accommodate thin days and fat days — add up what you'd spend on hair and make-up and new shoes to make an ordinary dress fabulous, and it's not so expensive.

We found ourselves in the headmistress's office, where Lord Tallimore sat behind Miss Thorne's desk, looming awkwardly over her knick-knackery and mint imperial bowl, not quite sure where to rest his arms for fear of breaking something.

It was the first time I'd been in this room without Paulette stumbling in with a tray of coffee at just the wrong moment — and I had to fight the temptation to go out and make some.

"Where should we start?" asked Lord T, and his lack of training in difficult conversations showed. His shoulders were somewhere up by his ears.

"How about with me?" I suggested, half-hysterically. I turned to Nell. "Forgive me for coming out with a straight question, but are you my mother?"

I could see it now — there was something in her oval eyes and tilted eyebrows that wasn't unlike my own, though her dark hair wasn't anything like mine. I wouldn't mind if Nell was my mother, I thought. At least she was fun and had a job . . .

"No," she said, and pulled her generous mouth into a tight sad line. "Sorry."

The simpering crowd of drug-addled bimbos and stupidly named boys reappeared before my eyes. I leaned back in my seat and shut my eyes.

"I'm your aunt," she went on, and my head spun so fast I nearly cracked a vertebra. She smiled ruefully at my obvious shock. "Believe me, it was as much of a bolt from the blue for me as it is for you. Shows what you know about your own family, eh? What next, Lord Lucan hiding out in the attic? No, sorry, should be serious."

Nell composed herself, as if rearranging a complicated list in her head. When she spoke again, it was in a more sober tone. "My elder sister Rosalind called me last month when she heard about Lady Frances's memorial service, and said she had something to tell me. She lives in Switzerland now, runs her own company supplying staff for chalets — none of us see her very often. I thought she was going to ask me to pass on some kind of message to Lord Tallimore here, because she always adored Lady Frances, thought the sun shone out of her lead crystal sherry glasses . . ."

"Rosalind was one of Frances's favourites too," added Lord T. "Beautiful handwriting. Very quiet. Never had to worry about her at social events, unlike some of the little trollops in her year . . ." He caught himself and put three mint imperials in his mouth to prevent further comment.

Nell coughed. "Anyway, Rosie dropped a bit of a bombshell. She told me, quite calmly, that *she'd* been the one who left the baby on the step. I had no idea, I swear to you! Couldn't believe it — my own sister, who only read the horsey bits of Jilly Cooper and skipped the sex!"

"How?" I asked. "And . . . who? And . . . when?" I pleaded with my eyes. "Please tell me that it wasn't anything . . . against her will . . ."

"No! No, it couldn't have been more romantic, darling," Nell insisted. "Rosie was an innocent from Buckinghamshire and your father was a Guards officer called Henry. Captain Henry Hargreaves. Apparently Rosie met him at a formal dining evening, upstairs in the ballroom. We used to have these nights with crowds of eligible men, putting our skills into practice," she explained, "with Vanders and Lady Frances watching us like hawks, and the bursar invited officers from his old regiment to be our other halves for the night. They were rather dashing in uniform, even the ones you wouldn't normally give the time of day in civvies. Brave too. Much more the sort of chaps we were supposed to be aiming for, not like slimy Hector and his dreadful cronies."

Nell flashed an apologetic glance up at Lord T. "Sorry."

He tilted his head in acknowledgement, as if he couldn't really disagree.

"What was he like?" I asked curiously. "Henry?" It felt too weird to call him "my father".

"I never met him," Nell admitted, "and Rosie only had one photo, but she said he was like something out of *War and Peace* in his uniform: gorgeous eyes, broad shoulders. Red hair. The works. He'd already got some decoration or other for valour, but she said she fell for him when he admitted that he was terrified of Coralie Hendricks and what she might do to him on the balcony."

"And they fell in love over dinner?" I asked, as the images spilled across my mind like scattered pearls. The best silver. Bare shoulders. Roses.

"Oh yes. Who wouldn't?" Nell smiled nostalgically. "What with the candlelight and the champagne and everyone flirting like mad, I can see why Rosie got carried away. She wasn't too experienced in the old romance game, God love her. Imagined you went from eyes meeting over the centrepiece to the announcement in *The Times* to a house in Gloucestershire all in one go. No one really explained the stickier bits in between — despite Coralie and Sophie carrying on . . . Anyway, I was at school still, had no idea what was happening, apart from her letters raving about this dishy soldier who made her laugh and cry and God knows what else, but the next thing we know, the aged parents get a letter from Rosie to say she's upped and gone to

Meribel for a few months to learn how to make fondues."

"Sorry?" I frowned, wondering if I'd missed something.

"No, we didn't get it either." Nell lifted her shoulders and then dropped them so hard her earrings jangled. "But that's what girls did, went off on courses. Two months learning Tartiflettes here, three months on ancient crocks at Christie's, two months ruining your nails touch-typing . . . Rosie sent us the occasional postcard, the parents weren't too bothered, considering she seemed to be in with some jolly nice people. And then she reappeared around Christmas, and she couldn't even use a fondue properly. That's when I knew something wasn't right."

I rubbed my eyes. "She hadn't been in Switzerland?"

"No. She hadn't. She'd been hiding in Cheltenham the whole time." Nell looked guilty, as if she should have known. "She'd seen the divine Captain Henry for a couple of weeks, and they'd been absolutely head over heels, and he'd given her that lovely bee charm for Christmas, with a ring to follow, but then his regiment got their marching orders and he couldn't tell her where they were going, because it was all so hush-hush. You see? Terribly Battle of Waterloo. But she'd carried on writing, and then one day all her letters came back in a bundle. She couldn't find anything out, since she wasn't family or anything, until there was a little obit in *The Times*. He'd been killed in Northern Ireland, in a terrorist operation that went wrong."

Nell's eyes filled up, and mine did too. "Rosie was in a real state, and then the poor darling found out she was in the family way. Took her long enough to work it out, but when she did, she panicked and decided that if she didn't tell anyone, she could pretend it never happened. Our parents would have gone berserk, and she hadn't even *met* Henry's, so she found herself a nursing home, like you could then, and said she was away at a Cordon Bleu course."

"And then popped back and left me on the steps," I said hollowly.

Nell nodded. "She knew Lady Frances adored children, and she thought she would look after you better than she could. Make you into the lady poor Rosie had decided she could never be."

"But that's so ridiculous!" I protested. "It's not a crime to make a mistake! People have unexpected babies all the time! Why didn't she just *tell* someone?"

"Because . . ." Nell struggled to find the right words. "She felt she'd spoiled everything. We were in a Cinderella frenzy that year — the royal wedding seemed like our *own* fairy tale, a nice finishing-school girl like us, friend of a friend, no O-levels but awfully sweet, no previous success with chaps, bags a prince! We thought, *well*, if it could happen for Diana *Spencer*, it could happen for us too. And poor Rosie . . . She'd dreamed of that. I mean," Nell added, "if we'd known then what we know now, she'd doubtless have acted a bit differently, but then . . . Well. Rosie did what she thought was best, and made herself live with the consequences."

It was a lot to take in at once. Suddenly I had a real mother, and a real father that my real aunt seemed to know as well as I now did.

I turned to Lord Tallimore. "Didn't you try to find out who'd left me? Franny must have recognised the necklace."

"Quite tricky, asking parents if their daughters have mislaid any newborn babies recently," he said, mildly. "Of course we made enquiries — I gave Hector the third degree, just to be sure, but he claimed not to know a thing."

"He didn't," added Nell. "Henry wasn't one of his friends. He barely even *drank*."

"And what happened to Rosie?" I asked. "What happened after she left me?"

"She went abroad, and got herself a job, which was pretty unheard of back then." Nell seemed proud. "She built up her own business in Switzerland, organising chalet girls for ski parties, and making sure they didn't get into trouble. Turned into a right bossy boots, curfews and checks and everything. The Mother Superior, we called her then." Her face fell, and she looked anguished. "Of course, if we'd known . . ."

I tried to make sense of it all in my head. "So, when you met me at the memorial . . . did you know who I was? Did you go there to find me? How did you know what I'd look like?"

Nell fiddled with her cuticles, a habit I'd struggled with for years myself. "I was going anyway, but Rosie asked me to work out whether you wanted to be found. She was too scared to come along herself — worried that you might be there, and you'd think her a bit of a crasher for turning up and spoiling your real mother's day."

She gave me a self-deprecating grin. "Not the *best* manners, really, for you or for Lady Frances. Bit of a scene stealer, don't you think? So she sent me to find out, as best I could, what sort of feelings you had, if any, for the frightened girl who'd left you on the steps." She paused, apologetically. "Her words, not mine, there."

I tried to remember exactly what Nell had said to me, when she'd accosted me by the photos. All I could remember was her feathery hat, and her friendly face and her sense of fun. "Why didn't you tell me? Why did you pretend not to *know* who my mother was?"

"Because I didn't know whether you even cared about her," said Nell, suddenly serious. "For all I knew, you might have wanted to track her down to give her a piece of your mind. Or Frances might have told you a different story, that you still believed, and I wasn't sure if it was the right place to start telling you that you weren't actually a royal love child or what have you."

"And did you spot me straight away?" I held my breath, hoping that some family connection had drawn us together, even if we didn't know.

Nell nodded. "I thought I wouldn't, but I knew, once I saw you. You smile like Rosie does, and you start conversations with strangers in the same brave 'what can we talk about?' way. But you're more like Lady Frances in everything else."

"Really?"

"Oh yes." Nell nodded. "You stand the same, with that lovely straight back, and you have the same mannerisms, the way you tip your head when you're talking, and that adorable smile . . ."

"And you walk the same," added Lord T. "And you laugh just like her."

Because Franny taught me to walk, and laugh, and smile. My eyes filled with tears again.

"When I said that you'd made us proud, I meant it," said Lord T. "God knows I'm not one for this touchy-feely business, but you were the absolute light of Frances's life. And mine. The most precious gift we could have had, and I'll always be thankful to Rosie for giving us the chance to love you." He blinked hard, and for a moment I thought I could see tears around his eyes. "And what you've done with this place . . . She always knew . . ."

I couldn't let him get away with that. It was one thing being proud of me now but if we were going to start dishing out home truths, I had some of my own.

"But you didn't always think I was so precious, did you? I wasn't good enough to be finished off!" I said. "You said the Academy wasn't for girls like me!"

Lord T's face crumpled as if I'd hit him. "Did you think that's what I meant?"

"Yes!"

"That is harsh," agreed Nell. "Oh dear, Pelham, not well done at all."

"And you covered up the scandal, brushed it under the carpet as if I was something to be ashamed of." My face was getting red now. "OK, so I tried my best to make you proud of me, but didn't you just take me in to stop the gossip getting out? Was that why you didn't think I was good enough to go?"

"I thought you were far *too* good to go!" Lord T exploded. "You didn't need finishing off, Betsy! Finishing off is for thick girls who can't even get out of a car without instructions, for God's sake!"

"Oh, thanks," said Nell. "Touché."

Lord T rubbed a hand over his face. "Betsy, the reason I didn't want you going anywhere near the Academy was because I wanted there to be more in your life than just men and marriage and flower arranging. I had no idea until about an hour ago who your mother was, but I knew it was a girl who'd been let down in some way. A girl who wasn't in charge of her own life. I didn't want that to happen to you."

He got up and started to pace back and forth in front of Miss Thorne's photo gallery of grinning debutantes. "I'm not ashamed to say that I was all for closing the Academy down that year — the awful car crash and the girls and what have you. Utter, *utter* nightmare. Frances did her best to influence Coralie and Sophie in a positive way, but we weren't their parents, most of that hell-raising went on outside term time, and Hector . . . How could we lay down the law when he was the worst of the lot?" He stopped and looked at me in the eye. "It was only because Frances wouldn't let me give up on a low note that this place carried on at all. Maybe

I shouldn't have listened to her. But I made a promise that under no circumstances would I allow your future to be risked mixing with girls who didn't care what happened to them. You were too precious, to me and to Frances."

"That's not what it felt like to me," I said, hurt.

Lord T looked mortified. "I can see that now. I should have let Frances handle things, but I didn't want you to be angry with her."

"But that's why I moved to Scotland! That's why I stayed up there!" I pressed my lips together, trying not to let my emotions boil over into tears. "I've never thought I was good enough. I've spent my whole life wondering who I was, and what I was meant to be, but mainly what was so wrong with me that I wasn't even allowed to arrange flowers with those girls."

"Then I've failed," he said, quietly. "I didn't want you to care. I wanted you to realise how much *better* than that you were. I'm so sorry."

Lord T's shoulders sagged, and I knew he wasn't just thinking of me, he was thinking of the years I'd spent away from Franny, who'd already lost one child to disappointment and misunderstanding.

"It's asking a lot," said Nell, breaking in with cheerful forthrightness, "but can you forgive a well-meaning old duffer with no idea of how to handle emotional issues, and a naïve schoolgirl who got most of her guidance from the pages of Georgette Heyer? And tactless old me, for not telling you the entire ghastly tale the very instant I clapped eyes on you?"

I looked between them both. I thought it would feel different, the moment when I found out who my parents were. But in the end it was just like reading the final scene in a detective novel; a part of me was going, "ohhhh, now I understand" as the pieces clunked into place, but the greater part of me felt exactly the same as I had done when I walked in.

The truth was, it didn't make any difference. I was still me. I was still Betsy, still Liv's friend, still Franny's daughter, still BA (Hons), still not a ballerina's child or a rock star's drunken secret. Only now I could stop wondering what I *might* be.

I always thought I'd be disappointed, but actually the relief was incredible.

"If you can't forgive me, and I can understand why," said Lord T, looking me straight in the eye, "then please, tell me you can forgive Frances."

I blinked back hot tears.

"Yes," I hiccuped. "Of *course* I can forgive you. I can forgive you both. You *and* Franny. You're my real parents."

And for the first time since I was five years old, and his Great Dane dragged me the length of the garden like a rag doll, Lord Tallimore opened up his arms and hugged me tightly to his chest.

Epilogue

Always keep a bottle of champagne in the fridge for special occasions. Sometimes the special occasion is that you've got a bottle of champagne in the fridge.

"You're seeing three of these women before lunch, and then two after, but you're having lunch with Mr O'Hare so I haven't booked the last two in until three thirty, just in case you decide to, you know." Paulette gave me a juicy wink. "Have a long one. If you know what I mean. Hahahaha! Oh, and I've scored them all out of ten, thought it might help. What with them being Work Life tutors."

I looked at the CVs she'd just handed me. The top one had a Post-it with "Photo looks like a bloke — was Simon, not Simone?! Bad roots. 3/10" on it in capitals.

"Scored on what basis?"

"Clothes, appearance. Amount of boasting they did. I was going to write on it direct, then I remembered what you said about Post-its," she added. She tapped her nose. "More discreet."

"Thanks, Paulette," I said. I was getting through on the discretion front, albeit slowly.

I'd been in charge for a month, but it felt like a lot longer. I'd be telling a solid gold lie if I said it had been easy to gloss over the terrible publicity: for two days in a slow news month, it had been seriously grim. Heavy breathers calling the office with "proposals", photographers lurking outside, the lot. If it hadn't been for Anastasia offering to get her dad to buy the offending newspaper — as in buy the business, not the physical object — "and see to the woman who wrote those lies!" I don't know if I'd have found a funny side.

I was touched by the deputation of three that turned up on Tuesday morning, their privacy protected by massive sunglasses and hats, and their "no photos!" body language whipping what had been two snappers and a bored hack into a veritable scrum. Jamie's coaching in how to get a good paparazzi snap had definitely sunk in.

Venetia wasn't with them. She'd "gone into hiding", or as Clemmy put it, "She's staying with her mum while she tries to get hold of Max Clifford."

"I'm starting to feel sorry for Venetia," said Divinity, sitting up in the bursar's office where Mark and I were trying to deal with the refund calls and the general enquiries. It wasn't all bad news; some people had phoned to enquire about getting on to the marrying a millionaire course, and were very disappointed to find there wasn't one.

"Venetia? I don't feel sorry for her at all!" Clemmy flicked her hair back; she'd toned herself down from

Raven Black to Mellow Crow since Liv's makeover and now looked dramatic rather than downright scary. "All right, so she's skint, and her family are total climbers, but she didn't have to marry some fat old arms dealer."

"She hed the contacts — she could hev dealt her own arms," agreed Anastasia. "Twice the profit."

"Can you help her?" Divinity gazed at me with her brown eyes full of pity. "Can't you ring her and tell her what to do? I don't reckon as Miss Buchanan's going to be much help, not now."

"Help Venetia? Are you mad?" demanded Mark, looking up from his calculations. "I'm looking at these figures and it's touch and go, frankly. One more cancellation and it's all over."

I'd been thinking about Venetia since the smaller follow-up piece on Monday had caught her emerging make-up-less from "her shamed bankrupt parents' home in South London". It turned out that her dad was a lawyer with an unfortunate poker addiction and even more unfortunate conviction for fraud; her resourceful mother had sunk her savings into Venetia's fees as a last attempt to salvage the family fortunes with a hefty marriage. If it had happened to someone nicer, Nancy agreed, it would have been almost romantic, Venetia plumping up her bosom, slapping her thigh, and setting forth to do what she could to save her parents from negative equity.

"I've got a plan for Venetia," I said. "What she needs is a job doing something she knows about, like fashion, somewhere out of London where she can start again. Maybe somewhere like . . . Edinburgh."

Clemmy looked at me strangely. "You seem very chipper for someone whose business is about to shut down."

"That's the best part about a disaster," I told her. "Once the worst has happened, it can only get better. As a wise woman once told me."

Clemmy raised both her thumbs, sarcastically. "Good luck with that."

After that, it did get better, but slowly. I decided that the only way around the Curse of Google was to start again under a new name: The Finishing Touches. I rented out my flat in Edinburgh, invested in some decoration for Full Moon Street, and threw myself into making manners for a modern age seem like the best secret boost a smart girl could give herself since platform heels.

Miss Thorne took "early" retirement, at very much the same time as Miss Adele Buchanan also regretfully resigned from the teaching staff "to spend more time on her charity work". Venetia hadn't held back in revealing who'd been tutoring her in the art of marrying well, and although I'd heard rumours that Adele was thinking of starting some kind of anonymous Springboard Marriage coaching blog, she denied them passionately — but then she would.

"I'm a very private person," she told me, when she called from Aspen to tender her resignation. "I can't have my personal life raked over, it's too cruel for those close to me." Then she asked for her term's invoice which she needed, she claimed, to fund a spa holiday to the Caribbean; with a heavy heart I noted that it coincided with a test cricket series.

So I lost two teachers, and gained two — Liv became a part-time style consultant for me, Jamie taught a couple of very popular classes a week on whatever he wanted, and I was almost at the point of employing a proper member of staff, to coach new students in preparing for the work place.

Which was why, one month on from the day I'd found out exactly who I was, I was sitting upstairs in my newly painted office, wearing my new green suit and my hair swept into a chic chignon I'd paid Liv's hairdresser to teach me how to do myself, and, most importantly, Franny's lustrous pearls. I was a real pearl convert. Everything she'd said about pearls coming to life on a woman's skin was true; from the moment I fastened the clasp, they glowed against my pale skin like tiny moonbeams. The only addition I'd made was to fasten the little diamond bee on to the clasp, so it hung like a charm. I felt I'd got the best of both mothers then.

The phone rang on the desk next to me and I answered it with a happy flourish.

"Is that the School for Common Sense?" enquired a familiar teasing tone.

"Why? Are you looking to acquire some?" A smile curled round my lips and I knew it showed in my voice. Liv said I had a particularly pukey smile when I talked to Jamie on the phone. When I was with him, I was too preoccupied with other things to notice what my face looked like.

"Nope. I leave the common sense to my girlfriend. She has enough for both of us. I'm just checking she's still on for lunch," Jamie went on. "We could go to a new Greek place that's just opened in Knightsbridge or we could try out a party venue in Soho — bit dodgy, very fashionable — or we could get sandwiches and eat in the park."

"Park, please," I said, sounding a bit village idiot but not caring.

"Good," said Jamie. "I don't know what you're teaching there, but I hear that most restaurants frown on public displays of affection. And I'm not driving all the way from Islington to Piccadilly if I can't at least have one kiss before coffee."

"I'm sure it's very bad manners not to offer one," I agreed. "Park it is."

Paulette had appeared at the door and was pointing at my desk, then at me.

"I have to go," I said. "I've got staff to engage," and hung up before I said anything a passing personal assistant might find embarrassing in her new boss.

"Shall I show her in?" Paulette asked.

I straightened my jacket and smoothed my hair down. "Yes," I said. "Oh, hang on, Paulette, which one's . . ."

But she'd vanished.

OK, I thought, checking my reflection in the mirror I kept in my drawer. Buttons, done up; lipstick, poppy red and fresh; teeth — I bared my teeth — fine.

Or was that a bit of granary toast stuck in the side of my . . . I pulled my lip back to check.

"Hello!"

I dropped the mirror in my haste to get up and nearly spilled cold tea on myself.

The first candidate was standing in the doorway — a tall woman, late forties, in a green suit a bit like mine, and lovely pale skin. No make-up, just red lipstick.

Chic, I thought, approvingly.

"Sorry," she apologised, "your assistant said to come right in."

Your assistant.

Deep breath, be calm, be friendly, I reminded myself, and held out my hand. "Hello, I'm Betsy Tallimore," I said. "And I should be sorry, Paulette hasn't actually told me which of these CVs is yours."

The woman had a good handshake — firm, three shakes up and down, lots of eye contact. She had lovely eyes too, with long lashes, and laughter lines feathering the edges.

Her hand lingered in mine for a second or two after we'd finished shaking and she didn't break off the eye contact.

"It's the one without the photograph," she said. "Very boring CV, really, just the one business for the last twenty years. I'm not sure how qualified I am, but I'm very keen. As soon as I saw what you were doing here, I wanted to be part of it."

"Right," I said, shuffling through the papers. I tried to hide Paulette's frank Post-it assessments from view.

If she decided to give up as a PA, I thought, there would be a job for Paulette with Simon Cowell.

"What lovely pearls," she said.

"Thank you," I said, proudly. "They were my mother's. I'm sorry, I can't seem to find . . ."

"I've been running a chalet business," the lady went on. "In Switzerland?"

I looked up, suddenly realising.

"And I've got some first-hand experience of the old Tallimore Academy. As a graduate."

She smiled, nervously, but hopefully — a smile I recognised as very like my own.

Something began to burn and flutter in my chest at the same time, pressing out and up into my throat until I didn't trust my voice to speak. Instead I turned my necklace slowly round, so the little bee was visible.

"I'm Rosalind," she said, holding out her hand again as her voice cracked. "Rosalind Howard. I've come for the job."

I slipped my hand into hers but this time, I didn't shake. I just held it.